SPECIAL MESSAGE TO READERS

THE ULVERSCROFT FOUNDATION
(registered UK charity number 264873)
was established in 1972 to provide funds for research, diagnosis and treatment of eye diseases. Examples of major projects funded by the Ulverscroft Foundation are:-

- The Children's Eye Unit at Moorfields Eye Hospital, London
- The Ulverscroft Children's Eye Unit at Great Ormond Street Hospital for Sick Children
- Funding research into eye diseases and treatment at the Department of Ophthalmology, University of Leicester
- The Ulverscroft Vision Research Group, Institute of Child Health
- Twin operating theatres at the Western Ophthalmic Hospital, London
- The Chair of Ophthalmology at the Royal Australian College of Ophthalmologists

You can help further the work of the Foundation by making a donation or leaving a legacy. Every contribution is gratefully received. If you would like to help support the Foundation or require further information, please contact:

THE ULVERSCROFT FOUNDATION
The Green, Bradgate Road, Anstey
Leicester LE7 7FU, England
Tel: (0116) 236 4325

website: www.foundation.ulverscroft.com

David Ashton was born in Greenock in 1941. He studied at Central Drama School, London from 1964 to 1967, and most recently appeared in *The Last King of Scotland*. David started writing in 1984 and has seen many of his plays and TV adaptations broadcast — he wrote early episodes of *EastEnders* and *Casualty*, as well as the *McLevy* series for Radio 4.

You can visit the *McLevy* website at www.inspectormclevy.com

and discover more about the author at www.david-ashton.co.uk

NOR WILL HE SLEEP

1887: The streets of Edinburgh seethe with anarchy as two gangs of students rival each other in wild exploits. After a pitched battle between them, an old woman is found savagely battered to death in Leith Harbour. Enter the Thieftaker — Inspector James McLevy. Robert Louis Stevenson, author of *The Strange Case of Dr Jekyll and Mr Hyde*, is in the city to bury his deceased father, and the two recognise each other as observers of the dark side of human nature and hopeless insomniacs. But glimpses of the murderer indicate a slender figure with a silver cane — a dancing killer not unlike Mr Edward Hyde. Is it just a coincidence that Mr Stevenson is back in town?

Books by David Ashton
Published by Ulverscroft:

SHADOW OF THE SERPENT
FALL FROM GRACE
A TRICK OF THE LIGHT

DAVID ASHTON

NOR WILL HE SLEEP

An Inspector McLevy Mystery

Complete and Unabridged

CHARNWOOD
Leicester

First published in Great Britain in 2013 by
Polygon
an imprint of Birlinn Ltd
Edinburgh

First Charnwood Edition
published 2018
by arrangement with
Hodder & Stoughton
An Hachette UK company
London

A catalogue record for this book is available
from the British Library.

ISBN 978–1–4448–3672–1

Published by
F. A. Thorpe (Publishing)
Anstey, Leicestershire

Set by Words & Graphics Ltd.
Anstey, Leicestershire
Printed and bound in Great Britain by
T. J. International Ltd., Padstow, Cornwall

This book is printed on acid-free paper

To Graham and Michael —
fellow travellers

1

If you want to be a wolf, you must howl.
                    Rousseau to James Boswell

A deathly hush had fallen on Leith Harbour as a horde of white faces stared up into the dripping sombre sky. The drops had smeared and caused the chalked make-up of the young men to run, giving them the appearance of distorted circus clowns, the dark rings round their eyes sliding like black tears as they held a collective breath.

The object of their scrutiny was a slender cane projecting like a stray moonbeam towards the top of a stately ship's mast. In fact an official vessel of Her Majesty's Revenue Service, but for this moment trembling on the edge of being the recipient of an equally stately corset that dangled from the tip of the cane.

The underwear swayed as if shying away from the jutting masculine naval staff and then coyly wreathed itself in fond embrace to surrender her charms, helped by an impatient prod from the conductor's baton.

But would she stay the course?

The stick removed itself, the wind fluttered straps and buckles but the corset held steadfast, gleaming pale as streaks of water ran down old satin in the dark night.

'She has found her hero!'

A disembodied voice rang out in the damp air,

1

and the crowd below burst into wild cheers to hail the slight figure who shinned nimbly down the mast, mission accomplished.

As the shape landed awkwardly on the deck and hopped to the harbour flagstones, it was now obvious that the cane was no affectation — one leg lagged crablike behind the other — but despite this, the young man executed an agile caper as he accepted the adulation.

His name was Daniel Drummond, also white-faced but with jet-black hair, long and swept-back, that framed the alabaster visage in a dramatic casing.

A medical student with exams successfully passed, Daniel was soon to be qualified like the rest of his fellows; and also qualified as leader of the White Devils, who at this moment vied with the Scarlet Runners, deadly rivals in derring-do and anarchic acts aimed at creating havoc in the public domain.

Three days of mayhem were the city's reward for the begetting and nurturing of these young bloods who would, in time, become respectable and frown upon the antics in which they now revelled.

A solid chunky figure led the congratulatory throng, Alan Grant. Drummond's best friend, he played, with some relief, Sancho Panza to the other's Quixote.

'Corsets on the topmast — a beautiful sight!' Daniel announced with gusto amidst much cheerful bedlam as the two friends embraced.

'I hope your mother doesn't miss them,' was the more deliberated response.

'She has such fripperies in abundance!'

Alan shook his head as he gazed up whence his comrade had newly descended.

'You are truly mad, Daniel. On such a night to climb so high.'

'Too cautious, my friend. How are we to win else?'

A refrain of agreement from the rest of the students milling around them brought a smile to Alan's face.

In truth both young men were to some extent acting a part, as were most gathered here, but whereas Alan possessed a ballast of sorts, the prudent inheritance from generations of a cooperage-owning family, Daniel had a reckless streak. His eyes glittered like the silvery cane he twirled in triumph.

Alan nodded judiciously.

'The Scarlets will be hard pressed to match such an exploit,' he admitted.

'And the White Devils will triumph — '

A hail of wet dungy clods, sky-propelled but now earth-bound, contradicted this bold assertion as they landed with smelly spattering impact on the gathering.

This was accompanied by a chorus of catcalls from a crowd of equally garishly attired young men who had emerged from one of the taverns, their tribal marking a livid scarlet, which covered the face and glowed diabolically in the dark like a satanic challenge.

A howl went up from the white ranks and as the scarlet horde whooped their jubilant way towards the narrow wynds that spread off the

3

harbour, the corset-worshippers set forth in hot pursuit.

Daniel paused once more to admire his handiwork atop the mast and Alan loyally kept company. The crippled leg would not allow his friend to keep up with the whirling limbs of their companions and these two would perforce follow at a more measured pace.

If there was any acknowledgement of his disability, it certainly did not show in the eyes of the slender figure as he bowed solemnly to Alan and they prepared to go where the noise of the fracas would lead them.

Then a cracked voice from the shadows stopped them in their tracks.

'*I saw ye.*'

A momentary fear showed in Daniel's eyes, as if some deep unrest had been provoked by a force of conscience but then some movement from the darkness revealed an old woman who stepped forward, clutching her large handbag like a shield.

A thin face, cheekbones sucked tight in rectitude, the small figure quivered with indignation as she confronted the two miscreants.

This was Agnes Carnegie, as the youths would find out at a later juncture, much to their regret.

'I saw ye,' she repeated. 'Profane a woman's undergarments, ye sinful godless creatures.'

Daniel threw out a riposte, though Alan was already trying to edge them away from further entanglement.

'I merely moved them to another location,' he replied.

'Ye have no shame!'

As Agnes spat out this verdict, some virtuous saliva joined forces with the rain falling alike on the blameless and culpable.

Nature has no favourites.

While Alan tugged at his elbow, Daniel peered with some humour into the accusing mouth.

'No shame indeed, but yet I have my own teeth.'

The tiny form shook angrily.

'A godless sinner!'

'He does lack a certain pious inclination, madam. You are correct in that observation,' said Alan earnestly, though a gleam in his eye betokened an inherent comicality to the situation.

Agnes's hat was saturated and had folded itself around the small pointed pate like a dismal pancake. She wrenched her head right and left to scatter the seeping raindrops, and moved forward to remonstrate further.

'Decent folk cannot walk the streets these nights without a student rabble making their life a misery.'

'I would imagine yours to be a misery in any case, madam,' Daniel responded ungallantly. Then, with aplomb, he limped forward and offered with outstretched hand what he thought to be a placatory gift.

It was a crudely formed rosette of white — the emblem of his faction, and indeed one of the same rested cosily in the bosom of the billowing corset above.

'You may have one of our favours, madam.

5

White. For purity of purpose.'

She snatched the rosette and with a vicious tweak of her clawed fingers, tore the fragile fabric in two.

Christians have never hesitated to proclaim their virtue by indiscriminate cruelty and Agnes held true to her belief; indeed the action released a further vein of moral invective sown in the Old Testament and reaped by Calvinism.

'Ye dare insult your elders,' she observed with tight-lipped relish. 'Look at you. A deformed soul. See God's punishment for your wickedness.'

Daniel's face flushed and his hand gripped tight to the cane. 'Go to hell,' he muttered and allowed himself to be moved away by Alan's restraining hand.

But Agnes had more to convey, clutching at the light grey sleeve of Daniel's suit, a colour he wore to distinguish himself from the common herd.

'You will wait till I have ended!' she shrieked.

'Take your hands from me — '

'You will wait my pleasure — '

Alan had by now walked some paces on, thinking to be followed, but now looked back to see the struggling pair.

'Daniel, come on with you,' he called somewhat desperately. What had been an amusing entanglement now appeared to have a vicious aspect.

'Let me go!'

The young man wrenched away and Agnes fell onto her backside in a puddle with an unholy splash.

'See how I am treated, God help me!' she cried

as both youths disappeared into the darkness.

For a moment Alan looked concerned, but Daniel hauled the larger man onwards, shooting back a vindictive glance, and then all that was left was the sound of the rain.

A distant howl indicated a faraway melee as the rival students joined battle.

Agnes sat, feeling the noxious damp spread around her nether regions. It seemed an eternity passed before she gathered the strength to lever her bony form upright.

She once more clutched her handbag and muttering a deal of possibly uncharitable imprecations, moved slowly off into the darkness.

Mistress Agnes Carnegie had lodgings in Salamander Street, where the slaughterhouse welcomed most dumb animals to its bloody bosom; every night she walked the length of Leith Harbour safe in the arms of the Saviour, but this evening the inner conversation was informed with a certain malicious righteousness.

Despite her damp posterior she considered she had won the joust with the crippled reprobate — had he not fled the battle? Scuttled away like a dirty wee rat?

Agnes laughed aloud in the silence. But what was better was her discovery from an earlier time — an open book had revealed the dark secret that would give her power to use or withhold, depending upon her Christian conscience.

Oh, the pleasure to be found as fearful haunted eyes begged silently for mercy and her avoiding gaze twisted the sin deeper, like a nail in the flesh.

Then a wetness where her fleshly tissue had rarely if ever known such brought her wandering thoughts back to present circumstance.

Daniel, the other had called him. A fell disgrace for such a holy name —

The rain had stopped for a moment and something fluttered at her feet. It was the favour she had previously torn, now lying on the moist flagstones.

Agnes looked swiftly around but saw nothing save darkness and shadow. Then a chirruping whistle sounded from behind her and she turned to see a slim figure emerge from one of the wynds that spread like wormy fissures from the body of the harbour.

Her eyesight was poor but she could see that he held a cane and skipped with an odd halting gait towards her.

Had the old woman not been so wrapped up in her vengeful musings, she might have observed this strange being to have dogged her footsteps for some time.

She peered as he whistled once more like a discordant meadowlark. His face was chalk white, his suit a pale colour, hair plastered flat, eyes dark and hidden as his countenance was averted at an angle from her sight.

He pranced up merrily like a March hare, struck an attitude with one dainty foot to the fore, then flipped back the tip of his cane to land on the shoulder and smiled, the teeth a little yellow against the white mask of his face.

Then he deliberately allowed himself to become still and presented his appearance close

8

towards her, as if in invitation.

Finally, her jaw dropped in recognition.

'You — ' she began as the cane whipped across and took her full in the throat, crushing the windpipe to stanch the flow of air.

Words need air.

As her head lurched forward, the cane cut viciously down in two blows to the sides of her unprotected neck and then welted down upon her pathetic, pious hat to penetrate her cranium.

She fell like a stone and the blows rained down with hideous accuracy and no little brio as the figure danced around the broken-backed doll that had once been a woman of some upright quality.

With her dying breath Agnes tried to form a word to name what she had recognised, but a swordsmanlike hit cut precisely between her eyes like a sabre and — as it were — she gave up the ghost.

A dying spasm finally loosened her grip on the bag and amongst its contents, now spilled out onto the slippery stone, was a heavy bible, solemn with usage, but the spine loose and flapping like a duck's wing.

The figure riffled through the pages till, coming upon a suitable passage he ripped free the leaf. Having perused then marked a line in it with a thumbnail, he wrapped the white favour within this holy covering and stuffed the whole inside the old woman's mouth as if she were a Christmas turkey. He then jammed the jaw shut.

So, like a jack-a-dandy, bible in hand, he danced off into the night, leaving his erstwhile partner a numb, lifeless wallflower.

The rain began to fall again, diluting the trickle of dark blood coming from the ears of the corpse.

A seagull high above let out a screech.

To signal a soul departing, or was it just a bird on the wing?

2

I've seen sae mony changefu' years,
On earth I am a stranger grown:
I wander in the ways of men,
Alike unknowing and unknown.
                Robert Burns, *Lament for James,*
                                Earl of Glencairn

James McLevy regarded himself in the rust-flaked mirror and came to the conclusion that he resembled a ruined castle.

The cheekbones still held their place but above and below were a scene of near desolation.

Where was the wolf these days?

He leant forward and peered into the slate grey eyes almost concealed in the folds of lidded flesh; a yellow light might still burn in them somewhere but damned if he could see it.

This revelation caused the nostrils to flare in the broad pitted nose. What teeth remained were like tombstone stubs hidden behind the thick, curiously ripe lips.

It aye puzzled the inspector why his lips might appear so lush with promised joy and perhaps to disguise this, he had recently grown a bushy moustache, which was flecked with some grey and an indeterminate colour like charred ashes that gave him the appearance of, in the opinion of Constable Mulholland, 'a walrus with the mange'.

Beneath the dimpled, or in more manly terms,

11

cleft chin was where the real trouble lay.

The heart.

Some years before, the inspector, after laying low a brute of a killer by dint of shooting the bugger on top of a roof while receiving a simultaneous battering, had commenced to experience various shafts of pain in the chest and innards. These shafts were sharp and took the breath away.

After suffering for many years as a man is apt to do with what he does not wish to acknowledge, this thorn in his flesh became more insistent and harder to disguise from such as Mulholland and Lieutenant Roach at the station.

McLevy began to suspect that Roach, not a man noted for his perception of other's woes, was giving him the odd little sideways look, so the inspector decided enough was enough and went to see the doctor.

A doctor in Glasgow of course; Edinburgh was a village for gossip and there's nothing the Scots enjoy more than the cataloguing of other folk's ailments.

Alexander Pettigrew was the reconnoitred specialist: an attenuated yet boisterous fellow whose false teeth flew in and out of his mouth with alarming rapidity.

The inspector had grudgingly bared his upper body to be poked and prodded, suffered an interrogation as regards his dietary habits, and even at one point been cross-examined on the subject of sexual activity.

Pettigrew clacked his teeth happily at the baleful glare this question produced — nothing

12

irritates the male Caledonian more than enquiries into the activity of nether regions.

The doctor finally sat down at his desk while McLevy donned his shirt and jacket, then put his medical fingers together to form a barricade and then beamed.

'Your heart,' he pronounced, 'is like an old carthorse that has been hauling a heavy load up too many braes, its poor hooves striking sparks from the cobblestones, the beast frothing at the mouth, badly fed and worse treated.'

This created a vivid picture in McLevy's mind except that it was himself he envisaged, lugging a scaffie cart up Coal Hill while the criminal classes of Leith jeered and threw big dods of mud at his suffering carcass.

But who was driving the vehicle? When he looked back, he saw a bulky figure silhouetted against the dull sky — the man was wearing a low-brimmed bowler and brandishing a whip.

Pettigrew at the desk bore a fixed smile on his face as if it were cemented; in fact the only time the doctor had frowned in any way was when McLevy had described his plethora of tavern provender augmented by many mugs of coffee, each furnished with four to six large sugars, that he gulped during the day and especially at night.

Having exhausted his carthorse simile, the physician moved in for the kill.

'Mend your ways,' he declared with a hint of the Old Testament, 'or the Grim Reaper will mend them for you.'

His patient seemed unimpressed. Pettigrew clarified.

'Death. Will strike you down.'

'I deal wi' death every day,' muttered McLevy.

'You are an undertaker by occupation?'

'Of a kind.'

McLevy had volunteered nothing in terms of his job.

'It causes you a measure of strain?'

'More like mortal trepidation — from time to time.'

The healer shook his head in cheerful sorrow. 'Then you must give up the profession!'

The atmosphere in the consulting room changed suddenly as if an icy ghost had slid in, and the doctor found himself pinned back by the bleak menace in the opposite eyes.

'My profession is my life.'

The flat statement lay on the desk between them like a fallen angel, until Pettigrew leapt to his feet and pointed an accusing finger from his tall lanky frame.

'Do you sleep?' he demanded.

'Whit?'

'With such caffeine ingestion — do you *sleep*?'

The inspector considered this.

'But rarely,' he replied.

The doctor waved his arms in triumph as if he had diagnosed the disease.

'Then worry no more about your aforesaid life. Either change your ways my dear sir, or you will attain the longest sleep known to man. An everlasting quiescence. Oblivion!'

On that dramatic note, a sour-faced McLevy had paid the Messenger of Doom, quit the scene and travelled back to Edinburgh as fast as the train could take his newly maligned shell of humanity.

The present incumbent of this cracked and fissured carapace left a grumpy face plus Glasgow memories in the mirror and crossed to a recessed cupboard, there to unlock the door panel with the gravity of a parish priest about to delve into the sacraments.

Here he kept mementoes of past cases all related for the most part to homicidal intent; either accomplished or abandoned depending on which way the hangman's rope had swung.

In pride of place was a narrow red ledger, itself a product of the relatively innocuous crime of embezzlement though it did involve a respectable suicide; this he carefully removed to lay upon the scratched surface of his battered old table-cum-writing desk.

Above the table was a large window that looked down from a height over the gleaming, mysterious city — this was his family, his keeping and his fate. Auld Reekie.

He sat, pursed his lips solemnly, slugged back some cold coffee from a mug, dipped his pen and began.

Diary of James McLevy.
7th May, 1887.

It has been some years since I ceased to write in this book and my motives for stopping are as puzzling to me now as the reason why I recommence.

The past wreaks vengeance on the present.

15

These words have been running in my head all day. If I set them down on paper, perhaps they may let me be.

They are accompanied by a dull feeling of dread, nothing you could pin with a finger but lurking as though perceived by someone else who has deposited the pending catastrophe with me for safe keeping.

Lurking.

And another thing.

Why is it that iniquity reveals nothing in the visage?

Here's me, a bastion of law and order looking like a demolished edifice compared wi' Jean Brash who keeps the most notorious bawdy-hoose in Edinburgh, revels in all levels of corruption and yet has the appearance of a milkmaid at dawn. Well, nearly.

Is there some toothless old harpy in the Just Land to whom she transfers the marks of sin? Who sits sookin', plook ridden, at some crumbly sugar biscuit in the darkness of the cellar? I must take scrutiny, next time I visit.

Jean Brash. The woman is untouched. Like a picture in a frame.

But I bear the scars of every murderous crime I have set my seal across. They sear me. Old yapping ghosts.

Scars of body and soul.

A curious innocence in my heart yearns for redemption.

There is a wild energy prowling in the city. Young. Dangerous. A roving, vagabond energy. The devil is on the loose and who knows what

16

flavours he will throw in the pot?

As usual I am in the middle but I feel the ground shaky as if the centre lacks cohesion.

Oh to be young again. What a foolish thought.

McLevy carefully blotted this guddle of half-baked insights and closed the book.

A noise from the streets below brought him to the window and he looked from his attic room over the black slates drenched by the slant rain of May, down at the torches flickering in the distance by the harbour.

A youthful reckless energy. Hazardous to itself and other folk or was that just the opinion of an old man whose voice echoed in the fumbling darkness?

Ach tae hell with it. He defiantly poured some tarry dregs from his fire-scorched coffee pot into the mug and let the humid tincture trickle through tombstone teeth as the enamel rim brushed annoyingly against the stalwart bristle of his moustache.

But there was scant doubt. Heart or no heart, pain or no pain — the devil had come to town.

What mask was he wearing?

3

Watchman, what of the night?
Watchman what of the night?
The Watchman said,
The morning cometh, and also the night.

                    Isaiah, ch21, v11. *The Bible*

A more piratical hirsute adornment under a very different nose, long and finely shaped, sifted the fumes of nicotine through its filaments as the owner of both neb and fusker gazed thoughtfully out at the respectable street below.

Heriot Row was a fine example of rectitude rewarded; it may have led at one end to the slightly suggestive curves of Abercrombie Place but of itself was straight as a die.

His father would have approved, no doubt still did approve, lying himself undeviating in the coffin, hands folded, good book closed for the journey, cold white face arranged so that demonic senility had left no trail.

An empty space.

Thomas Stevenson, father of the miscreant Robert Louis, was waiting for his burial in some days' time.

Patience father. It will come. And I shall see to it. A splendid affair. No expense spared. Clouds of glory.

Stevenson sucked a long draft of smoke deep into his waiting lungs, a blessing they still

18

functioned to purpose, and held it close like a lover. It crept into the crevices of his bony shipwrecked chest, calming the nerves, soothing the feelings, until released with a whoosh.

Leaving behind?

Another empty space, my friend.

He tapped the cigarette ash off into his palm, regarded the tiny mound gravely, then blew it away towards nowhere.

The whole house was asleep, thank God; his wife Fanny no doubt engaged in phantom operatic adventures provoked by her instinctual organs; his mother Margaret hopefully not actually slumbering in widow's weeds, though she had taken to mourning like a duck to water, slept the righteous sleep; and Lloyd, Fanny's son but not his, would be snoring like a log.

Like a log.

Good boy. A consecration if he but knew it. Sleep.

And Robert Louis? The famous Robert Louis? Left with and by himself, which, to tell truth, was no great hardship.

Peace to torture himself with guilty imaginings, amuse same with the observed traits of humankind, or bear witness to the wellspring whence the strange beings that peopled his tales of adventure and woe issued forth, unbidden, at times most terrifying, but never unwelcome.

From the depths they arose and to the depths they descended.

All grist to the mill.

He sucked once more upon his self-rolled,

19

Papier Persan, tobacco conduit to the stars and murmured in the half-light.

Come lend me an attentive ear,
A startling moral tale to hear,
Of Pirate Rob and Chemist Ben,
And different destinies of men.

Indeed. Different destinies.

They had arrived and for two days the old man had stared at Stevenson as if he had sprouted from the moon.

Then Thomas passed over to that blessed veil where along with the Almighty, various Presbyterian dignitaries would no doubt be waiting to hail him for a life well spent, consult their pocket watches and congratulate the devout traveller for arriving bang on time.

Pre-destined.

Or an empty space.

Faites vos jeux.

Louis shivered suddenly; someone had walked over his grave. To see that face empty of meaning, eyes dilated, jaw agape, made a brutal mockery of conscious existence.

In many ways he had feared his father, especially the irrational rages that contrasted with the decent generosity and kindness shown to his wayward son.

The dark forces he rode like a rider in the storm, in his father had been buried under pillars of rectitude.

And at the end, had they not taken vengeance? Put his senses to fire and pillage, destroyed the inner essence, gouged out the soul and left a vacant carcass to rattle and creak like a haunted house.

Ahh!

Tobacco had burnt to the stub and singed the tapered authorial fingers. Stevenson swiftly extracted another cigarette from his case and passed the immortal flame from one to the other. *Cigarettes without intermission, save for when coughing and kissing* — both of these carry sufficient danger by themselves, wouldn't you say, old chap?

He flipped the stumpy remnant out through the open window and watched with some malicious glee as it sparkled like a sinful firefly upon the respectable flagstone before a drenching rain put paid to further adventures.

Edinburgh rain was like no other. He had returned but a few days and already his body ached, nose constantly dripping.

How could this hero, creator of *Treasure Island*, *Kidnapped*, and *The Strange Case of Dr Jekyll and Mr Hyde* into which it was rumoured that Queen Victoria herself had inserted royal fingers to ruffle these pages of charted depravity, how could this hero stand before his household gods with a snottery nose?

Louis caught an errant nasal effusion in a large white handkerchief and regarded himself in that part of the window pane not covered by the heavy curtains. It was a ghostly image: pale, long face like a disappointed donkey; drooping but sly moustache; prominent bony forehead; and dark eyes that darted right and left before settling

21

once more into a fixed perusal of the countenance, heart-shaped; the hair long and brushed back from the somewhat large ears.

Earlier that day, in his father's desk, he had come upon some cached photographs, posed formally with Thomas who stared at the camera as if preparing for a life of filial disenchantment over the doleful creature with an old man's head on a young body standing there beside him.

Stevenson had felt a sudden piercing to the heart, replaced the images and closed the drawer.

Enough. Enough regrets for this night.

He struck a sudden comical pose, cigarette held aloft like a holy relic, and pranced like one bereft of wits before inhaling once more with bravura.

That's more like it. That's the ticket.

A wry smile spread across the other's face in the window pane — what a fool to behold.

A dolt. And a workhorse.

He ignored the faint sneer that had appeared in the visage opposite and peered past it into the dark night. The young men who had gathered earlier to jostle in Heriot Row for a glimpse of ghostly legend at the upstairs fenestra, had been driven away by the incessant rain, or perhaps they had better mischief in mind.

As a law student he had prowled the streets in licentious drunken gallivants, but these medical boys would seem to have codified their pursuits into tribal lines.

Somewhere in the house a clock chimed midnight and in the silence each separate sound spread dark vibrations that permeated one after another, into his very being.

A sound of foreboding.

As if something was being cradled and created, an evil likeness in his name.

And then wrenched from him to have another life and spread atrocities in the wet and bitter night.

The man known to one and all as Robert Louis Stevenson pulled himself out of that particular pit to drag some more emollient tobacco into his lungs, let it seep into every possible pore and then stood quietly in the shrouded room.

Let it come. Whatever it be. Above or below nature. He did not fear the unknown.

It lay within him like a hungry beast.

Let it come.

4

Death like a narrow sea divides,
This heavenly land from ours.
Isaac Watts, *Hymns and Spiritual Songs*

Four faces were to be observed in the Cold Room at Leith Station.

One belonged to Lieutenant Robert Roach, an elongated snouty affair, not unlike an irritated alligator. His long jaw twitched unhappily as he glanced at his erstwhile subordinate who shook the raindrops off a heavy coat and sucked thoughtfully at one end of his moustache.

James McLevy. Roach had known him for nigh on fifteen years and still the man was a mystery. There were rumours the inspector was a secret Papist, frequented opium dens, most certainly had a strange and twisted relationship with Jean Brash who ran the best bawdy-hoose in Edinburgh, and had killed men with his bare hands.

The lieutenant was prepared to discount the opium since he was the one who had sent McLevy in under cover; as regards bare hands the level of violence he had witnessed unleashed, even at a distance, would always make such a possibility, and as long as it was directed at the criminal classes Roach was prepared to grant a little leeway — but in his Presbyterian bones he sensed a strange otherness of religion in the man.

24

It might be a mere Jacobite leaning but with Pope Leo XIII daring to celebrate his priestly version some months after the oncoming Golden Jubilee of Queen Victoria, it was as well to be on guard.

The House of Windsor had been making conciliatory moves in the Vatican's direction but these moves had not crossed over the border.

Nor would they ever.

As regards Jean Brash — that was a mystery beyond all powers of deduction.

One thing was for sure. The man might look like a midden, scorn authority like a street keelie, ignore the wise advice of his superior officer to the point of blind insolence, but James McLevy was a Thieftaker. The best in the city, the best Roach had ever witnessed.

A combination of the aforesaid violence, fierce forensic intelligence and weird insight cut through murder and crime like a knife through butter.

Not that Roach would ever admit it. Or deal praise. But nothing pleased him better than seeing his Chief Constable Sandy Robb at the Masonic monthly gathering, to murmur such as . . . *The Pearson case is closed. The poison the judge used to kill his butterflies was utilised by his own wife. As my inspector observed . . . hoist with his own petard.*

Of course this deadly ability was buttressed by the owner of the face on Roach's other side.

Martin Mulholland towered a good eight inches over the inspector and four over his own lieutenant. He had an open candid countenance

25

that bore no trace of the myriad murders and bloody adventures through which he had trailed his large boots. The bar-room brawls he had taken part in alongside his inspector with lethal hornbeam stick to hand was part of Leith legend. Still a humble constable, he had refused promotion many times because he preferred to be on the saunter with McLevy to any other activity.

His Irish blue eyes and soft spoken ways had lulled many a female criminal into an unwise move, though it must be said that his luck with women was just terrible unless arresting them.

Which is why he had recently taken up bee-keeping.

So there were three faces, all with a tale to tell.

The fourth belonged to a female body that lay on the slab. It was waxy as a dead moon, already shrivelled, and covered with a sheet to hide the poor naked form with livid bruises that marked her at regular intervals.

This face was empty, the eyes staring and the jaw tight shut.

'Found by the early morning constable down by the docks, brought in with the carry-wagon.'

The lieutenant sniffed in disapproval at the faint musky smell coming from the inspector's coat — was there a whiff of rodent?

'I was here to receive it. I arrive on time for my bounden duty.'

McLevy grunted and peered more closely at the corpse; in his experience there was never any hurry to view a dead body, after all they weren't going to make a run for it.

He had much on his mind and so had taken a circuitous route to the station to mull over a strange and jagged dream that had invaded his few hours of repose.

No sooner arrived than he had been summoned in to gaze upon the latest murderous offering from the parish.

The inspector tossed his low-brimmed bowler onto a little table supposedly reserved for the medical instruments of the police surgeon.

Roach sighed.

'Well?' he enquired snappily.

'I think I know the face,' Mulholland announced from on high.

'Ye should,' McLevy muttered. 'Some years ago, a wee keelie stole the poor box from St Stephen's Church.'

'You're not wrong there,' replied the constable, coming over a little Irish as his memory sparked into life. 'Ran like hell up Forres Street, pursued by the devout.'

'Right intae our worshipful arms.'

'What were you doing in the vicinity?' the lieutenant asked with a suspicious gleam in his eye. 'That's Heriot Row and the environs. Respectable citizenry.'

'We got lost,' was McLevy's stolid response. In truth when he and Mulholland went on the saunter only the devil knew where the journey would end.

'She was in the van of pursuit, I remember now. Put on a fair turn of speed for her age,' offered the constable.

'Not any more,' said McLevy, lifting aside the

sheet to display the inert body.

'And the poor box was empty,' Mulholland recalled.

'A' that palaver for nothing.'

'A decent devout soul on the path of righteousness,' Roach muttered querulously. 'How does she end up dead as a doornail in Leith Harbour?'

'God's mystery, sir.'

McLevy moved to stand at the top of the cold slab behind the head of the corpse; for a moment, to the disconcerted Roach, he took the appearance of a minister at the pulpit, but Mulholland knew his man better and merely straightened up a little.

Facts were about to unfold.

'Agnes Carnegie,' the inspector pronounced. 'Lodges somewhere in Salamander Street, a deal o' distance from St Stephen's but she made the pilgrimage.'

A quirk of black humour twisted McLevy's lips.

'Ye'll know her son, Mulholland. Sim Carnegie. An auld freen of yours.'

The constable's face tightened as he made the connection.

'The newspaper man?' Roach said. 'That's all we need.'

The lieutenant took a deep breath within his immaculate uniform and set the official investigation on its way.

'Now we know who she is — *why did she die?*'

'Not robbery,' replied Mulholland crisply, the memory of his last encounter with Sim Carnegie pushed to the side though a vestige of anger lingered. 'Her handbag still had the purse. Intact. Not much to send home but intact.'

He stopped to see if McLevy had anything to add but the inspector's attention seemed to be still fixed on the rigid shrunken face of the departed Agnes.

It brought back a memory of the dream. Himself as a young man. Lost in a forest of insinuating ferns and female laughter and then looking into a pool of water to see there reflected an old wizened apparition.

He had come awake sweating like a hog.

'Cold blood,' Mulholland said suddenly. 'Murder in cold blood.'

'How so?' Roach questioned.

'If you look at the blows. Even spaced. Like a tiger's stripes. Matched on each side. That takes precision.'

'And precision,' agreed McLevy, 'demands cold blood.'

He had spotted something at the side of the corpse's jaw, the merest sliver of paper of some sort and, without a by your leave, abruptly wedged apart the mandibles and stuck his fingers inside.

'Open Sesame!'

Roach let out an outraged yelp.

'That is the function of the police surgeon!'

'Doctor Jarvis isnae here, sir,' replied McLevy, delving industriously. 'If he were, we'd smell the claret. Now see!'

With the air of a magician the inspector had produced from the sunken mouth a wodge of wet paper, which he neatly picked open to disclose a white, crumpled relic of sorts.

He slid the relic to the side with a damp forefinger and squinted hard at the paper.

'It is a page from the Bible,' he announced.

One part of the writing that had a line scored underneath seemed to jump from the segment and McLevy quoted it with due solemnity.

Ye are like unto whited sepulchres, which indeed appear beautiful outward, but are within full of dead men's bones.

Roach blinked his eyes in disbelief.

'Sacrilege!' he reproached the bare, uncaring walls of the cold room. 'To desecrate the Holy Book and stuff it in a poor woman's God-fearing mouth!'

'And her no doubt dying at the time,' observed McLevy dryly.

'No sign of such in the handbag,' Mulholland observed. 'Perhaps the killer carries pages with him.'

'A calling card,' said the inspector.

The lieutenant shook his head.

Though both faces before him were set in solemn lines, he felt as if the whole event had moved into a weird divergent universe where Satan's hooves were scudding on the rooftops.

He took refuge in scrutinising the crumpled relic.

This he could name. Upon this he could contribute hard-earned knowledge.

'A white favour,' he almost spat out the words. 'These damned students were down the harbour last night and left a female undergarment atop the mast of the Excise ship!'

'It also had a white favour I am reliably informed, sir. Stuck in the breastworks.'

This poker-faced statement from Mulholland set Roach's mind spinning in an ever more tempestuous gyre.

'The harbour last night was swarming with the White Faction. Is it possible their wild behaviour overstepped the mark?'

'It's possible,' allowed McLevy. 'All things are possible.'

The inspector replaced the sheet and, as one man, the three, McLevy nipping up his bowler on the way, suddenly strode from the Cold Room like the end of an Act upon the stage. Agnes was left sole remnant, the white sheet spread over like a shroud. McLevy had forgotten to close her mouth and she looked cheated from a last word.

The main hall of Leith Station seemed like a complete other world; Sergeant Murdoch near somnolent at the public desk as usual, the constables just changing shift and a deal of good-natured horseplay amongst the young men giving the impression indeed of animals in a field.

Normally Roach would frown upon such behaviour, but at this moment he welcomed the earthy normality; then just as he was about to slip into a more comfortable role, his roving attention was caught and the lieutenant's eyes near popped.

'Ballantyne!'

The addressed recipient, a young gawky constable whose face was marked by a livid scarlet birth-mark that extended down the neck, turned with a faintly bemused air.

Ballantyne was a strange mixture of unconscious innocence and the occasional cryptic remark that caused the listener to wonder whether this boy was as gormless as he appeared to be.

At first he had been relentlessly bullied by the herd but, without in any way cosseting or making exception, McLevy and Mulholland had put the boot in hard against a few backsides to alter that particular situation.

The young constable often amused McLevy, but this did not apply to the lieutenant now, who pointed an accusing finger at Ballantyne's reasonably well-ordered tunic.

'What — what is that — there?'

The constable looked down at the small emblem tucked into one of his top buttons.

'I found it in the street,' he replied cheerfully enough. 'It's a nice wee colour.'

It was in fact one of the favours from the Scarlet Runners; perhaps the boy had picked it because the hue matched his own marking, but in Roach's case it was the red rag to a bull.

'Remove it from your person and let me never again see such a monstrosity festoon the decent environs of this station!'

The constable's mouth opened and shut like a goldfish, his pale blue eyes blinked, then he slowly removed the favour and slid it into his trouser pocket.

A snort of suppressed laughter brought Roach's head whipping round but McLevy and

Mulholland were graven images.

'An old woman lies dead,' said the lieutenant bleakly. 'I suggest you begin an investigation.'

'We'll do that right away, sir,' McLevy averred.

'And you might start with the White Faction!'

'That's immediately on our mind, lieutenant.'

Mulholland's dutiful response failed to satisfy Roach, who felt that these two found some secret amusement in all this tomfoolery, but a piercing stare produced no discernible reaction and so he turned back to the hapless Ballantyne.

'Never — again!'

With that apocalyptic warning the lieutenant strode off into his office, slamming the door behind.

'That'll shake Her Majesty,' said McLevy.

Roach's beloved Queen Victoria had pride of place in various portraits on his office wall, but despite best effort she was forever hanging on the slant.

The inspector turned to Ballantyne, whose fair hair had flopped over a downcast face.

'Try no' tae annoy the lieutenant, eh?'

'It jist seems natural,' came the reply.

McLevy shook his head, a smile that might even have been mistaken for affection on his face.

'Away ye go and save the cockroaches.'

Ballantyne nodded and off he tootled. He had a great interest in the insect world, and spent much of his time at the station shepherding invertebrates into small boxes to be shaken out into a quiet byway, safe from the marauding boots of the constabulary.

A thoughtful silence fell between McLevy and Mulholland.

'The lieutenant's in a rare bate.'

'There was of course the recent incident,' Mulholland responded, 'where a woman had her posterior pinched in Constitution Street and the lieutenant got the blame, he walking behind at the time.'

'A student prank no doubt.'

'I believe so. But he was sore offended.'

This deadpan exchange over, McLevy's mind flitted back to the body in the Cold Room.

He had seen Agnes Carnegie sometime in the harbour streets, a small, grim, dark-clad figure; that sort of dismal denying rectitude was everything he detested in the baleful essence of the unco' righteous.

Nevertheless the woman was dead. Most cruelly murdered.

Had she blundered into this by accident or had the cause, as so often in his experience, risen from the dark roots of a blighted past?

Time would tell.

Yet the wizened, shrunken face, like a trophy on a cannibal's belt, stayed with him.

Was that to be *his* fate?

Love gone. Life fled.

Too late now. Was it Confucius said that?

He became aware that Mulholland was regarding him curiously, a habit the constable had fallen into of late.

'Murder most foul,' he said, jamming on his low-brimmed bowler. 'That's our profession.'

Mulholland also stuck his helmet aloft, which

34

resembled a pea on the crest of a mountain, and they left swiftly.

Ballantyne, trying to coax a small beetle into a Lucifer box, watched them depart the scene. One day the constable dreamt of being an intrepid investigator, feared by many and envied by all.

He glanced round to make sure there was no untoward observation and teased out the favour from his pocket.

It was still a nice wee colour.

5

Anger is one of the sinews of the soul.
Thomas Fuller,
The Holy State and the Profane State

The magpies of the Just Land leant out its neatly painted, neatly grooved windows and tried to suppress laughter that shook them like rag dolls.

A demanding night afore; the May Cattle Tryst when the heavy-boned men of the Lothians bulled their way into the city, sold their stock, and kicked over the traces, before lowing back o'er the lea towards their muddy farmyards.

After a wild series of reels to greet the world of nature, there was many a rutted furrow and many a swollen plough-graith primed to dig high or low; loud were the cries and deep were the bellows.

Some of this would have been better employed in the marital bed, but it is aye a mark of the male animal that he makes his loudest noise away from home.

After such ramstam milling — they may not have been Gallic but by God these men could give it laldie — the magpies had lain late abed wondering idly what it might be like to be a farmer's wife, then rose at the same time as if linked by some satiated cycle to consider the garden of the Just Land.

It was a sight to behold.

36

There was their mistress Jean Brash, still in her elegant morning décolletage, flitting about like a demented moth and getting wetter by the second in the rain, as she and her right-hand woman, Hannah Semple, keeper of the keys, attempted to gather in a most unusual harvest.

It falls out as follows.

To prevent unwanted impregnation or passing of the pox from one precipitous plunge to another, the most learned scientists and engineering talents of Her Gracious Majesty's realm had produced — the sheath.

Animal intestines soaked and then tied with a piece of ribbon. French Letters, English Overcoats, name them as you wish, they were to be attached to the erect male member with the requisite amount of firmness, though a too-tight ribbon might stem the flow and numb desire.

But that was where they belonged.

On the aforesaid member.

Not festooned round the bushes and rose banks, stuck arbitrarily upon a naked twig, flaccid and glistening in the rain save for a number that had been inflated by unknown means and pinned at height on branches to wave gaily in the conniving wind.

The Scarlet Runners had struck in the night, leaving their red favours to provide safe convoy.

Jean had risen to discover this, let out a howl for Hannah, and been hard at harvest since.

The sheaths had been left high and low, so she was forced to use long bamboo sticks to knock them off like so many fairground trophies.

'Ye'll catch your death o' cauld,' Hannah

panted, hauling at one guilty specimen which stretched like a sausage skin before pulling free with a sodden twang. 'The Lord be thanked, at least they're empty o' purpose.'

Jean's own red hair was plastered to her face, the dressing gown of fine silk moulded to and slithering round her lean shapely body in what might well have been deemed erotic invitation had it not been for an expression that would have stopped a charging satyr in his tracks.

'I'll kill the swine,' she muttered, her green eyes narrowed to a pin-point of rage.

'Oh mah Goad,' exclaimed Hannah. 'There's wan on the boy Cupid.'

Jean recently had overseen a small statue to the son of Venus installed tastefully in a shady nook, but now to accompany the playing of his pipes, Cupid had a wrinkled embellishment upon his stubby appendage.

As the mistress of the Just Land jerked the thing from its locus with a furious twitch the magpies above could contain themselves no longer.

A loud peal of hilarity rang through the damp air.

Jean looked up and all was sudden silence. Nothing is more terrifying than a beautiful woman in a rage.

'You girls come down here,' she said coldly. 'And get tae work gathering.'

As the windows slammed shut in chorus, the back door to the garden opened and Lily Baxter emerged.

Lily was a small, sunny-natured creature, deaf

and dumb since birth, but a bundle of attractive curves.

She and her lover, Maisie Powers, who appeared behind, had been comparatively underused the previous night, due to the fact that in the Just Land cellars they catered mostly for inflicted pain with, if requested, lacerating bondage.

The farmers got quite enough of that in the calving season, so the two women, expert with whip and thistle, had rested on their laurels yester-evening.

Lily's face was grave and she pushed the large, somewhat lumpy figure of Maisie to the front. The big girl also held one of the offensive casings.

'I found it stuck tae the front door knob,' she said.

Jean closed her eyes for a second.

'Take it away,' she ordered. 'It's bad for business.'

Lily meanwhile had picked up one of the bamboo sticks, used for supporting plants, and was swishing it through the air with a thoughtful expression on her face.

'Take it away!'

The two vanished and there was silence in the garden, broken only by the soft hiss of rain.

'We could maybe reconnoiter some o' the better quality,' suggested Hannah helpfully. 'Waste not, want not.'

Her mistress made no reply. They made an odd couple in the wet grass, Jean graceful as a swan despite her bedraggled ensemble and

Hannah a clumpy figure in her woolly gown and rubber boots.

The old woman was in her own admission weather-beaten by the bitter winds of misfortune and had been no raving beauty to begin with, but the bond of trust between the two of them, though stretched many a time, had never broken.

'Ye should get McLevy in and show him the evidence,' volunteered Hannah after deep thought. 'That would be a sicht worth seeing.'

'I'm sure he has a passing acquaintance,' Jean said quietly.

For a moment there was a strange, lost look in her eye, but then the garden door opened and as the magpies spilled out to scatter all over the garden, Hannah rushed off to supervise and Jean was left alone.

'I'm sure he has acquaintance,' she repeated to herself as the rain ran down her face and the scarlet favours lay scattered round like so many discarded blossoms of desire.

6

See how love and murder will out.
    Congreve, *The Double Dealer*

What James McLevy had acquaintance with at this precise moment was a mounting irritation, though not a flicker of this showed on his features, which had settled into what Mulholland knew well as the inspector's *a wee bit out of his depth, self-important but not-too-bright* official persona. This had its uses.

They both stood in a well-furnished respectable room, in a well-furnished respectable house in St Andrew Square, whence had one a telescope one could gaze a long way down at the teeming wynds of Leith.

McLevy could not stand wiseacres, especially with youth on their side and Daniel Drummond qualified mightily on both counts.

The young man was trying to disguise the obvious superiority of his intelligence as best he could, but it issued from the very pores. His companion, Alan Grant, appeared a more decent type not quite so comfortable with such supremacy of class and education.

Mulholland stood slightly back observing the play and noticed that McLevy had not shaved very well that morning, the moustache unfortunately remaining, but the chin nicked by razor and upon that feature various hairs celebrating their escape.

There was a heaviness to the inspector's limbs and general demeanour that was not pretence; the animal vitality that fuelled that investigative hunger, and was the bedrock of the violent outbursts that terrified the criminal fraternity, lay it would seem in abeyance.

And yet. And yet.

What was it his Aunt Katy was wont to say?

There's nothing darker than a wolf's mouth especially when he's yawning fit to burst.

Drummond and Grant had been identified from sources as the ringleaders of the White Devils, with address supplied by a professor at the university who owed McLevy a favour of a different kind, by dint of one wayward sister rescued from the toils of a blackmailer.

The sister sadly continued being a laudanum addict but the blackmailer ended up in a fishcart headed for Stranraer.

A fate worse than death.

And so here they were. Four figures in a room.

'A bit of fun, inspector,' Daniel announced airily. 'Think of it as letting off steam.'

'*Steam?*' repeated McLevy ponderously.

'A figure of speech, sir,' said Alan.

The inspector nodded his head as if enlightened and Daniel was encouraged to elucidate further.

'We have passed all medical examinations, and are soon to be qualified men of repute, but in the meantime . . . '

'You create havoc, Mister Drummond,' Mulholland interposed.

Daniel smiled proudly.

42

'We are the White Devils. The Scarlet Runners sniff at our heels. Daring deeds — in that we compete!'

'Like breaking shop windows?' asked the constable.

'It does go a bit far at times,' Alan allowed judiciously, 'But compensation was paid.'

'Whit about murder?'

At this sudden and blunt assertion from the grizzled specimen on the patterned carpet, both young men stopped as if something unseemly had been deposited on the thick pile.

'An old woman was found by the Leith Docks, vicious assaultit, most certainly dead, her body bruised tae hell from the terrible beating it received. She lies on the cold slab in our station — like a plucked chicken.'

'On her corpse was found a white favour,' Mulholland slid in as a less lurid addition. 'Your colours, Mister Grant.'

'I — not me — personally,' was the confused response.

'We had a crowd down the harbour last night,' Daniel offered swiftly, 'but — I mean — a bit of a fracas with the Scarlet barbarians, but — no old woman.'

'That's whit you tell me?'

'That is the truth.'

'Is that *your* experience, Mister Grant?'

McLevy ignored Drummond and his eyes were piercing deep at Alan.

For a moment all was frozen and then Daniel's right arm jerked involuntarily, breaking the stillness.

43

Alan Grant took a quick breath and nodded.

'It is. Indeed.'

There was a feeling of palpable unease, possibly the result of murder being thrown in to mar the boyish pranks but McLevy's attention was suddenly fixed elsewhere and an almost imperceptible movement of his head signalled Mulholland to provide distraction.

'Who stuck the underwear up the mast, sir?' the constable enquired with guileless curiosity.

'Not a clue,' answered Daniel. 'Someone in the crowd. Dark, you see.'

'Were they purloined?'

'What?'

'The corsets.'

Daniel roared with laughter and Alan, who had been silent since his statement, managed a half smile, but then McLevy came back into the fray with blood in his eye.

'The old woman was scourged raw with some implement. It left narrow welts. Deep in the flesh.'

His attention had moved to a gloomy corner of the room where he had remarked a glittering object.

'Like a cane,' he said slowly. 'A thin whippy cane.'

Daniel flushed at the insinuation and, despite his impaired gait, moved quickly to return with the stick that he presented without some irony to the inspector, holding it out in both hands.

'A gentleman should never be without one,' he remarked.

McLevy took it and rubbed his hands up and

down its surface as if prospecting.

'My sister had it made specially for me. A birthday present. Silver Birch.'

The inspector's hands were clear of any traces of dirt or blood from the stick and he deliberately brought it up to his nose and sniffed through his moustache like a dog at a bone.

There was something intentionally crass in the action and Daniel's lip curled a little.

'Ye polish it well,' McLevy muttered.

'A gentleman should always look after his cane.'

The inspector handed the stick back and Daniel in a weird excess of spirit brandished it skilfully in the air.

'Have at you, sir!' he exclaimed, thrusting the tip towards McLevy, who did not move a muscle. Mulholland's hand crept to his own hornbeam stick which had its lodging in a long pocket on the inside of his coat.

The end of the cane had come to rest precisely over the inspector's heart, beating in muffled animosity behind the thick coat, and McLevy yet did not budge, while his hands hung limply by his side. The very stillness was itself a warning that Alan Grant was alert enough to register as he stepped forward to twitch the implement aside with an assuaging smile.

'Daniel is the university champion,' he explained.

'Whit at?' was the obdurate response.

'Fencing, of course!' Daniel announced, twirling the cane in the air to tap against his crooked leg. 'Despite the handicap. One can

45

always overcome handicaps.'

'Unless one is dead,' said McLevy.

A gleam of battle in their eyes, youth against authority, boy to man, young bull to old; wrap it up how you will, a challenge had been issued. And for the inspector's part he had contemplated ripping the cane away to prod it into a socially unacceptable place but, happily, had thought better.

Mulholland blew out a breath. The same thought had crossed his mind about his inspector's next move.

In the tense silence a door opened and into the room stepped a striking young woman, not beautiful, but charged with such energy that the whole atmosphere lifted, as it often does when a female enters the male domain.

She had rich chestnut-coloured hair that strayed from its confining bun so that some strands curled around her ears and neck in a most becoming fashion.

Whether accident or artifice was hard to tell.

'Ah, Jessica,' her brother welcomed. 'Perhaps you can help us? These gentlemen are wondering where the White Devils may have laid their hands on some corsetry.'

'I rarely make use of it,' was the cool reply.

Alan's face relaxed into an admiring smile, Daniel laughed and struck a pose, Mulholland noted a quicksilver resemblance between brother and sister, but Jessica's focus had fixed firmly on the bulky figure that seemed glued to a spot on the carpet.

Recognition, it would seem, had struck and

caused her no particular pleasure.

'You are James McLevy, are you not?' she said.

'Uhuh,' was the dour response.

'The Thieftaker?'

'I have been so described.'

He looked slightly downwards at lively dark eyes set in a broad face. She was obviously younger than her brother but had a more settled appearance.

Her form was not at all lacking in the contours that interest the opposite sex but it was the feline quality in her movement combined with a restless intelligence that drew McLevy's attention.

Many expressions flitted across her face, rather as the moon might show through an edgy night, but for this moment the predominant one was of dislike.

'A friend of mine,' she remarked crisply. 'Lucy Clayton. Her father. You arrested him for embezzlement.'

'He deserved it.'

'We arrest people all the time, ma'am,' Mulholland volunteered, leaning in like the Tower of Pisa.

'Mister Clayton committed suicide.'

'Hanged himself. In the office of his bank. He had gone tae clear out his desk before trial,' said McLevy.

The pair had not taken their eyes off each other from the beginning of the exchange.

'You have a fine recollection.'

'I was there when Mulholland cut him down. His reach is higher — a matter of elevation.'

The tone was matter of fact but the constable noticed that McLevy had sparked into life suddenly, the dark ironic humour provoked by her incisive thrusts.

'His name was Andrew — did you know that?'

'I saw it on the death certificate.'

'It broke her heart. Lucy. It broke her heart.'

McLevy smiled grimly and, for almost the first time, moved to put himself directly in her line of fire. He could smell fine quality soap from her skin; God knows what she was getting from his.

'I do not make the law, Miss Drummond. But I come down heavy on those that break such. That's my profession.'

With that he jerked his head at Mulholland and they both made for the door, where McLevy wheeled round to address Alan Grant.

'Her name was Agnes — did ye know that?'

'What?'

'Agnes Carnegie,' said Mulholland quietly. 'The dead woman. That was her name.'

'She was a miserable wee body,' McLevy added. 'But she had a life. And now it's gone.'

His eyes bored a hole into Alan's, and then he looked back to Jessica, lips holding to the strange twist of that dark humour.

'However I will find the killer,' he said. 'That's my profession. Born and bred.'

Daniel, perhaps missing being the centre of attention, threw in his pennyworth as the policemen reached the door.

'Oh, inspector?' he called cheerfully. 'I intend to specialise in forensic science. Who knows that

48

we may not meet in an official capacity?'

'A prospect to savour,' was the dry response.

'What think you to anthropometry?'

'Anthro-whit?'

'Pometry,' Daniel supplied with an innocent air. 'I'm sure you know the work of Bertillion?'

'Oh, foreign by the sound,' replied McLevy with what Mulholland recognised as his glaikit face. 'Aye — aye — right enough.'

He jammed the low-brimmed bowler on so that it came far down, as if to emphasise the idiotic cast of his features.

'Uhuh. Right enough. Alphonse Bertillion. The method of identifying habitual criminals through recorded measurement of their physical bodies. Useful wi' recidivists and the like, but too prone tae human error for my liking. No!'

He suddenly held up a stubby thumb towards the three young people.

'Fingerprints. That's the prize. Henry Faulds is your man. No two are the same. They are left everywhere. Record them with printing ink. Compare. Theory at the moment but find a way to do that and not one criminal will sleep easy ever again.'

In the silence, Jessica suddenly spoke.

'I agree with you about Bertillion, inspector. It is but a step along the path.'

'Are you of a medical bent, Miss Drummond?' was the almost courtly response.

'I study privately. Many doors of the university are closed to women.'

'Then kick them down.'

'That is our intention.'

49

An unexpected smile appeared on his face.

'Mulholland will show ye how. He's an expert.'

Mulholland looked down modestly at his huge feet; in female mythology they betokened a corresponding largesse in other appendages, but that fancy aside, had indeed battered down many a felonious portal.

McLevy saved his last words for Daniel as he held up his thumb towards the young man.

'Not one criminal,' he said softly. 'Not one killer.'

Then he was gone, followed by the silent Mulholland.

Jessica Drummond's laugh was a full-throated, most unladylike affair.

'Well, my darling brother,' she announced. 'Put that in your pipe and smoke it!'

'A lucky guess,' was the somewhat illogical answer, but Alan Grant was more troubled.

'That man worries me,' he said quietly.

'Why?' Jessica queried. 'You have nothing to fear.'

In the interval that followed the remark, she marched over to a polished sideboard, selected an apple from the bowl of fruit, and bit in like a true daughter of Eve.

'What about this poor old woman?' she asked a little indistinctly.

Daniel's response was light and smooth.

'Oh? An accidental death down by the docks, we the prime suspects!'

She frowned.

'You two must pull in your horns.'

'Agreed,' said Alan quickly.

Daniel wheeled round from the window, where he had been watching the figures of the two policemen disappear along the side of the square.

'Nonsense!' His eyes were glittering with temper as he confronted Jessica; he had been excluded since the advent of his sibling and the pique this had bred was augmented by a darker underlying emotion.

'You, my dear sister, pretend to be wild at heart but underneath you are nothing more than a . . . conformist!'

Jessica was stung.

Nothing stings like family.

'Am I really?'

'Yes, you are!'

A somewhat childish exchange, but it produced a frozen silence, which was broken by a loud authoritative call from the next room.

'That is our mother's voice,' said Jessica, throwing the half-chewed apple at her brother, who caught it neatly. 'In case you do not recognise the timbre.'

She swept out through a side door, while Daniel flipped the apple, which landed tidily on a small salver.

'Mater will give it me in the neck,' he grinned, but Alan had other matters on his mind.

'Daniel? Why did you not mention our wrangle with the old woman?'

'More trouble than it's worth.'

'In what way?'

'Use your noddle, my dear chap,' drawled Daniel, in the affected tones he and Alan were wont to employ while in heroic mode. 'Once they knew that, never get them out the door.'

Grant was not quite at ease.

'Last night — we were separated quite a time. After the chase.'

'Yes,' said Daniel, sighting down his stick like a rifle. 'Press of the crowd, old chap.'

'I wondered — where you had gone?'

'A duel to the death,' replied Daniel carelessly. 'With one of the Scarlets. He had a wheelbarrow and I my cane.'

Alan nodded acceptance as the door opened and Jessica emerged with a malicious smile.

'Our mother would like to know,' she murmured, 'the whereabouts of a certain set of corsets?'

'They were decrepit,' protested Daniel.

'And fitted all the better. She is waiting.'

Daniel took a deep breath, limped towards the door, and slid it shut behind himself.

Appraisal from a woman can contain many elements. Jessica looked at Alan's solid frame, decent demeanour, then had certain thoughts she kept to herself.

'You are a good friend, Alan.'

'I hope so.'

'Because of his . . . infirmity, Daniel feels he has to prove himself. Twice over.'

'I realise that.'

'You must watch over him.'

'A difficult task — at the moment,' Alan replied wryly.

Jessica's eyes widened innocently and she moved a little closer so that he could inhale, however faintly, the odour of sweet apple.

'Perhaps,' she breathed, a glint of mischief in her eyes, 'I may provide assistance.'

7

For commonly, wheresoever God buildeth a
  church,
The devil will build a chapel just by.
> Thomas Becon, chaplain to
> Thomas Cranmer

John Gibbons heaved at the heavy pew, trying to
wedge it back into the straight. It was a mystery
how some mornings these solid receptacles for
the nether regions of the worshipful congregation were skewed out of true.

Older member's of St Stephen's Church
muttered darkly it was the devil dancing in the
dark of night that moved the benches, his cloven
hooves beating a rhythm that resonated then
translated into sinful shifting; John, though he
nodded politely, kept his own counsel.

As he did in most things. A quiet watchful
young man bound to follow his father Jonas into
the ordained ministry of the Church of Scotland,
he was of average height, a stocky build,
sandy-haired with a calm disposition.

A certain quiet humour occasionally informed
his words but in contrast to his father's more
public persona, he was a private soul.

He looked across to where the wiry figure of
Jonas Gibbons stood talking with the two
policemen, one indeed rising like a steeple above
the minister, and then John knelt down not in

prayer but to run his eye along the line of the next pew.

It was also out of true.

Satan's slant in the House of God.

On the outside St Stephen's Church faced the elements with the usual equanimity of Craigleith stone, hewed sharp to cut through inclement weather.

A broad flight of steep forbidding steps provided occasion to contemplate myriad sins as the faithful laboured upwards to the main door, above which, rising a good 160 feet into the air, was the bell tower.

It pointed uncompromisingly to heaven and set at the top was a clock face to inform the passing citizen just how much time was left in this life.

St Stephen's resembled not so much a house of worship as a fortress of religion. Had there been slits for the archers of God to shoot through at the unbelievers not one devout eyebrow would have been raised.

For this was a deity who valued defence.

Preferably in advance of attack.

The interior shunned ostentation; it was set in octagonal lines with doors leading to staircases that spider-webbed upwards to mysterious destinations. At the back similar doors opened onto descending stairwells that guided to rooms where children schooled and mothers plotted sales of work. After that the stairs plunged into the murky depths of the foundations.

What was hidden in those depths?

Something forgotten or still remembered?

Jonas Gibbons stood below the high-imbedded pulpit whence, in deep resonant tones, he preached fiery sermons that attracted the godly from his dreich rivals all over the city, and bowed his head in sorrow.

'Poor woman,' he murmured, though it was close to a rumble. 'She has gone to the bosom of a merciful Lord.'

'It's not where she's gone that concerns me,' said McLevy. 'So much as who sent her there.'

The minister seemed to accept the remark at face value.

'Thou shalt not kill,' he responded.

'Not if I've got anything to do with it,' grunted the inspector and signalled to Mulholland, who produced a crumpled piece of paper from his tunic pocket, which he smoothed out best he could and then presented.

It had been agreed between them that the constable would retain any pieces of evidence, since McLevy inevitably misplaced them in the crevices of an untidy attire or lost them in his station cupboard.

'Would this bring anything to your mind, sir?' asked Mulholland.

Gibbons peered down at the scrap and then brought it up closer; he was somewhat short-sighted but considered glasses a vanity. Which way the vanity worked was open to question, however he let out a cry of recognition.

'I am almost certain. It is from my own bible!'

'Is it missing a page then?' enquired McLevy suspiciously.

'No. But — oh — poor Mistress Carnegie.'

'If you might just — proceed to the nub, sir.'

Gibbons nodded at Mulholland's polite dig in the ribs and sighed.

'The Good Book. Its back-binding had come loose.'

'No doubt through reputable usage,' encouraged Mulholland.

'No — it was the moths,' replied Gibbons. 'Mistress Carnegie offered to take it home for repair. She was very handy with a needle. And thread. My own wife, Martha, lacks that ability.'

'Very sad,' said McLevy. 'Well there was no sign of any book, good or otherwise.'

'I'm afraid that is correct, sir,' added Mulholland. 'The killer may possibly have taken it.'

'My personal bible? In the hands of a murderer?'

'Unless he chucked it in the harbour,' McLevy hazarded.

The minister's head came up sharply at this but Mulholland diverted potential indignation.

He had summed up Jonas Gibbons as a man who admired the sound of his own voice, The man was small of stature and had a handsome broad face, with mutton chop whiskers luxuriant in the Lord's name that formed a furze under the neck but left the strong chin bare. A formidable personality, but despite all this a certain childlike need for attention.

Women are often sore attracted to such men and the older ladies of the church no doubt fluttered around like insects to the flame.

'Are you absolutely certain sure, sir,' ventured

the constable, 'that the page is from your book? It may be vital as the case unfolds.'

Gibbons nodded acknowledgement, then called over his son and acquainted the young man with the sad facts. John, after strong scrutiny, confirmed the provenance of the page.

'It is from my father's bible I have no doubt,' he said gravely. 'The spine had weakened.'

'Was the page clutched in her poor hand?' asked the minister.

'Not quite,' answered McLevy, who had a sudden flash of the open mouth and his own hooked, inserted fingers.

All four of them looked down at the stone floor as if the body had been transported there.

Agnes Carnegie's presence lay before them and each saw a different spectral version of the crumpled corpse.

In McLevy's mind, she looked up accusingly, her mouth still gaping from his horny-handed intrusion and her voice rasped out.

I wait tae be avenged. I demand it. Whit kind o' Thieftaker are you? Where is my vengeance? Sappie-heid!

'The Lord gives, the Lord taketh away,' the elder Gibbons intoned.

'And the police have to aye be finding the solution,' the inspector muttered. 'We'd be obliged if you might provide us with the woman's address — '

'Wait!'

Gibbons held up his hand as if struck like Moses on the mountain.

'Were not the students by the harbour last night?'

'A known fact, sir,' Mulholland replied tersely.

'Could not their wild and immoral behaviour have led to this unfortunate pass? Striking down the godly in their jealous frenzy? Satan knows no bounds!'

'That is true, father,' said John quietly. 'But there is perhaps a distance between wild behaviour and the taking of a life.'

He looked McLevy straight in the eyes, an unusual act for a member of the public in the presence of a policeman, and nodded.

'I will fetch the address from our records.'

As John moved off his father smiled proudly.

'A good boy,' he announced. 'Fruit of my loins.'

Trust you tae take a' the credit, thought McLevy somewhat unkindly. It was to the minister's good name that he toiled hard amongst the poor in the extremities of the city, but he had, to McLevy's thinking, the fault inherent in most men of God.

What was it Mulholland's Aunt Katy would say?

Once you think you've got the inside track, there's no gettin' past you.

The constable's consideration, however, had shifted once more towards the accuracy of the blows meted out to the pitiful Agnes. What kind of mind would produce exaction of such violence?

Was it purely accidental or had she somehow provoked the attack?

If accidental, the investigation would be a long haul but if not? The blows, the insertion, might

59

well betoken an amoral, cold and calculating mind.

From which direction?

Another long haul.

He looked around this church where everything seemed to have its place.

'God and Satan — a similar precision,' said McLevy aside, as if he had somehow read Mulholland's thoughts.

A side door opened and three women came through with blameless tread. In the lead was a frail birdlike creature and it was to her that Gibbons directed a heartfelt cry.

'Martha — a most terrible happening!'

He moved swiftly over to the three, spoke softly, raised his hands as cries of outrage and fear came in response, and then bowed his head.

The women fell to their knees before him as if stunned, Gibbons clasped his hands together and the sound of prayers arose like bees buzzing around one of Mulholland's hives.

John, who had returned with a slip of paper, took one glance at the scene, another at the police, then also fell dutifully to his knees and prayed for the departed soul.

McLevy and Mulholland stood there.

It was too far down for the constable, and the inspector lacked the inclination.

They also serve who only stand and wait.

8

Ah, Raleigh! you can afford to confess
yourself less than some, for you are greater
than all. Go on, and conquer noble heart!
But as for me, I sow the wind and I suppose
I shall reap the whirlwind.

Charles Kingsley, *Westward Ho!*

Stevenson watched the backs of the two figures
as they moved along Heriot Row, and regretted
he had been unable to glimpse the faces.

One, like a beanpole, was crowned with an
absurdly small helmet, while the other bore a
heavy coat and had the rolling gait of an animal
new emerged from its lair.

Police, from the uniform of the tall one, but
what struck the writer was the unhurried stroll of
both, as if they had all the time in the world.

'Louis?'

Fanny's voice buzzed in his ear like a wasp and
drew him away from the window.

She and his mother Margaret were seated in
two armchairs, one ensconced in mourning
weeds, the other with a black silk scarf draped
round her neck but other than this, more
accoutred for a climb up Arthur's Seat.

No, he was being unfair, but his wife's dress
sense would never chime with respectable
fashion any more than his own. Fanny was a
buccaneer; in his imagination he saw her

61

boarding a grappled ship, cutlass atween the teeth, ready to loose forth rapine and riot —

'Louis?'

This time the wasp had grown mightily and almost filled the room with angry vibration.

Stevenson lit a cigarette with great care and deliberation, knowing this would provoke but unable to help himself. He had been immured in the family home for days now and felt a most profound desire to have a tantrum, kick the polished furniture, disgrace himself by passing water in the aspidistra and generally behave like a spoiled child.

'Yessss?' he drawled.

The bone of contention was that Robert Louis had decreed that his father's funeral was to be a grand affair with over a hundred guests and at least forty carriages.

A heartfelt tribute or compensation for a meagre internal mourning?

Not an easy question to contemplate or answer.

The reception would be here, hands shook, heads shaken, plenty of manly forbearance and womanly lace handkerchiefs; then it would be on to the New Calton Burying Ground on the other side of the city, where Thomas would be laid to rest in a manner befitting a man of constructional bent and strong Christian beliefs.

His own father Robert already lay there with the inscription, *there remaineth therefore a rest in the people of God.*

Another lighthouse engineer.

It had, on a recent feverish night, occurred to

Stevenson that he might propose the erection of a small pharos near the family vault that would act as a warning beacon 'gainst grave robbers but he had thought better of it when dawn laid her grey, grim fingers in the sky.

This was the problem.

Stevenson had started the task full of vigour and vim, organising, overseeing, full of the traditional ancestral energy that supposedly descends on the son when his father slips the leash of life, but Messrs Phlegm and Mucus had begun to follow him round like a black dog, so that he felt every breath was like drowning in a catarrhal mud flat.

Now the arrangements were being borne by his mother, wife, and cousin Bob who was remarkably unaffected by the noxious clime and seemed to have taken over the role as man of the house.

He and Louis had been inseparable as young rascals, but as men grow older they do not necessarily improve, and Stevenson could sense a certain tension. It cut him to the core that fame and good fellowship do not easily walk hand in hand.

Jealousy lies dormant even in the best of friendships.

Yet for the moment, Bob was captain of the ship, with Fanny an extremely reluctant figure-head as baleful mermaid, and his mother a steady hand upon the tiller.

This image comforted Stevenson, but it had to be admitted that though the crew had accepted responsibility that did not mean they liked the charter.

Yo ho ho and a bottle of rum.

Not at all.

He came out of this reverie to find the gaze of both women firmly fixed upon him; Fanny smouldering like a pre-eruptive volcano and his mother's regard tinged with worry that there might be two funerals instead of just the one.

To augment the point he took a deep draught of his cigarette and coughed like a gutter drain.

Margaret closed her eyes and Fanny narrowed hers. She was well aware of the manoeuvrability of her spouse, and while she did not doubt he was indeed internally affected, he was not quite at death's door.

Not yet, and she hoped not ever.

For she loved him dearly, in her way.

But he was tricky as Mercury.

'Louis — you have not said a word?'

'Haven't I?' he murmured. 'I expect so.'

'There is much to do.'

Stevenson swallowed along with the phlegm a waspish retort that he could not fail to be aware of this since it was pushed in his face on an hourly basis. He contented himself with a non-committal, 'I expect there is.'

Fanny was not to be deflected.

'You spend your time looking out of the window.'

'I'm hoping the weather might change.'

Margaret, who was a decent, sweet soul and in time to come would prove to be as hardy an adventurer as the two in her presence, sensed there might be a storm brewing that had nothing to do with weather.

She had developed this intuition through near forty years of marriage with Thomas, whose sudden intemperate outbursts of rage often directed at or caused by his wayward son had to be subsumed and cradled, but, of course, never dealt with directly.

That was not in her marriage vows.

A soft answer turneth away wrath.

'I wonder if you remember, Louis,' she remarked gently, 'a saying of your father's — *All hands to the pump?*'

'Maritime, I believe,' replied her son. 'He often went to sea. To tame the wild ocean. I myself enjoyed being under the surface. The vasty deep.'

Twenty years before, he had gone diving. In Wick of all places, where half the population spoke Gaelic and the other half didn't speak much at all.

Despite bone-crushing weights and great bolted helmet he had found the experience exhilarating.

Weightless, womblike.

Like a world of dreams.

All hands to the pump, eh?

Stevenson had a sudden onrush of anger and grief; his father's face swam before him, slack-jawed in his dying bed like an imbecilic gargoyle, like a gargoyle!

He wrenched away from the women back to the window lest hot tears betray a wounded heart.

From the presented back view they watched a lazy plume of cigarette smoke rise into the velvet curtain while his voice floated, itself like an insubstantial vapour in the air.

'Where is Lloyd? Where is my bonny boy?'

This was Fanny's son, who had recently declared he might wish to follow the compromised occupation of story-telling despite, in truth, being somewhat lazy by nature and showing little gift or talent for the calling.

He adored Stevenson as a father figure and the older man revelled in such adoration, returning a deep affection of rare quality.

The young man was possibly and wisely staying out of the firing line.

'He is occupied,' Fanny answered briefly.

'At what, pray tell?'

'Writing. Lloyd is writing.'

'Dear me.'

Stevenson watched the streaks of rain slide grudgingly down the glass and swore inwardly that by hook or by crook, he would be out on the streets tonight.

The darkness might be his disguise.

Enough of the four walls of rectitude.

By hook or by crook.

'Writing?' he said with grave intonation. 'Dear me. What a strange and unrewarding pursuit.'

9

Haste thee nymph, and bring with thee
Jest and youthful jollity,
Quips and cranks, and wanton wiles,
Nods, and becks, and wreathèd smiles.
John Milton, *L'Allegro*

The operation had been performed with near military precision.

A grimy carriage whose driver wore a shapeless hat pulled down over his eyes, drew up near the immaculate, gold tipped wrought iron gates, which stood sentry over the back garden of the Just Land.

Some six young men disgorged, all muffled up, two carrying most carefully a small cauldron of tar, the other four each a bulky sack that they bore with ease.

The cauldron was set down on the wet pavement, not fissured, not cracked, for this was an area well kept by the authorities whose officials at the end of weary day's vigilance over the heaving city might well enjoy forbidden fruits at a somewhat reduced price. Be that as it may, two heavy brushes were dipped in the mixture and the sticky pitch lathered onto the elegant ironwork.

This took a matter of moments and, due to the murky weather, there were no witnesses to record the shaking out of the large bags of cheap red feathers, which sailed gracefully through the damp air to land on and adhere to the tar like stranded leaves in Autumn.

A bare spot had been left in the centre and onto that was firmly pressed a scarlet favour.

Had outside photography reached sufficient development, no doubt a posed group beside their handiwork would have ensued, but the young men had to content themselves with a brief moment of shared glory then a quick leap back into the carriage, which disappeared down the hill into the lower reaches of Leith.

The operation was over.

Some time later McLevy and Mulholland came upon the scene from the opposite approach. On the saunter, back from St Stephen's where the kneeling mourners had finally stopped praying for the departed soul long enough to hand over the address in Salamander Street.

'So,' Mulholland said, to break what had been a long silence in the falling rain, 'according to the Reverend Gibbons' wife, after the women's church meeting, as was her wont, Agnes Carnegie left St Stephen's around ten thirty in the evening.'

A muffled grunt came in response.

'That would work out with the time of death by the time she got to the harbour, an old woman not fast on her feet.'

A seagull landed on the opposite side of the street and waddled over to investigate something that had caught its eye. It turned out to be some land of red feather and not worth the poking of a beak, so the bird flew off again.

'The purse still in the handbag,' continued the constable doggedly. 'No robbery. Only thing missing is the bible. Why take a bible?'

'Maybe it had a treasure map inside.'

Not much of a deduction but at least a response.

Mulholland waited for further pieces of eight.

'One thing I noticed,' said McLevy as they trudged along. 'Though much was made of devout and devoted and holy dedication I didnae sense any real affection for the woman.'

'Perhaps affection and the Church of Scotland do not go hand in hand,' was the constable's thoughtful rejoinder.

The inspector shot him a glance; this was an unexpected remark from a Presbyterian Son of Erin.

'These bees are having an effect,' he observed.

They then both went back to their thoughts.

Fragments of that dream from the night before kept surfacing in McLevy's mind. It was not at all unpleasant in repetition; the fear and dread previously experienced at the wizened apparition had been replaced by a vague scintilla of guilty pleasure as a picture replayed the naked female forms flitting ghostlike behind the writhing fronds.

Of course he was a young man in the early part of the dream — the wizened apparition had taken a back seat till later — that would explain the pleasure.

Did one of them not now bear a fleeting resemblance to Jessica Drummond?

McLevy wrenched his mind back to the case

69

but the naked carcass of Agnes Carnegie had limited charm.

Mulholland sneaked a look at his inspector and noticed him wincing as if in some pain and rubbing at his arm. The rain had reduced to occasional drops as if the clouds could not squeeze out any more liquid for a while, but McLevy seemed oblivious, as if caught within some internal strife.

It was a worry to the constable. What was this pain? Was it the same old hurting McLevy had suffered for a while or was this agony new-minted?

The constable wanted the previous persona back to blight his life. Bellowing the odds, terrible shafts of illogical temper, wild humour, weird flights of fancy, blaming all and sundry except himself for the mess into which he inevitably blundered like a bull at the peat-bog.

In other words, human.

James McLevy.

This withdrawn though insightful creature was no fun; a bit like that skull in Hamlet.

'Whit's goin' on up there?'

Withdrawn or not, the inspector had noted something a little down the road in front of the gates of the Just Land and as they approached what looked like a rammy of sorts, a voice could be heard like the master on a slave galley.

'Ye thought it funny hingin' out the windows, eh? See ye laugh on the other side of your face now!'

Mulholland nodded solemnly. 'Hannah Semple as I live and breathe,' he announced.

'Either that or a warwolf,' McLevy remarked with a burgeoning glint in his eye; he and Hannah had knocked spots off each other many's the time.

The melee at the gates was revealed to be the magpies of the Just Land in plain workaday dresses, sleeves rolled up, scrubbing with hot water and rough soap at a sodden but defiant sludge of feathers and tar that clung to the hallowed portals.

They had started with gusto, thinking it to be quite an adventure, but hard labour and broken fingernails now a burdensome reality, the air was full of lamentation.

This changed with the advent of the policemen, and Mulholland's fetching stature gave rise to appreciative giggles plus a more graceful movement of stiff brush and slithering lather.

Hannah shook her head at such levity and spoke aside to the inspector.

'The mistress will want a word wi' you, McLevy. By God she will!'

McLevy blinked at her. Could this be the toothless harpy who took on Jean's sins? He had noted the possibility down in his diary but best not speak it aloud to Hannah's face.

It was common knowledge she carried a cut-throat razor.

Through the gates three figures could be seen approaching. Lily and Maisie lugging a huge washing pan of hot water and behind them a tight-lipped Jean Brash.

The gate was shoved open with a big pole, washing pan laid down, then Jean and McLevy set to it like two actors on a stage with a captive audience at hand.

'See whit's happened here!' said Jean without bothering to greet her fellow thespian by name.

'Sticking out a mile,' was the response.

'The Scarlet Runners!'

'That would explain the hue.'

'Hue?'

'Of the feathers.'

There was no discernible trace of humour in the inspector's big bap face so Jean had to accept this at local value.

'Whit're you going to do about it?'

'Observe from a distance.'

The green eyes snapped like a dragon's jaws and she moved in for an exchange at close quarters.

Mulholland slid out of reach and Hannah crooked her arm through his then looked up at him. She aye relished a rammy between the inspector and her mistress.

'How's my big handsome laddie?' she whispered.

She enjoyed teasing the constable about his attractive manly qualities including the large feet, which he was now shuffling uneasily. The magpies took advantage, scrubbing less, ears cocked for the fray.

'I pay your wages, McLevy!' Jean opened up.

'Indirectly, I suppose you do,' was the mild response.

'I pay my taxes, my Parish Charge.'

'Which gives succour unto and supports the Force of Leith, your civic protector and guardian,' announced the inspector with a pomposity guaranteed to irritate.

'So — protector, what do you intend?'

'Intend?'

'You heard me.'

McLevy pondered, stroking a moustache that Jean considered would have looked better on a dromedary.

'I could send Constable Mulholland back tae the station for tweezers.'

'*Tweezers?*'

'Evidence gathering. We could pick the feathers, one by one. Take time, though.'

McLevy's face gave nothing away. Jean nodded as if her worst fears had been confirmed.

'Hannah — d'you hear this lunacy?'

'I do, Mistress. Typical.'

Mulholland once more adopted the role of peacemaker.

'The trouble is, Mistress Brash,' he said earnestly, 'the feathers are stuck on the tar. And the tar is stuck to the gates. We're all sort of . . . coagulated.'

As a statement, thought McLevy to himself, it was worthy of Ballantyne at his most cryptically ingenuous.

Jean shot Mulholland an evil glance.

'I just had these gates painted. With gold leaf.'

'Ye can still see some wee bits,' said McLevy.

Jean's eyes narrowed; it was still difficult to tell from the inspector's countenance whether he actually knew how obtuse he appeared.

She tried once more.

'Why, may I ask, are these little swine picking on me?'

'Possibly because their fathers spend more time at your bawdy-hoose than they do at home.'

'That surely would be a blessing.'

'It is certainly to your profit.'

The two had provoked each other beyond their normal bounds, but underneath there was a mutual bafflement, as if they were two ships that had been cut loose and kept bumping into each other in the dark.

As if something deep had lost touch.

'What — are you going to do about it?' Jean asked coldly.

'I shall file report,' was the stolid answer. 'Gates painted, bawdy-hoose in uproar. Scarlet woman.'

Jean leant forward till their faces were almost touching.

'You go tae hell, McLevy,' she said intensely. 'You go straight tae hell.'

With that she swung round, signalling Lily, who had been lip-reading the exchange with mounting disquiet, and Maisie, who would most cheerfully have seen the inspector in Satan's Palace, since he had once arrested her sister for the minor crime of shoplifting a bridal dress and the poor girl about to get married, to pick up the spare empty washing pan.

Jean Brash marched off without a backward glance, spine stiff as a poker, followed by the pan-bearers.

A baleful look from Hannah set the magpies back to scrubbing, while Mulholland carefully disentangled his arm and addressed his inspector.

'I don't think she's very pleased, sir.'

'Ye could be right.'

Hannah shook her head.

'That's you buggered for ony coffee in the Just Land,' she observed. 'If the mistress offers I'd check for poison.'

'I'll bear it in mind,' replied McLevy.

He felt oddly out of sorts at the culmination to the exchange, as if he was somehow in the wrong.

But surely not?

Why was Jean so upset?

After all, what had he said?

Mulholland had that funny look on his face again as he gazed over, not unlike the Glasgow doctor.

An unearthly wailing sound startled McLevy, but it was not a troubled conscience, merely the ornamental peacocks in Jean's garden.

'These bliddy birds,' muttered Hannah. 'Whit for did they no' steal them awa' the other night, instead o' leaving them French sodgers?'

The inspector had heard of the happening but chose not to delve into the details.

Besides he had been struck by an idea that might make amends.

We all like to make amends after the event, rather than own up at the time.

An easier contemplation.

He beckoned the other two over and huddled them together like conspirators.

'Hannah — have you heard the notion that things happen in threes?'

'Ye mean the buggers will be back?'

'Uhuh. And what could be their next target?'

'Damned if I know.'

The peacocks wailed morosely as they pecked around in the damp grass and Mulholland began to get the drift.

'Where *were* the birds last night?' he asked.

'In their cages in this weather, right under the bedroom windows.'

Both policemen nodded. That would explain why no attempt was made — the noise would waken the dead.

'Whit's on your mind, McLevy?' questioned Hannah warily.

There might have been a smile on the inspector's face, thought Mulholland, but it was difficult to discern under that glaikit thing on his upper lip.

'From the tail of your Orientals,' McLevy murmured. 'A feather in their caps.'

'*That's the target?*'

'Could be. If you set a trap.'

'*How?*'

'Tether the peacocks in the middle of the garden. Trip wires all around.'

'Tie something in that makes a sound,' added Mulholland, bringing country lore into play. 'Little bells or the like.'

'We hae such left over frae Christmas.'

McLevy lowered his voice another notch.

'But don't tell Jean it's my idea, otherwise she'll reject it out of hand.'

'True enough,' said Mulholland. 'Especially after that terrible joke.'

'Eh?'

'Wait now,' interrupted Hannah. 'Once the bells go tinkle, tinkle. Whit do we do then?'

'Let fly. Small-shot is best. Hurts like the pox.'

'I wouldnae know,' was her stolid response.

'Bang, bang,' Mulholland said. 'Bang, bang. But you never heard it here.'

He straightened up and the three moved apart in a casual fashion to deceive any watchers.

'Better be on our way, sir,' he announced loudly. 'We have a murder to investigate.'

'Aye, right enough,' McLevy responded. 'On our way.'

They moved off, leaving a thoughtful Hannah gazing at the peacocks.

As they picked up speed downhill, the inspector's short legs working twice the rate of the loping constable, McLevy frowned at his companion.

'I considered it quite a good joke,' he said. '*Scarlet Woman.*'

'Hilarious,' replied Mulholland.

Jean Brash stood meanwhile in the kitchen of the Just Land while Lily and Maisie heated then poured water into the washing pan. The smaller of the two flicked cold water at her companion's neck and darted out of retaliatory range.

Maisie shook her fist and Lily grinned.

They were in love and all is forgiven in that exalted state.

Their mistress felt an unaccustomed emptiness inside.

The boy Cupid was now unsheathed to disseminate his arrows in any direction.

Too bad they kept missing the target.

10

Thus we must toil in other men's extremes,
That know not how to remedy our own.
            Thomas Kyd, *The Spanish Tragedy*

Lieutenant Roach looked across the desk at a
man he detested but who had the privilege to be
obnoxious for the moment.

If a son lose his matriarchal lodestar, may he
not be entitled to howl at the heavens?

Or at least bullyrag an officer of the law.

Roach's own parents had lived a respectable
distance from his heart, died within months of
each other, and concealed their disappointment
in him as best they could.

He had no children of his own, his wife being
more interested in tragic opera and cultural gath-
erings.

His own secret passion was the game of golf,
at which he was not untalented save for the
matter of putting.

But with putting there is no illusion. The ball
must go in the hole. And for Roach it would be
easier to contemplate shoving a camel through
the eye of a needle.

Therefore when he sifted for compassion, not
much was to be found, even had he been sincere.

Which he was not.

Because he just did not like the man.

'You have my total sympathy, Mister Carnegie —'

'I don't want your sympathy,' Sim Carnegie interrupted. 'My mother is dead. I saw her poor body.'

'At your own insistence, sir.'

'I wanted to make sure!'

A possibly ambiguous statement, but the man had seemed shaken enough when he stood there in the Cold Room and gazed down at the emaciated corpse, wrapped up in the blanket which covered her like a larval skin.

Sim Carnegie was a lean, whippet-like creature with a face that seemed to have a permanent sneck of doubt settled upon its features. A bony body, tall, with a long neck and a prominent Adam's apple, his clothes not exactly grubby but worn from sneaking through so many doors sideways.

In other words, a member of the press.

His voice was high-pitched and his mirthless laugh not unlike a dog's bark; there were hard little eyes, a clean-shaven face with a long protruding upper lip and sparse brown hair slicked close to the pink scalp.

But he was sharp; and his attention was fixed upon Roach, who could see Queen Victoria behind the complainant high upon the wall and regretted that Her Majesty was unable to come to the aid of an obedient servant.

Victoria's face gave nothing away. She had an empire to rule and little spare time.

'My mother is dead,' Carnegie repeated. 'A savage, brutal murder. Why? And who? Who is the killer?'

'The investigation has scarce begun,' said

Roach in what he hoped was a comforting but firm tone.

'I am a journalist, sir, and I know the pace of investigation in Leith. Like a snail!'

'The race is not always to the swift,' Roach replied, concealing his indignation at this downright calumny.

But denial would not help. Better to bow the head and wait for the storm to pass.

'Not always to the swift,' he muttered.

'That is by the by!'

Carnegie now began to talk in banner headlines.

'I intend to write a scathing indictment of your force, sir. And the *Leith Herald* will ask the question why you have not acted upon the evidence!'

'Evidence?'

'A white favour, found upon the body!'

The lieutenant almost jack-knifed in surprise.

'How do you know this?'

'I have my sources.'

As Carnegie treated Roach to a sly and secret smile, the door opened and James McLevy poked his head inside.

He and Mulholland had sneaked in before they went to Salamander Street to snaffle a cup of Sergeant Murdoch's execrable coffee and share a piece of honeycomb the constable had planked at the station.

When told the contents of Roach's office they had decided to come to the rescue or, in the inspector's case, to indulge his nosiness.

For one thing would always be true about

James McLevy, high or low, dead or alive — he was nosy.

In fact it was his recorded wish to have this inscribed upon his tombstone.

Here lies a nosy man.

With the constable behind, he stood impassive as Roach brought them up to date.

Since he and Mulholland had had their ears casually pressed to the door and eavesdropped the end of the conversation, McLevy was unimpressed by the repetition of Carnegie's little bombshell.

'The streets were littered wi' these favours,' he averred. 'Your mother could have picked it up anywhere by pure coincidence.'

He did not, of course, mention hooking it out of the corpse's mouth; only the three of them knew that, though there was another question to address.

Who the hell had informed Carnegie about the favour?

'Aye, but try this for size,' Carnegie shot back with a twisted grin. 'These students are spoiled rotten, no moral compass worth a damn. Strive tae outdo each other. A murder. That would be the ultimate, eh? Win at all costs.'

'A good headline,' McLevy allowed. 'But there is the small matter of proof.'

Sim Carnegie stood and pointed an accusing finger.

'Proof? Proof is whit you believe to be true.'

With that corrupt aphorism he made for the door, only to find it filled by the form of Mulholland.

The constable showed no sign of moving and the dislike in his eyes was palpable.

A girl's shrunken body lay face down the cobblestones, her face white, neck broken by one single deadly blow.

Like a rag doll.

A young constable, not long begun his shift, knelt down beside the pitiful wreckage and gently turned her to the light.

He knew that face and his insides lurched.

Rose Dundas.

A pretty name for a pretty wee girl.

Pretty no longer.

Carnegie did not budge either, hard bright eyes full of self-justification.

'Still bear a grudge, eh, Mulholland?'

'Only till my dying day,' was the reply.

'I was just doing my job. Pure and simple.'

'Like Judas Iscariot.'

'Ye blame me for your own faults.'

Both McLevy and Roach knew the history of this exchange, but that was not the issue at moment as the constable stood slightly aside, forcing Sim to squeeze past.

While the man's hand reached for the door handle, McLevy slid out an apparently idle question.

'Where were you last night, when midnight chimed? At prayer, I suppose.'

Sim turned, his smile a slit in the face.

'I waited for you to get round tae that. Big Susan and Mae Dunlop. In their loving arms. I spent the night.'

'Whores can be bought.'

'Like policemen?'

'Get out,' said Mulholland tightly.

'Yours tae command,' Carnegie answered ironically. 'Oh by the way — wait till you read the paper. It'll make your toes curl.'

But McLevy found the last word.

'Sim?' he called softly.

The mail turned, half in, half out of the room.

'Your grief for your mother,' the inspector tilted his head in acknowledgement. 'It's gey overwhelming.'

For a moment Sim blinked as the shaft went home, then he slammed shut the door.

There was a heavy silence.

'We have an informer in the station,' said Roach grimly. 'Either careless or in Carnegie's pocket.'

McLevy nodded.

'We'll smoke him out.'

A knock at the door and at Roach's behest it opened and Ballantyne poked in his head.

'Lieutenant? Ye told me tae report any more bicker wi' the students?'

Roach inclined his head to indicate agreement.

'Well,' Ballantyne announced earnestly. 'A woman jist came tae the desk to put in a complaint that they've stolen her parrot.'

'Why would they do that?' the lieutenant asked wearily.

'It had red feathers.'

For a moment McLevy had a vision of the students plucking the parrot naked to augment their deluge for the gates of the Just Land, but then shook his head.

Madness is catching.

'She left the cage on the window sill,' Ballantyne added to help the investigation, 'and the wire door was broken into!'

'More likely she forgot to close it and the parrot flew away,' Roach dismissed. 'She can tell all to Sergeant Murdoch, I'm sure he can manage that much criminality.'

The constable nodded jerkily and was about to leave when McLevy stopped him with a sudden question.

'Ballantyne — do you know anything about a white favour on the corpse?'

'Aye. I saw it!' came the proud response.

'Tell me a wee thing, eh?' the inspector queried, fearing the worst while Roach's face set like stone.

'Yesterday. After you left. I went into the Cold Room tae view the deid body. It's important tae look at cadavers, tae get used tae the sight in case you come upon them on patrol.'

Mulholland had been lost in a bitter past, but the thought of Ballantyne on the saunter through a slew of corpses brought him back to the present.

'So,' continued Ballantyne. 'I saw the favour, I saw the deid body and I put two and two thegither!'

'And who did you tell about this?' asked Mulholland.

'Only the boys in the station,' replied the young man, beginning to grow somewhat uneasy under the questions.

'Not Mister Carnegie by any chance?' inquired Roach, whose face was like thunder now.

'I jist saw him come and go,' replied Ballantyne simply. 'He's not in the police, is he?'

'So only the boys,' McLevy pursued. 'Why tell them?'

The red birth-mark pulsed on Ballantyne's neck as he began to realise that he might not be the hero of the hour.

'They're aye making fun o' me, because I don't know anything. So I wanted tae let them see. That I knew.'

Roach waved an exasperated hand at McLevy as if to say, *you deal with it*, and walked off to contemplate his Queen as the inspector took a deep breath.

'Constable, if you ever have knowledge of something as regards an ongoing investigation, you must inform no-one but Mulholland or myself.'

'Whit about the lieutenant?'

'He has enough on his plate,' replied McLevy while Roach kept his back to proceedings.

Ballantyne was a picture of misery.

'Did I do wrong, sir?'

McLevy shook his head.

'Silence is golden, jist keep that in mind. Now — away back to the desk and deal wi' the missing parrot.'

The young man nodded gratefully and shut the door.

The inspector and Mulholland looked at each other and both bowed their heads slightly, perhaps to conceal a smile of sorts, but Roach was not amused.

'How did that boy get into the force?'

'His mother's a nurse,' said McLevy.

'So, all knew and someone spilled over,' the lieutenant mused, face still averted.

'We'll find the guilty party.'

Mulholland's intended emollient remark unleashed a torrent, because Roach had not enjoyed Carnegie's jibes and knew that his Chief Constable Sandy Robb was an avid reader of the *Leith Herald*.

'We have anarchy on the streets, dead women littering the gutter, the press on our backs and you two wandering about like lost souls!'

Roach swung round, his jaw jerking from side to side like an irritated alligator.

'You have accomplished nothing!'

'The murder only happened last night,' McLevy pointed out reasonably enough.

'That is not good enough. Call yourself a Thief-taker!'

Roach cut an immaculate figure, uniform pressed to a knife edge, shirt white, shoes gleaming — those he insisted on polishing himself, being of the opinion that you can always judge a man by his shoes.

His subordinates made a sorry contrast. McLevy looked as if his clothes had been thrown at him by a sloven, and Mulholland seemed always, despite his best efforts, to be growing out of whatever official attire he possessed.

From a high moral and apparelled ground, Roach spoke with principled vehemence.

'By God, I am tempted to come out on the street, roast these students and show you how to

86

pursue an investigation!'

To the lieutenant's eyes, his inspector looked embarrassed or even alarmed at this possibility.

Of course being shown up is never a pleasant prospect.

McLevy scratched behind his ear for a moment.

'Funny ye should mention this, sir. Mulholland and I were not long ago discussing that very notion.'

The constable managed to keep his face straight at this assertion; they had discussed nothing of the sort.

'We have interviewed the leaders of the White Devils, and it is our belief that they conceal something.'

Mulholland nodded. This at least was true; both he and McLevy had sensed something awry in the depiction of last night's events from Drummond and Grant. Of course it might be relatively harmless, but both policemen felt it could have a darker tinge.

The problem was how to shake it out of them.

That much was agreed upon, but what else was fermenting in McLevy's mind?

'We need tae catch them in the act,' the inspector continued smoothly. 'Breaking the law. Stick them in the cells, hammer at the pair. Find the truth of what transpired last night.'

Roach nodded wisely. This made sense and it still rankled, the woman shrieking in Constitution Street that he was a lecherous pincher of her posterior.

His thumb and forefinger twitched.

'A night in the cells will do them no harm,' he concurred. 'And if it aids the investigation — '

'Exactly!' said McLevy, eyes gleaming.

There was a long silence before Roach asked what seemed an obvious question.

'How do we go about it?'

Mulholland sensed his inspector moving in for the kill as sincere assurance throbbed in the air.

'With your valuable assistance, sir. This very evening. All things are possible.'

11

Time, the avenger! Unto thee I lift
My hands and eyes, and heart, and crave of
    thee a gift.
           Byron, *Childe Harold's Pilgrimage*

His hands were cleansed, perfumed with rose water, and in the darkness of the small windowless room like a monk's cell, the single candle lit was suffice illumination.

The Golden Book lay on the bare table; he had wrought the cover himself with such skill as he could bring to bear.

It bore three initials and he traced them with a loving touch.

This was his Tanakh, Talmud, Kabala, Koran, his holy scripture of inner thoughts and dreams.

His charted destiny.

Those who insulted, those who laid on impure hands, would suffer retribution.

He had given the dull stupid one the slip and the idiot would wait with bovine patience until summoned once more.

He pulled back a curtain and hidden in the comer hung his pale suit, no trace of blood bearing testimony to the accuracy of his blows.

The cane at a certain louche swagger of angle, lay elegantly against the wall. It brought a smile to his lips.

Glittering.

Eager for more adventures.

But first.

Open the book.

He did so and the grainy image that stared out at him brought tears to his eyes.

As they flowed in a never-ending stream down his face, he had a strange practical thought of how to explain a wet shirt to curious eyes.

This made him laugh and the tears stopped.

No water had fallen on the page, it never did, and so he turned the pages again till the formal photograph of a child stared out at him, well attired, hand in pocket, with a sidelong disinterested gaze.

This was his favourite. Stolen from under the eyes.

He leant forward and planted a tender kiss upon the innocent lips.

Not long now and he would be known, accepted, held within a warm embrace.

But first there was work to be done. The unworthy, the dirty stink of the past must be expunged.

Another not worthy to live must die and be left on a doorstep as a cat would leave a mouse.

As an offering to its owner.

He closed the book and his eye was caught by a tattered book thrown into the corner.

Somewhere he would find in its pages the very word, the apposite reference.

Had to be good for something.

But after that, he would burn it — so that no trace remained.

Oh, tonight would be such fun.

But not yet though. He would allow the dullard some pleasure of his company, then leave him in the lurch and the fun would begin.

The white face, the suit so elegant, the donning of which would cause his very molecules to writhe and twist into an unrecognisably splendid being.

Who ruled the world.

The rising tide in his blood brought him to a sinuous caper ending when he slid the cane up between his legs in phallic salute.

The laughter bubbled inside him.

Every day he was more powerful, running rings round them all, especially the dullard.

And soon he would meet his Destiny.

But not yet.

First there was work to be done.

He would put down a sign. He had planned this for a long time. Nothing must go wrong.

But how could it?

When you ruled the pendant globe.

12

Man is the shuttle, to whose winding quest
  And passage through these looms
God ordained motion, but ordained no rest.
       Henry Vaughan, *Silex Scintillans*

Lieutenant Robert Roach shivered a little in the cold, damp air and wondered to himself how such had come to be.

'Are you certain this will work, McLevy?' he enquired somewhat plaintively.

'Rest assured, sir,' was the bracing reply. 'Ye wanted to be out on the streets, and here is the place!'

From past the rim of a rather large top hat the lieutenant looked up at the grim sky and blinked as the heavy rain spattered onto his skin.

He could have been at home, in the warm, by the fire, listening to his wife describe the latest gory opera she had witnessed full to the brim with dying abandoned women and bellowed catastrophe, but no — somehow his inspector had persuaded that the lieutenant's vital presence would anchor and buttress a stratagem for bringing these damned students to heel.

And perhaps move on apace the murder investigation, because McLevy and Mulholland had reported a distinct lack of success from their visit to Agnes Carnegie's lodgings.

A bare, wee room full of religious artefacts, no

sign of a personal life of any kind. No letters, no books of any dimension save assorted mildewed holy tracts, no pictures except Moses and the Ten Commandments, and a gloomy looking Son of God who had to stare at his father on the opposite wall, sitting on a throne and casting sinners into hell.

In the drawers, her clothes threadbare though neatly folded, intimidating underwear, three pairs of shoes, heels worn but lined up like soldiers.

Nothing out of place, yet both policemen had a strange impression that the room may have been recently searched.

Nothing you could put your finger on, though they had rifled enough chambers in their time to sense when something may be amiss. But then who could have entered the place?

They had unearthed the door key in Agnes's handbag and the respectable landlady confirmed that she had the spare and there was no other.

So — it remained just an impression.

One small, wooden chest had its fastening pulled askew and the scrape seemed reasonably fresh, but it may have just been wear and tear; the contents were more church papers.

The woman would seem to have had no life save the church and now she had no life at all.

Roach had sniffed — impressions did not interest him — proof did and there was nothing to indicate a murder motive.

That left a haphazard kill.

The worst kind.

The three men were now standing in the

shadows of the harbour with some constables in support loitering unseen in one of the nearby wynds.

As a sudden gust of wind blew squalls of rain over the watchers, a random thought popped into the lieutenant's mind.

'Did you find out if Sim Carnegie's alibi held?' he asked hopefully. It would be a great relief to one and all if it turned out that the fellow had killed his own mother; a touch Greek but a great relief nonetheless.

'It held, sir,' McLevy dashed such hope. 'He spent all night wi' the whores as provided. Underpaid them though. Big Susan says the man's as mean as hell.'

'Good for Big Susan,' said Roach disconsolately.

He peered into the darkness and could see nothing on the streets. It was the inspector's contention that the White Devils would return this night, but not a sign so far.

And even if they showed, would the plan work?

Mulholland detected the unease; he had been silent this while because he was concerned about his bees. The hives were not relishing this constant precipitation and their citizens seemed as dismal as the lieutenant.

Yet here they were all gathered and it was time to rally the troops.

'The inspector is a dab hand at setting up ensnarement, sir,' he encouraged quietly. 'You're the second this day.'

'And what was the other mark?' muttered

Roach, beginning to think that he was catching a cold.

'Ornamental birds.'

'That gives me great comfort,' was the grumpy response, but a sound at the far end of the harbour put paid to this unsatisfactory exchange.

In the mirk could be distinguished fleeting daubs of white, as shapes moved in the night. This was accompanied by a babble of distant excitement as a group of young men came into view, their faces almost glowing in the dark.

'The White Devils,' McLevy announced softly. 'I thocht they'd be back.'

He whipped out a spyglass and trained it on the jostling crew. In the front he could make out the limping Drummond and Grant with a smaller figure between them.

This wee birkie had a pair of old fashioned long johns draped over a shoulder; obviously the intention would be to replace the corsets, which a jolly jack tar from the Custom ship had removed that day, with a male equivalent, on high.

McLevy had a notion something of that ilk might happen but as well as male underwear atop the mast, the crowd would be out for any kind of mischief.

Which is where the lieutenant came in.

Roach stepped forward and took a deep breath.

'Well, how does the target present itself?'

The inspector nodded gravely.

'Tall. Proud. A top hat of the most perfect proportion.'

Then he slightly diminished this exalted description by adding a mischievous rider.

'Pure invitation for a dod o' mud.'

'Mud?'

'Figure of speech, sir,' Mulholland said hastily.

The shouts grew louder as the students approached.

'Best of luck, sir,' McLevy proclaimed as Roach hesitated then began to move off. 'Tall and proud!'

'Not how I am feeling at this precise moment,' said the receding Roach. 'Not remotely.'

As the lieutenant veered at an angle to the crowd, in fact heading for the wynds where the other constables were lurking, a host of bitter thoughts ran in his mind.

How had he allowed himself to be persuaded into this foolhardy exploit? Somehow McLevy had twisted a tale that the inspector and Mulholland were too familiar landmarks to tempt rash action.

They needed someone of mystery, enigmatic, unknown to the leaders of the White Devils.

A towering presence.

How had he swallowed such palpable nonsense?

One thing for sure. McLevy might be more subdued and taciturn than usual these days, but he was still a sly, manipulative, conniving, deceitful hunker-slider!

Meanwhile the man himself watched through his spyglass as Roach's tall outline presented itself side on to the pack, like a ship about to exchange or receive cannon-fire.

He saw Daniel Drummond stoop to pick up something.

'That's it, my mannie,' he murmured. 'Ready, aim, fire.'

'Even if they hit,' whispered Mulholland. 'What is the charge?'

'Assault of a police officer,' was the solemn response.

A sudden howl of pain rang out in the night and Mulholland gasped in dismay.

'My God — they've missed the hat and hit the lieutenant!'

'Even better,' grunted McLevy, still glued to the spyglass.

A police whistle from the wynds blew to signal the hidden constables.

McLevy pocketed his spyglass.

'The ringleaders are splitting up; you take the first two I'll awa' after the third!'

Just as the two parted company, Roach's slightly strangled voice roused the herring-gulls on the harbour water from their dreams of silver fish.

'McLevy — I have one in hand — aghh!'

The lieutenant had obviously been kicked in an unofficial spot.

'That's *double* assault,' McLevy shouted back as he disappeared into the darkness.

Mulholland paid no heed and legged it at a rate of knots towards the melee, which was further complicated by the arrival of the constables who came pouring out of the wynds like a mob of assassins.

Roach rose aloft in the struggle with a

triumphant roar, holding a wriggling form by the front lapels though the lieutenant himself had lost his hat.

'Holy Moses,' Mulholland panted to himself. 'I didn't know the man had it in him.'

Then he lifted his own voice, coming over a bit Irish in the wild shenanigans, hornbeam stick upraised.

'Guard your skulls! I'm comin' at you — ready or not!'

The herring-gulls circled dispassionately above; from their point of view there was nothing edible in the writhing wormy mass beneath, so they turned attention to a single figure below that was running into one of the narrow wynds. It threw aside a white flaccid object with trailing legs but this was of no interest either, so the birds flew back to the more sensible motion of the sea.

On its bosom they might find rest.

The single fugitive the birds had observed and dismissed stumbled onwards in the narrow darkness, feet slipping on the wet treacherous surface, a trembling of fear in every limb. But there — there was light ahead at the top of the wynd. Safety. A few more steps —

Then a foot shot out from a narrow side alley and tripped the fleeing form.

As it crashed painfully onto the sharp stones, James McLevy looked down — unlike the gulls he had found something to satisfy the appetite.

'You run, I walk,' he pronounced as if beginning a sermon. 'Yet I know these wynds better than any living being therefore hangs the reason I stand and you fall.'

He stooped to turn over the recumbent figure.

'Now — let's hae a wee keek at you, my mannie — '

The prone body suddenly jerked into life, squirming frantically to escape, and the unexpected motion unbalanced the inspector to topple onto the figure below.

McLevy grunted in pain as a sharp knee dug into his leg, perilously close to the crown jewels, then he pinned the arms back so that he straddled the tricky wee swine.

His chest pressed upon the other's torso and the whole of his body pushed down hard to contain the wriggling form.

'I said — let's have a look at you!'

He managed to contain both his opponent's hands in the one of his own and pulled off the tweed cap that concealed the other's countenance.

Rich chestnut curls tumbled down to frame the flushed and hectic face of Jessica Drummond.

13

And most of all would I flee from the cruel
  madness of love,
The honey of poison flowers and all the
  measureless ill.
          Alfred, Lord Tennyson, *Maud*

Time stands still. Time flies. Time will tell.

For a moment that seemed eternal yet fleeting,
their lips, hers aquiver, his dry as a bone,
hovered over each other's; her breath was sweet
from some lozenge and he cursed the intake of
Sergeant Murdoch's coffee which had swirled
around like a digestive dervish no doubt creating
a sour emission from his maw.

But why was he worried about breath?

Their faces had not moved an inch, both
registering a somewhat bewildered ambushed
surprise as if they had together fallen into a pit.

Her dark eyes possessed, on close scrutiny,
strange green flecks, which put him in mind of
Jean Brash.

And the aforesaid torso, come to think of it,
had a pliant, yielding quality.

His whole body felt curiously weak, as if
someone had pulled the plug.

From Jessica's point of view, she saw a pitted
parchment face with grey, slatey, lupine eyes, and
a moustache that looked like a hedge of sorts.

She was also conscious of a strange feral

energy in the damp air.

Finally, as if a curtain had lifted, McLevy abruptly hauled himself off and hoisted her upright.

They still had not spoken.

The inspector broke silence and a different reality settled around them.

'Miss Drummond!' McLevy rebuked the bedraggled shape, whose countenance was streaked with markings of the White Devils, giving her the look of a market clown. 'Whit're you doing wi' all this gallivantation?'

She flinched at a shaft of pain from the fall.

'I am not — gallivanting. I am a fool!'

'I shall give you no argument there.'

Having delivered this formal remonstrance, he watched in some concern as she massaged at her ribs.

'Did I hurt you?'

'Only my pride.'

'It often comes before a fall.'

'Are you being droll, inspector?'

McLevy pondered and then came to the conclusion that he was being deadly serious.

But who was proud and who had fallen?

He shook that thought aside and assumed a part of his personality easier to access and more apposite to the event.

'Explain yourself,' he commanded tersely.

Jessica hesitated, then stooped to pick up the tweed cap to crumple in her hands. There was something childlike and appealing in the gesture, but he hardened his heart.

A policeman's heart is adamantine is it not?

101

Second only to the Sphynx.

'I — I wanted to — protect my brother.'

'So that he can throw gobbets of mud at folk?'

She winced either at the remark or another shaft of pain.

'And,' Jessica admitted, shoving at her hair, which was wet and clinging to the face, 'to tell truth — I suppose I came also because I was — challenged.'

'To conduct yourself like a man?'

'Yes.'

'That is with great stupidity.'

She blinked at the unexpected observation; it was beginning to dawn on Jessica that this bulky individual was perhaps a more subtle entity than she had presumed.

In her brother's old suit, which was at least a size too large, the young girl cut a forlorn figure.

'And were you tae climb the mast and attach the long johns?'

She shook her head, embarrassed at the prospect.

'No. Daniel just — stuck them on my shoulder.'

'Yet you swaggered well enough.'

Jessica could not deny the truth of that. She had been swept up in the fever of a mob.

'As I said. I am a fool.'

Silence followed this candid admission.

'Pit on your bonnet,' said McLevy suddenly, 'or ye'll catch your death.'

A meek acceptance, then she took a deep breath.

'I suppose you will arrest me now?'

It would be the talk of the tea parties and her

mother would hardly forgive her.

Ever.

'You tell me my job as well. Thank you.'

His face was like stone beneath the low-brimmed bowler.

'No, but I mean — you must.'

'Is that a fact?'

He reached out abruptly and drew her towards him by a vice-like grip upon the arm.

My God, was this how they arrested people?

'You lack the gentle touch, inspector,' she announced with as much dignity as a potential jailbird might muster.

'Do I really?' he muttered angrily, a fierce light burning in the grey eyes — a light, did she but know it, that had not flamed for some time now.

'Get going,' he said.

'What?'

'You heard me!'

These words were accompanied by a hefty shove that sent her sprawling up the wynd.

Outrage battled with relief as she discovered distance between herself and incarceration.

'You should treat me with respect sir,' she managed. 'I am not a street keelie.'

'Uhuh? There's a big dod of mud on your neb.'

'I didn't know that, did I!' she snapped in response, and wiped the nose with the back of her hand. 'There. Gone.'

'As should you be before I change my mind.'

McLevy stood forward threateningly, as if about to charge after her, but Jessica held her ground.

'What about my brother?'

'He'll take what's coming. Now, on your way!'

She scrambled up towards the head of the wynd and at the top, a safe measure between them, attempted to find some dignified comment on her circumstances.

'I thank you, inspector. But you are not a civil person.'

'And you're a very lucky girl.'

'I am not a girl, I am a woman!'

With that she was out of sight while McLevy bawled after her.

'That is a matter of debate!'

As McLevy walked down in the opposite direction, conflict raging in heart and mind, he muttered inside.

A matter of debate.

'Inspector?'

The damned female was back again, shouting from the top of the wynd like a fishwife.

'You should remove that ridiculous fungus from your face. It puts years on you!'

Then she was gone. This time for good.

Now it was McLevy's turn to feel tripped and winded.

That was a low blow.

'Women — they like to have the last word,' a voice commented from the shadows. 'Nature of the beast.'

The tone was wry, from the man who stood in a doorway, tall with a long, dark coat, and an exotic soft hat which nevertheless seemed to repel the rain.

He had a gambler's face, long, pale, almost

horse-like, and he was sucking thoughtfully at a cigarette.

'I came to the harbour for old time's sake,' he murmured. 'It used to be tarry-breeks for the odd riot, but it's a better class of hooligan these days.'

The man laughed quietly and drew a little circle in the moist air with the glowing tip of his cigarette.

How much had he heard?

McLevy had a maelstrom of feelings with which to deal and it took a moment before he identified the countenance, from both past and present.

'You're Stevenson, the writer!'

The man bowed his head and stifled a phlegmy cough.

'At your service, sir.'

He drew aside and indicated with an elegant movement of the hand that they might walk together.

This they did towards the main body of the harbour, the inspector thinking that the further away from recent events, the better.

'And you are James McLevy, the Thieftaker. A man of many adventures, I am told.'

There was a light, ironic tone that unsettled McLevy; it was hard to fathom this fellow's thoughts.

How much had he witnessed?

The inspector had of course read the notorious *Jekyll and Hyde* and been deeply impressed by the insights.

In his own nature he had felt these murderous

contradictions and McLevy could only assume Stevenson had experienced the same.

The duality of man. Saint and sinner.

'Tae tell true,' the inspector said out of the blue. 'I prefer Edgar Allan Poe.'

'So do I, sir. So do I!'

Stevenson laughed infectiously and linked his arm through McLevy's in familiar fashion as they neared the lights of the harbour taverns.

'A woman dressed as a man berates the famous Thieftaker upon the state of his upper lip,' he teased. 'Is this the beginning of a tale, I wonder?'

'I doubt it,' muttered McLevy in response and, part to change subject, part because he felt a sudden aggressive urge to put this mannie in his place, went on the attack.

'I remember you. Climbing up a drainpipe in the Lothian Road. I was a constable then and you a daft student.'

Stevenson blinked for a moment, then his face cleared as a memory surfaced.

'I was making for a widow's window. To offer comfort and solace.'

'You were dressed like a pirate,' McLevy said firmly.

'I had been performing in a play. The Daemon must have seized me.'

Stevenson suddenly assumed the manner and delivery of an actor as he quoted his own doggerel poetry with relish.

The silent pirates of the shore
Eat and sleep soft, and pocket more

Than any red, robustious ranger
Who picks his farthings hot from danger.

'So, which are you, inspector?' he asked, flipping the bright tip of the cigarette in an arc to expire hissing in an oily puddle. 'Silent pirate, or robustious ranger?'

'Neither. Though I arrest both.'

This deadpan response set the writer of into a burst of laughter, which deteriorated into a hacking cough.

He wiped his mouth with a large white handkerchief.

'I never did arrive near that widow's window.'

'That's because I pulled ye down.'

'You thought I was a burglar.'

'It was the eye patch.'

By now they had come near to the harbour taverns. From one, the Rustie Nail, a commotion of sound arose, angry voices slurred by ramstam ale and inferior whisky.

'Some things change, but rarely,' murmured Stevenson.

'A dirty dive. Helter skelter.'

Robert Louis swung to a stop to light up another cigarette, huddling at the wall to preserve the flame.

'And yet,' he puffed out a thin entrail of smoke, 'I remember you in there. On the floor. A fight. With a certain Henry Preger.'

McLevy nodded. Early days. A young man then.

'He was a vicious brute,' he replied. 'A pimp.'

In truth he could not now remember why the

fight had started, only that Preger had heavy boots and used them well. Kicked his fill.

'I was . . . observing,' said Stevenson. 'At the back. Keeping clear of the blood, you know?'

'Enough of it,' McLevy responded. 'Maistly mine.'

For a moment the inspector seemed lost in memory as the rain fell and the writer inhaled, fingers poised.

'Preger's woman. A certain Jean Brash. Stepped out.'

'She didnae step out. She was always there.'

As he had looked up at the blur of hostile faces, one stared back, red hair like a flame, a cool, dispassionate look like a gravedigger.

The writer leant forward to peer curiously into McLevy's eyes.

'What did she do to get you off that floor?'

'She winked.'

Another roar of laughter, another fit of coughing.

'Well, it did the trick, my friend. You wiped him from one end of the bar to the other.'

'I've never been back down there,' said McLevy solemnly. 'Tae the floor. It's a bad place.'

'They say Preger was never the same man.'

'That's because he died. In my view poisoned.'

'By whom?'

'Madame Arsenic.'

The men appraised each other and a measure of wary approbation rose between them.

McLevy came to the conclusion that for a gabby man, Stevenson was a canny bugger and whatever he saw in that wynd might well stay with him; Robert Louis thought it had been a long time since he'd met a psychology that chimed in such a strange way with his own.

'There was an old woman murdered here last night,' said McLevy suddenly. 'Battered tae death.'

'Life is cheap,' replied Stevenson sombrely.

'Aye. And it willnae gang on forever.'

The inspector watched as Robert Louis took another deep drag of smoke down into his lungs.

'Ye're about tae bury your father?'

'That would seem to be the situation.'

'I read about his death in the papers. Mind you they often lie.'

'Not this time.'

A burst of fiddle music from a well-lit tavern signalled that there might be more to existence than a father's demise or lying on the dirty planking with someone about to kick hell out of you.

'The Old Ship,' Stevenson announced. 'A fine establishment — tell me, does it still have private booths?'

'If you've onything to hide.'

'I am an open book, sir. But I was wondering, given that I am chilled to the bone by Auld Reekie's dismal inclemency — if you might join me in a hooker of whisky?'

Of course the correct and proper procedure would be a stern shake of the head and a course set for Leith Station, but McLevy had a deal of wild thoughts careering through his mind and no wish to catalogue a mob of boisterous, drunken students in the cells.

Plus he'd have to explain how his quarry had slipped out from under the long arm of the law.

So he nodded assent and de'il tak' the hindmost, though he put in a caveat.

'I cannot linger long, though.'

'Excellent!' cried the writer. 'We can lift a toast to the female of the species no matter how much trouble they may bring to a quiet life.'

Rumour had it that Stevenson's own wife Fanny was a handful and McLevy had his personal besom riders whirling in the air.

So he nodded again. Robert Louis took his arm once more, and the two men walked through the swinging doors of The Old Ship to disappear into the generous light and leave the darkness behind.

Indeed. Let the devil take the hindmost.

14

Now is the woodcock near the gin.
William Shakespeare, *Twelfth Night*

The birds were miserable as they endured the cold dripping night, the sheen of the males dulled and tawdry, the smaller females making a slightly better fist of it, pecking around inquisitively, while their erstwhile lusty overseers shivered feathers and wailed like a tribe of lost souls.

Of course this shivering with wings outstretched at other times was intended to hypnotise the female, until a precarious mounting and mating had been accomplished, but for now the wings were clamped close to keep the cold at bay.

Not intelligent at the best of times, the peacocks lamented being so unexpectedly tethered together in the garden of the Just Land in the middle of the night.

Who might save them from this fate?

Where was the hero?

In the shadows, Hannah Semple, Jean Brash, and her taciturn Aberdonian coachman Angus Dalrymple waited by the back of the gazebo, hidden from sight, each perched on a wooden kitchen chair.

Angus was a giant and the small-shot firearm looked like a toy in his beefy hands.

Jean held a smaller version, but both guns were capable of scattering a stinging fusillade of pellets that could give a painful wound even from a distance.

The victim would then, if lucky enough to find a physician, spend an excruciating passage getting the flinty missiles extracted from beneath his skin.

They may not be cannon fire but could cut and gash with the best of them.

Behind the watchers the Just Land itself was suspiciously placid, while at the back of every curtain the magpies rested, ready to play their part.

Lechery had been given the night off.

A sacrifice must aye be made.

Jean was fretting at the inaction.

She imagined what if it was McLevy out there, come to pay one of his late night visits to scrounge a cup of the best Lebanese?

How justified would it be if, in the course of defending her property, as is the right of every law-abiding citizen, she put a load of buckshot into his fat backside?

Hannah mistook Jean's silence for disquiet, and whispered encouragement regarding the motionless Angus.

'*He used tae be a poacher, mistress. He will not gang agley.*'

'Good,' muttered Jean grimly. 'I don't want my birds in jeopardy.'

'*Whit about your own aim?*'

'I'll manage.'

'Black as the devil's hint-end out there,' Angus suddenly grunted.

'Wait!'

Jean's delicate ears, admired by many a suitor, had other functions such as acute perception.

They all listened as a faint tinkling registered through the mournful ululation of the tethered targets.

'Might be a fox,' Hannah offered.

Then there was a louder jangle, followed by a mumbled curse.

'That's no' a predator,' Jean concluded with a wicked smile. 'That's an idiot.'

She called back softly to the house.

'Girls — at my command.'

Excited giggles came in response as more bells rang and more muffled profanity followed in the darkness.

'One, two, three!'

As Jean's voice rang out, every curtain in the Just Land was jerked back to reveal an artillery of oil lamps, which shot illumination into the garden like a lightning flash.

It revealed a bunch of young men, feet trammelled by the trip wires, panicked at the sudden exposure and terrified by the wild screams coming from the magpies, who sounded like avenging Valkyries girding up to choose the slain.

In a blind funk, the Scarlet Runners kicked off the encircling ropes and ran to scale the walls — thus presenting a tempting target.

'Like heidless chickens.'

While Hannah delivered this verdict, Jean and Angus were sighting with great care.

'Careful of the peacocks,' warned Jean. 'Backsides if you please.'

113

'They're well enough presented,' answered the coachman.

'Then fire and be damned!'

A roar of small-shot from him, followed a moment later by Jean letting fly, screams of pain, cat-calls from the girls, another discharge, frantic scrabbling at the garden wall, then the last of the Scarlet Runners yelped over the top and all was quiet except for distant sounds of limping agony.

'A cauld day in hell afore they come back.'

Jean nodded agreement to Hannah's words.

'They'll be picking pellets out their rear-ends for weeks. Well done, Angus!'

The giant rose, flexed his limbs in satisfaction, then walked off to join Lily and Maisie, who had run out of the house and were freeing the peacocks, both being fond of the glaikit birds.

Jean and Hannah also stood. The garden was now peaceful and by some miracle the rain had ceased.

The Mistress of the Just Land sighed at a job well done and cast an appreciative gaze at the woman beside her.

'I must confess, Hannah Semple,' she said fondly. 'You are aye my good right hand, but you have excelled yourself this time.'

'And I must confess,' replied Hannah, who never mind all the depredations life had visited upon her, still maintained a firm sense of right and wrong, despite the odd manipulation of a razor, 'that it wasnae my notion.'

'Don't tell me,' Jean said warily as the peacocks filed past heading for their cages, with Lily in the lead and Maisie bringing up the rear.

Angus was picking up the bells from the grass with surprising daintiness.

'The notion. It was McLevy's,' continued Hannah.

'If I'd known that!'

'Exactly. That's whit he said.'

Jean felt a sudden rush of hot anger.

'Oh that bugger of a man!'

Hannah sniffed. She had been about to suggest peaceful overtures but now was obviously not the time.

Twa wasps fighting over a dead worm.

Such was love in Hannah's opinion.

'A wee cup o' coffee wouldnae go amiss, eh?'

On the nod from Jean, Hannah stumped off towards the Just Land, calling back over her shoulder as she disappeared, 'Aye, some sore erses picked over the night, hell mend them. May they fester like the Canongate ripples!'

This pithy reference to a species of venereal disease, associated with a certain area of Edinburgh, that affected the back and loins, passed Jean by — her attention had been drawn to the massive Angus, who had found something at the foot of the garden wall and, like some well trained retriever, brought it back to his mistress.

'It's a photie,' he announced. 'Fell out the pocket mebbye. Nae blood though, nae holes shot through.'

Handing it over, Angus then headed for the stable to feed his beloved carriage horses. Each to his own.

A family photograph. The proud father in military garb and, with a young boy dwarfed by

115

this giant, the mother in between them.

The boy looked angelic.

Jean was tempted to tear it up but stayed her hand.

Now all the action was over, she felt a curious emptiness.

What a pity it hadn't been McLevy amongst the bells.

She looked out into the garden and then back to the Just Land where the peacocks rooted contentedly in their cages.

All this she had.

What more could there be?

15

For it is your business, when the wall next door catches fire.

Horace, *Epistles*

The cells in Leith Station are not clean and neat like a honeycomb matrix. Some trace of every bedevilled felon that has fed the fleas and protested his innocence lingers in the lumpy bedding, in the very pores of the blank walls where initials are scratched, in the very dank and airless atmosphere that lies there inert — a prisoner behind the bars as much as any criminal.

One cell in particular was small like a square coffin, separated from its fellows at the end of a long, bare, winding corridor.

Those of a dismal disposition might think that here, hidden from sight, the police could wreak vengeance or wield violence in order to gain confession.

No-one would hear the cries of pain.

As is commonly perceived, all are innocent until proven guilty, and let us hope the forces of law and order are never too tempted to hurry the process along.

Such subtle discriminations were by no means running through the mind of Daniel Drummond.

The inhabitants of this cramped space were

117

four in number. Two could leave, two could not.

McLevy and Mulholland, Daniel and Alan Grant.

Of course the policemen might have remained on the other side of the bars to post their questions through like letters, but they had preferred to squeeze inside and, as far as Mulholland was concerned, literally, for his head, minus helmet, scraped against the knobbly roughcast ceiling.

But he bore the unwelcome friction manfully, because it brought himself and the inspector into the very air the suspects breathed.

Nose to nose.

McLevy loomed in the centre, an immovable object, even with what might be the faintest odour of whisky fumes detected by the sensitive nose of Mulholland. The two young men, still with traces of white smears on their faces, sat on a crudely formed bench, pinned in the corner.

The policemen had been questioning the pair for near an hour, not yet getting to the nub, more concentrating on the petty acts of vandalism whilst cocking a snook at the law.

But imperceptibly, because the questioners were skilled in the black arts, the tension was growing.

Daniel was sweating like a Turkish Bath attendant, his voice more high-pitched by the minute; Alan Grant seemed a touch more in control, but he had his hands clenched between his knees, like a truant schoolboy.

Both were bruised, Daniel with a mouse under the eye where Roach's bony elbow had made contact, and Alan Grant with a sore and stiff neck where an enthusiastic constable had hammered down his baton.

McLevy shook his head solemnly, a sardonic light in the eye. Time to raise the stakes.

'Assault of a police officer, Mister Drummond.'

'I didn't know that!'

'Well, ye know now.'

'Twice as a matter of fact,' Mulholland chimed in helpfully. 'You also, Mister Grant. Naughty boys.'

'I was trying to help Daniel get free — '

'Freedom is something ye will not contemplate for a good wee while,' the inspector interrupted. 'Ye face charges of vicious and premeditated assault with worse tae come.'

'What?'

'You heard me!'

This sudden roar from McLevy straight into Daniel's face brought Alan off the bench. Mulholland was swift to shift also, the hornbeam stick out in a flash.

'No physical violence, if you please, sir!'

Of course the constable knew there was little or no danger to McLevy, and he had no intention of unleashing the mighty power of the weapon on such insubstantial sprats, but the very fact of the movement ratcheted up the pressure.

He had also enjoyed the bellow, more like the old McLevy.

'I — had no intention,' Alan protested.

'Then sit down,' Mulholland said evenly.

Grant did so meekly enough, but Daniel was

119

made of sterner stuff, at least in his own eyes.

'All this will be resolved,' he protested. 'No harm done.'

McLevy moved so quickly it was as if he had appeared like an ogre in the fairy tales, towering above the seated pair with hardly a span between himself and them.

'Worse tae come,' he repeated in a quiet controlled tone that was somehow more threatening than any roar.

The inspector dragged over a chair and sat so that he was on the same level as the other two.

'Agnes Carnegie. Yester-night,' he said gravely. 'Whit really happened?'

'Nothing,' said Daniel quickly.

'You're a liar, sir.'

A simple enough statement, but the enormity seemed to take Daniel's breath away. His face whitened under its layer of that same colour and his mouth opened and closed without sound.

At that moment he bore no resemblance whatsoever to his sister, and the inspector was grateful for that as he went in for the kill.

'Beaten tae death. Her body — battered and bruised frae the blows. Lying there like a bag o' bones.'

In the silence created by this macabre image, Daniel shook his head in denial, not, it would seem, trusting himself to speak.

McLevy suddenly turned on Alan Grant with a direct gaze, almost impersonal, that pierced into the fraught conscience of the young man.

'Whit about you, Mister Grant? Do you still deny crossing paths with this poor woman?'

Alan replayed the moment when, pushed by Daniel, the old lady had toppled backwards into the dirty puddle — but that would not harm her surely? They had left her sitting, a crabbit old biddy but alive. Yet soon afterwards he and Daniel had become separated. But that was just happenstance. There was no way his friend could commit a gruesome murder . . .

Yet they had not told the truth.

What was it Daniel had said?

More trouble than it's worth.

But was it?

He glanced sideways at his companion in arms. Would it be classed as betrayal? Surely innocence can reveal itself just as readily as guilt?

Alan became aware that while these thoughts had passed swiftly through his mind, he was still under the scrutiny of the inspector's gaze.

A moth trapped by candle flame.

How could the man know in any case?

But he did. He knew something was not being told.

'I am waiting, Mister Grant,' said James McLevy.

To the watching Mulholland, this was the moment; a moment he had witnessed many a time.

It teetered in the balance as the young man hesitated, the inspector held silence, the companion glanced sideways as if to counsel against revelation. And from his great height, at the three seated figures, the constable looked down like a judge in court.

Or were he inclined to grandiose speculation,

121

like Zeus from the heavens.

A voice broke the silence — however it was none of the aforementioned.

'May I have a word, inspector?'

A sour-faced Lieutenant Roach had approached quietly up the corridor. Bad news often comes in silence.

McLevy almost growled in frustration, and snapped his head round as if to dismiss his superior officer, but one look at the lieutenant's countenance put paid to that idea.

The inspector swung out of the cell, followed closely by Mulholland, who slammed the door shut with a clatter as if to promise that this was only a temporary respite.

But it was, in fact, a cessation.

Roach drew them both far enough away so that their voices could not be heard, and spoke in low, bitter tones.

Unlike the look of triumph with which he had greeted McLevy on his return to the station, jubilant that he had hooked his quarry while the inspector had come back empty handed, and commenting gleefully that McLevy had lost his touch compared to the street expertise of one Robert Roach, the lieutenant's face now bore the appearance of a man who had swallowed a slug with his curly kale.

'I have two of Edinburgh's most notable lawyers in my office,' he muttered bleakly. 'And they have served me with judge's papers demanding the release of all who were connected to the recent affray, most especially a certain Daniel Drummond and Alan Grant.'

'Judge's papers?' said Mulholland incredulously.

'One of the students has turned out to be the offspring of Judge Bennett,' was the acid response. 'He dotes upon the boy. And to save you further query, the lawyers have been retained by the Drummond family.'

'How did they know we had them here?' asked Mulholland like a dog worrying at a bone. 'Hardly three hours gone.'

'That,' Roach replied, 'as the inspector is often wont to remark, may be one of God's little mysteries.'

The lieutenant noted that the man himself had become curiously silent and mistook this for disgruntlement.

'Not my fault, McLevy,' he admonished what he imagined to be a sulking subordinate. 'It would always have been hard to hold these students for an affray, but I hoped if we kept them in the cells overnight it might at least have put the fear of God into them.'

The inspector still did not say a word, and now it was Mulholland's turn to misinterpret the lack of response.

He and the inspector, of course, had been angling for bigger fish, and who knows what Alan Grant might have said if they'd kept the pressure on?

Everything or nothing — who knows?

Too late now.

'Well,' opined Roach, turning away, 'I have to deal with my learned friends. You, Mulholland, can help organise release of these upstarts

— take Ballantyne and tell him to imagine that he is unleashing a nest of dung beetles.'

He signalled Mulholland to follow to the door and had a last word for the entity they had left behind.

'McLevy, once you have finished standing there like Patience on a monument, perhaps you might join us lesser mortals in the humdrum life of Leith Station.'

Then he had another thought.

'Oh by the way — my top hat has a large dent. Who is going to pay for that, I wonder?'

The door closed and both men were gone.

Of course Patience did not stand in the various memorials, she was on her backside and struggling to get away from a confining bond.

Not unlike Jessica Drummond in McLevy's grip.

And the inspector had let her go. To trump himself.

Hoist by his own petard, to bring in another fanciful and unwelcome figure of speech.

The girl had moved fast. Roust the lawyers, get them to the judge, serve the papers, don't look back.

Move fast. It helps when you're young.

Betrayal is like ashes in the mouth.

Under an impugned moustache.

He felt such a pain inside — a sudden shaft, as if he had been pierced to the bone.

Was this love or some illness in the marrow?

Or is it much the same thing?

The inspector moved slowly to the door and slipped through it into another life.

The corridor was once more silent.

Inside the confines of the cell Daniel and Alan waited, not realising what was happening beyond their sphere and for the moment, it seemed, forgotten by the forces of justice.

Both had a jumble of thoughts running in their minds.

Daniel finally rose and dragged his twisted leg, which pained considerably after the night's exertions, across the floor to peer up the now vacant corridor.

'Thank God my sister was not taken,' he said finally, his face hidden in shadow. 'Think of the disgrace.'

'Yes,' came Alan's voice in the dim uncertain light of the cell. 'Think of the disgrace.'

16

With a heart of furious fancies,
Whereof I am commander;
With a burning spear,
And a horse of air,
To the wilderness I wander.

Anon, *Tom o' Bedlam*

The Old Ship tavern divides into two dominions separated by a small door, the bar itself in a horseshoe shape where the publicans ply their trade.

One kingdom is that of the rougher element, where the young street keelies and their fancy girls with bright ribbons huddle thegither to pledge undying love, and plot mischief against a society for which they have nothing but contempt; where washed up nymphs of the pavé watch this youthful parade, envy the gay sparkle of eyes and avoid such mirrors where they might contrast what once they were and have now become.

Ghosts at a feast.

Sim Carnegie was in his glory in such a world; he trawled the various dives to pick up from informers what tit-bits of scurrilous gossip and petty crime had floated like scum to the surface, often ending up at the Old Ship where he entertained his cronies with such tales.

It was noticeable that he rarely bought a drink,

126

perhaps thinking his adept company and fine stories were payment enough, but this night his companions were well nigh astonished to find Sim's hand disappearing into his pocket and emerging, not with a grubby handkerchief, but coin of the realm with which he proceeded to buy not one but two rounds.

When twitted about this sudden largesse Carnegie tapped the side of his nose in a self-mocking gesture and mentioned a certain Mister Herbert Lawson whose letter had arrived at his office address with welcome news.

His mother's lawyer and a dried up wee specimen, but honest enough considering the profession.

The news? Ah, that would be telling, but welcome enough that he had borrowed a sum to augment the miserable pittance he received at the *Leith Herald*!

Sycophantic laughter greeted that remark and as Sim turned to survey his empire from the top of the horseshoe bend his attention was caught by two figures sitting at a table through in the other room.

This was where the more respectable visitors to the tavern sat, occasionally sipping their tippeny ale and cocking their wee finger in the air.

Nonsense, of course; the other bar was marginally less noisy and had private booths where business might be secretly transacted, but the tobacco fumes were just as thick and the faces just as flushed with strong drink; perhaps a better brand, peat-whisky as opposed to spiel-the-wa'.

Such distinctions meant little to Sim; at this

moment he was monarch of all he surveyed.

He swaggered through the connecting door and with a grin like a tipsy shark stood before the two figures.

They had seen him coming, but continued their deliberate ingestion of some much needed belly timber.

'*Leith Herald*. The Monday edition,' Carnegie said. 'It will make bonny reading.'

From his salt herring and tatties, the poor man's supper, Mulholland preferring a dish of sheep's heid broth, James McLevy looked up at the puddock before them.

Both policemen had for the most part been silent since arrival, ordered, drank, ate; it had been a tiring and for the most part, unsuccessful day.

They had sadly been unable to procure a booth, which might have spared them this unsavoury invasion.

Since the inspector had continued masticating, while removing the odd small fish bone from his moustache, Sim put one hand in familiar style upon their table and leant in.

'So, sir,' he remarked, with the solemn timbre of someone who has imbibed well but not, in his opinion, too much. 'How proceeds the investigation?'

'It proceeds.'

The inspector went back to his meal. Mulholland had never left his, but Carnegie was not to be ignored.

Headlines were running in his mind.

'My poor old mother lies in the morgue, her

murder cries out for vengeance and the police pass time in a tavern. Draw your own conclusions.'

'A man needs his provender,' replied McLevy mildly enough, 'and I didnae notice you flooding the station wi' filial tears.'

'I loved my mother,' Carnegie declared indignantly. 'And my mother loved me!'

'D'ye have that in writing?'

'Indeed I do!' was the triumphant response. 'I have just received legal notice that I am her sole inheritor.'

'That's nice,' McLevy said blandly. 'Well, I have something tae tell you, sole inheritor.'

The inspector flicked a silvery piece of herring-bone in the direction of Carnegie's greasy shoes.

'If you don't bugger off, I'm going tae pit you on the deck.'

Mulholland had found a strange shaped shard of bone in his broth and wondered idly if it was an eye socket, as Sim Carnegie took a prudent step backwards.

But then the constable's attention was attracted by something behind Carnegie's distasteful and unwelcome form.

'God almighty,' he muttered. 'It's like Waverley Station this night.'

Three young men had entered the tavern and at least one of them was not unknown. He wore a light coloured suit and dragged his leg like an unwilling dog.

They froze at the sight of the two policemen, but an imp of mischief charged by a sudden rush

129

of fury possessed the inspector, and he beckoned the arrivals over. 'Mister Drummond,' he boomed. 'May I introduce ye to Mister Carnegie, son of the dear departed Agnes, gone but not forgotten.'

And like a master of ceremonies, though still not budging an inch from where he sat, McLevy earned on with his spurious bonding.

'Mister Carnegie — here stands afore ye, the dauntless leader o' the White Devils.'

Daniel, who had foolishly shinned down a drainpipe from his room to celebrate his unexpected release with friends, thence returning to a location he should have avoided like the pox, pressed his cane to the floor, drew himself up to full height, and bowed.

Sim Carnegie was not impressed. In truth he had been surprised by a shaft of sudden fear at the look in McLevy's eyes, but now was a chance for him to void his wrath against what he considered an inferior opponent.

The newsman took in the dandyish appearance, the silver cane, long hair, and filled his lungs.

'You rampaged the night my poor mother died!' he accused loudly and the words caused a silence in the crowd.

'I know nothing of her death,' replied the young man stiffly, conscious he was the focus of all eyes.

'Oh, I wouldnae say that,' offered McLevy, adding fuel to the flames. 'I told you all about it, Mister Drummond.'

Daniel choked back a retort, thinking the inspector manifestly unfair and manipulative, but unable to deny the literal truth, and finding when he looked to Mulholland, that the constable's eyes were calculating and not friendly.

'I remember it well,' announced Mulholland. 'In your own drawing room. The gory details.'

What an idiot, Daniel cursed himself, *to fall amongst thieves, but now if he could just extricate himself with a little dignity intact — dignity was everything!*

'A liar as well, eh?' The tall, angular Carnegie looked down a long, slightly dripping nose, then raised his voice.

'Educated thugs!' he informed the whole tavern. 'Creatures o' privilege. Money buys learning, eh?'

In truth there might have been some veracity to that statement no matter the dubious source, but as various jeers added boozy support and Sim raised his hands like a Roman gladiator, Daniel bit his lip, turned, and limped off.

'Like a whipped dog,' crowed Carnegie and a chorus of mocking yelps followed the three young men as they hastily quit the tavern.

But there was an equally calculating look in the journalist's eyes.

Gardy loo.

It's best to beware when the press and the police find any measure of agreement, no matter how remote.

Outside Daniel tore himself free from his companions' restraining hands, his face puce with humiliation at being such an object of ridicule.

'That was a foolish venture!'

A furious assertion that would have brought

131

little argument from the rest, save perhaps for the fact it had been his own idea. But they knew the mercurial whiplash to his temper and held their tongues.

To a certain extent he did inspire fear when in one of these rages, skin taut across the bones of his face, seeking for someone to blame other than himself.

'I shall find my own way home. Leave me!'

With that, he turned abruptly and moving rapidly despite his crippled leg, was lost in the night.

A burst of noise from the tavern brought the other pair's heads round, but it seemed more connected to a screech of music than derision, so they slid off into the shadows.

Music soothes the savage breast.

In the rough bar, an old shipwreck of a fellow with no teeth to speak of and one rheumy, glistening eye, had whipped out a battered fiddle to launch into a lively jig.

Two of the girls had started to dance, raising their skirts enough to provoke an equally lively reaction.

Sim grinned at all this, but then became aware that he was still the focus of McLevy's hard stare.

'I meant what I said. Bugger off back where ye belong.'

The very stillness of his form, flatness of tone was warning, and the journalist was not a stupid man.

But as he retreated, Sim could not resist a parting remark.

'Mulholland? A wee piece of news. I hear tell that Gash Mitchell is back in the city.'

The constable's face betrayed nothing.

'You heard the inspector,' he said quietly. 'Get out.'

The fiddler had switched to a slow air as Carnegie made his exit. Folk had gone back to their business and he was no longer centre of attention as he called back from the door.

'Monday edition, gentlemen. Well worth the read.'

'Oh, one thing?' McLevy called in response. 'Big Susan confirmed your whereabouts.'

'Only right.'

'Gave her word. But she might have given you something else as well. As a bonus. She's a generous girl.'

The journalist's protuberant Adam's apple jerked spasmodically for a moment, then he managed a dismissive sneer and left the scene.

Big Susan had said nothing of the sort, but it's all grist to the mill.

Both policemen were silent. Mulholland's mind was full of jagged images.

The young girl lying, limbs askew, neck broken. No sign of her assailant, no proof to hand.

Rose Dundas. Still dead. Still lying there.

On a dark night. Such as this one.

The fiddle's tune was slow and stately. Grief hung under the strings. A funeral air.

'If Gash Mitchell is back,' the constable said softly. 'All he needs to do is make one mistake.'

'And you'll be there wi' bells on.'

133

'That I will.'

There was a moment of silence before the constable made further utterance.

'One thing. Carnegie was right. He may have let the name loose. But I should have hung her murder round that bastard Mitchell's neck.'

To McLevy's knowledge it was the first time he had ever heard his constable swear.

'The proof was lacking.'

'In my head. It is proven.'

The exchange over, Mulholland stood and gestured towards an empty glass.

McLevy nodded.

'If you're buying, I'm drinking.'

When the constable returned with a hooker of whisky and sma' beer for himself, the inspector had sunk back into the reverie that had taken possession of him since they entered the tavern.

He sooked noisily at the dram, fell back into silence, and then asked a sudden and surprising question.

'Whit d'you think tae Jessica Drummond?'

Mulholland considered. Surely she was not a suspect?

'Stands her ground.'

'A cow does such. In the field.'

There was an odd look to the inspector's eye that put the constable in mind of a child lost at market.

'I noted she kept looking at you,' he remarked finally.

'Did she? That would be forensic.'

'And you kept looking at her.'

'That's my job. Scrutiny.'

Mulholland sighed. It had been a day interminable.

Thank God tomorrow was Sunday.

He'd be glad to get back to the bees.

17

Teach me to feel another's woe,
To hide the fault I see;
That mercy I to others show,
That mercy show to me.
Alexander Pope, The *Universal Prayer*

There is a kind of rain in Edinburgh called 'skelp-the-wean's-backside', where a fiendish wind, usually from the East, drives the downpour horizontally above the ground.

If coming from behind, it hurls the victim headlong into lampposts, sharp corners, or sends him careering helplessly down a steep hill to meet some watery fate.

If from the front, it blinds the vision and cripples the joints, so that the very effort of walking seems an affront to nature. A stark convulsion. No mercy.

Such a vicious monster had been unleashed by the city gods for reasons of their own; it had commenced some fifteen minutes before and cleared the roads like the Great Plague save for one tiny, whimpering figure that made its way down the broad unprotected expanse of North Charlotte Street.

The figure left behind a trail of little spots of blood that were swept to instant oblivion by the elements.

Thomas Archibald Carstairs, known because

of his diminutive frame to his fellow students as 'the Runt', had canvassed hard and earnestly to be allowed into the sacred fraternity of the Scarlet Runners and to take part in his very first raid.

This had proved no more successful than that of the James Gang robbing the First National Bank of Northfield, Minnesota.

The Runners had shinned up the walls of the Just Land, Tom being thrown up first to provide a fulcrum with rope for the rest, and then found themselves in the pitch black of the garden with only the peacocks' cries to guide them.

For this was the objective. To pluck feathers from their tails and add them to the stash of trophies and deeds of derring-do that would be valued and judged against the paltry exploits of the White Devils.

Tom had tried not to grin in the dark lest his nervous teeth gleam and give away position — this was the Just Land, a bawdy-hoose, full of danger and disease — but he was a man among men, hat pulled over to hide his blond hair and blue eyes, mouth tight shut and fingers ready to lift the booty from these effeminate wailing willies.

What an adventure!

As may be gathered Thomas was not a natural cutthroat; a studious good natured boy often the butt of his boisterous fellows, now was the chance to show his mettle.

A hero in the making.

In other words a born innocent and defence-less destination for a load of buckshot.

As are we all.

Everything went well at first, as it so often does.

After that, the devil took a hand.

They stumbled over what seemed like myriad snakes in the grass, setting off a tinkling sound as if the fairies had been disturbed in their nocturnal pursuits, and then?

All hell broke loose.

A sudden terrible light shone from the windows like a lighthouse to expose the valiant invaders, which was followed by a fearsome female screeching and then, as they bolted for the escape of the garden wall upwards to clamber and gain safety, a thunderous noise split the heavens with shrieks of pain from the climbing Runners.

Tom was frightened out of his wits but, being to the rear, had missed the salvo.

Was Dame Fortune on his side?

No. She can be a fickle creature, tending to side with bawdy-hoose keepers, and so as Tom and some other laggards clawed their way up the brickwork, a second noise burst forth.

Not as loud as the first, but just as deadly in consequences.

A piercing sting as the pellets ripped through his coat and trousers took Tom's breath away, and then the pain, as shock subsided, made him howl like an animal.

His flanks and buttocks were a mass of fiery agony.

He managed to scramble over to the other side and then they all ran for their lives, limping, lurching, squealing like a herd of pigs, jostling in the frantic effort to put distance between them and lethal pursuit.

Not a hero to be found, which is often the case when small-shot takes a hand.

To his surprise, Tom, who cried easily, had not shed a tear. That happened later at his best friend's house in Queen Street, the parents fortunately God-fearing and already asleep, when a shivering decimated band of wayfarers attempted in the cellars by wavering candlelight to extract the imbedded fragments from violated flesh.

They had the instruments and supposed skill, exams passed in medical matters, but the hands were shaking and the whisky they employed to numb the pain, clean the wound, and then swallow to provide enough nerve for another operation, had left Tom with a horrible taste in his mouth.

The injuries had been dressed as best they could but he had felt them open again as he struggled in the onslaught of this pitiless bitter wind and rain, most of which seemed to be beating into his right ear while he negotiated Forres Street like a wrecked ship.

This was, without doubt, the most miserable night of his life. More to come.

As he turned finally into Heriot Row, the wind and rain hit him full on. Body blows. He had lost the hat a million years ago and his hair was flattened to the skull.

Tom had been flogged by the gale part out into the road and then heard a wild scream above the tumult.

139

A carriage was heading straight for him, the driver muffled up but brandishing what seemed a shining stick and howling in weird delight as the horse careered towards the isolated young man.

Tom threw himself to the side and the wild-eyed animal rushed past, the driver now standing to shake his stick defiantly at the elements, screaming like a banshee, paying no heed to anything in his way.

For a moment the covering clothes slipped and Tom caught a glimpse of a pale material underneath before the carriage swept past and was gone.

Vanished.

As if by magic.

Had that been the devil himself? There was something indeed beyond this world in that vision.

A nightmare figure from the Apocalypse, seeking vengeance on all who crossed his path.

A vicious gust of wind and rain brought Tom back to his present woes; his knees were now skinned from the fall to add salt to the wound.

His family house was in Albany Street, not far, he could do it. Best foot forward.

But as he attempted to press onwards, his limbs collapsed under him and he sprawled sideways to lurch into a stone pathway leading to a front door. The impetus forced Tom down on his hands and knees to gain a moment's respite.

There were heavy bushes on the other side of the iron railings to provide shelter of sorts from the watery blasts, so he sat up against the metal, hugged arms round his legs, knees under his chin and tried to count his blessings.

He was still alive.

The wounds would heal.

He could feel, even in all this turmoil, the warm blood trickling down the back of his legs.

Eventually. They would heal.

But what of his parents?

He would have to tell them, or they would find out.

Either way. A rum proposition.

Tom's face changed as he realised that the hand he had pressed inside his coat and jacket for warmth had not found the usual contents of his inside pocket.

His lucky photograph.

It must have fallen out in the stramash.

Damn!

It never rains but it pours.

A wry, pained smile at that thought and then he looked up to see the number solidly fixed to the equally unmoved front door. Seventeen.

The very number of the Great Judge!

Though no trophy from this night would be worthy of his judgement.

Tom took a deep breath and prepared to rise. 'Steady the buffs' was one of his father's favourite sayings and to a certain extent, despite the horror of the night, tears, the throbbing pain, the looming shock and disappointment of his mother especially, he felt a curious resilience.

Steady the buffs.

In the top buttonhole of his jacket there was still the loose remnant of a scarlet favour — he was yet a member of the gallant crew.

As he stood somewhat waveringly, Tom's eye was attracted to a large bundle that lay by the left of the stalwart portal.

A blanket of sorts, wrapped round something, a grey huddled shape; he had been too concerned with his own woes to remark it until now.

For a moment the young man considered leaving well alone, but since when has humanity ever followed that course?

He reached out a cold, inquisitive hand to twitch aside the top of the blanket.

It fell away like a rotten fruit to reveal the lifeless face of a woman.

Her neck and face were welted with blows, the skin was mottled, painted like a maypole, and the mouth gaped open in a cruel parody of surprise as if to say, *Unhand me, sir. I'm a good girl, I am!*

He put trembling fingers to her skin to feel for a pulse, but she was dead. Dead as mutton.

The verdict of a medical man.

A sudden spew shot out of his mouth, doubling him over on hands and knees, to jet the contents of stomach plus medicinal whisky over the glistening path that led to the front door.

The young man wrenched away and ran off as if the hounds of hell were after him.

Resilience went only so far.

18

The world is full of care, much like unto a
    bubble;
Women and care, and care and women, and
    women and care and trouble.
    Nathaniel Ward, *The Simple Cobbler*

James McLevy took a large draught of
reasonably hot coffee, ignored the flakes from his
tin mug that had set sail upon the surface, and
tried to make sense of events.

It was like looking at a fast, boiling river and
attempting to follow a scrap of silver paper that
had fallen in, and now was part of the swirling
foam.

Momentary glimpses that might well be
illusions lifted the spirits for a second, but then
disappeared, leaving only the hypnotic movement of the current.

Whit a caper, eh?

Yet somewhere there was a pattern, he could
sense it. A composition with little or no logic,
where nothing fits but from the deep fissures of
the past, some misbegotten Caliban was clawing
his way out into the air.

Perhaps not ugly and deformed, perhaps a
more seductive killer. Like Ariel. But a killer
nonetheless.

The inspector shook his head and treated
himself to another slurp. All fancy conjectures,

dancing like witches round a cauldron, but he welcomed these weird insights.

A while since they had honoured him with their company.

A shaft of pain struck him amidships and he bent over to quell the sudden agony.

Finally, after what seemed an endless moment, the pain retreated sullenly and left him alone.

Very alone.

The attic room was a naked proposition; no warming portraits of a beloved family, no cushions where one might lean back to puff a leisurely hookah, no tokens of affection left by a passing maenad.

Just sharp corners and bare wood of a bachelor life, where books and forensic periodicals littered the floor like discarded snake-skins.

He took another slurp and braced himself, but nothing happened.

How long since the old woman had met her unexpected Maker?

Hardly twenty-four hours and the inspector had been run ragged, a cork in a whirlpool, scraped along like dung on a boot-heel, as if the Fates had decided they would throw everything that came to hand at James McLevy.

What had he done to deserve such projectiles?

Had the world gone mad or was it just another day in Leith?

The only moment of respite had been that stolen sojourn in the Old Ship with Stevenson.

They had said little, had sat in a booth sipping at their drinks, best malt whisky, this being the writer's treat, and watched the bar trade to find similar points of observation.

McLevy rarely met anyone who could glean character and foibles of folk up to his own exacting standards, but Robert Louis came close.

Are a writer and policeman not kindred souls? Always somewhere behind the eyes a calculation being made that might help the case.

Or add a chapter to the book.

Stevenson parsed a man who stood by the bar nursing a pale beer, and came to the conclusion the fellow had fallen on hard times. Once prosperous by the cut of his now shabby clothing, his hand trembled as it grasped the glass, and his eyes shifted here and there as he sought out salvation.

The writer prophesied a tale would unfold.

It came in the form of a scabby mongrel dog that slunk in through the doors and scuttled to the man's feet before the barman took action.

This was obviously not their first meeting.

The dog made no attempt to ingratiate itself and looked around in much the same manner as the man.

The man poured a little of his beer into a saucer and set it down before the dog.

The dog licked up the beer, the man finished off his drink, and they left together.

Stevenson drew thoughtfully on his bent and bedraggled cigarette and murmured, 'Not exactly a happy ending but it will have to suffice.'

Then he glanced slyly sideways at McLevy's impassive countenance.

'Henry Preger. A sudden acquaintance with

Madame Arsenic, you said?'

'That I did.'

'Self-induced?'

'I doubt it.'

'Then who might be the purveyor?'

'There would be a long queue — he was a nasty piece of work, but . . . '

McLevy looked over to the clock above the bar. Half an hour had passed. Time to go.

' . . . Jean Brash was his business partner. All the money came to her, along with their bawdy-hoose. The Happy Land.'

McLevy's lips quirked in a smile of what might have been reluctant approbation.

'Then she closed that and erected the Holy Land. It burnt down and lo and behold, wi' the insurance money she bought the Just Land.'

'A woman of backbone,' Robert Louis commented.

'Ye might say that. I must leave you now.'

The inspector rose and pointed to Stevenson's glass, but the writer covered the tumbler with long tapered fingers.

'It has been a pleasure, sir.'

'Unexpected, I'll wager,' grunted McLevy.

For a moment the two shared a sardonic glance and then the inspector's face grew solemn.

'My condolences for your father's death,' he said out of the blue.

Robert Louis extinguished the paltry remains of his cigarette in a small tin tray.

'He died. Not knowing who he was. Already in another world. The Unknown.'

A careful statement that hid a welter of feeling.

'Do you sleep well?' asked McLevy suddenly.

'Never.' Stevenson blew out some smoke. 'You?'

'Likewise.'

McLevy nodded as if some revelation had been made between them, and prepared to depart.

Stevenson watched as the inspector pulled fretfully at his moustache.

'A recent acquisition? The fuskers?'

'Eh? Oh? Aye.'

'I shall not ask the whys and wherefores of the earlier advice from the ragamuffin hermaphrodite.'

'Good. I wouldnae tell you anyhow.'

McLevy was inclined to be disappointed that the subject had been raised again, but then realised that in similar circumstance he would have done the same.

Amongst the traits they seemed to share was that of the nosy man.

Stevenson smoothed at his own whiskers.

'I have had mine for years. An old friend. It grants me gravitas.'

He suddenly roared with laughter at that idea, but then his own face became solemn.

'Good luck with your murder.'

'I may need it.'

As McLevy, on the move, pulled up his collar and jammed on his low-brimmed bowler, Stevenson called softly after.

'I may not stay in the city long myself; this climate marks me like the Black Spot. But I have a feeling we will meet again, inspector.'

For a moment McLevy hesitated and then, on impulse, hawked out a scrap of paper and wrote something down with the stub of a pencil.

'My lodging address. In case you're passing by at midnight. The attic room. If the light's on, that's me.'

'A kind offer,' smiled Robert Louis. 'I'll keep it in mind.'

The inspector had then left him; a wraithlike figure as the smoke of the tavern curled round with loving tendrils.

An indignant scratching at the window brought McLevy out of this memory. His familiar, Bathsheba the cat, a royal presence that visited late at night to claim her privileges.

The rain was still falling, but the cat was dry as a bone as she slid through the opened frame — how did she do that?

He carefully poured out a little weak coffee into a saucer and shook his head in customary amusement as it was delicately lapped up.

A cat that craved coffee.

Another nocturnalist, perhaps.

The inspector picked his way over the scattered books towards the table where the red ledger of his diary lay precisely in the centre.

Unavoidable. No getting away wi' it. There it was — lying like a stone in his path.

What the hell was going on in his heart?

Perhaps if he wrote it down, it would make some sense.

Diary of James McLevy.
10th May, 1887.

I did not expect to see a woman, that's the problem. It should have been a man. With a hairy face.

Fragrance unexpected can hit below the belt.

Jessica Drummond.

Her eyes are dark and deep; there might even be gypsy blood in the family.

Her brother is a murder suspect. He's hiding something and so is his friend. But I will find it out.

Dearie me.

Jessica Drummond.

Her face swims before me like a jellyfish and produces the same feeling of inner disquiet as when such a creature is encountered.

You meet them on the edge of the shore and when you poke them with a boot, they quiver in the most alarming fashion.

McLevy suddenly raised his head from the page and let out an anguished bellow.

'Why am I talking about jellyfish?'

In answer, Bathsheba hopped up onto the sill, spared him one inscrutable yellow-eyed feline glance, and then ghosted off into the damp night.

McLevy closed the window after her and strained for a moment to trace her whereabouts, but she had already vanished.

Leaving him with what refused to disappear.

He returned to his labour.

I have been reading Edgar Allan Poe, 'The Tell-Tale Heart', a murderer betrayed by guilty imagination when his victim's beating heart sets up a racket under the floorboards.

The past come back to haunt him.

But that is only a story, this is the real world. Is it not?

Jessica Drummond.

Was she already in that dream or did I put her there?

Is my heart pounding under the floorboards? What has been buried?

McLevy laid the pen aside, blotted carefully and closed the diary. He could take this no further.

The red ledger had been gifted to him by a grateful bank manager at the successful discovery of an embezzlement case.

Pity the man concerned hanged himself.

The past aye comes back.

If he had just not looked direct into her eyes, things would have been fine.

But he had, and they were not.

The coffee was cold now, but he held it against his chest as if it were a source of warmth before dispatching the contents in one gulp.

Let us face the facts and draw conclusions.

His insides were churning with strange fragmentary feelings of a sort never before experienced; an emptiness in the bread-basket that had little to do with absence of black pudding; visions replaying in his mind of parted lips and sweet breath that issued therewithal.

Conclusion?

Could it be that he had fallen in love?

The symptoms fitted what might be read in books but had never been felt.

Until now.

James McLevy in love? Or more accurately — infatuated?

Dearie me.

In the morning it might be gone like the lifting of a wizard's wicked spell.

But in the meantime.

It was going to be a long night.

And he was damned if he'd shave his moustache.

19

I within did flow
With seas of life, like wine.
        Thomas Traherne, *Wonder*

For the corpse in the doorway, time had no meaning. It had fled like a young man from ugly death.

The rain beat down and washed the caked disguise from her face, revealing an age of suffering.

Once she had been a flickering nymph of the pave, but it seemed in the twinkling of an eye her life had altered to that of scavenging.

Delving deeper in the wynds, later and later in the darkness, waiting for passengers of the night, often fu' as a puggie, a quick dunt against the wall or even better a flutter of the fingers, easy milked, then the pretended passion run its course, money in hand and move on apace.

Cold dreary winter found her in the low dives, howking out the odd auld randie, or hanging at the edge of tables on the look-out for an unfinished drink or oddments of food.

All the barmen knew her and mostly turned a blind eye for she was not a quarrelsome soul.

But it was not a proud life.

Once she had been a real beauty, creamy, with a soft, curved body where men desired to bury their passion. All the young bucks. One especial

— for a while her regular till he ran out of money.

Even then she favoured him, but a girl has to live.

And move on apace.

Then the hard knocks came.

One after another, queuing up.

She lost the prize, her bonny boy.

Not long ago she'd seen a face brought all the memories back, but when she poured out her heart, the drink had taken over and she ended raving like a loon.

When she awoke, she was alone.

This evil night her luck had run out in the Foul Anchor when she had tried to sneak a wee nip from the glass of an auld birkie who had shuffled outside to driddle agin the wind, and Mary had been caught by a sharp-eyed young barman.

He shoved her rudely to the door and a boot in the arse sent her skelping headlong into the dark, where she limped through the harbour cursing bad fortune.

Then she saw the figure skip towards her with an odd halting gait, light on his feet, face a white mask shaded under a wide hat, a silver cane in hand — a real dandy.

'Are ye searching out adventure, young sir?'

To her slightly croaking enquiry, he bowed his head and moved closer. She pulled up her threadbare rags and arranged her mouth into a smile of welcome.

The wind was biting but thank God the rain had lost interest.

'What is your pleasure? I ken them all.'

The first cut is aye the cruellest they say, and when his cane slashed through the air at her throat, it was indeed a savage but surgical slice that drove the breath from her lungs with rendered agony.

She fell on her knees and, as the blows rained down with deadly precision, was mute like an animal to the slaughter.

At the very last, she looked up and through swimming eyes, a vision of the countenance above swirled like an illusion changing shape.

But — but — *she knew that face!*

She cried out a name that stopped him in his tracks for a moment. Then he struck deeper.

And then she knew no more.

Legend has it that the victim's eyes will retain the murderer's image on the retina.

But all that was reflected in her eye was the darkness.

And so she lay there.

Waiting for the morning light.

20

Ah! from the soul itself must issue forth,
A light, a glory, a fair luminous cloud
Enveloping the Earth —
Samuel Taylor Coleridge, *Dejection: an Ode*

'Death waits for every man and woman who walks this world, and those who have sinned and fallen short of the glory of God will be unredeemed! A Lake of Fire they will see before them but to the faithful what says the risen Christ?'

At this point the Reverend Jonas Gibbons — his rangy figure clothed in the robes of his Faith, unruly locks combed severely flat from a side parting, furze of face hair that framed the leonine features bristling with holy intent — paused and looked down from his pulpit at the packed congregation huddled together and steaming from the rain like a herd of cattle, before raising his hands to buttress the answer to this rhetorical question.

'Be faithful unto death, and I will give you the crown of life!'

A quiet murmur of accord, which for the Church of Scotland was equivalent to a full-blooded Hallelujah plus angelic choirs followed by heavenly thunderbolts, came in response and the minister nodded gravely, then began anew.

'For if we live near to God, if he is ever present on our right and left hand, by our side constantly, shall we not share in a blessed communion with heaven?'

The simple sincerity in his words and the resonance of delivery were evidence of an ability that drew the righteous from near and far.

Of course it is fine and worthy to hear the word of the Lord in all its glory, but if there is a charismatic appeal that might gild the sacred sensibilities of the female of the species, then may she not make the pilgrimage and drag her husband along for good measure?

One might have mistaken Lieutenant Roach for one such freighted accompaniment as he sat there beside his wife, for indeed their church lay a good three miles distant and the incumbent minister dry as grave-dust.

Roach's presence on this day had, however, a perverse duality.

He was profoundly split, not unlike the old Adam, but instead of a tempting apple, his attention was torn between murder most recent and the word of God.

Matters were not helped by the fact that the pews in this church were apparently designed to cause maximum discomfort to those of a bony posterior. This was possibly meant to keep a reverent mind focused on the sermon, but in his case was having the opposite effect.

Why must worship be always couched in pain?

In the Deep South of America it was not so, but in the East of Scotland, it would seem, it was par for the course.

Of course golf was the other subject never far from Roach's mind, but he rounded up his migrating thoughts and tried to concentrate.

Gibbons leant over and spoke softly, for he was intending to launch into the main body of his sermon and it was always wise to gather in the fold first and foremost.

'For what says the 23rd Psalm? *Yea, though I walk through the valley of the shadow of death, I will fear no evil: for thou are with me; thy rod and thy staff, they comfort me. Thou preparest a table before me in the presence of mine enemies; Thou annointest my head with oil; My cup runneth over.*'

The words rested like a blessing on the bowed heads.

Now he had them in the palm of his hand — now he could talk about sin and redemption. Nothing crude or manipulative, for Jonas was far from an exultant revivalist. No — together they would walk the road.

The road to a sober Salvation.

Sadly, Roach's mind had veered back to murder.

He had been roused from his bed at an unearthly hour of the Sabbath Day to be informed that a corpse had been found on a reputable doorstep, bearing the exact same marks as the one in the harbour.

By the time he'd got there, McLevy plus Mulholland were already on hand, the path scoured for evidence, all of which was bagged. Roach had then made a decision to keep all of this under wraps, for a variety of reasons.

Luckily the corpse had been discovered so early that there were no witnesses to the police activity. Heriot Row, in any case, prided itself on the avoidance of neighbourly contact. An Englishman's home may be his castle, but for the Scots, a net curtain will suffice.

And for such Roach was profoundly thankful.

Of course discreet enquiries would be made up and down the street, but they would be couched as if concerning a night-time incident, a disturbance of the peace, and due to the aforesaid net-curtain mentality Roach could almost foretell that nothing would emerge.

Under wraps. As far as possible. For the moment.

If someone like Sim Carnegie got a hold of this story, the investigation would be hopelessly compromised.

It involved a world-famous son of Edinburgh, so until such time as guilt was ascertained, unwelcome and unsavoury publicity should be buried in the pit of the dunghill where they belonged.

He had informed the City police; they had agreed with his conclusion and in fact were delighted to let Leith run with the investigation.

Because if something went wrong, they, the City police would be in the clear and he, Roach, would be buried deep in the bunker of shame.

But McLevy had his teeth firmly into this new murder by the time his lieutenant had arrived, so it was too late.

Besides the original crime was in their parish and Roach had somehow become personally embroiled in the whole atrocity — that's the trouble when you take to the streets.

And that dent in his best hat demanded vengeance —

'*Robert* — *stop talking to yourself*,' his wife's whispered tones broke into this internal symposium.

'*I was praying*,' he muttered defensively.

Mrs Roach shot him a look. She knew fine well that in common with most men he only prayed when in a predicament or was bidden to from on high, and neither of the cases applied because the sermon was still proceeding.

The minister had traversed the valley of the shadow of death with his congregation, guided them to the sunny uplands of a potential heaven should a decent Christian life be lived, but he was careful not to make it sound too easy a task.

The devil was aye on hand. Though if you looked him full in the face he would wither on the vine.

Auld Hornie would come again, though. Reborn. An eternal vigilance was needed.

On the watchtower of his soul, each man must scan the horizon for dark riders.

Live near to God that He might say, *Well done, my good and faithful servant; enter thou into the joy of Thy Lord*.

The minister bowed his head for a moment in deep thought, his strong sinewy hands resting on the huge reading bible that lay before him on the pulpit.

As Roach shifted uncomfortably once again on his persecuted rear-end, a hand tapped him on

159

the shoulder. They were sitting in one of the side pews and the lieutenant was at one end, somewhat marginalised from the main body of the kirk.

A young man had stepped forwards from the shadows, and Roach recognised the sandy hair and open, broad face of John Gibbons, son of the manse.

'Here,' said John quietly, a glint of humour in the light brown eyes. 'This may provide assistance, sir.'

He slipped Roach a small cushion, which proved to fit neatly under the suffering flesh, and then stepped back out of sight.

When the thus-relieved lieutenant brought his attention back on course, the words of Jonas Gibbons had an uncanny pertinence.

He at last raised his head, solemnity etched into his face like fissures in a holy statue.

'A good woman has died,' he announced. 'A devout spirit who worked night and day for the Lord and for the church of St Stephen's. Her reward will be in heaven and all who knew this dear soul can attest to the good deeds and worshipful diligence that was her way.

'Kind to her neighbours and believing in the true path, Agnes Carnegie will be sorely missed by all her friends in this place.'

If amongst the godly females who had shared duties with Agnes there might have been some reservations, due to the fact that the woman was a terrible gossip, aye poking her nose intae other body's business with a tongue sharp as a pike's teeth, they were nowhere manifest upon their

160

countenances, and indeed the fate of the poor sowl was sorrowful enough to allay any such qualms.

'Murdered!' Jonas Gibbons suddenly thundered, tacking somewhat towards the Old Testament. 'An innocent lamb tae the slaughter! May the vengeance of the Lord descend upon the godless sinner who perpetrated this vile act. May the forces of law and order bring this killer under the heel of justice and let him suffer the due and severe consequence of stringent retribution!'

More than a few glances, including his wife's, were cast Roach's way, but his attention was fixed on a separate pew, reserved and paid for by the Stevenson family.

There sat the mother-widow Margaret, beside her a striking woman with beautiful but heavy features and eyes that seemed to be fixed beyond this world. The youth on Margaret's other side was thin-faced, with a straggly moustache, and bore a self-generated semblance to the most absent member of the clan.

Despite the convulsion at Heriot Row, after all how many decent households find a dead body on their doorstep, Margaret Stevenson had insisted upon going to church.

This was her habit. This was her rock. And besides, the Reverend Jonas Gibbons would soon be officiating at the funeral of her dear husband.

It was inconceivable, when the minister looked down, that she should not be looking up.

Fanny had reluctantly agreed to accompany her, and Lloyd was press-ganged to be the representative male of the family.

The titular head was conspicuous by his absence.

It was well known that wild horses could not drag Robert Louis Stevenson into a church, especially this one, where his youthful rebellious spirit had been whittled at by the notched blade of Holy Scripture.

His declared atheism at the age of twenty-three had provoked his mother into agonised distress and his father into the grim prophecy that eternal damnation had just walked in the door.

Be that as it may, the possibly eternally damned Robert Louis had other business on hand, not completely disconnected to the man who now sat more comfortably upon a cushion.

Police business.

Margaret caught Roach's stare upon her and returned it placidly, before fixing her attention once more in a heavenly direction.

The lieutenant had walked them all down to the church, thinking it was the least he could do, then was astonished to find his own wife waiting for him by the bleak vertiginous steps of St Stephen's.

In all the stramash he had completely forgotten that she had persuaded him to come and hear this preacher who had inspired such pious admiration throughout the city.

But there she was. And here he was also.

As far as Mrs Roach was concerned, he had left early on some police errand and would turn up on time.

Her husband was never late.

Which he was not, and since his inspector was taking care of business at the station, it was as well to carry on in the direction of Sabbath travel.

And so, in they all went together.

And here they all were.

Within the fold.

John Gibbons emerged from the shadows to kneel, accepting silently Roach's nod of thanks for posterial deliverance, as Jonas Gibbons, having at length praised the late Agnes and commended her to a guaranteed deliverance, raised both arms in the air.

An unexpected, pallid streak of sunlight burrowed through one of the church windows and illuminated him like an angel, as his strong voice rang amongst the flock.

After all, he was their Shepherd.

'Let us pray,' he said simply. 'Let us pray for the departed soul.'

He began the opening words of the Lord's Prayer and the congregation joined in the swell of heavenly tribute.

Here endeth the lesson.

21

The way out is via the door. Why is it that no one will use this method?

Confucius, *Analects*

He had slept badly. Dreamt a wasteland of dead trees where he, as a shivering young man, fled for his life, pursued by yelping hounds. His father appeared and promised to help but only if the youth gave God a barley-bannock as payment. This he refused to do and the old man shook his hoary locks, tears of grief running down his face.

He took the young man to the edge of a grey stone stairway that led to an iron-studded door dripping with candle grease and gobbets of red melted wax. The old man then vanished with a sorrowful prophecy that the barley-bannock sin and other such iniquitous transgressions would return in the form of a beast with two heads.

The young man opened the door to find a dark void, and when he peered far below, saw a white slab, luminous in the surrounding shadows.

There seemed to be a body on the slab, but he failed to construe the features.

Then he heard the beast. Heavy in tread, smelling like an addled midden, grunting as it lumbered upwards.

He could see its shape, but not yet clearly if it had two heads. And if so, which to cut off first? For the hero had suddenly been granted a sword in hand, rusty and mottled with age, but sharp enough surely to hack through a throat.

The beast let out a terrifying roar. It had smelt the prey. Its breath was like a poisonous gas and the young man was now pinned to the very last step that led to nowhere.

He raised the sword, but it melted in the heat.

Stevenson woke in a fierce sweat, which rapidly cooled, leaving his night-clothes wrapped clammily around his thin body like a shroud.

He leached out for his tobacco pouch and muttered an oath on finding it empty.

Were dreams of such nature from bad conscience as the preachers would prate, or a darker, deeper place that took no account of such paltry concepts?

One way or another, they were his constant companions.

By the night-light Robert Louis could make out Fanny's outline buried under blankets in the other bed, safe in the arms of Morpheus. So he slid out quietly, donned dressing gown and slipper's, then padded off to find his mistress.

Madame Nicotine was in the hall within his jacket pocket, sheathed in leather and waiting with open arms.

He quickly rolled a life-saving cylinder, lit a Lucifer and smoked at once where he stood.

An addict knows not time or place.

A clock somewhere chimed a muffled tribute

to five o'clock, beyond the witching hour but according to some smack dab in the middle of Auld Clootie's temporal reign.

The front door rattled in a gust of wind and Stevenson regarded it thoughtfully.

It lacked a flight of stone stairs but what was behind?

The void?

Eternity?

Or just a wee, wet street?

With cigarette in lips like a Mexican bandit, Stevenson turned the heavy key that secured the house against Satan's legions and threw open the door.

He had hoped to find the void, the unimaginable inchoate darkness, where all possibilities branch off in disparate directions like so many shooting stars, giving rise to other possibilities, other worlds, where anything might happen at any moment, an ever-changing kaleidoscope of shapes and events that might change in Protean splendour.

But no. It was a wee, wet street.

The rain had stopped and the wind blew a sour fetid odour through the tobacco smoke.

Was it the Monster?

Nothing so outlandish.

His eye fell upon a spattering of vomit upon the path that the rain and wind had failed to clear. Some drunken juggie no doubt, for Stevenson's sensitive long nose could detect the lurking dregs of John Barleycorn in the smell.

For a moment he felt a childish disappointment: no adventure, no treasure, no malevolent figures in the fog — just a dreich Edinburgh morning, where the only battle was between lamp-light and the grey tinge of looming cloud.

And then he saw the Beast.

Almost at his feet, huddled to the side, wrapped in a blanket like some obscene cocoon, the face washed clean by the air, white and staring.

Not at him, the neck jerked askew, livid brand on the flesh, eyes averted, staring wide at death's door.

For a moment, the sight so unexpected, Robert Louis forgot to inhale.

Then he let out a stifled shriek. Not of terror, more as if something he had expected in the depths of his psyche had arrived to greet the wanderer.

A visitor at the gate.

22

Bad as he is, the Devil may be Abused,
Be falsely charged, and causelessly accused,
When Men, Unwilling to be blamed alone,
Shift off those crimes on Him, which are
    their own.
           Daniel Defoe, *History of the Devil*

Stevenson smiled a little wearily. He had recited the more prosaic version of *the finding of a corpse upon my doorstep* and wondered whether Queen Victoria, from her high vantage on the wall, was entertained and believed the story.

Or did Her Majesty harbour secret doubts?

He shifted to another pair of eyes that had probably witnessed more lying than a politician's mistress.

'My first thought was to lug the cadaver away from the house and disclaim all knowledge,' the writer admitted with disarming honesty. 'But then — I thought — what if it were me lying there? Would I not wish a more ethical observance?'

'On the other hand,' replied James McLevy. 'Being dead, you might not give a damn.'

'True,' came a somewhat florid response. 'But, taking my first assertion as proven, I suppose there are scraps of conscience not yet pulverised by the grinding hypocrisy of our civilised world and so — I thought of you, inspector.'

Indeed McLevy, sleepless at his attic window, chewing hard upon his moustache, had heard his name called from the streets below.

He gazed down to see Robert Louis who had battled through the city in the biting cold, bare-headed, his hastily donned clothes and velvet jacket a poor protection against the knife-edge cut of an East wind, clutching the scrap of paper with the inspector's address given in the tavern under very different circumstances.

Stevenson resembled nothing so much as a character in a threadbare adventure tale, beckoning urgently as if to invite the watcher to join in some dubious enterprise.

They had knocked up Mulholland on the way back, and everything had followed on.

Now all were cosily tucked away in Roach's office, the interrogation room being deemed a touch brutal for the frail personage of such a world-famous creator, and the cold slab, now in possession of the corpse, an equally grim prospect.

From the inspector's view, Stevenson was holding up fairly well after what must have been an exhausting time, but was there a tremor that might be exploited?

Just in case ought was hidden.

For the writer and the policeman are aye on the look-out for something hidden.

It might even be concealed from the subject himself; that makes no difference.

Kick over the stone — see what crawls below.

'The vomit is not that of the corpse,' said James McLevy. 'No marks on the clothing, no

169

traces of sick in the mouth.'

He did not mention the other contents of the mouth. Keep that up the sleeve.

'Clean as a whistle,' said Mulholland cheerfully, well aware of his inspector's intent.

'Might it have been from the killer — the vomit?'

A reasonable question, as Stevenson fidgeted somewhat having been told that Lieutenant Roach frowned mightily upon the smell of tobacco in his quarters.

'I doubt it,' said McLevy. 'The murder too precise.'

'Precise?'

'The blows, sir,' chimed in Mulholland. 'On the nail. The distance between them. Exact. A cold measure. Even the Police Surgeon couldn't miss it.'

'Precise folk don't tend tae vomit.'

Having delivered this judgement, McLevy sat back in Roach's leather chair and folded hands over a corporation that grew a little rounder with every passing year.

It was a comfy chair; he could get used to being a lieutenant. Stevenson sat across the desk from him and the constable, as usual, stood like a giraffe in the corner.

Mulholland looked at the writer with a curiosity that he made no effort to conceal.

The Irish have always admired writers, unlike the Scots, who regard them with deep suspicion, and the English who try to pretend they don't exist.

The fellow was thin as a rake, but had darting,

lively eyes and a turn of mind that seemed never still — now what kind of animal would Mulholland place him to be? Some kind of thoroughbred that's for sure. Greyhound or horse.

Unaware he was being thus translated, Stevenson offered another contribution to the debate.

'A drunkart blown in by the wind?'

'Time will tell.'

McLevy leant forward. Kick over the stone.

'The woman — do you know her?'

The writer frowned.

'I am not sure. Something in the face. I glimpsed it but briefly.'

'We can go back tae the cold slab. She's laid out like a dish o' fish.'

The inspector laughed coarsely and Mulholland knew well the technique: innocent or guilty, stir the pot.

Stevenson's fingers twitched. He was gasping for a cigarette, and feeling oddly under siege.

He had been delighted to accompany the police; it avoided the inevitable wrangle over his refusal to toe the line of God even with his father due to be interred.

Also he had been intrigued, and revelled in the chance to observe the mechanics of a real investigation.

What he had not reckoned on was being the centre of it.

'Something in the face,' he repeated slowly, and indeed in his mind a tantalising elusive recognition was swirling.

'Mary Dougan.'

To this flat statement Mulholland nodded accord. They had both known the woman at first sight, though the face was drawn by death and the mouth no longer smiling — in spite of the blows fate had dealt, Mary had always found a smile.

'She was a good-natured soul, but a little on the weak side,' offered the constable.

'A whisky diver,' said McLevy bluntly.

At the name, Robert Louis had flinched, his worst fears realised. What he did not wish to see in the ruined features came rushing back into his mind.

'I knew her in that case,' he stated simply. 'My God, how she has changed.'

'Life and death. Mark ye deep.'

McLevy's sardonic comment struck a flicker of light in Stevenson's eyes, but then the inspector signalled that the floor was his and the writer, in a strange gesture, raised an imaginary cigarette to his lips, took a deep drag, and then blew out as if to release memory.

'A threepenny whore. I was a young man. Her regular. She was modest and decent for all that. The other girls were . . . wild. I knew them all.'

A dispassionate tone, but the sigh that followed told a different tale.

'I had to leave Edinburgh. *Ae fond kiss and then we sever.* She clung to me. That bonny face. Awash with tears.'

'Did she love ye then?'

'Who knows?' Stevenson hesitated for a moment. 'Love is a mystery, is it not?'

172

He gazed down at his long fingers, stained yellow at the ends from tobacco smoke, as if they were either to blame or might provide an answer.

'I was desperately ill. And had to leave the city. I never saw her again until this sorry day.'

This rendition of lost affection, even with a threepenny whore, had silenced McLevy strangely, and the constable hastened to fill the gap.

'How long ago was this, sir?'

'Eighteen years or so, I would estimate.'

Mulholland looked at McLevy, who roused himself from some inner contemplation and waved his hand.

The constable produced a crumpled, damp piece of paper, which he then smoothed out.

'This was found inside the mouth of the corpse.'

He carefully read the text; again it seemed as if underscored by a nail.

Naked came I out of my mother's womb, and naked shall I return hither: the Lord gave, and the Lord hath taken away; blessed be the name of the Lord.

'Does that ring a bell, sir?'

'Other than the anatomical accuracy. Not remotely.'

'It seems to have a religious bent.'

'Unless it is meant ironically.'

McLevy grunted what might have been an agreement to this, but then fixed Stevenson with a direct stare.

'There is, however, one question that must be answered.'

'And what is that?' asked the writer, before

suddenly erupting into a racking cough, which he finally stifled with the aid of a large white handkerchief.

'My lungs crave the blessed weed,' he murmured.

'Well, they'll have tae wait.'

No hint of any former intimacy, no matter how fleeting, was displayed on the inspector's face, and it stirred the steel of Stevenson's nature.

He cocked his head to the slant and Mulholland realised that he'd got the animals wrong. Neither dog nor horse — but a bird.

Magpie, jackdaw or crow. Bright, glittering eyes and always a deceptive move ahead.

'What is the question, prithee, kind sir?'

To this gently mocking repetition, McLevy's face changed not a jot, and Mulholland grasped that there was another conversation taking place, one that with all his experience and knowledge of the inspector might still be a mystery.

'Why was the corpse left at your door?'

Now it was the writer's turn to stop in his tracks while McLevy pressed forward.

'You admit that you knew her from the past?'

'A long time ago.'

'Time is a creature wi' its own rules. And the other woman, Agnes Carnegie, murdered in exactly the same fashion, a piece o' bible page stuffed in her gob, she worshipped at St Stephen's Church where your own mother kneels to pray.'

Robert Louis desired a cigarette most fervently, but he could not refuse the challenge.

'You see a connection between the two?'

'It's possible.'

'And you think I may be the bridge between — the bridge this murderer walks upon?'

Mulholland looked up at Queen Victoria — like himself she was listening intently.

'Again, it's possible. Is there nothing more you can tell us of Mary Dougan?' asked the inspector.

'Only what I have said before. She was part of a different life.'

Both men sat perfectly still.

'Of course it might all be coincidence,' remarked the writer finally. 'In the long process of time.'

'I'm not a great believer in coincidence,'

'Neither am I. Unless it suits me.'

Stevenson smiled wryly. McLevy nodded assent to that.

A soft knock at the door and on the inspector's call, Ballantyne entered. He kept his eyes carefully averted from their famous guest, and in fact was one of the few at the station who, had noticed him being sneaked in at the back.

A man who tracks the movement of scuttling insects is hard to sidle past. Also he had been given a task suited to a particular talent for discrimination.

'Ye told me tae report anything of import amongst the sick bits, sir?'

Indeed Ballantyne had been handed the evidence bag and told to exercise his forensic capabilities.

'I found this.'

He proudly unwrapped a piece of tissue paper to display a small fragment of material.

It was scarlet in colour.

Mulholland leant over from his great height and made an educated guess.

'Could be a piece of . . . a favour.'

'The students?' queried Stevenson alertly.

'They . . . may have a hand in it somewhere,' muttered the inspector. 'Hard tae tell. All things are possible.'

This had brought McLevy's thoughts back to an uneasy terrain, so he laid them aside for the moment.

'Ye've done well, Ballantyne. Away ye go now.'

But as the constable reached the door, another call.

'Ballantyne!'

McLevy nodded towards Stevenson and then to the fragment on the desk.

'Silence is golden, eh?'

The young man stiffened with pride or outrage, his birth-mark pulsing in the throat.

'Not a word will pass my lips, sir.'

However, he could not then resist, since he had earned a modicum of praise, taking part in what he perceived to be the grander scheme of things.

He turned back and addressed Stevenson as if on equal footing.

'I liked *Treasure Island*. We don't have any pirates in Leith, though. Not any more.'

Robert Louis nodded sagely. 'And which is your favourite passage, sir?'

'When the boy was in the barrel.'

'What kind of barrel?' asked Stevenson, to test the mettle of this admirer.

'Apple. Jist as well it wasnae herring.'

One of the constable's oddly placed remarks, where a man was none too sure whether to take literal or ironic import.

Having delivered his plaudit, Ballantyne finally found the way out.

Stevenson caught a moment of humour between the other two policemen as the door closed.

'A valuable helper,' he remarked.

'He has his moments,' Mulholland replied.

The writer suddenly experienced a shaft of pure addiction that sent him bolt upright; a wrench of desire that took him out of this world into another.

It is often so with smokers. As if part of their body is elsewhere. In thrall to Madame Nicotine.

'If there is nothing more at present, then I shall bid you farewell, gentlemen,' he announced with some force.

'Aye. Ye need your wee indulgence, eh my mannie?'

'Indulgences are what the Pope sells,' snapped back Stevenson.

He rose, strode to the door and then, struck by a thought, turned to face the inspector.

'This killer — is a picture forming in your mind?'

Mulholland was impressed by the tenor of that question; it was a side of McLevy not many perceived, but Stevenson had instinctively grasped the workings of that odd intelligence.

The inspector gave this query serious consideration.

'He is a man — obsessed. But concealed. And cunning. His obsession may be yourself. What you represent. Or something else completely, I do not yet know.'

The words touched a vein of thought that had been plaguing Robert Louis regarding those he had once considered close to him but who now were not so.

'Might it be . . . a jealousy of fame?'

'All things are possible,' was again the response. 'But he is — separated. Apart from himself, even. You will never know to look at him. Such killers are hard tae fathom.'

'Like Jekyll and Hyde?' Mulholland threw in suddenly.

'Marcus Aurelius,' the writer replied, 'held that the arts merely imitate natural forms. Not the opposite.'

McLevy grinned and abruptly banged the desk, throwing Roach's immaculately assembled inkwells out of true.

'Aye. You pair are far too langheidit for me!'

He let out a whoop of laughter, as if some tension had been released and pointed at Stevenson.

'We'll try tae keep our own secret and get you out of here without a soul seeing save Ballantyne.'

'I thank you for that.'

'And you — Mister Stevenson — must make sure that not one of your household breathes a word.'

'It will be done.'

'It had better be. If this case breaks, we'll have the press delving intae every orifice.'

The inspector scowled at that notion and looked down, as if Sim Carnegie might yet shelter in some intestinal duct.

'I would appreciate the privacy,' said Stevenson soberly. 'I have a father to bury.'

'We all have our duties,' McLevy retorted dryly. 'Now — there's a hansom cab rank at the back of the station. Ye can puff yoursel' tae death all the way home.'

Robert Louis nodded meekly enough and made for the door, but the inspector had not quite called it a day.

'One thing more. The bible page. It was ripped from a holy tome that Agnes Carnegie was taking home tae repair before she met up wi' the devil. Guess the owner of that Good Book?'

'Someone of a religious bent?'

'The minister of St Stephen's church. Just round the corner, eh?'

Stevenson frowned in thought. Indeed it would seem there was a malevolent convergence — was he the centre where all roads met, or was it just the writer trying to pull all threads together?

As he made finally to leave, the inspector had yet one more straw to lay upon the camel's back.

'And you, my mannie — you being such a clever bugger wi' your Roman emperors — see if ye might delve back and find something that might help wi' this investigation.'

Stevenson turned to grin.

'All things are possible.'

But then his face changed in memory.

'Mary Dougan. She was a bonny girl.'

With that he was out the door to follow Mulholland.

For a moment McLevy pondered deeply.

If there were an informer at the station, as had happened when Sim Carnegie finessed them with finding out about the white favour on his own mother's corpse, keeping the enquiry in hugger-mugger would be a hard task.

But he had his own thoughts on that.

The inspector glowered up at Queen Victoria as if she were personally responsible for all this, and then swept out of Roach's office to march through the main body of the station, paying no heed to the respectful silence greeting his entrance. He then disappeared into the cold room.

Mary Dougan was still dead.

Her face did not seem so bonny now.

She was a good-natured soul and, as far as he knew, had never wittingly done a single person harm.

See where it gets you.

23

For the life of me, I could not understand
why a woman should not have as much right
to enter a canoe as a man.

Herman Melville, *Typee*

Jean Brash leant back and let an envious wind
blow through her hair so that it flew like a
standard trailing behind as the coach clattered
noisily in the Sabbath silence.

They had gone hell for leather through Leith
Links, found their way to Bonnington Road, and
then hammered along Henderson Row, as she
revelled in the freedom a wee blink of sun could
grant a woman in sore need.

Angus had been instructed to haul back the
top of the carriage, give the cuddies a good
skelp, and off they went.

'Whee-hee!' shouted the owner of the Just
Land in a most unladylike fashion, causing her
companion Hannah Semple to shake her head in
a *nae good will come of this* manner, a phrase
she often thought might look well on her
tombstone.

In contrast to Jean's vivid lavender dress
ensconced inside a cream coat, Hannah was
dressed in dowdy hues, with a hat shaped not
unlike a dropped scone, that she clung onto
grimly as the wind pegged wickedly at her body.
On the Links, Jean's own hat, which took after a

181

French cake, near whipped off her head and she had taken advantage to pull out the pins, loose it from her head and give best to nature.

In truth she knew not why her spirits were so high — perhaps it was the success of repelling boarders at the bawdy-hoose — those cries of pain echoed yet in her joyful ears — or just the fact that the sun had managed to fight its way through the clouds to bring a moment of luminosity to the browbeaten stone of the city, but she felt a rush of elation not even the thought of McLevy's boiled dumpling of a face could spoil.

Even Angus sneakily extracted from his pocket one of the sugar lumps he kept for the horses and crunched it in his teeth with what passed for Aberdonian abandon.

They had swung up sharp left from Henderson Row, heading for Queen Street, where Jean planned to veer to the right and confront the Castle.

She never failed to thrill at the mass of rock that looked as if it had been deposited there by a giant hand, and nursed a secret childlike fear that one night it would take off like a rocket firework and speed off into darkness, never to be seen again.

But not today!

'Faster, Angus! Pit some beef intae it,' she called loudly, as Hannah winced.

Sometimes Jean went back to the good old days, which as far as Hannah was concerned were the bad old days where murder and mayhem broke out before your eyes if not under your very feet. That stramash wi' the Scarlet Runners had got the mistress's blood boiling — God knows where it would all end up, but the woman was *steamin'* wi' tomfoolery.

It didnae help that she had no-one in her bed at this minute. Her last lover, a handsome and eminent surgeon, had been in the habit of describing in grisly detail the workings of his latest operations upon the gall bladder. This, as Jean told Hannah, may have set the man's corpuscles moving, but did very little for hers.

It had been a clean cut.

He might return to his wife and gall bladders.

The coach suddenly jolted to a halt, as Angus pulled hard on the reins. They had encountered a crowd of folk newly out of St Stephen's Church; not an uncovered head to be seen, even amongst the weans. The scene was like something out of a moral tract, as the congregation gazed at Jean and she looked back at them.

A shaft of bright sun played lasciviously with the tousled locks of her red hair, her white skin shone like a beacon of temptation, and the green eyes sparkled with a fire that few loins in that gathering had ever experienced.

As the shut faces of the women froze to a rigid righteousness and some of their husbands, who may have known Jean's bill of fare a little more closely than they might concede, shuffled behind to avoid scrutiny, the imp of mischief possessed her and she called out a name to a face in the crowd, known from previous exploits.

'Lieutenant Roach — isn't it a beautiful day?'

A hiss escaped the lips of Jonas Gibbons. *Harlot!*

Roach's face at first went puce then drained to a putty white. He seemed to be the object of all eyes, especially the uxorial pair on his immediate left.

Jonas Gibbons's strong hand gripped Roach's upper arm as if to restrain him from leaping into the carriage and driving off in answer to Jean's daemonic sexual invitation.

For indeed the woman was the embodiment of the siren song, and the minister's face registered anger and disgust that she should thus profane the Sabbath Day.

And as for Roach?

What could he say?

You must excuse me but I have had professional dealings with this woman, not at all of a lecherous nature, more to do with murderous activities, and mainly through the offices of my inspector James McLevy who is sadly not on hand at this moment otherwise I could point him out and you might all gawk in his direction.

I can also honestly say that I have never set foot in the Just Land! I much prefer the opera in the company of my good wife. Opera being such a cleansing experience.

No. It would sound like a feeble justification, and one look at the minister's countenance made him think that the Mercy of God would stretch only so far.

Better to say nothing, lower his head in a way that might be interpreted by Jean as acknowledgement and others as a pious dismissal, and hope that either the woman quit the scene or the

184

ground might open up and swallow him.

For a moment Jean registered the secret hatred of the gathering, but then her laughter rang out again.

She boldly sought out the hard, unforgiving eyes of Jonas Gibbons and smiled.

Then, almost comically, a face peeped out from behind the obdurate man of God. A sandy-haired youth, mouth slightly open, eyes wide.

Jean winked at him and the young man turned bright red and disappeared.

'For Goad's sake, Mistress Brash,' Hannah said urgently. 'Can we get tae hell out of here before they burn ye at the stake!'

Jean sat back demurely, ran a hand through her hair, and signalled Angus to drive on past the worshippers.

'See Hannah,' she murmured as the horses jangled up South Charlotte Street, steam rising from their flanks in the sunlight. 'All gone. Jist like a bad dream.'

Indeed the way was clear and the grim audience far behind; don't look back, eyes straight ahead.

Jean had always felt sorry for Orpheus. Poor man, doing his best but the Gods are a sleekit bunch.

'Whit's fur ye will no' go by ye!' she added.

This being one of Hannah's own sayings, the old woman had to give best to this remark, but she had noted a moment of pain on Jean's face before the defiance appeared.

They were outsiders.

Their profession more honest than the dirty tricks of commerce and the lying hypocrisy of the unco guid.

The Law, the Church, and the Body Politic — three snakes slithering round each other as they climbed the greasy pole.

No — they were more honest than that slime.

But they would never be accepted.

'Angus — stop!'

Jean's cry jolted them once more to a sudden halt.

'Sorra mend ye!' Hannah expostulated. 'Are we never getting' up this brae?'

But what Jean had noticed was a passenger in another carriage that had just turned off Queen Street. The gentleman in the hansom cab had also shouted his driver to a stop.

Angus carefully backed the coach so that when the fellow leaned out, he and Jean were face to face.

He took a deep drag of a slim cigarette and coughed elegantly behind an upraised hand.

'Jean Brash — as I live and breathe. Near twenty years and still as beautiful.'

'Robert Louis,' Jean smiled. 'I wish I could say the same for you.'

Stevenson laughed.

'How so that you recognised me then?'

'That lang neb. And shifty outlook. Doesnae alter.'

Another burst of laughter, joined this time by Jean.

Hannah observed them both with narrowed eyes. Were they once lovers? She doubted that

— Henry Preger had his brand on the young Jean until McLevy beat the hell out of him and arsenic finished off the job.

Jean reached out a hand to lay upon the sleeve of the man's velvet jacket, just above the immaculate white cuffs held in place by diamond studs. His tie hung loose and the whole appearance was of someone more at home on a Mississippi river-boat.

'Ye should have been a gambler, Robert.'

'I am.'

Implicit in the statement was that Stevenson wagered on life itself rather than money, and Jean bowed her head to the point before she gave a more formal response.

'I was sorry to hear about your father.'

'Yes. It has been a sad time. But he will shortly be . . . in more welcoming surroundings.'

A sly, humorous droop to the eye and she could not restrain an answering smile.

'Have you enjoyed your visit so far?'

'It has been . . . eventful.'

'Will you stay longer?'

'No.' He coughed once more. 'Otherwise I shall finish this sojourn in the company of my ancestors.'

The horses were becoming fidgety and Hannah was obviously in sympathy. Jean smiled once more.

'Come see me afore ye go. The Just Land. A'body knows it. For one reason or another.'

He bowed his head and she let out a call, signalling Angus to gee up the horses, then shouted back as the carriage moved off.

'In the afternoon. I aye take coffee in the afternoon!'

'I'll bear that in mind!'

With his answering cry the carriage was gone and his last view was of Hannah's dour face glowering, as if to threaten arsenic of her own should he take up the offer.

Stevenson grinned to himself, then nodded to his driver to carry on down the hill, as the toiling faithful, like a stream of black ants, made their way up each side of the road.

No doubt Fanny would be in a blinding post-pious bate, being more bohemian by nature than even he might aspire to, but a cleverly pitched version of his ordeal at Leith Station, where her ailing husband had found himself at the mercy of a menacing Edgar Allan Poe fanatic, would move her to pity or at least curiosity.

So long as she had not witnessed a conversation on the brae between a beautiful red-haired bawdy-hoose keeper and himself. An innocent conversation, but the pure at heart can often be lumped in with baser elements.

Besides and to be truthful, with all her irretrievable faults, he put Fanny Osbourne above all women.

Not on a pedestal, however.

The cab turned into Heriot Row and he could see her on the road ahead hanging onto Lloyd's arm, with Margaret, his mother, on the other side.

It would make a man of the lad.

Meanwhile on Queen Street, that bawdy-hoose keeper dangled one arm out of the

188

carriage and enjoyed the encounter of cool air with her bare skin, as the wind sneaked up her sleeve.

She smiled to herself and met Hannah's wary glance with an artless countenance.

'He's a happily married man,' she remarked.

'That's whit they a' say,' was the sardonic response as they turned the corner to confront the immensity of the Castle.

Surely it put human machinations into some kind of proportion?

But on the other hand had the massive edifice seen into the future it might have warned that even a sunny encounter in the street might bring about a death in the family.

24

Give me, kind heaven, a private station,
A mind serene for contemplation.

John Gay, Fables

Sim Carnegie tried not to let the unwholesome glee he felt inside show upon his face. Things, other than the sad death of his mother, of course, had never before gone so well in his life.

He had something up the sleeve that was going to cause panic and perturbation plus supply sufficient headlines to make a bonfire.

Who knew? Perhaps one of the bigger newspapers would pick him up; only what he deserved.

Furthermore it was not long now before he would sit in Herbert Lawson the lawyer's office and once again keep the warm glow of pleasure to himself, as he inherited the fruits of his mother's frugality.

She had been left a decent amount when his father, an antiquarian book-keeper, had collapsed and died while poring over a large tome of *Pilgrim's Progress*.

Giant Despair of Doubting Castle.

The shop plus contents were sold and Sim had never got a sniff, but he played the part of the attentive son, calling every Wednesday evening, tholing Agnes's disapproval of his dubious profession and lack of religious observation.

She would unlock the chest where she kept all her 'treasures', pull out some holy tract and declaim aloud in the hope that it might convert the ungodly.

Sadly, it had not worked. But he bore it. And nodded. Even went to church a few times. But his hypocrisy and greed could only endure so far.

And after her reading, Sim would repair to the tavern, find a couple of murky whores and rut it out of his system.

Now all these sacrifices would be proved worthwhile.

She never spent a penny and he would be a rich man with money and headlines to burn.

His only concern had been if she had changed her will for any reason; occasionally his dear mother would mutter darkly about *to those that hath, it shall be given*.

But as soon as he had heard of the death, Sim had slipped into her lodgings using a copy he had waxed and made from her own door key, then searched the place from top to bottom.

Nothing found. Safe as houses. And the only will at the lawyer's was the original.

All this and the sight of Lieutenant Roach's face as he read the front page of the *Leith Herald*.

'I thought it only fair to bring you a copy of the Monday edition. I am proud of what I have produced and must warn you in all decency that there is more to come.'

Having delivered this fastidious rebuke, Sim leant back in his chair and watched the effects of the written word.

Since Roach still said nothing, Carnegie felt it incumbent upon him to quote from memory.

'*The dead body of my dear mother will no doubt join a list of unsolved crimes that litter the history of our far from gallant and supremely inefficient police force.*'

The lieutenant imagined Chief Constable Sandy Robb casting his bloodshot, bulging eyes over this sorry farrago, and it was not a pretty thought.

His attention was caught by another part of the article, which was more fuel to the flame.

It is more than rumoured that a white favour was found upon the poor corpse. That very night, the Murder Night! the White Devils faction of these warring students who have made our streets such a cauldron of unprincipled violence had a pitched battle with their fierce rivals the Scarlet Runners.

Was this decent soul caught in the middle? Was the favour left as a mark of contempt upon her lacerated body? The leader of the White Devils is known to the police — after another fracas in the dark, he was taken into custody but released almost immediately. Why is he not arrested and put under the hammer like a common criminal until the truth emerges? Is it because he is a different class with lawyers to hand? An educated hooligan?

Where is my mother's murderer?

Why is he running free?

The lieutenant blinked tiredly, however his mind was racing — so Carnegie knew that Daniel Drummond had been hauled in and let go.

Again the man seemed to have information

about the inner workings of the station.

Of course there were many constables involved and it was possible careless or boastful talk might have gone the rounds but — it was more likely an informer.

And that was a hellish prospect.

Who was it?

'Well?'

At his opponent's impatient interjection, Roach pushed the paper aside with one finger as if fearing contamination.

'You ask a great many questions, Mister Carnegie,' he muttered.

'And I want them answered.'

'They will be. In good time.'

Sim had stood since he entered the office, and to look down on Roach was no great hardship.

'Just how *is* the investigation?'

'It is . . . proceeding,' replied Roach warily, glad of the small mercy that the man had so far not caught whiff of the second murder — but that would only be a matter of time.

Again Carnegie fought against the outburst of malicious glee; better to let it drip into his system drop by drop as he watched events unfold.

'I have a great deal of ammunition,' he contented himself with saying. 'Solve this soon, lieutenant, or you will feel the impact.'

'Impact?'

'There is more to come. You have been warned.'

Roach had suddenly had enough; he had toiled most of Sunday and the evening was spent listening to his wife's bridge group in the adjoining room, where few cards were played and most of the talk was of Jean Brash's Sabbath insolence.

His wife, though not ignoring him entirely, had not been rushing to fetch pipe and slippers. A cold supper. Ham and pickles. He detested pickles.

'I observe you to be still standing, Mister Carnegie,' Roach said frigidly. 'Perhaps you might oblige me by turning on your heel and making use of the door.'

Sim opened his mouth to make retort, but Roach snarled like a cross-grained reptile.

'I said the door!'

Carnegie exited without another word, but a sly smile was spread across his face; the plan had formed and he had found a lever for the job.

Now the fun would begin.

As he came out he looked for a particular countenance, but the constable was keeping out of sight.

A wise precaution.

And so Sim Carnegie went on his merry way.

Left alone in his office, the lieutenant looked up at a beloved queen.

'It's a sair fecht,' he said out of the blue.

Victoria did not blink an eye at this colloquial expression of malign fate.

She had a Golden Jubilee next month. Forty years on the throne. Empress of India.

Could she have survived the same term at Leith Station?

Roach doubted it.

25

*You strange, astonished-looking, angle-faced,
dreary mouthed, gaping wretches of the sea.*
　　　　Leigh Hunt, *The Fish, the Man,
　　　　　　　　and the Spirit*

Two bedraggled figures hauled their weary bodies along the street towards the lower reaches of Leith, where they had their official dwelling.

A sea-haar had suddenly fallen upon parts of the city and, though not heavy, was enough to dampen the spirits and limit vision of the way ahead.

A clouded prospect.

What remained of yester-Sunday had been spent trawling the deepest dives of the harbour, hammering on doors until the moment evil-tempered publicans and barmen answered, then firing questions without respite until satisfied the truth had been extracted as far as possible from these unpromising candidates.

The subject covered any events concerning Mary Dougan on the previous Saturday night and the dispiriting response negative in the extreme.

At one point an old lag, who seemed to be close-hingit with McLevy, took the inspector aside, but though the exchange clearly gave the policeman food for thought, it seemed not to pertain to the murder.

Finally at the Foul Anchor, a tavern second only to the Rustie Nail in terms of base criminality, where priggers, pocket-delvers, pimps, and sharpers touched elbows in fine companionship, they had found a young keelie just taken on as live-in bar tender, who proudly admitted the following:

'I saw her, see? Fidgin' up tae a table, the auld gangie awa' out tae pee wi' the wind and left his dram at the board. She liftit and swalleyed — but me, I was wise tae her tricks and bootit her right oot the door!'

His pride faded somewhat when told the fate of the whisky delver, but he maintained she had been moving well enough for someone propelled by a hefty kick and that, to his memory, no-one from inside had followed out after the woman.

The other barman and the innkeeper confirmed this story though the latter, a man of few words and hard knuckles, had expressed a moment's regret for her passing.

'A harmless soul. Mary. Jist — fallen on bad times.'

The publican also had a vague memory of some months before when she had tried to claw herself round some man, but the tavern had been mobbed to the gunnels at the time, so he saw nothing of the fellow and the only upshot was that Mary had ended drunken-fu', collapsed upon a table.

That aside — nothing more.

Her expulsion from the tavern was near ten o'clock that Saturday night, and the Police Surgeon Dr Jarvis, wrenched by the urgency of the case from Sunday lunch, greasy chops bearing witness to the roast and innocent lamb, claret fumes round him like a halo, estimated the time of death between that instant and some hours after midnight.

Therefore, there seemed no reason why Mary should have ended up on Heriot Row, unless she had been killed and taken there.

Lo and behold one small advance in the investigation — because they knew, at least potentially, how that might have happened.

Lo and behold!

Mulholland glanced at the whey-faced, stocky figure barrelling doggedly along beside him and shook his head, if not in complete wonder at least in appreciation.

When they had met this Monday morning the inspector looked as if a runaway railway train had hurtled over him and he had muttered about a bad night's sleep.

But then, on some weird instinct, McLevy had insisted that they carry on the door-to-door enquiries that had been called to a halt at the end of Abercromby Place.

To the constable's mind it was for the want of something better to do, since the only witness they'd managed to find so far was a keelie-barman.

But then they found another.

From a much more respectable source.

Albany Street third door along. Upon their knock the woman opened, took one look, then her face whitened and she called for her husband.

Down he came.

A large bull of a man, ex-military by the carriage, a proper, curled moustache that put the inspector's to shame, and piercing blue eyes; augmented by an impression of integrity coming not from outward rules but inner ballast.

He was dressed to go out into the world, overcoat still open, no doubt about to be buttoned.

One of his arms hung rigid to the side as if frozen inside the sleeve.

'You would represent the police,' he said while the wife exited, shutting the kitchen door behind her as if wanting to be quit of the scene.

'We would indeed, sir,' answered Mulholland, adjusting his helmet to prove a point.

'You've saved me a journey,' said Archibald Carstairs.

'Have we?' replied McLevy. 'That's nice.'

The man straightened his back a fraction more as if coming to attention and announced, 'My son is waiting.'

He beckoned them inside and they followed him upstairs to a pleasantly furnished sitting room where a young man, also dressed to leave, was standing by the window.

He was diminutive in frame, with a candid face, and he flinched when he saw the visitors.

'These gentlemen are the police,' the father addressed to him gently. 'But there's no need to worry, Tom. Just tell them what you told me. The truth never hurt a living soul.'

On that somewhat contentious affirmation, the story was told without interruption.

Tom's voice was hesitant at first but as the events of the evening unfolded, it grew in strength, save for the ending where he described his flight.

'It was cowardly,' he faltered.

McLevy's eyes had never left the young man's face during the whole recitation.

'I'm sure your father can tell you,' he responded quietly, 'all elements are inside a man. And most of them are opposites. Cowardice and bravery just two of a great multitude. Like love and hate.'

For a moment there was a ghost of a smile on his face, but then he clapped his hands loudly together, a shocking sound in the stillness of the room.

Mulholland recognised the signal.

Now the questions would begin.

They took the boy through the whole night, all over again.

Every moment was scrutinised, though the account of the botched sortie into the Just Land had the father shaking his head in military disapproval, and rendered the faces of McLevy and Mulholland into impassive neutrality.

The long, painful walk down South Charlotte Street, the hurtling carriage, the finding of the corpse, to the moment when Tom boaked up the contents of his stomach.

'Were ye sporting a scarlet favour?' McLevy asked suddenly.

'I may have. I think I might'

'Where is it now?'

'I was on all fours. It may have — joined the rest.'

The two policemen exchanged glances. At least that was one mystery solved.

'The corpse. Did you know the woman?'

'I did not. Poor soul.'

Tom's mind flitted back to the moment when he had twitched the covering aside to reveal the empty, staring face, like a death mask.

'The blanket, you touched it?'

'I did.'

'Was it sodden from the rain?'

The young man thought for a moment.

'No — just a wee bit damp. Hardly anything.'

The father watched both policemen lean back for a moment.

They were sitting at a table facing his son, who was also seated and in obvious discomfort from his lesions; though the questioning had been intense, there had been no hint of bullying or violence.

Of course had Carstairs ever seen McLevy at full torrent in the interrogation room, or he and Mulholland in action when taking on a villainous gang of felons, hornbeam stick and fists whirling in concerted ferocity, then a different opinion may have been formed.

But for this moment they were unmoving.

Their thinking thus.

If the blanket, thoroughly examined and found to be a cheap, common covering with no identifying marks, such as was used on stored furniture or perhaps the odd dead body — if such were comparatively dry, then this rough casing and contents had been dumped there not long before.

Which brought them to the carriage and driver.

Tom had glimpsed them for only a brief moment but the image had burnt itself into his brain.

That was good.

So, tell us all over again.

'The carriage — it was roofed?'

That way the corpse would be hid from prying eyes should the blanket slip.

'Yes. It was small, I think, though. More like a trap.'

'And the horse? Colour, size — any wee thing?'

'No. It was dark. So the horse must also have been dark in hue. I could hardly make out. It was screaming.'

'You mean neighing — loud maybe?' Mulholland probed.

'No. A scream. Or perhaps it was him. Howling.'

Now we get there. Now we pray for a detail, anything, a scrap that might point the finger.

'The driver. Whit was he like?'

'The devil.'

This response stopped the investigators in their tracks. A fallen angel would be a tricky mark

'The devil takes many forms,' McLevy said cautiously. 'Ye might elucidate, sir. And keep it simple.'

'It was black as pitch. Wind and rain, in my face. I could hardly see but . . . he was standing. Howling — as if in some form of madness. Raving. Moon-struck. A chronic rapture of the cerebrum.'

'Tom is going to specialise in diseases of the brain,' his father offered.

McLevy was more interested in other dimensions.

'Height? Weight?'

'Hard to tell but — not tall. Nor heavy. He was wrapped in a cloak, with a hood.'

Hood?

Mulholland's heart sank — for here was the question they had been inching towards.

The face.

'Face?'

'It was — white.'

At least a beginning.

'White?' McLevy queried. 'A natural complexion?'

'No. Painted. Gleaming white. Like enamel.'

The young man shivered and shifted in the chair.

'Features?'

'It was all so fast. I could not tell.'

'You would not know that face — should you see it again?'

'No.'

'Not even a wee toaty bit?'

'In all honesty. I would not.'

Tom sensed that his words had not transported the policemen into the realms of delight and hastened to help all he could.

'One moment the cloak fell aside, the colour of the cloth underneath — it was pale. Like a pale grey.'

'Uhuh?' grunted McLevy.

'And of course . . . the stick.'

'*The whit?*'

'The stick. He waved it in the air and howled. It was silver. Even in the dark it glittered. A silver stick.'

And that, for the moment, was that.

At the door McLevy and the military man spoke aside while Mulholland towered over the mother and assured the worried lady of the house that her boy Thomas upstairs would not be hanged by the neck until certifiably dead.

The constable was good with women, so long as not romantically involved — then his luck was beyond the trials of Job.

'He'll have to come intae the station to make a formal statement,' said the inspector, 'but apart from his sore arse he may get off light.'

Archibald Carstairs nodded briefly.

'Tom was desperate to join the Scarlet Runners. One of the gang. On the coat-tails.'

'I've never been a great believer in gangs,' replied McLevy. 'I aye prefer solitary.'

'You'd not make an army man then?'

'Only in front of a firing squad.'

A moment of sardonic and shared humour, then Carstairs lifted one huge hand and laid it oddly across his heart.

'He's a decent boy.'

'That guarantees ye nothing.'

Then McLevy's attention was caught by the rigid arm still hanging to the other side.

'How did that come about?'

'I was sliced in ambush. By one of my own men.'

'Dearie me. Whit happened to him?'

Carstairs's regard moved to a rectangular glass

203

case on the nearby table. Inside was a service revolver that gleamed in the light.

'He died in battle.'

The blue eyes were like ice and McLevy recognised when best to let well alone.

He jammed on his low-brimmed bowler.

'If anything occurs further . . . ?'

'If something returns to his memory, I will let you know at once.'

'I thank you for that, sir.'

A brusque gesture of the inspector's hand and Mulholland was signalled to join them at the door.

Just before the policemen left, Carstairs had one last thing to ask.

'Has this been of any help?'

A strange expression crossed McLevy's face, as if he had suffered some piercing shaft of pain, and then a bleak smile appeared.

'Now there's a question,' he said.

And indeed it was.

Both policemen were thoughtful as they walked Great Junction Street with the eventual objective of their station in mind.

They now at least had some kind of description of the killer — the white face, pale suit and especially the silver stick pointed towards Daniel Drummond, but it wasn't enough to haul him in again — they would just look like fools —

'Jaysus!'

This exclamation from Mulholland, who was not wont to take the Redeemer's name in vain, stopped McLevy dead in his tracks.

The constable's body had stiffened as if a bolt

of lightning had struck him from above, and when McLevy followed the direction of his staring eyes, all became clear.

The sea-haar had fixed into a thick, cloying mist and four figures were to be glimpsed on the other side of the street travelling in the opposite direction. The one in the lead appeared as if he had emerged from the primordial soup; a large head with straw coloured hair, that hung in dirty hanks around the pouched and loose lipped face, topped a shambling frame that was massive — once perhaps hard-muscled but now going to fat, though he moved with a simian ability that hinted at a former quickness of hand and foot.

His arms were abnormally long and the knuckles of his spade-shaped fists brushed against the knees of greasy oil-skin trousers.

He wore a sailor's reefer jacket pulled up to the neck, and the eyes, hooded like a cobra's, had flickered open to lock gaze with Martin Mulholland.

Gash Mitchell.

A murderer for sure, and a monster for certain.

He smiled, rubbery lips stretched till they almost split his face.

'Well, well — see whit we have here!'

The other three men were not known to McLevy, but they were hard-looking types, and bulges in their pockets suggested that it wasnae sugar biscuits kept there.

None of this worried the inspector.

What worried him was his constable.

Mulholland was yet rooted to the spot, but it

would take only one wrong word, one sneer, one jab into the scar tissue that had filmed over a failed investigation.

Mitchell knew this and that the odds were with him — yet he hesitated.

McLevy's hand had moved inside his heavy coat. It was well known the inspector carried an old service revolver that fired heavy bullets, which strangely enough often found their mark.

And being a policeman, he could get off with killing folk.

Gash had an animal cunning that had served him well over the years. If he could sneck the lanky bastard over the road to make a wild foray, then use him as cover in the dank fog, then there might be some fun to be had.

The street was deserted, no witnesses, a good kicking keeping the constable's body between them and the bullet, then disappear into the mirk.

Wiser to wait maybe? For a better time?

Mulholland's eyes were boring a hole through the film of damp air; Mitchell grinned to show how little this affected him, and then spat a huge gobbet of saliva as far as he could across the road.

No harm in trying.

As Mulholland jerked forward in response, his jaw tight with anger, McLevy grabbed him by the arm.

It was like taking hold of an iron bar, but he did not let go and wedged himself in front.

A carriage rattled past and the coachman glanced idly right and left before leaving the scene.

The inspector hissed into his constable's ear like a veritable tempter, Auld Hornie himself, but the message was not to court damnation.

'Not now. Later. A better time.'

Both parties seemed to agree on that decision.

Mitchell because he would prefer to isolate the constable in a dark wynd, bodily violence or even murder better not conducted in an open space; and McLevy because he was genuinely concerned that Mulholland might sunder the man's skull and kill him in public view.

They had enough on their hands.

Mulholland let out a gasp as if some tension had been spat out of his body, and his eyes suddenly found focus as if coming back to some kind of known world.

A child's voice was heard and, like a figure in a fairy story, a little girl all muffled up against the elements, with a bright blue Tam o' Shanter on her head, emerged from the fog in pursuit of a hoop, with her parents close behind.

She laughed at the erratic progress of her toy and sped past the two policemen, heading down the hill.

The parents followed, blissfully unaware of what they had almost stumbled upon.

As these innocent wayfarers vanished, McLevy turned to face the baleful presence of Gash Mitchell.

'Go,' he said quietly. 'Not one word. Or it will be the worse for you.'

Mitchell smiled malevolently, but McLevy's hand had slid inside his overcoat once more, and while Mulholland might always play fair like a stupid Irish bastard, the inspector was not to be trusted.

Had he not killed people with bare hands, shot them down like a dog, drowned them in the open sea, even though the man couldnae swim?

And chopped down a killer with his own axe?

These were the stories told.

Wait for a better time, when such a slaughter merchant was nowhere to be found.

And so Mitchell turned on his heel and left, his three men trailing after.

They were gone. Simple as that.

To leave silence and the sea-haar.

'Come along, constable,' McLevy commanded breezily, as if nothing had transpired worth a damn. 'A double murder waits for no man.'

Mulholland uttered his first words in a long while.

'I used to have a hoop,' he said. 'When I was that size. Round and round it went. Never stopped rolling.'

26

If we could read the secret history of our enemies, we should find in each person's life sorrow and suffering enough to disarm all hostility.

Longfellow, Forgiveness

George Dunwoody splashed the water from the basin up into his face, dried it with a scrap of towel and lifted a square of reflecting glass up to see the effect.

'Ye have a coontenance like a monkey,' he informed the image. 'A fusty auld monkey. I cannot tell a lie.'

Indeed his face was small and pinched, his eyes wrinkled, wisps of hair hung down from a bald pate and the false teeth on the upper half of his mouth stuck out as if permanently bared in a welcoming smile.

He was proud of these teeth; he had found them on a market stall and the previous owner may well have been a man of substance, for they were good quality. The bottom set not so well fitting, therefore shoogled to and fro uneasily, but they were white enough.

They wouldnae tempt a rich widow mair's the pity, but a man has to take comfort where he can.

George was in truth not a gloomy old birkie, lively enough in his limbs despite them creeping together with age, with a brightness to his gaze, and his small body tidily framed with clothing of a frayed but decent character, again from the market stalls where he used to deal himself; so he knew all the sellers.

In fact when he thought of it, there was not a thing he wore apart from singlet, drawers and socks that had not at one time belonged to someone else.

Dead men's vestments.

They wouldnae mind.

It aye went down well to present a decent front.

His small room in a wee close off Broad Wynd was kept clean, with everything in place.

Not that he had much with which to wrestle.

Save for the hoped-for bounteous widow, every old sailor's dream, his carnal needs were few and far between, so therefore he might keep a tidy ship.

For women were messy creatures, best left to their own devices or admired from a distance.

Naked on a photograph say — Eve with the Serpent.

George gathered his thoughts. He had a task to perform as circumstance dictated. His mind liked to jump about, but this was not the occasion.

He had lived so long alone that he wondered at times if other folk in the world existed at all, or if he just made them all up like a raree show.

But no. They did. All to his benefit.

He would sit in the tavern, nurse his one sma' beer and listen tae the gossip.

For George loved to gossip.

His agile mind would link all the tittle-tattle thegither and store it away, for you never knew when it might come in useful.

Secrets are money.

But now he had a task to fulfil.

His own wee secret.

A servant of justice.

He put on a coat that was ower long, but not by too much, and might have once belonged to some office clerk who had stabbed himself to death with his own pen, or perhaps run away to sea with a mermaid and never been seen again.

All things were possible when you wore other folk's clothes.

He cackled to himself at that thought, then snuffed out the candle and left.

As the door closed and was carefully locked, the spiral of smoke from the meagre wax sentinel rose in a spiral like a will o' the wisp.

Hanging in the air.

* ★ ★

At the station, Constable Ballantyne was beside himself with excitement.

When McLevy and Mulholland had arrived back, the tall constable, white as a ghost, had been dispatched in the direction of Roach's office to bring the lieutenant up to date with recent discoveries.

Ballantyne had been keeping his head low, having discovered a nest of centipedes amongst the dirty socks in the constable's boot room, then swiftly transferring them to an empty apothecary's box of which he received a never-ending supply from his mother's work at the hospital.

This one had a label specifying the treatment of gout, which he trusted would not adversely affect the centipedes, since they were endowed by nature with a multiplicity of feet, but since it was a cure not a curse Ballantyne felt relatively at ease.

He would wait for a quiet time to sneak outside and shake away the insects, but felt a quiver to the backbone when he looked up from his desk to see the inspector's menacing face, part hidden by the low-brimmed bowler, like a gibbous moon.

McLevy said nothing.

Ballantyne also remained silent, but he was almost certain he could hear a scratching noise as the centipedes writhed indignantly in their prison.

Just then a new shift of young and noisy constables surged out as the street patrols came in like a herd of bullocks.

'I have a job for you, Ballantyne,' remarked the inspector quietly. 'I want ye tae listen. Shake your head if anything is beyond comprehension, but if you hae understood nod like the devil and do not fail me upon your life.'

'Are ye sure I'm the right man for the undertaking, sir? There's bigger than me and mair clever.'

To this worried response McLevy nodded agreement.

'True. But there's no-one with your ability to look daft and act the opposite.'

The inspector took a swift glance at the boot room door, behind which the constables were throwing smelly socks and letting rip wind at each other in the time-honoured fashion that young men mistake for wit.

He then leant in close.

As McLevy began to whisper, Ballantyne began to nod.

* * *

Mary Dougan might have wondered what all the fuss was about as she lay in the cold room. Sadly the fact that her death was being treated with more decency and care than her life was an irony that she could not appreciate.

She lay under the sheet, her body sponged clean the day before by a respectable Police Surgeon; her fate had been discussed by highly regarded officers of the law; and then a benediction of sorts pronounced by a world-famous writer who seemed both to mourn her passing and commend her bonny face.

What more could a girl ask?

A light in the eye perhaps? A lark's song in the morning mist? A silly wee lamb in the cold frost?

Too much to hope it would seem.

She did not hear the door to the cold room click softly open, nor see a figure slip inside.

The room was poorly lit, with a few high windows and a small oil lamp on a nearby table where the surgeon laid his tools.

He had cut her open, found little of interest in the stomach and guts, and then stitched her back together again.

Her wounds had been catalogued, the evenness of spacing noted, plus keen similarity to the first murder and then with no more to divulge, Mary had been left in merciful peace.

Until now.

Now a hand peeled back the sheet, and her body was hastily turned to the side and over, so that she lay without dignity on a surgically sliced belly, her buttocks exposed without so much as a by your leave.

Unhand me sir, I'm a good girl, I am!

Before she might suffer further humiliation a voice sounded in the empty silence.

'Aye, Billy. The marking is not upon the flesh. It never was. Greed is a terrible thing, is it not?'

Constable Billy Napier froze as if caught by an icy hand — he replaced the sheet but his breath puffed out in the cold air like a spoor of guilt.

James McLevy stood at a door he had opened equally quietly. Just behind him stood Mulholland, and a grim-faced Roach had slipped in to make up the trio.

Napier opened and shut his mouth but no words emerged, so the inspector continued talking as he entered further, the other two following, Roach closing the door as if cutting off an artery of escape.

'I've had my eye on you for a wee while, Billy,' said McLevy softly. 'But I did not wish to believe the stories. A few o' the street kitties tellt me that you had been asking benefit of their charms as part of your shift and lifting a wee touch money or you'd run them in.'

For some reason he whistled the old Jacobite tune, 'Charlie is my darlin'', through his damp moustache before carrying on.

'Of course some of these girls make up fictions for fun jist tae pass the time so that might not hold water, but one o' the auld lags this morning passed me word that he'd glanced one of my men lifting glass wi' Sim Carnegie. The fellow had a heavy coat over his uniform but it fell aside enough that our station badge was seen and his big polis boots stuck oot a mile.'

A mirthless chuckle came from the inspector but inside he was boiling with fury.

'And here is the description. Hefty big callan, loud voice, laughed a lot, wavy black hair, kept running his hand through the foliage front tae back.'

'You never told me this,' muttered Mulholland.

'How much aggravation do ye need these days?' was the edgy retort. In truth the inspector had kept this under his hat because the very thought of it had made him nauseous.

McLevy stepped forward and carefully turned the corpse over on her back so that she was more decorously arranged, while talking in an almost conversational tone.

'The portrait fitted you, Billy, but it could do others in this station; fair is fair, however that made two counts.'

He meticulously pulled the sheet up so that it was just under Mary's chin.

'And this — makes three. Three — is one too many.'

Napier, despite the cold, broke out in a sweat as he tried to bluster his way out of the chasm.

'I wis jist — curious. Tae see. A deid body. Ye'd want tae see — '

'Liar.'

One word. Flat and cutting. But not from McLevy. It came from Roach.

Mulholland had seen them once before have this strange accord, but that time it had been turned on him.

He was younger then. Now he would fight his corner.

It was a dark corner at the moment, because he could not get the leering face of Gash Mitchell out of his mind.

'Greed,' repeated McLevy. 'Sim Carnegie paid you to pass information as regards the white favour on the first corpse, so when Constable Ballantyne told you that he had heard Mulholland and I talking that the killer had left a strange sign, Masonic even, carved upon the woman's back — ye couldnae resist.'

With a sickening jolt, Napier realised he had fallen into their trap.

Word had got round there was another corpse in the cold room but no more than that. When Ballantyne had blurted out what he claimed to have overheard and the three now facing him were supposedly ensconced in Roach's room in deep discussion, it took a matter of seconds to sneak in when no-one was looking, turn the body and find out the secret.

That would be something to sell!

Greed.

The four half crowns Carnegie had slipped into his hand with the promise of more to come.

'I only did it the once,' was his pathetic excuse.

The contempt was palpable in their eyes.

'Get out of this station,' said Lieutenant Roach, the words like coal-spit in his mouth. 'Thank God you are now out of uniform — you can disgrace it no longer.'

'Ye can keep the boots,' added McLevy with a feral grin. 'They played their part in your undoing.'

He and Roach stood aside so that Napier was forced to walk between them like a man on the way to the hangman's noose, and as he went by Mulholland he received a final malediction.

'Your name is mud in this city. Not one will respect you. Not the keelies, not the Fraternity, not your own kind. Not even scum like Carnegie. Ye've lost it all.'

Napier finally passed through, Mulholland closed the door behind and there was silence for a moment.

'A clever ruse,' Roach said without pleasure. 'And why did the sign have to be Masonic?'

'Gave it a particular . . . application,' McLevy replied.

'A clever ruse right enough,' Mulholland remarked thoughtfully.

'Greed is aye stupit.'

A sudden sound of a raised voice in the station tailed on to this dismissive remark of the inspector's and the three made their way quickly out into the hall.

Napier, whose humiliation had been complete and who had cowered under the contempt heaped upon him, now looked for some way in which to redeem himself in his own eyes.

His gaze had fallen on Ballantyne, who was sitting quietly at his desk wondering what had transpired next door. Billy saw in the constable's vulnerable form the source of all his misfortunes.

It is aye a mark of humanity to blame others for their own sins and the weaker the target might seem, the louder the flood of vituperation.

'Ye dirty traitor!'

This screamed, he hauled Ballantyne up and tried to land a vicious punch on the scarlet birth-mark that spread down the side of the constable's neck.

Ballantyne managed to block the blow, but the force of it sent him sprawling to the floor.

For a moment Napier felt a brief exultation. No-one dare meddle wi' him — see whit ye get —

The whole station was staring and he gloried at the fear in their eyes before realising that its focus was something else.

James McLevy stood quietly; Mulholland and Roach eased off to the side.

'Ye're hammering at the wrong door,' the inspector said. 'It was my idea, I jist tellt Ballantyne tae keep an eye on the cold room portal and let us know if ye swalleyed the bait. I'm the one you need tae batter.'

Billy Napier was a hefty specimen. He had

been a bully at school and never beaten in a fight. Nor had he been bested since, for he made it his business to aye land the first smash, hard and true. Fell them where they stand.

Then the boot can go in. No quarter given.

His blood was up now — he had been tricked and cheated and he saw before him a man of older years, tired and slow, and who knows but one stave of his big fist might shatter that reputation and leave Billy a heroic figure?

If he could take McLevy in his own back yard?

It would be the making of him.

A giant among men.

The inspector had not moved, his hands hanging limp by the side; through his open overcoat Billy could glimpse a soft, round belly straining against the watch-fob.

If he could sink his fist there!

McLevy wheezed and sniffed in the silence like an old seal at the circus.

'I'll give ye first swing,' he remarked — and still he had not budged.

Billy made his move sudden. Give no warning, yell at the same time to startle the side of beef, pull back and hammer in!

Indeed a fist did sink into an exposed gut but it was McLevy's hand — as Billy shifted weight to deliver the blow, the inspector hit him so fast his fist was a blur.

Full in the breadbasket. Bent him over and then hit him again, full in the face, one, two, three times, straightened him up but broke the nose, bent him back over with one more savage sinking punch; then grabbed him by the collar and the belt of his pants and ran the gasping wretch out of the station headfirst into a lamppost which, unluckily for Billy, was directly opposite the station door.

There was a sickening distant crunch, then silence.

After a few seconds McLevy walked back into the station, and for a moment regarded the massed ranks of his young constables.

They would not be human if somewhere they hadn't hoped to see the old bull brought down; now they knew better and all the stories they had heard were no doubt true.

The violence they had witnessed, however, was nothing compared to the violence they had never seen.

So not one was prepared to meet his eye, save for Ballantyne who, though rubbing at his neck, was not avoiding that stony stare.

'Billy Napier sold out this station,' the inspector proclaimed, his voice calm as if he had just gone outside to check the weather. 'He received his just deserts as would any person of a similar proclivity. A word tae the wise, eh?'

To their credit the assembled motley crew scratched their heads before nodding assent; it would seem the thought of betrayal had never occurred to them.

Besides Billy Napier was not a popular man. A tormenter of the weak whose farts would fell an elephant.

Good riddance tae bad rubbish.

'Whit happens here, stays in here!'

Lieutenant Roach had his own silent caveat to

this last declaration from his inspector. Word of the fight would get round Leith in about thirty seconds.

All grist to the mill.

Though it did not solve a double murder.

However, one way or the other, time for a superior officer to take command.

'One of you constables search out a bucket and mop,' he announced crisply. 'There may be blood on the paving outside and we must discharge at all times our civic duty.'

'There's some on the flagstones here as well,' added Mulholland, equally unperturbed. 'Ye don't want it to be soakin' in. Blood is terrible for that.'

One of the constables sped into the boot room to do as commanded and the rest began to break up and return to their normal duties, save for Murdoch at the desk who had scarcely stirred as he watched Billy Napier leave the premises with such unprecedented velocity.

Stasis is a kind of duty, is it not?

The three wise men disappeared into Roach's office on legitimate business this time and Ballantyne, who had received a brusque nod of approval from his inspector for his part in the unfolding morality play, let out a long breath and calculated the time when he'd be able to loose the centipedes.

As he looked over, an old fellow entered the station, shuffled around uncertainly, then plonked himself on one of the wooden benches by the front door.

The constable with bucket and mop went

221

past, heading for the bloody lamppost. Napier by now had no doubt dragged himself into the depths of Leith to lie upon his death bed.

Murdoch had vanished under the desk, with only one meaty hand remaining on top, having been, it would seem, grafted on to that piece of furniture. Ballantyne levered himself up and walked across.

What a time so far: corpses, centipedes, information false-drappit into another man's ear for the good of the cause and getting a sore neck for recompense.

Surely that would do for the day?

'Can I help you, sir?' he asked politely.

George Dunwoody looked up and smiled. At least the teeth did, whatever his inner inclination.

'Ye can indeed,' he answered. 'And I can help you!'

'That would be a nice change,' responded Ballantyne a little warily, wondering if he had come across someone bereft of their wits — but the old boy had a sharp glint to his eye and was well enough attired.

'Ye had a murther — in the harbour — a nicht o' last week.'

'That we did. More's the pity. An old and decent woman.'

'I noted her picture in the paper.'

George brought a crumpled edition out of his pocket and unfurled it with care.

Sim Carnegie had topped his splenetic article with a family photo of his mother. Younger, but unmistakably Agnes.

The old man's finger tapped upon the image.

'I saw her.'

'What?'

'And him.'

'Eh?'

Ballantyne's exclamation was high-pitched enough that a few glances were thrown their way — whit the hell was daftie up to now?

'They both passed me. On my way home. Later than my preference because of thae damned students.'

George shook his head in disapproval and Ballantyne resisted the temptation to seize the old gadgie and shake the truth out of him.

Think of the man as an insect. A nice shiny insect.

'Him? You saw a him?'

'Tracking her. Behind a distance. A real Jack o' Dandy.'

George smiled again and the constable tried to compose his face into nothing that might alarm a murder witness.

'If you might just wait here. I am certain Inspector McLevy would like a wee word.'

Ballantyne set off then changed his mind, returning almost to haul George off the bench.

'No — better you come with me — things can disappear in this station.'

As they made for Roach's office, the boy with the bucket came in.

He looked down at the flagstones and began to scrub at some reddish marks that might have been blood or remnants of a rusty nail.

All grist to the mill.

27

I am destined by the mysterious powers to walk hand in hand with my strange heroes, viewing life in all its immensity as it rushes past.

Gogol, *Dead Souls*

Under a covered gazebo, two elegant figures sipped at their coffee as peacocks strutted the immaculate lawns. In a nearby large pond, various heavy-bodied tropical fish dunted up against each other, their bright yellow and orange providing a brilliant contrast to the dreich skies above.

A soft, insidious rain had begun to fall, which made no odds to the fish and enhanced the vivid blue of the male birds — it trembling on the edge of the mating season, the men o' parts were spreading their wings a little gingerly for an exploratory shiver while the dowdier females pecked around like wifies at a greengrocer display.

The rose bushes now mercifully free of preventative sheathing were coming into bloom; along with other drenched but vibrant flower beds, Cupid was glistening; and the fecund whole might well have been an ideal scene to augment the gardening column in *Ladies' Companion Magazine*.

Save for the fact that the equally elegant

building that cradled the grounds like a loving mother might require the caption *Bawdy-Hoose. Proprietrix Jean Brash, all tastes indulged up to the eyeballs.*

Stevenson laughed aloud at that notion, but shook his head at Jean's enquiring glance.

'Not worthy of you, my dear,' he murmured, inhaling the delicate caffeine aroma of the Lebanon, which combined aesthetically with his pungent tobacco to produce a Leith version of Yin and Yang, opposite yet entwined.

Once more he had slid out of Heriot Row while the rest of the house pondered tomorrow's funeral arrangements, heads bowed over lists; it was an odd twist in his temperament, but the more unreliable he became in other's eyes, the happier he felt inside.

To be somewhere other than in one's appointed place lifts the spirit, and do we not all feel this?

A great deal is made of freedom, but perhaps it is no more than an absence from the ties that bind.

Or would we be lost without those ties?

On a whim he had disguised himself in a long, shabby coat and one of his father's old outdoor sea hats, and fancied that he might flit unseen through the busy streets without recognition.

Of course he had laid away the coat and wafted the hat aside in Jean's presence.

A velvet jacket with white cotton shirt collar, cuffs that encased those thin wrists at the end of which dangled the surprisingly large hands, and a long pale face that hung in the shade like a

225

mocking portrait. The least he could offer a beautiful woman.

Jean had told him of the adventure with the Scarlet Runners and they had laughed over that.

All the while they appraised each other in not unfriendly fashion; two artists at the height of their profession.

He coughed in the damp air and flicked at some moisture that had gathered by the end of his long nose.

'The rain never leaves for long,' Stevenson murmured.

'A constant companion.'

This wry observation made, Jean suddenly let out a very unladylike snort of laughter.

'It might have been your backside I let fly at once upon a time, for you were a wild rogue, Robert Louis!'

'According to many, I still am.'

Many impulses, overt and hidden, had lured him towards the Just Land, all to do with the past, but the present had sparked into life when he had seen the surprised smile on Jean's face.

A man aye likes to surprise the female.

It is a rare occurrence.

'Whit a life we've led.'

'And see where we've ended, with no discernible trace of sin.'

They both laughed at this sardonic comment, but then he surprised her again, not quite so pleasantly.

'And we are both in thrall to James McLevy.'

'How so?'

Jean's countenance did not alter a jot and she

slid a delicate china plate towards him.

'Sugar biscuit?'

'I don't mind if I do.'

He pronounced this in a ridiculously affected English accent to take any sting out of his following words, as he carefully stubbed out his cigarette in an ashtray that, for some reason, had the shape of a squatting bulldog, and nibbled at the biscuit.

For Robert Louis was on the prowl. The dark insights he lived by had forewarned him of a beast of sorts on his trail and it seemed to have moved from the realms of imagination into a grim reality.

It was not his nature to be passive unless stricken with illness or faced with a funeral.

The demise of the father? Had that delivered some malignant shambling fate?

'Death they say is a great release,' he announced with as much gravity as a sugar biscuit might allow. 'For instance, Henry Preger was an evil God. James McLevy brought him crashing down to earth. You were thus released from a dire and hateful bondage.'

'McLevy certainly started the process,' Jean replied, intrigued to see where all this was leading. 'But he's scrounged enough cups of coffee on it — another biscuit?'

'Thank you.'

They were both disturbed when one of the peacocks let out a mournful wail as the oscillations of his plumage had proven an abject failure; the female seemed to have discovered a long, yellowish worm more to her taste.

Yet again the call of Madame Nicotine was too strong to resist. Thank God he had rolled a day's supply, for his fingers were covered in a fine sugar dusting and trembling to boot.

Stevenson lit the Lucifer and drew in a soothing draught of high-grade tobacco leaf.

For a moment he created a cloud in front of his face, but when it cleared he found himself under scrutiny from those beautiful but piercing green eyes.

The question to ask of course was, what was *his* own thralldom, but the woman was too intelligent for such an obvious response.

'Mary Dougan,' he said. 'Do you remember her?'

'I do. Well.'

'Can you keep a secret?'

'If necessity demands.'

She poured out more coffee for both. It was still warm and faint wispy steam rose from the surface.

'Mary is dead. Murdered.'

The green eyes did not change.

'I had heard. Another body at Leith Station. But not the name. Poor Mary. A decent soul for all that.'

Stevenson resolved to keep the doorstep discovery to himself; the less divulged the better, with women.

'McLevy seems convinced that part of the answer may lie in my past.'

'Then I would pay attention,' replied Jean. 'He's seldom wrong.'

Though she was drawn by this turn in the

conversation, Jean was also conscious of a prickle of annoyance. Could a man not come to visit without an ulterior motive?

Or was that all they were good for?

Blissfully unaware that he was, for once, conforming to a stereotype, the writer continued his line of enquiry.

'I have been away so long. Mary. What happened to her?'

'The usual,' responded Jean with a shake of the head. 'I offered her a wee place here, looking after the girls, for she was kindly by heart and would have been a good balance to Hannah, but — she was too set in her ways. The damned circle had closed. No way out.'

Then she smiled suddenly, for she had been struck by a memory of a time before the arsenic had worked its wonders and Henry Preger went floating somewhere in Leith Harbour, when the fiddler had sawed a slow air in the tavern and a young Mary Dougan had danced with a gawky, coltish man.

For a moment it was just the two moving somehow in time to the tune, as if magic had descended on the rough planking, Mary looking up with a shining light in her eyes and the tall youth gazing into a different future.

Robert Louis had been the favourite of all the threepenny whores, due to deferential manners and assiduous provision of pleasure. Give and take.

'You were her poutie,' said Jean slowly. 'I don't believe she cared for any other man.'

Stevenson bowed his head.

'I went into business,' said Jean. 'And lost touch with her. Years later I saw Mary in the streets. A shipwreck.'

He blew out a long trail of smoke and hunched his shoulders, lost in a distant recollection.

'It was not your fault,' Jean continued. 'A different fate before you. But you were her poutie.'

That was the trouble, thought he, *with returning home. All the ghosts come back to life.*

His silence lengthened and though Jean felt no real wish to comfort, she considered it only fair to stitch a different button upon the garment of regret.

Besides, out of the corner of her eye she could see Hannah Semple hanging her head out of an upstairs window to signal that time was flying and the looming evening lechery must not be neglected.

Supply and demand.

'It happens sometimes, with unlucky women, that they fix upon one man. A lifetime obsession.'

His agile mind switched to his own Fanny Osbourne.

'And men?'

'Oh, they can get obsessed. But it doesnae last.'

'What if it happened to you, Jean Brash?'

For a moment, a certain unlovable face swam into her mind, but she shook her head like a horse getting rid of an annoying fly.

'If it did. I would bring the mannie before me,

and shoot him right between the eyes.'

The watcher across the street, hidden by the heavy, low-hanging branches of a late blossoming cherry tree, hissed like a snake, as the man threw back his head in laughter, while the woman laid a lascivious hand upon his sleeve.

She had no right. She was a whore. Flaunting herself like a painted doll. He imagined the cane beating down on that face, the mouth twisted in pain as she sought for mercy but no — there would be no mercy.

See there! Her head was close to his — what secrets were they murmuring?

He had followed Stevenson from his house to this palace of whoredom, this Babylon.

He must leave this scene because he had many other deeds to perform in another life.

But now he knew where to burn the roots of sin.

A page would be found in the tattered and crumpled book.

Then a price would be paid.

And the harlot would squeal like a pig.

28

For surely this Mastiff though he was big,
And had been lucky at fighting,
Yet he was not qualifi'd worth a fig,
And therefore he fell a biting.
> Alexander Broome, *Songs and
> Other Poems*

Now was the moment of truth. The Judas Hole
was too high up for George Dunwoody to reach,
so a stool had to be brought for the old man to
perch upon.

He had waited patiently in the station for many
hours until the suspects had been rounded up.

Now they had. Now was the moment.

Inside the cell off the corridor two young
fellows, not for the first time, sat disconsolately
on narrow beds.

But they were not yet unveiled to George. At
the moment all he could see was a panel of wood
with a knob of sorts, upon which rested the long
fingers of Constable Mulholland.

On George's other side was a fell-faced McLevy,
his pepper-and-salt hair tangled like seaweed from
a recent stramash with the students.

'I envy ye the growth,' said George out of nowhere.
'Whit?'

The old man pointed to his own sparse locks.

'The cauld in winter. Straight through the
cranium.'

232

McLevy fixed the man with a bleak stare.

'This is a matter of identification, Mister Dunwoody. Craniums have bugger all to do with it.'

'Fix your mind, sir,' Mulholland interjected calmly, though his fingers tapped impatiently at the knob, 'on the murder night. Fix the face of the man you saw and tell us, if you please, whether you see it inside.'

George nodded and squinted his pale eyes.

'Are you ready?'

The old man inclined his head.

Mulholland looked at his inspector, who tugged once at his moustache, which was now sprouting in many directions, perhaps suggestive of the twists and turns of their investigation, and then McLevy also nodded.

The panel of the Judas Hole was snapped back and the noise caused both young men in the room to jerk their heads up. What they saw was a slit of light and what George saw was like a framed picture of two distinct faces.

'The rain was battering in my coontenance, mind ye,' he muttered, squinting the whiles.

'Well it's dry now.'

'And there he is!'

The old man's teeth jutted out in triumphant confirmation, as he pointed a cautious finger towards one of the seated men.

'Him. Large as life. See. No' a pick on him. A Jack o' Dandy!'

The other two crammed their heads in from each side to follow the direction of the accusatory digit.

It was pointed at the drawn but defiant countenance of Daniel Drummond.

★　★　★

And yet they began the hammer at Alan Grant, once Roach had given his reluctant permission.

The lieutenant had interviewed Dunwoody himself and been grudgingly impressed by the old man's mental alertness, even if it was allied at times to a slightly askew slant at the world.

But the witness was sharp as a tack, and now insistent that the man he witnessed on the murder night and then in the cell was as claimed.

The Jack o' Dandy.

He had earlier given an accurate description of the man, including the dragging leg, and made his present case by holding up a single forefinger of each hand.

'One like the other. Peas in a pod!'

The old fellow had signed his statement and been packed off home with Ballantyne for company to guarantee a supposed safe passage, and then Roach, before the lawyers descended, though this time they would not be so mysteriously forewarned, took a deep breath and set the dogs loose.

Or was it, in McLevy's case, more the wolf?

Regarding Alan Grant, he was once more pitchforked into a strange jagged world.

He had been at the forefront of the motley crowd of students, more to keep an eye as promised to Jessica on her wild and wilful brother who yelled encouragement beside him as one of the tribe was climbing up the spiral staircase of the Scott Monument in Princes Street to plant a white favour on top of one of the many turrets that festooned this strange Gothic tribute to the Great Man.

Sir Walter himself had been awarded another white favour, on his quill of stone, and the writer's dog Maida had a collar fastened round his neck with more offerings.

It was a matter of some speed before the public show of such derring-do attracted the forces of repression, and once the squad of police had arrived a reasonably good-natured scuffle took place before the students scattered to the four winds.

That is except for Daniel and Alan. Just as they sneaked round the side, it seemed the crowd parted like the Red Sea, and there before them were the implacable figures of James McLevy and Constable Mulholland.

The inspector had lost his low-brimmed bowler for a moment as somebody careered into him, but he jammed it back on his head with a degree of force.

Both young men had the light of adventure in their eyes, no harm done, a cheeky foray up a well-known landmark. Surely such mischief was permissible as the day of reckoning approached for the Scarlet Runners and themselves?

Yet the policemen had solemn faces like unto Wattie Scott himself as he contemplated a graven eternity.

As the whooping students and pursuing

policemen left the scene, it was only the four of them in mutual regard.

'Aye, gentlemen,' said McLevy with grim relish. 'A wee caper awaits ye at the station. Ye'll know the way.'

And now Alan sat in the cold, bare interrogation room, the walls of which were covered in liverish yellow stains, and what seemed like scratch marks, where unavailing nails might have clawed desperately for freedom.

He sat in the middle on a small chair more appropriate for a schoolboy. Or the dunce of the class.

McLevy loomed over him while Mulholland leant nonchalantly against the locked door.

The inspector had decided to invoke the Old Testament and assume the persona of Moses on the Mount.

'You have lied to me once, sir,' he proceeded with a sombre magisterial air. 'Kindly do not do so again.'

Grant swallowed hard.

'I must confess I do not understand the import of your words, inspector — '

'I said, not again!'

This sudden roar from McLevy, which would have set the followers of the Golden Calf running for the hills, startled the young man out of his wits, but was precisely calculated, as Mulholland knew well.

The constable unfolded his long form from the door and pointed an admonitory finger at the young man.

'Don't try a move, sir,' said he, as if Grant was

236

about either to flee or make some aggressive motion.

'I shall give you the benefit of a mistaken impulse of loyalty, Mister Grant,' McLevy announced gravely. 'But take it no further, lest you yourself become accomplice.'

'Accomplice?'

'To murder.'

In the silence that followed these words, a seagull somewhere in distance let loose a series of high muffled screeches, as if mocking Alan Grant's efforts to hold firm to his resolution.

'To conceal the truth is to deliver the blow yourself, as Cain tae Abel from the beginning of time. One falsehood — and you ally yourself to the slaughter of the innocents.'

McLevy was pitching it high, thought Mulholland, *but Grant came from good stock and that can often be a weakness.*

'Agnes Carnegie. Whit really happened?'

The inspector pulled another small chair over and straddled it somewhat comically, as if they were twa auld gadgies sittin' thegither in the park.

Grant thought to deny once more that they had at all come across the woman, but somehow it seemed simpler to tell the truth.

Or at least — part of it.

'Nothing. We — had words. And parted company.'

Not by a flicker did the inspector's face give away the fact that this might be a floodgate.

'But ye did — cross her path?'

'We did. As I said — we — exchanged words.'

237

'Whit kind o' words? Insults?'

'She — upbraided us.'

'And you replied in kind?'

'Daniel did.'

'You were the peacekeeper?'

'I suppose so.'

McLevy addressed Mulholland out of the blue.

'Is it the peacekeepers that inherit the earth?'

'I think it's the meek, sir,' came the straight-faced response.

'Oh? Right.'

Then with a friendly wave of the hand to Alan, McLevy indicated that he should carry on. All friends now, havin' a wee gab.

'And then — we left her.'

'In what condition?'

Alan blurted out an unexpected answer.

'On her bottom. In a puddle.'

'That's a awkward place to find yourself,' Mulholland threw in idly. 'With the rain and all.'

'It is indeed,' agreed his inspector. 'How did that transpire, I wonder?'

'Daniel pushed her. And she fell.'

'So there was physical violence?'

'She — grabbed at him.'

'Agnes was an old woman,' McLevy corrected in matter-of-fact tones. 'But he pushed her off anyway?'

'Yes.'

'And you left her there? In the wet? On her backside?'

'I — I — I was further away. Daniel was closer.'

McLevy's face betrayed nothing, but Alan Grant found it difficult to meet those lupine eyes.

'Yes, we left her there,' he managed finally.

And now it was coming.

Mulholland sauntered across the room to occupy a place on the wall diagonally behind McLevy, so that wherever Alan Grant looked, the frame was filled with interrogators.

'And was he angry, Daniel? Insults, you said. Of what kind?'

Alan had a sudden flash of Daniel's white, furious face as he dragged his companion into the darkness.

'She — the old woman — mocked his infirmity. Said it was God's punishment for his sins. He has a temper.'

McLevy leant back as if satisfied with this, and Mulholland slid in like a friendly snake.

'So — off you went on the randan with the rest of the gang, all boys together, eh?'

'Yes.'

'And you never returned to the scene of the crime, as it were?'

Both policemen laughed at the turn of phrase, and Alan felt curiously nettled, as if not being taken seriously.

'I certainly did not!'

'And what about Daniel?'

'No — he — neither.'

'With you all the time, was he?'

'Yes.'

This occasion it was Jessica's face that flashed before him.

'All the time.'

Liar. I can smell it from your pores.

'You will remember,' said McLevy quietly. 'That I spoke to you of lies, the truth and misplaced loyalty.'

Mulholland felt an odd urge to dance a little jig — this time there were no lawyers — this time, no escape.

'We have a witness who has identified Daniel that very night, on the trail of Agnes Carnegie.'

'But that's not possible!'

'It is if he went back.'

McLevy did not add the murderous ramifications such a return might signify, that might muddy the waters, no — all he wanted was a simple admission.

'Mister Grant. On your honour, on probity of family, on the Holy Book itself — can you swear Daniel Drummond was by your side for the rest of that night?'

Break this alibi and the game is on.

Alan opened his mouth, but his tongue could not form the words of denial. Instead another creature emerged.

Truth, at times, like murder, will out.

'I — lost touch with him.'

'For how long?'

'An hour or so.'

'What was his explanation?'

'A duel. With one of the Runners.'

'And you believed him?'

'Yes.'

McLevy blinked his gaze almost comically, as if he had been told a tall tale. A child's fable.

Mulholland's Irish blue eyes had never seemed more innocent as he posed a last question.

'And why did you not tell us all of this, sir — when we first came to visit?'

'Daniel. He said — '

More trouble than it's worth.

29

That garret of the earth — that knuckle-end
of England — that land of Calvin, oatcakes
and sulphur.
Sidney Smith, English clergyman, *Memoirs*

The Scarlet Runners charged down the quayside
to see what misdirected mischief they might
cause on a wet afternoon.

As is the manner of a mob, they mistook
boorish behaviour for high spirits, and had
already spirited off a lady's lace bonnet that one
was wearing to some effect.

The Runners had licked their wounds after the
fiasco at the Just Land and felt themselves to be
falling behind their rivals, witness the recent
scaling of Scott's statue; so they had taken to the
streets with no great plan of campaign of which
to speak, three of their leaders lying dolefully at
home to nurse perforated buttocks that rendered
them *hors de combat*.

The Scarlets did not notice the absence of the
small figure of Tom Carstairs, who still slept
fitfully after an encounter with death, while his
father sat in a nearby room and cleaned a revolver
from which he had fired upon a blood-crazed
killer.

One of his own. Once a good friend. Now a
madman who had cut a sword through his
commander's flesh and would have cut once

more but for the bullet.

Archibald Carstairs looked back into a different world and cursed the arm that lay limply by his side.

The army was his life and this life was nothing — he loved his son, paid dutiful homage to his wife, but the reality he had known made the present seem like a nest of shadows. What was out there but shadows?

In the darkness, all shadows die.

Out there.

Like a crowd of bullocks the Runners jostled down the ancient thoroughfare, perhaps fuelled by the thought that tomorrow was the day of reckoning and their revels would be soon be over.

No more bellowing, lambasting, no more the heady brew of untethered rampant howling at the moon.

No more.

All glory diminished into a confining narrow life; respectability would take them by the throat and squeeze flat as if a pitch macadam roller had passed over.

And so there was an underlying desperation as they hunted targets that might satisfy the lust for one last moment of compromised grandeur.

'Loony, loony!' they chanted as a weird figure loomed up ahead like a stranded ship.

Tall, emaciated, a long shapeless coat flapping round his ankles, an equally shapeless hat folding apprehensively round the head — he turned to see the source of such jeers and lost his footing on the wet cobbles.

The horde was onto him like a flash, buffeting

the thin figure from side to side, and a cry went up.

'Oh dear me — throw him in the sea!'

The water in the harbour would be cold and deep enough to shock the unwary recipient, but the weakness of the man's flailing limbs incited desire to attack the vulnerable — as if a shabby form invited such molestation.

And yet if singly they had been confronted by the bestial ferocity of such behaviour? A sorrowful shake of the Christian head as the civilised man views the savage.

A fragment of this was darting through Stevenson's head as he felt himself lifted from the ground, unable to gasp protest because of a hefty arm clamped round his windpipe.

He kicked viciously and had the satisfaction of smashing his foot into someone's face, but the howl of pain served to spur on the hellish legion, and he was transported bodily towards the very edge of the quay.

Robert Louis cursed the meandering ways that had led him from the comfort of the Just Land to slope down the hill, appetite sated with excellent coffee and a plethora of sugar biscuits, wander an hour under the guise of his father's hat and then, as a fish returns upriver to spawn, find himself walking Commercial Place by the side of the harbour.

As he was hauled at from all sides, a racking cough welled up from his lungs, which was most surely not to be improved by the plunge, but was it too late to plead a special case?

I am a renowned man of letters, dear sirs, and

if you baptise me in the murky waters of Pud-
docky Burn, might I not catch my death of cold.
And think of the great works you may destroy
that yet repose in my phlegmy bosom?

The arm, however, was still hooked stiflingly around his neck and with dread he heard the concerted cry of — 'One — Two — and — '

Then a muffled thud interrupted the projected launch, and Stevenson tumbled to the ground as another thump caused a cry of pain, and he found himself wrenched off to the side and a most welcome anchorage.

A square-built, sandy-haired young man with an older, leaner, but strong specimen who sported a minister's collar, had obviously disrupted proceedings.

One of the Runners was on the ground nursing a sore jaw, courtesy it would seem of the younger fellow, while the older addressed the students in terms that would have abashed the very Vandals themselves.

John Gibbons helped the shabby, gangling tramp to his feet as his father unleashed his best pulpit tones.

'I know your fathers, many attend my church and I will make it my business to inform them that this is how their sons take their pleasure!'

Jonas Gibbons positively bristled with authority as he pointed the chastened mob back whence they came.

'Go to your homes, study your actions and feel the shame for what you have done. You persecute the weak amongst us when you should pray for their salvation!'

Stevenson was not quite so sure he appreciated being lumped in with the halt and the lame, but as he peered over at the glutinous, sullen waters below and imagined his body landing like some disenfranchised starfish, he decided that a gracious thanks was more in order than piffling personal concerns.

As the students slunk off, the writer removed his hat and was gratified to see a shock of recognition strike in the younger man's eyes.

'Father — see who this might be — Mister Stevenson!'

Jonas Gibbons turned slowly like a stately galleon and nodded gravely, as if he had rescued a sinner from the depths of hell.

'It is your good fortune, sir, we were on our charity rounds for the needy of this parish. Lord knows there is much necessity in the broken lives that litter these wynds.'

Stevenson gave his heartfelt thanks, Jonas and John made their introductions and as the younger man slipped shyly into the background, Robert Louis realised that the Reverend Gibbons was not only a person with whom to reckon, but the man had a part to play in coming events.

'It will be my honour and duty to officiate at your father's funeral,' intoned Jonas. 'Thomas attended church with your mother these many years and was a beacon of good Christian observance.'

Obviously the reverend had never witnessed one of his father's violent tantrums but, more uncomfortably, his son had been noticeable by his non-attendance in the family pew as the years went by, and more recently especially, absent for the funeral discussions at St Stephen's.

If it came to a choice, would Stevenson have preferred a dangerous dip in the sea to a Sabbath sermon?

Not much in it.

The sea might have killed him through pneumonic complexity, but the Church did the same for his spirit.

However, this little bantam-cock of a man had saved the day, and there was no doubt of a powerful charisma that not only cowed students but probably raised the faithful to the heights of worshipful admiration.

Stevenson noticed light flecks in the man's eyes and revised his metaphor to a more leonine slant.

The furze of hair that framed the broad face added more than a touch of the lion, the wiry body had a coiled catlike quality, yet could he not sense something?

A tremor behind the certainty?

An emptiness of some kind?

Or was he just looking for an excuse to denigrate the man of God?

From Jonas's point of view he saw a dishevelled, wraith-like creature so insubstantial that a strong wind would blow him aside. The minister had made it a point of duty not to read *Jekyll and Hyde*, considering it a work that delved into the darkness of the human soul and brought no great hope of salvation; it would seem that the production of such a bleak viewpoint had obviously taken its toll.

'I thank you once more,' said Stevenson, to break the somewhat uncomfortable silence. 'For your strength in my adversity.'

'God gives me strength,' was the stolid response. 'From His Presence, cometh all things.'

Robert Louis put his hat back on and resisted the temptation to light up and then blow smoke, lest it be misinterpreted as Satan's breath.

Jonas bowed gravely. 'We must be on our way — there is a great deal of work to do and little time to do it.'

Now that was something Stevenson could agree on. He nodded vigorously, almost causing the ill-fitting hat to flop once more over his face, and pulled himself upright to indicate that he was more than ready to enter the fray.

As the minister marched off down the quayside, his son nodded also, but Stevenson had a question to deliver.

'The ruffian who found himself on his backside — did you punch him?'

'Only the once,' was the solemn reply. 'And that was because he resisted reformation.'

Robert Louis grinned.

'I owe for that. What may I give in response, sir?'

John Gibbons hesitated.

'I have a copy of *Treasure Island* — if you might sign your name?'

Stevenson hid a smile. All the works he had created and wished to explore, all the splits in the psyche fermenting to be born — yet in his home city, both admirers met so far had eyes only for a boy's adventure.

At least that is how it was regarded.

'It would be my pleasure.'

Then an elfin sprite of mischief, one of his brownies, caused him to add.

'And who, prithee tell, is your favourite of the tale?'

The young man shuffled uneasily for a moment, because he could see his father waiting impatiently along the quayside. 'Ben Gunn,' he managed finally.

'Why?'

'Because he suffered for his sins and the sins of others. On his own. A solitary desolation.'

Stevenson forbore to mention that the man had spent all his treasure money, one thousand pounds, in nineteen riotous days. However, the fellow had ended up in church and sang to the Lord of Pirates plus their prey.

'And what did he say that you most remember?'

A slow smile crept reluctantly over the young man's face.

'Many's the long night, I've dreamed of cheese — toasted mostly.'

Stevenson's laugh and the father's shout coincided to send John Gibbons on his way, his eyes showing a shaft of feeling that was oddly touching.

'Bring the book,' called the writer. 'And I will sign it with the utmost alacrity!'

He smiled as he watched both men disappear into one of the crooked wynds that spread out like broken blood vessels from the main thoroughfare.

Then Robert Louis finally lit up a deep-desired cigarette and coughed so long and loudly that the skittering seagulls of the harbour waters took to the skies in alarm at such hideous discord.

Homeward bound then, the writer turned his steps.

Oh, that he might dream of cheese.

30

The time I've lost in wooing,
In watching and pursuing
The light, that lies
In woman's eyes
Had been my heart's undoing.
Thomas Moore, *Irish Melodies*

James McLevy stood gazing at Jessica Drummond, wondering why he had volunteered himself for such a twist in the gut.

At the station they had battered away at Daniel, but the young man, while finally admitting that he had obscured the truth as regards discordance with Agnes Carnegie, stuck firmly to the assertion that he had not returned to wreak a murderous vengeance.

He maintained his absence was due to a ridiculous duel with one of the Runners, where the two had chased each other in and out of the wynds, the other wielding a wheelbarrow, himself a flailing stick, until they had both collapsed in laughter and called truce.

Yet he could not name or identify his opponent under the masking scarlet, and that was all he had to offer by way of alibi.

When confronted with his own identification by a casual passer-by, a man with no axe to grind, a man who had pointed a finger at his culpable countenance, who had seen him trail the old woman — Daniel shot bolt upright in the same small chair that Alan Grant had found so uncomfortable, his eyes blazing with fury.

'Bring me this fellow and I'll wring his damned neck!'

'Will you now?' said the inspector.

'Without mercy!'

'You could do it easy, he's a wee bit timorous fellow.'

'Easy meat,' Mulholland agreed.

'He's a liar!'

This very anger more than hinted at an uncontrollable temper, which might well have fuelled a killing frenzy, and Drummond was intelligent enough to realise the fact.

'You try to provoke me, sirs,'

'No,' replied McLevy. 'But you are a deep suspect in murder. You had motive, the instrument to hand, which you well may have cleansed later, and you were witnessed on the poor woman's heels.'

'The man is a filthy liar!'

Another flash of that temper and Daniel bit his lip.

A tremor of weakness and McLevy was on it like a shot.

'You pushed an auld woman so she fell to the ground, is that not so?'

Daniel crunched his eyes together for a second; Alan Grant had betrayed him — a man he had considered his true comrade. How could he have done this?

'I don't deny it.'

'Are you proud of such?'

'No, but — '

'Yes?'

'She — provoked me.'

'An auld wifie? You're gey easy provoked!'

Mulholland in his guise as treacherous peace-maker, stepped into the ring.

'She drew attention to your impairment, is that not so sir?'

'It was mentioned.'

'In what way, I wonder?'

'She — suggested it was God's punishment.'

'For your wicked ways, perhaps?'

'Stupid but — yes.'

'And that's why you shoved her?'

'She hauled at my coat!'

'A terrible sin,' said McLevy, firing in from the side with some heavy irony.

'I've seen murder committed for less than that,' said the constable thoughtfully.

'True enough,' replied McLevy. 'Ye remember the man wi' his neighbour's pig?'

'Oh, that was terrible. Blood as far as the eye could see. This is much tidier.'

Daniel found himself almost totally ignored, as if his guilt had been taken for granted.

'I did not murder the woman!'

'Agnes was her name,' Mulholland offered helpfully.

'Agnes Carnegie,' added McLevy. 'And I can understand how it would happen.'

'What?'

The inspector pursed his lips and smoothed at his moustache like a satisfied beaver.

'Ye went back tae correct her misapprehension,

253

her lack of intelligence. Stupid, ye said. How dare she invoke the authority of God to poke intae such a sensitive issue.'

'So you followed her to bring her attention to the offence she had caused,' added the constable.

Mulholland was wide-eyed with earnestness and McLevy took up his tone.

'But she would not accept her responsibility in this matter, perhaps provoked you further, insult to injury and when you tried to reason, you were met with scorn. There's nothing worse than the scorn of the unco guid, eh, constable?'

'Oh, it's a fierce aggravation!'

The inspector puffed out his cheeks.

'So you tapped her sharp with your cane. Then again to bring her to heel. Then harder, as she would not yield. And harder again — until — she lay — admonished.'

'A hard lesson. Hard delivered, hard learnt.'

Both policemen nodded at the summation, as if the matter had been laid to rest, and for a moment Daniel was almost hypnotised into the same state of mind.

Then he shook his head, as if to clear a fiendish spell.

'I never tapped the woman with my cane. I never went back. I left her there.'

'In the puddle?' Mulholland asked, as if guile was the last thing on his mind.

'Yes. I am afraid so.'

'On her nether regions?'

'That as well.'

'Not a gentlemanly act, I'd say.'

'I was — provoked.'

Now the gloves were off. The inspector's eyes bored in.

'Agnes Carnegie met her death. Your violence began the process. And it is my contention that ye finished it off as well.'

But Daniel did not flinch.

'You are mistaken, sir.'

'What did you do with the book?' asked Mulholland suddenly.

'Book?'

'The book you took from her. With the bad binding.'

Daniel shook his head.

'This is like a nightmare,' he said quietly.

Now they moved to the second murder. All grist to the mill.

'Ye have a carriage?' McLevy's turn for the unexpected query.

'Carriage?'

'Wheels and a cuddy, that sort o' thing.'

'In the family. Yes.'

'Describe same, if you please.'

'It is ordinary. Small. Roofed.'

'The horse?'

'Brownie.'

'Eh?'

'Name and colour.'

'Saturday night. Where were you?'

'In my room. All night.'

'Why?'

'I had a . . . dreadful headache. I get them sometimes.'

'Convenient.'

A silence descended. Both policemen had

255

previously decided that they would withhold accusations of the Mary Dougan murder until they might think of bringing Tom Carstairs to peep through the Judas Hole, but the boy had been scrupulously candid that he could not distinguish the killer, and it would be a rough call at best.

For the moment they could get no further.

Leave him victim to his own guilty imaginings and then return, all guns blazing.

But leave the laddie something to chew on.

While the fleas nipped his blood.

McLevy pushed up close and almost whispered the words in Daniel's ear.

'Somewhere. Somewhere deep in you, my friend. The devil has his dwelling. I can smell the sulphur.'

A fine farewell.

Now, standing with bowler twisting in both hands, it was the inspector's turn to feel the prod of Satan's pitchfork.

He had related, with just sufficient detail, circumstances of Jessica's brother's plight — Lieutenant Roach had decreed that the family must be informed, according to the rule of law; there were also one or two sly investigations Mulholland might perform elsewhere in the house, though that had left the inspector face to face with Jessica.

A prospect both desired and distempering.

At first she had been like her brother, the temper flaring, but she was without the dark undertow McLevy sensed in Daniel Drummond.

'This cannot be true.'

'I'm afraid so, Miss Drummond, a witness — '

'A snake in the grass!'

'An old man. Whit motive would he have? We questioned both boys separately — '

'Boys?'

'So they seem tae me.'

Jessica assumed a haughty demeanour.

'My brother is not a child.'

'He belongs tae a class. Too much learning, no common sense. Spoiled rotten.'

The inspector growled out the words, then Jessica made a move that left McLevy punching air.

'I'm sure the same might apply to me,' she murmured. 'I regret my lack of manners, inspector. Please continue.'

She moved a bowl of fruit, plucked out a red apple this time, and bit into the flesh, teeth white against the vivid skin of the fruit.

Not realising this to be an already utilised feminine ploy, which may have been accidental with a younger man but now had perhaps a more deliberate nuance, McLevy tried to gather his scattered concentration.

'Under questioning, Alan Grant has confirmed, as I have previously informed you, that your brother has no alibi for the time of the killing.'

'Poor Alan. He must have felt dreadful.'

'Why?'

'To . . . inform upon his best friend.'

'He told the truth!'

'And the truth is your lodestar, is it not, inspector?'

That was when she had simply looked at McLevy and he felt that twist in the gut.

When a woman, no matter what age, simply gazes at a man, especially if she holds an apple in her hand and he has been close-gripped to her in a murky wynd, then a certain contortion of the heart might well ensue.

As if the bottom has dropped out of the known world.

She spoke gravely, in equality, or at least as equally as it can ever get between the woman and the man.

'Daniel is boastful, inconsiderate, hot-blooded and selfish — but he is not a murderer.'

'In hot blood. He might be.'

'No. You are mistaken. He — an accident at birth left him with this crippled leg. His compensation is — '

'To win at all costs? De'il take the hindmost?'

'I know him to the core. He is innocent.'

'There is a darkness to your brother. I can sense it.'

Jessica took another bite and moved closer, as if what she had to say was a confidence beyond all others.

'Our father died when we were very young. Heart attack out of the blue. I was just a baby, but Daniel suffered . . . a terrible loss.'

McLevy's private thought was that such an original wound may well be the suppurating source of a homicidal response when opposed or affronted.

As a child will lash out at the enemy.

Blindly. Without care or regret.

But Jessica had moved so near that he could sense the sweet fragrance of fallen fruit mixed with the odour of — woodsmoke?

Was that woodsmoke he could smell?

'Did you light a fire this morning?' he blurted out.

'In the garden,' she replied. 'The dead branches. I love to see the flames. Fire is my element.'

'The devil's gey fond of it as well.'

Jessica laughed at the remark and her dark eyes sparkled for a moment before the face grew serious. Then she heaved a sigh that moved her bosom in perilous proximity to his official chest.

Had she said she didnae wear a corset? Surely not.

Every woman did. Somewhere.

'It would break my mother's heart.'

Of course the mother had a corset, but it ended up on top of a mast.

Why was his mind fixed on corsets?

'My brother is innocent,' Jessica said softly. 'I know it.'

She put the apple aside to lay her hand upon his sleeve and McLevy jolted as if galvanised by some promiscuous electrical charge.

'Help me, inspector. I put my trust in you.'

'Whit does that mean?'

'In the wynd. You let me go.'

'I got distracted.'

'You let me go.'

'Only the once.'

'I saw it in your eyes. You are a good person.'

'I'm jist a policeman!'

As McLevy made this panic-stricken assertion, the door handle clicked and they sprang apart. Well, at least the man sprang. The woman stood her ground.

Constable Mulholland entered, still on the case.

'Well,' he announced, apparently oblivious to the unstable atmosphere. 'Searched his rooms and found nothing.'

He inclined his head gravely towards Jessica.

'Thank you, Miss Drummond, for letting me — poke around, as it were.'

'My brother has nothing to hide.'

'I'm sure I hope that might be true,' replied the constable in a diplomatic but somewhat Irish fashion.

'What were you seeking out — another body?'

'No, ma'am. Biblical artefacts.'

'Taken from the dead woman,' McLevy butted in. 'Perhaps as trophies.'

Jessica ignored the implication that this might possibly be linked to the dubious honours list of the White Devils.

'Find these and you'll find the killer perhaps.'

'You tell me my job once more.'

She smiled at his grumpy countenance.

'It's a bad habit.'

'Perhaps,' muttered McLevy. 'Oh jist one thing? Saturday night. Your brother's where-abouts?'

'That's easy. In his room all night.'

'For what reason?'

'Headaches. They plague him. He has to lie. In the dark.'

'Did you visit?'

'No. He is never to be disturbed. Until the morning.'

'Uhuh?'

For a moment their eyes met again, then the inspector stuck on his hat and made for the door.

'I assume you will tell your mother and she will instruct the lawyers.'

'I would imagine so.'

'No' be so easy this time.'

'We may not need them.'

As both policemen turned in surprise at this enigmatic comment, Jessica once more held McLevy's gaze.

'Do not forget your promise, inspector.'

'Whit promise?'

'The one you made. Goodbye.'

Mulholland glanced sideways at his superior officer, who blinked as if stung by one of his constable's bees, and then made a jerky movement of one arm to ward off some imaginary foe, but Jessica still had a last word in mind.

'And Mister McLevy?'

He had stopped, comically, one half in, one half out of the room.

'I'm sad to see you did not take my advice,'

'Advice?'

'As regards the . . . fungus?'

She twitched fingers under her nose like a pantomime villain.

Mulholland coughed to disguise the amusement best he could, while McLevy scowled like a child and strode huffily out of the door, followed by his lanky subordinate.

Jessica listened to their footsteps go down the stairs and waited till the front door slammed.

Only then did she let the tears flow.

They poured down her face in a stream, and she placed her shoulder blades against the nearest wall to let her body shudder.

Because she was not sure.

McLevy was right. There was a darkness and had always been. A violence that ripped at the surety of their life.

She would always have to watch. To guard. Until perhaps the day dawned when her brother could take command of that darkness.

But was it too late?

There seemed such a split in Daniel. He would talk about himself in a contemptuous off-hand way when alone with her, never at any other time.

As if he were worth nothing.

Her mother's voice sounded once more in the next room.

Time to tell events so far and set the lawyers in motion.

Now she would be Jessica Drummond once more.

Mistress of her fate.

A great part of which was hanging in the strange brooding perception of a certain Inspector James McLevy.

31

The bell's main weakness was where man's blood had flawed it. And so pride went before the fall.

Herman Melville, *Piazza Tales*

Sim Carnegie near jumped for joy as he saw the policemen approach. The evening edition of the *Leith Herald* had just hit the streets and he had been savouring the imaginary appearance of Lieutenant Roach's face as the headline jumped up to smack him in the lugubrious official snout. 'ARREST IMMINENT IN CARNEGIE MURDER CASE!'

He watched McLevy pay good money for the paper then he and Mulholland, the constable craning his neck to get decent vantage, peruse the front-page story. This was a world better than a miserable lieutenant.

The inspector's face betrayed little, but Mulholland shook his head in a fashion that suggested the ground shifting beneath his feet.

'Aye, gentlemen,' Carnegie called cheerily, letting his disdain surface just enough to make it noticeable. 'Do my journalistic efforts strike fire from the flint?'

It had been an uncomfortable saunter for McLevy, what with a maelstrom of feelings spouting like hot jets from a previously peaceful though sullen lava field.

Mulholland had confirmed that, the room having been searched, he had also made a swift but thorough examination of the family carriage, finding it clean as a whistle and the horse indeed brown.

Daniel's alibi had been confirmed by Jessica, though that could be questionable, a drainpipe having been noted in close proximity to his outside window.

These two findings aside, the constable had moved on to tax his superior regarding the exact moment Miss Drummond had given McLevy advice on his upper lip, advice that Mulholland backed to the hilt. It was just that he could not remember hearing these words of wisdom delivered.

Obviously from a time before — but when?

Obviously he had not been on hand.

And what, more importantly than fungal removal, was the promise?

'None of your business,' was the curt response.

'Oh, is it personal then?'

A grim tread. A question not answered.

But not remotely abandoned.

'I noted a certain . . . resonance between you.'

'Resonance?'

'Like a bell.'

'A bell?'

'Chiming.'

Again the grim tread. McLevy knew fine well Mulholland's ability to irritate from the most apparently inept remarks denials that contained an unwilling hidden answer.

'Ding, dong.'

'Ding dong?'

'Chiming. Like a father and daughter, maybe.'

Luckily, before the inspector's wrath erupted at this age-implied insult, the newspaper boy called out his wares.

And now they read that two of the student leaders had been hauled bodily back into Leith Station, and strong evidence uncovered to link one of them to the recent foul and bloody murder of an innocent old woman. Who was, in fact, the writer's very own dear mother; and a charge was hovering like an avenging angel over the evil doer's, or doers' head.

Imminent.

All circumstantial, all adjectival magnification, but a deal of it, accurate enough to negate outright denial.

Not that it stopped McLevy as he glared at Carnegie. 'Who told you this blether?'

The man took out a pure white handkerchief and blew his nose fastidiously.

'I have my sources.'

'I battered one the other day.'

'So I have heard. I believe the poor boy is bedridden.'

'Let's hope it lasts,' said Mulholland.

'Oh, constable?' responded Sim, affecting only now to notice what in truth would have been an extremely hard figure to fail to see. 'I hear you had an encounter with Gash Mitchell.'

'We met.'

'Lucky the inspector was on hand to save your bacon.'

'Who said that?'

'The man himself. Gash. He also said that next time — you'd have nowhere to hide.'

Mulholland's face did not alter, but he snaked out one long arm to grasp the brushed lapels of Carnegie's expensive new overcoat, and drew the man close so that their faces were no more than a bruised fingernail apart.

'You tell Mitchell. Any time. Any place. I'll leave him face down. In the gutter. Dead or alive.'

It must be said for Sim Carnegie that though he was a venomous, slimy specimen, he did not lack nerve.

His furtive eyes slid sideways, but he managed to hold his water and nod the head.

Mulholland released his grip, and the newsman turned to smile at a stone-faced McLevy.

'Do you have a quote for me, inspector?'

'Talk tae the lieutenant.'

Carnegie laughed.

'That would be a waste of time. I'll see how events turn out. My readers will be waiting. With bated breath.'

He walked a short distance away as if continuing on a pleasant evening's stroll and called back cheerily.

'If you do nothing, I'll name the man in any case. I have it at my fingertips.'

'*Who told you?*'

Anger shot the question out of McLevy like a bullet.

'Ye think I have but a single informant at your

station? Mair than one way tae skin a cat, McLevy.'

The phrase was repeated as the man walked off into the gathering gloom.

'Mair than one way — tae skin a cat!'

He laughed like a rusty door wrenching open.

'I warned the lieutenant I had more ammunition. He should have listened!'

With that boastful rejoinder, he was gone.

Neither of the two left behind moved.

McLevy had an image of a giant hoop bowling down the hill, out of control, himself spread-eagled inside howling out some instructions to which no-one paid any heed. And yet, and yet . . . something at the back of his mind. Despite the chaos of feeling, a shape was forming, coming into focus. But it was blurred so far.

He wished to God it would hurry up.

Mulholland tried to shake aside a foul picture of the girl — her thin neck snapped like a twig. What was forming in his mind was vengeance. A bloody vengeance.

Finally they both returned to the normality of a damp street in Leith with seagulls screeching complaints to a heavy-browed sky.

'The lieutenant's going to be hopping like a Chinese firecracker,' said the constable.

And so it appeared as they entered his office.

Roach had the paper spread on his desk and the expression on his face could in no way be confused with a dancing moonbeam.

Yet he surprised both by speaking quietly — now and then the lieutenant rose above the estimation of his two main men.

'Tell me what transpired at the Drummond house, if you will?'

They did so.

'So we are no further on from this morning?'

Solemn nods.

'And Daniel Drummond has thus far resisted confession — if indeed there is aught to confess.'

'We have the identification — '

'I am well aware of that, inspector. But it's not enough without further evidence. And now?'

Roach rested his somewhat bony hands, palm down, on the offending headline as if he must block it from his view.

'How did this happen?'

'Buggered if I know,' was McLevy's response.

'That — though having the merit of honesty — does not advance the cause.'

The lieutenant jerked his head forward abruptly to indicate that they might sit.

The other two did as bidden, unlike Queen Victoria in her portrait, standing for eternity.

'This rag of a paper,' Roach again spoke in even tones, 'has caused a predicament. When Chief Constable Sandy Robb reads it, he will be over me like the Canongate pox.'

McLevy and Mulholland blinked; the lieutenant was not celebrated for his use of venereal simile.

'Drummond's lawyers will be here soon. I may stave them off for a while, but then I have to charge or release.'

The lieutenant continued his sequence of thought.

'If I charge, I will follow a course of action that

I do not believe is yet sufficiently supported by evidence in a court of law. If I release without opposite proof of innocence then Carnegie will slaughter us in the paper.'

Roach suddenly slammed his fist down on the desk in antithesis to the previous dry delivery, causing both his men to jump in their chairs.

'But the worst thing is how did Carnegie have knowledge of all this?'

All three fell silent. The idea of another traitor in the station was indeed a sickening one.

'Could the auld fellow not have been blethering untoward?' remarked Mulholland. 'He's gabby enough.'

'No,' replied Roach firmly. 'I have been considering that possibility. For Carnegie to get the story onto the presses and printed in an evening edition, he would need to have known by this day mid-afternoon at best.

'Dunwoody had scarce made his identification by that juncture and if you remember we then sent him home with Ballantyne.

'Ergo — he had no time to blether.'

The lieutenant had obviously given this matter deep study; McLevy seemed also lost in profound contemplation, so Mulholland asked the obvious question.

'When did Ballantyne get back, sir?'

'At least two hours later. Told Sergeant Murdoch that he had uncovered a nest of cockroaches in Dunwoody's room and thought to do the man a favour by clearing them out.'

'That sounds like the constable,'

'However — he had to find some small boxes

for the insects and was away for a short time while the old fellow made them a pot of tea.'

Roach sighed and wearily rubbed at his long chin.

'That might give opportunity, I suppose. The constable was out of sight, on the streets.'

'But he helped us catch Billy Napier!'

'I am well aware of that Mulholland — yet it is possible he may have met up with Carnegie or someone else and boasted of our success.'

'Have you asked him?'

'Not yet but . . . Ballantyne is . . . a weak vessel.'

'Not sure I agree, sir.'

'It is a matter of the given facts. Either the constable or — someone in the station.'

'Or — a wee thing else.'

McLevy had emerged from inward delving and a light of sorts was gleaming in his eye.

'When did you last see Carnegie, sir?'

'Some time after his mother's death.'

'And he warned you then — he had more ammunition?'

'Yes.'

Roach gazed at this strange man he had known for nigh on fifteen years who might as well at times be an island of the Outer Hebrides.

'How do you know Carnegie said those words, inspector?'

'Because he vaunted of it tae me.'

McLevy winced suddenly at an unwelcome shaft of pain.

Mostly he ignored such arrows of internal affliction, would do at this moment and would so again — one day no doubt there would be a reckoning.

But not right now.

Never right now.

'Give me this one night clear,' he petitioned. 'One night only. Hold Drummond until tomorrow.'

A timid knock upon the door and at Roach's command it opened to allow Ballantyne to stick in a tousled head. His birth-mark seemed unusually vibrant as it snaked down his neck.

Unaware that the three intent stares upon him might be weighing up his potential for dissimulation, indiscretion or treachery, the constable blurted out far from welcome news.

'These same lawyers are back. Hinging aboot at the desk.'

'Where the carcass is, there will the vultures be, eh?'

Ballantyne looked blank at his lieutenant's muttered response, and then nodded avian recognition.

'Like hoodie crows at the lambing season.'

The constable frowned at the cruelty of nature, before remembering why he had entered.

'Anyhow, they're scratching at the counter, sir.'

'I will be with them shortly.'

Ballantyne moved his lips as he memorised the message before departing.

Mulholland shook his head.

'If he's the one, I give up on the whole tin can.'

McLevy ignored this piece of folk wisdom, his

eyes still fixed on his lieutenant.

'Give me this night and one way or another I'll bring it home.'

Robert Roach was not a gambling man, save perhaps an occasional wager on Leith Links as regards his prowess with a mashie-niblick, and so he hesitated.

If wrong, his head might roll.

'And with a wee bit of luck,' added the inspector, 'I'll cut Carnegie down.'

The Queen looked down upon her three subjects. One of them had to make a move.

Surely?

32

Within the bowels of these elements,
Hell hath no limits . . .
. . . for where we are is hell
And where hell is, there must we ever be.
                                        Marlowe, *Faust*

He lay in the corner, huddled limbs together like a threatened animal.

From the outside he seemed still, inert, but in the depths of his being a change was taking place. The other was sleeping now, the idiot brute, and that was splendid because it gave him time to plan.

And paint pretty pictures in his mind.

For there was no evil to be found in this, no, what he did was a service — as a good husbandman would clear the stinking growths around a fine tree, so he frees the living creature to reach up for the sun.

And bless the child.

So.

One more before the awakening.

One more that stood between himself and the moment he had dreamt of for so long.

An ugly image lurched into his mind. The old witch in the tavern, mouth twisted and leering, trying to smile, slobbering tears, hands like talons, crying his name — *HIS NAME!*

He had pulled away, but she yowled and

clawed at him, then by fortune stumbled to the ground so that he might escape, out of the tavern doors into the fell, dank air of the harbour, with tears blinding him.

Yet she had revealed his destiny. So for that she must be thanked and for that she must be destroyed.

It was only right. Only justice.

Had he felt joy when he lashed down?

It must be admitted there was some delight, as if he was tasting the sweet, beginning fruits of freedom.

He had wrapped the witch in swaddling blanket and then left her at the glistening door as eliminated memory that could no longer harm the coming splendour.

He screamed with joy as the carriage cut through that dark night like a knife.

Soon he would be free!

And even with the first who had dared to threaten, to reveal the sacred book he kept so close, who was no more than a slug under foot, again he had felt such glory as the cane whipped its precise music upon her face and body.

Now there was a third.

Come from nowhere.

The last.

A viper, vixen, naked and wanton.

To tempt, seduce, suck out life and blood, her soul squalid as a leech.

The other two were old and ugly but she was exquisite, a doorway to depravity.

How beautiful are thy feet with shoes, O prince's daughter the joints of thy thighs are like jewels, the work of the hands of a cunning workman.

Thy navel is like a round goblet, which wanteth not liquor: thy belly is like an heap of wheat set about with lilies.

All this he would destroy.

It should not take long.

Silence the whore with a first blow across the fluttering pulse in her throat and then whip out the life.

He heard a sound somewhere, footsteps on stone perhaps, but he did not open his eyes.

While they were closed he was safe.

For the moment he could only plan, but soon he would be released to dance around the writhing harlot.

And strike down.

The blood in her mouth would be as blood upon his own lips, stripes upon her skin the flayed pain he had suffered since the advent of the witch.

Each welt an exact chastisement.

Patience and death.

The plan was made; the moment would arrive.

Only just. Only right. Only proper.

A joyful deliverance.

33

I am not in the least provoked at the sight
of a lawyer, a pick-pocket, a colonel . . . a
politician, a whore-master, a physician . . .
a traitor or the like; that is all according to
the due course of things.

Swift, *Gulliver's Travels*

George Dunwoody smiled a little foolishly as he
directed his wayward feet towards his own wee
door.

The crack had been no' half bad at the tavern,
men of a decent age all with tales to tell; most
stories George had heard before, but having the
pelf for a decent dram of whisky brightened the
prospect of an oft repeated anecdote, and he
himself had been accorded pride of place, having
brought in a healthy round.

Money cements friendship.

Of course, no mention, not a hint of present
events; this knowledge George hugged to himself, while regaling the party with the umpteenth
retelling of the blessed day he saw his teeth
smiling like a lover's promise from the market
stall.

All the time, though, his ears were cocked for
scraps of gossip or a remark made in drink at a
nearby table, for his hearing was sharp as a razor
shell.

Like a squirrel George stored these careless

remarks away, for who knows when they might come in handy?

But not this night.

Now he had money in his poche, and providing he steered clear of such as that big lump of a girl Susan Templeton who had winked her eye when he stumped up coin at the bar, safe in his pocket it would remain.

Mind you. She was a ripe temptation.

George laughed aloud at that idea, navigated the narrow hallway and turned his key in the lock.

Safe from all carnal incitement, it was the work of a moment to light the candle, banishing the darkness.

This he did, and then he blinked.

Did his eyes deceive, or was a man not sitting in the single three-legged chair?

And another leaning against the damp wall.

Men he knew.

But they did not belong in this neck o' the woods.

From the chair, one spoke.

'Aye, George,' said James McLevy. 'You seem in fine fettle.'

'Wrestle a bull to the ground,' added Mulholland.

'How did you get in here?' George asked, grinning in spite of himself.

'Magic.'

This remark of the inspector's was not strictly true, since he had utilised a set of lock-picks confiscated from a master craftsman many years ago, and now in McLevy's hands at the service of justice.

At least this is what he told Mulholland when the constable suggested, as usual, that his inspector might be sliding towards unlawful entry.

'Throw me in the jile then,' was the retort accompanied by a defiant glint in the eye. In truth McLevy relished the thrill of tickling ratchets, the moment of consummation and then the compliant click as the lock sprang open.

They had searched the place top to bottom without success, uncovering only a small cache of photographs involving a well-upholstered naked female with what seemed a remarkably versatile, large snake.

Mulholland had identified it as a boa constrictor, male because of its pelvic spurs.

All grist to the mill.

The photos had been replaced in their oilskin wrapping. McLevy continued the exchange.

'I've spent the night calling in favours, Mister Dunwoody. Some folk didnae even wish to make donation, being of a profession that is but one step up from the sewage rat.'

'Yet once we twisted their tails, they squealed a fine little tune,' Mulholland added cheerfully.

George said nothing, but carefully lowered himself onto a small stool, as if preparing for the long haul.

'Should have done this before,' remarked McLevy genially. 'But in my defence let it be said I have been somewhat beleaguered.'

'No-one is perfect, sir, not even yourself.'

The inspector ignored this sage comment from his constable, attention fixed upon the old man, who now sat forward alertly, as if about to receive a commendation of sorts from his betters.

Indeed, there was a curious innocence in his eyes, which McLevy was intent upon demolishing.

'George Dunwoody. Ye make a wee living, peddling to the papers. A dirty business.'

'Gossip, hearsay, all kinds of calumny,' Mulholland threw in.

'Scandalmonger. Paid informer. Muckraker.'

The old man blinked.

'These are gey harsh words, inspector.'

'And I didnae pay a penny for them!'

Indeed, though McLevy had canvassed and coerced the gentlemen of the press, to a certain extent his work had been made easier by the fact that a certain slimy rodent was loathed even amongst his own feral tribe.

'And an avid buyer of the scurrilous dross you peddle is none other than Sim Carnegie, I am reliably informed.'

George suddenly stuck his thumb into his mouth, chewed on it for a moment, then pulled it out with a pop.

'Now and again,' he announced.

'What?'

'A wee drap tittle tattle. Peyed buttons maistly.'

'By Carnegie?'

'Amangst other folk.'

'You didn't mention that,' Mulholland observed.

'I forgot.'

'Forgot what?' growled McLevy.

'I knew him, like. Carnegie.'

279

'That's quite forgetful.'

Dunwoody made no response to the constable's words, while McLevy struggled to contain a mounting ire.

Of course they had earlier, after George's first visit to the station, checked out the old man in the tavern where he drank and with his neighbours in the wynd, but Dunwoody kept a low profile and other than a fey disposition from time to time, seemed to lead, for Leith, an unassuming and ordinary life. A reliable witness then.

It wasn't till McLevy started to dig deeper this very night, especially with a possible Carnegie connection in mind, that a certain incriminating sideline had emerged.

But the inspector still blamed himself.

They say never look a gift horse in the mouth, but a good policeman should have been alerted by the teeth alone.

George sat like a jovial elf on the stool, eyes bright and shiny.

'All right,' muttered McLevy a trifle heavily, because there was something about eternal cheerfulness that he found very wearing. 'I'll lay it out how I think it happened and at the end all you have to do, George — is nod your head.'

'That's all I have tae do?'

'If you agree, that is,' Mulholland interjected for the sake of even-handedness.

McLevy shot him a look to indicate that further neutrality would not be welcome, and began his dissertation.

'Sim Carnegie, it is my conjecture, approached

you, George Dunwoody, with a plan for a great wee piece o' mischief, and there's naethin' you love more than mischief on the burner, eh sir?'

A nod almost came in response, before George remembered he was only supposed to perform that particular action at the end, and only if in concurrence.

'Mister Carnegie had already met with one of the suspects, as it were, in the tavern, so he was able to furnish you with a detailed description of the young man; the bad leg, the cane, the time you would have seen him that night.'

Nothing could be gleaned from the old man's face so far, other than he was enjoying this, as a spectator would a rollicking good play.

'Carnegie paid you — good money I trust and not buttons, George — to land up at the station and set the cat amongst the pigeons.'

McLevy let out a mirthless guffaw that sounded more like a bull walrus catching sight of a rival, and lest George take alarm, Mulholland sidled in.

'Great fun to be had watching the police chase their own tails. Great fun!'

'Only,' added McLevy with a savage grin, 'too true. There we were, hammering at this boy, worrying our guts about how Carnegie broke the story, and the answer was simple; he had started it in the first place.'

Dunwoody stuck his thumb back into his mouth.

'Whit a caper, eh? And you did a grand job, George — '

'First class!' chimed the constable.

'You could take pride in mission accomplished — is that not so, my mannie?'

There was a long silence. Both McLevy and Mulholland inclined their heads in enquiring but kindly fashion, as if they in turn were genteel spectators at a clever show.

At last George removed the fleshly digit, though for the moment afterwards was frozen in time and space.

'A chance tae be the hero, eh? Sim Carnegie — all his plan, his doing. But you were the champion.'

'The bold boy!'

Mulholland's Irish blue eyes were filled with admiration; the inspector winked in high regard.

The old man smiled at such approbation and then — nodded. Firmly. A man of mettle. A champion.

Neither by movement nor glance did either policeman indicate the importance of that inclination.

'Sim Carnegie is a clever chiel,' said McLevy. 'But you George, you went intae the lion's den.'

'It didnae feel like that,' replied the old man. 'It felt . . . righteous.'

Best not to quibble too directly with that; strike a solicitous note.

'But if you'd stood up in court, George. Sworn on the bible, eh?'

'Wouldnae have gone that far, inspector.'

Silence. McLevy took a deep breath.

'Tell me a wee thing more.'

'If it got anywhere near tae trial, Carnegie tellt me I was tae alter course before. Change of mind. Wisnae sure. Bleary auld eyes, dark night, rain in my face — a clever chiel, eh?'

The old fellow let out a peal of laughter, more of a dry, cackling sound, teeth up and down like a drawbridge.

Worried McLevy might revert to type, tear the man's head off and throw it out the nearest window, Mulholland made a more sobering contribution.

'Do you not think — it might have been — a little on the questionable side?'

'How so?'

'False witness.'

'No' exactly false. Sim was certain sure the boy had done it!'

'Was he now?' muttered McLevy.

'Certain sure. Whit he told me. Whit he desired wis that once startit, ye would find out the bona fide truth.'

'That's why he did it, eh?'

'Vengeance. His poor mother was dead. Every man loves his mother!'

The inspector could have cited at least ten murder cases contradicting that last assertion, but at least they had got what they wanted.

Or had they?

Carnegie would deny everything.

It would be George's word against his and the old man would, with a little skilful questioning, cut a dislocated figure in the witness box.

They could prosecute Dunwoody for perjury, but would Roach wish to dive into that particular midden?

He would not.

The lieutenant would gladly settle for official release, because the only witness now vouchsafed he was no longer able to point the finger.

That's what Roach would tell the lawyers, and conveniently forget to mention the fact the police had the wool pulled over their eyes.

Perhaps the law could confiscate the photos of the woman and the snake?

But that would just be evil-minded.

So they had everything and nothing.

Like so much in life.

34

It is impossible to love and be wise.
                    Bacon, *Essays*, 'Of Love'

The weather was unchanged, the gazebo held to its elegant lines, the peacocks wailed, Cupid took everlasting aim, the woman was unyielding — only the man had altered.

Jean Brash studied McLevy as he sooked noisily through his moustache at the best Lebanese coffee undulating in her delicate, porcelain cups.

He aye had problems getting his stubby fingers through the space between the handle and its rounded body. No doubt the man would prefer a large, tin mug, where his customary six lumps of sugar could dissolve with room to spare.

From McLevy's vantage, he would liked to have spent the rest of the day drinking this fine coffee, even with Jean's beady eyes upon him.

The inspector had a lot on his mind, most of it in a whirling storm.

His surmise about events had proved correct. Next day, in fact this very one that stretched before him, having been informed about everything except the boa constrictor, Lieutenant Roach had been undoubtedly relieved to set Daniel Drummond free, with adjusted and official explanation to the sharp-nosed lawyers.

Alan Grant had also been released, though there seemed to be an air of some restraint between the two students.

Plus the decision whether to prosecute George Dunwoody had been deferred, though the inspector wouldn't have bet his next black pudding on a positive verdict.

Another thorn in the side was that though in fact McLevy had brought the chicanery of identification into the open, his lieutenant, as is the habit of superiors, appeared to blame him for not spotting it in the first place.

'I seem to remember,' remarked Roach, with a mean cast to his eye, as they surveyed an emptying station, 'that you, inspector, made promise that you would *cut Carnegie down*. Or did my ears deceive me?'

'I will eventually.'

'Well you may recommence the process this very day.'

So he and Mulholland had been dispatched to trudge the damp streets and confront Carnegie in his newspaper office. As feared, they had been met with denial and disdain.

The man did not dispute knowing Dunwoody, but this was only as a contributor of insubstantial tittle-tattle, and most certainly not as a conspirator in supposedly manufacturing headlines.

But now, thanks to the police, Carnegie had another.

'*SUSPECT RELEASED. WILL MY MOTHER'S KILLER EVER BE BROUGHT TO JUSTICE?*'

McLevy noted the fellow's skin seemed dry-flaked, and there was a strong smell of last night's whisky, but that aside, there was little hint of fallibility.

The inspector also remarked a white shirt and damask waistcoat.

'Ye're gey well attired these days. Have ye come intae money?' he asked.

Carnegie seemed to find this very amusing.

'Not yet,' was the answer, a sneer never far from that long upper lip. 'Not yet, but my legacy is within reach.'

He held out his hand as if to grasp something and closed it into a triumphant fist.

And so they left Sim in all his glory. And outside the newspaper offices, while the dull rain of May fell alike on saint and sinner, Mulholland, who had remained silent during the exchange, on account of his intense dislike of Carnegie and the man's connection to a certain Gash Mitchell, was instructed to scour the taverns once more, and hunt up any of Mary Dougan's drinking cronies they may have missed first time around.

The second murder had been neglected and overtaken by the rapid events surrounding the first, but surely somewhere in the woman's past there must be cause for her vicious slaughter.

McLevy himself, niggled by the acid words of his lieutenant, had gone scouting round his financial contacts in the lower regions, but without success.

Carnegie's boasting to Roach had put the inspector onto the track regarding George Dunwoody, and he had wondered if the same might apply again with the new clothes and money to burn — *not yet* the man had said, about his legacy.

So what was the source of this largesse?

He had had no luck, however, and McLevy felt badly in need of a wee breather.

He had hardly slept the previous night, tormented by unsettling images of Jessica Drummond, hair tumbling down, deep dark eyes, white teeth biting into russet skin; all this provoked a churning welter of feelings.

A younger, more vulnerable self had appeared, and this scared him more than any homicidal maniac.

Was he awake or was he asleep?

He hoped to God he would not do something daft, as men in love were wont to do.

But he was not in love, was he? Jist — short of sleep and besieged by pictures.

Only in one place could a man find respite and response.

The Just Land. A bawdy-hoose.

Only with one person, acceptance despite all.

Jean Brash. A bawdy-hoose keeper.

Only with one taste, manna untainted.

The purest coffee. From the fragrant Lebanon.

So here he was in the garden. Peace on the cards.

But for how long?

'I had a visitor,' Jean remarked with an air of innocence.

'Oh?'

'An acquaintance of yours.'

'Such as?'

'A teller of tales.'

The gleam in her eye was indication enough.

'Stevenson?'

'None other.'

'That mannie travels near and far.'

Still not having quite forgiven him for the contretemps at the tarred gates, though this was mitigated by the fact that the tethered peacocks and small-fire had rid her of the students, Jean sowed a snap more mischief.

'A real will o' the wisp. Charming as ye like.'

McLevy's hand had once more found its way to the plate of sugar biscuits and he bit off a near half, before making an indistinct reply.

'Uhuh?'

There was definitely something on his mind; usually Jean could rely on the mere mention of an interloper to provoke a nippy retort, but the only further reaction was the disappearance of the remnant of the sugar biscuit.

'Robert told me you have a second murder on hand.'

'He didnae lie.'

'Mary Dougan. Puir soul.'

'You would know her?'

'She was once a sweet kittie. Fell amangst thieves.'

'Certainly did. Onything ye can say of her?'

'Her best love was him. He left. She declined. For close to a year, no-one saw her.'

'Put not your trust in writers.'

An edge there right enough, then his head came up, eyes fierce. No matter what had turned him inwards, a case would always bring out the wolf.

'You will keep this second murder to yourself.'

'I keep *everything* to myself.'

As they stared each other out, Hannah Semple stuck her head from one of the upstairs windows.

'Mistress,' she bawled. 'The horse has collapsed in the cellar. Wan o' the struts. Rough usage nae doubt.'

'Horse?'

For a moment McLevy was lost, before remembering that the Berkeley Horse was a piece of apparatus that was used for flagellation purposes, in the lower regions of the Just Land.

He knew it merely by name and wished no further acquaintance.

Jean had more intimate cognition, but the actual spread-eagling of clients, whipping and squeezing of hanging flesh, utilisation of cane plus thistle, then nettle in season and omnipresent leather with an edge to cut steel, was left to Lily Baxter and Maisie Powers. The big girl being new to the job, however, hefty, and occasionally over-enthusiastic, must have put too much strain on the device.

'All right, Hannah!' Jean bawled back. 'I'll be in directly,'

'Ye better. I'm no' a joiner.'

The window shut, though Hannah managed a ritual glower in McLevy's direction, as if he had been somehow responsible for the equipment malfunction, while Jean rose to her feet.

In a way she was oddly discomfited. Of course she was proud of her profession and the inspector, if not from a personal experience, realised fine well the inner workings of a bawdy-hoose. Yet at this moment, for some reason she could not identify, she felt strangely exposed.

As if under foreign scrutiny.

'Whit was Stevenson doing here anyway?' McLevy asked suddenly.

'I told you. A visit. Like yourself. On the scrounge.'

'For what?'

'Information.'

He frowned.

'I have a favour tae ask.'

'I might have known.'

The request was made and involved Jean's superior contacts with a squalid profession in the nether reaches of Leith's financial strata.

She nodded acceptance, but wondered if there might come a day when a man came to see her off his own bat.

Every woman born has thought this at some point.

What every man born thinks is a different matter.

'I'll see whit comes out the woodwork,' she announced as she turned to go, brushing stray crumbs from her dress. 'Goodbye, James.'

Then he shot out a question that stopped her in motion.

'Jean — have ye ever been in love?'

Cupid was now a staging post for various garden birds of late, and despite a regular morning scrub, had developed a streaked, worn-out appearance as if the job was getting too much for one demigod.

Finally the Mistress of the Just Land found a word or two in response.

'Whit — whit put that into your head?'

'Jist answer the question!'

'I have a broken horse tae mend.'

'It'll keep.'

Silence.

She came back a little and looked down at his face, which resembled a lost dog at the races.

'Well?' he growled.

Silence.

'Once or twice.'

'Whit was it like?'

'Terrible.'

'That's what I thought.'

McLevy took up the last sugar biscuit and crammed it whole into his mouth. The sight did not entrance.

'Why are you asking?' said Jean Brash.

'No reason,' replied James McLevy.

She peered closer. That damned moustache of his had hidden something, but now it was clear.

'Ye shaved gey close this morning.'

'Did I?'

'Usually by this time o' the day, your chin has a blue tinge.'

'That's nice.'

'And you have a clean collar, now that I think of it.'

He had muffled up in his heavy coat, but she caught a glimpse of unexpected colour.

'Is that a purple tie?'

'I found it in a drawer.'

Hannah opened the window again and banged it shut without uttering a word.

Jean took refuge in mockery.

'You have a' the symptoms of a braw gallant. Is it for my benefit?'

'It's no' for anybody's benefit,' he blurted out.

'That's sad.'

'I jist found it in a drawer!'

He had, in fact, in front of the breakfast mirror, swithered over the thought that he might visit Jessica Drummond to witness what he hoped might be admiration in her eyes at his part in the freeing of her brother; had thought to dress in such a way that might further augment his standing, but lost the inclination as the morning wore on.

Jean was certain now that something was going on in his heart in which she did not play a role, and it cut her right through to the core.

Guilt and hurt.

Both married to anger.

For a moment their eyes met, then she turned and walked away abruptly.

He did the same, but just as he reached the iron gate and wrenched it open, Jean called across the lawn.

'Oh and James — you asked about love? It's the very devil.'

Then she wheeled round and the house door slammed, followed seconds later by the crash of the iron gates.

One of the male peacocks suddenly leapt into the air and landed on a low-lying branch.

He let out a cry of strangled triumph and the

female lifted her head for a moment, no doubt wondering if his passionate assumption would last the course.

35

Lars Porsena of Clusium
By the nine gods he swore
That the great house of Tarquin
Should suffer wrong no more.
By the Nine Gods he swore it,
And named a trysting day.
Macaulay, *Lays of Ancient Rome*

Stevenson had been part of many strange situations in his life, witness his first visit to Silverado, where the deserted mining village perched like a rusty parrot on the shoulder of the North Californian hills, hemmed by rubble, abandoned machinery and poison oak. He had felt immediately at home.

Now he was a stranger at home and in a predicament that put other geographical vicissitudes to shame.

He had observed from the window, as the afternoon wore on, a crowd of students of both camps, scarlet and white, faces daubed accordingly, gather in numbers in the street directly before his house.

In the main the young men were silent, solemn, and though Fanny, Lloyd and his mother openly gawked at the other window, Robert Louis lurked behind the curtain like Polonius, trusting he would not meet the same Shakespearean fate.

He enjoyed the limelight, but the last time these ruffians had laid hands upon him it had taken divine intervention to save the day.

No matter they had not known his identity, it would have been small comfort as the cold sea closed around him to hear a distant voice

Oh dear — that man swallowing half the harbour water — did he not write Kidnapped? Is that the second or third time he's gone under? I'm sure I know the face!

A brisk rapping of the doorknocker brought him from this pleasant reverie and Stevenson quickly made his way downstairs lest one of the servants should have to face these looming troglodytes.

First he took the precaution of grasping one of his father's heavy walking sticks. It was of teak, with a brass fist at the top, and would serve the purpose.

When he opened the door, however, rather than a full frontal assault, he was met by the sight of two youths, one red, one white, who had already retreated respectfully half-way back down the path.

Both held long scrolls and bowed their heads towards him.

The White Leader was a small, dainty fellow with an elegant cane and curiously crooked leg, but the other was a large, hulking form, whose face Stevenson vaguely remembered hanging over him from the harbour incident.

Had he not in fact kicked this fellow? On the ear as far as he recollected.

The writer took a quick glance at the lughole

in question and was gratified to see the remnants of a large bluish abrasion.

As all this flashed through Stevenson's mind, the White Leader spoke in formal tones, though his eyes had a curious, almost predatory, glitter.

'We are honoured, Mister Stevenson, that you have agreed to act as our judge in these historic proceedings.'

Act? Judge? *Agreed?*

Then Robert Louis recalled with a sinking heart having received, hand-delivered through the letter-box not long after his father had died, an envelope with ornate calligraphy which he had ripped open, glanced at carelessly and thrown aside.

The words, jumbled in recollection, danced a riotous jig in his head — *privilege to Scotland — greatest living offer* — author? — *to judge between* — *ancient rivalry* — *of Runners and Devils* — *heartfelt thanks* — *Scarlet and White our final* — *your decision.*

He glanced up to the window and Lloyd grinned down proudly, excited to see so many of his contemporaries — though his own university studies of engineering theory had foundered on the rocks — on the streets.

Fanny looked as if she would prefer the company of man-eating sharks and the mother-widow seemed, as usual, to be prepared for an eternity of mourning.

But Stevenson dearly loved his stepson despite accusations of the youth being lazy, a philanderer and when it came right down to it, not all that clever.

So for Lloyd's sake, he nodded gravely and accepted the proffered role in this great drama.

A cheer went up, then there was silence.

The writer was presented with a judge's wig, filched from one of the student's own fathers, which he donned with appropriate gravity.

He cut a strange, frail figure, and yet there was a dignity to the man as he lit up a cigarette and waved a languid hand to begin proceedings.

Daniel Drummond, released from the confines of a prison cell, commenced to orate and minutely describe the exploits of the White Devils. He had won the tossed coin, so his rival Gregor Gillespie, a hulking fellow who had just scraped through his exams, but was indispensable in the front row of the rugby team, had to stand by and grind his teeth.

As Robert Louis listened to the various feats, one or two of which had a flavour of high adventure and most others being to do with scoring points off the opposition, he noted at the back a few policemen taking up unobtrusive positions.

The numbers of the students were not above a combined fifty, these being the hard core, but there was no doubt that if a riot took place they might well wreak havoc.

'That's a dirty lie!'

To Gregor's cry of deep indignation, Daniel paid no attention and ended the narrative with a flourish.

'Thus I respectfully commend to your lordship the deeds and derring-do of the incomparable White Devils!'

A ragged cheer went up from his followers, but the massive figure of Gregor Gillespie had not budged.

'A dirty lie,' he said loudly. 'We cracked that window and lifted the dummy!'

The dispute appeared to concern the breaking of a dress-shop window and the purloining of a partly clothed mannequin, which later had been deposited in front of the Register House.

'Indeed you did break the window,' replied Daniel calmly. 'But you then ran for your life pursued by the forces of law and order. And while you were thus occupied, we rescued the poor lady and left her where she might be inserted into the archives.'

More laughter and cheers from the white faction did not improve Gregor's temper.

'Ye performed such on our coat-tails, too feeble for strong action. Cowards to a man!'

Daniel's eyes narrowed and an insulted growl arose from his followers.

'I think, gentlemen,' said Judge Stevenson in conciliatory tones, 'you might leave the discrimination of events to your appointed officer and merely relate the facts.'

The tension faded a little but, though there had been at the outset of the contest good-natured horseplay between the factions, as the days wore on the physical striving had become more and more bruising. Now, at the end — though they may not even have been aware of it — both parties were spoiling for a fight.

Young men are often so.

Unaware and potentially violent.

Stevenson took another long drag at his cigarette, tapped the ash daintily upon the cracks in the family path, and waved his hand to indicate the renewal of proceedings.

He also remarked that a few more police had joined a few more police, which is never a good sign.

So — on with the motley.

Gregor coughed importantly and unravelled the scroll, which in truth was almost twice the length of his opponent's and looked more than a little absurd as it trailed to the ground.

The unravelling of subsequent events was, sadly, to do with a pea.

Nothing more heroic.

One of the White Devils had felt the force of Gregor's fist in the previous rammy by the harbour and borrowed his younger brother's pea-shooter that very morning.

He rested it lightly on the shoulder of the fellow in front, took aim, puffed out his cheeks and let fly.

It was a hard pea, nutritious in days long gone, but not unlike a miniature cannon-ball as it sped through the air and smacked into the tender flesh just by the ear, where a certain famous writer had already landed his boot.

Gregor let out an outraged howl and, since no-one but he and the shooter knew the cause, appeared to jump spasmodically as if suffering some delusion or perhaps had been stung by an early horse-fly.

A clegg is the name in Scots for something that sucks blood and leaves a lump.

The recipient cut a far from dignified figure, and Daniel could not restrain a snort of amusement.

Stevenson sighed, In his time he had experienced a student fracas or two and if this one took off, it would be a hell-broth.

Take off it did.

Gregor swiped mightily at Daniel. A punch that, had it connected, might have wrenched his head near off his shoulders — but it did not.

The slighter figure ducked nimbly, then lashed out with the thin cane he had used to support himself during the formalities.

It was aimed at the side of the assailant's neck, but glanced off the shoulder and hit the man flush in the side of the face, leaving a white welt as the scarlet paint peeled off under the force of the strike.

Gregor's second roar of anguish operated like a signal for hostilities to begin.

As Daniel skipped off into the street, pursued by the vengeful ogre, a rammy of mammoth proportions commenced.

Scarlets and Whites threw themselves at each other tooth and nail, all protocol forgotten, the scrolls dropped and trampled underfoot as fists and boots flew.

Whereas their previous skirmishes had an element of ritual posturing, this was savage and bloody.

Noses were broken, teeth were smashed, and to fall was to suffer badly damaged ribs as kicks rained in.

Stevenson lit up another cigarette and watched

quietly; it would seem that the primitive side of man was never far distant and that Mister Hyde was having a field day.

Further oil on the flames was the intervening of the previously undetected police; at first outnumbered and suffering a violent buffeting as they tried to separate the warring factions, then augmented by reinforcements led by two figures with which the writer had enjoyed some previous experience.

Daniel had been pushed to the ground, collar wrenched and torn as he looked up to see a Scarlet looming above, face distorted with anger and hatred.

'Smart boy, eh?' said the other, kicking Daniel hard in the gut and doubling him over in pain.

Daniel knew this man, had seen him in the university, a decent type, but now unrecognisable, a brutish adversary.

'See how you like this, smart boy!'

As the other lifted his foot to stamp down on Daniel's crippled leg, an iron hand smacked into the attacker's face, almost paralysing him with the force of the blow.

The man was then pitched into the arms of some waiting constables and Daniel hauled to his feet.

He found himself facing James McLevy.

'Ye're handy wi' that wee stick, I notice,' said the inspector with a sardonic grin. 'I'll keep that in mind.'

Daniel found he was still clutching the cane, but before he could make response McLevy hurled him contemptuously off in one direction before plunging back in the other to rejoin the fray.

An angry fire burned at the back of the young man's eyes, to be treated so, to be so humiliated — he saw the hulking shape of Gregor making towards him, but then was grasped firmly by the shoulders and hustled from the fever pitch of conflict.

Alan Grant was by his side, face a little bloody from a cut under the eye.

'We don't need any more trouble, Daniel,' he shouted above the noise. 'This is out of your control now.'

For a moment Daniel stiffened, remembering what he considered a betrayal by Grant, but he saw nothing in the other's eyes save concern and friendship.

Enough was enough.

Though the bitter anger still burned.

Always.

'I am inclined to agree,' he replied formally, and the two slipped away out of sight before a stray representative of the law might think them fair game.

Just before escaping, Daniel glanced back to where Stevenson stood, and was rewarded with an ironic bow.

He responded in kind, and for a moment there was contact between them.

Gregor meanwhile knocked a young policeman to the ground and howled like a Berserk.

Mulholland could scarce believe his eyes.

'Ballantyne!' he called out. 'What the hell are you doing here?'

303

'They ran short of numbers,' gasped the constable.

'Don't move!'

There wasn't much danger of that, since the boy was badly winded, but Mulholland had little wish to be distracted.

'I am afraid, sir,' he said politely to Gregor, 'that you may have stepped beyond the boundaries of the law. That being the case, I'll have to be arresting you where you stand.'

The big man had blood in his eye and saw only a bean-pole with a fair complexion like some country bumpkin.

He charged forwards and was hit precisely between neck and shoulder by a hornbeam stick that was as hard as the hand of God. As Gregor tried to haul great bucketfuls of air into his lungs, the stick came down on his other side with equal force and, like a stricken oak, the great leader of the Scarlet Runners fell to earth.

Mulholland levered Ballantyne up to his feet.

'Go and find a quiet corner,' he advised sternly. 'Do not move from there until I give you word.'

The young fellow hung his head, birth-mark pulsating down the side of his neck.

'Don't be hammering at yourself now,' said Mulholland in more kindly tones. 'The only thing you lack is the one thing I would never wish you to possess.'

'Whit's that, sir?'

Mulholland picked up the carcass of Gregor by the leg, and, as he prepared to depart, whispered a response.

'Violence. Terrible violence. But luckily or otherwise for yourself, you have to be born with it.'

'And whit about you, sir?'

'I'm never really quite sure.'

McLevy at that very moment was bringing together a Scarlet and White pair who had previously been fighting, but found themselves at the beck and call of a greater force.

This power crashed their bodies into each other with wounding velocity.

Both toppled to the cobblestones and as they did, the inspector looked around to see that the battle was losing intensity, bodies scattered round like a haphazard harvest.

He became aware of scrutiny and saw the figure of Stevenson, judge's wig slightly askew, regarding him from a distance.

'I declare this contest to be level-pegging!'

Having made this announcement to the unheeding throng, the man smiled, waggled fingers at McLevy, and then walked back into his house as if — the entertainment was over.

As if — and this dark thought occurred suddenly to the inspector — Robert Louis had brought it all into being.

Further down the road, towards Albany Street, three of the Runners ran for their life and crossed paths with a burly figure and diminutive companion.

One of the Scarlets, having been deep in the conflict and received more than a few merited vicious kicks and punches, had decided to leave war to its own devices, but nevertheless recognised the smaller figure.

'Tom Carstairs!' he shouted. 'You should have been there to support your brothers. You are a coward, sir!'

The burly man stepped forward, one of his arms hanging limply by the side.

Without further ado and with the good limb, he hit the accuser a blow on the chin that lifted the man off his feet and dumped him senseless upon the ground.

Tom stepped bravely forward, ready to defend his father lest the other two students attack, but they stood irresolute as Mulholland with some chasing younger policemen arrived to collect the fugitives who had made the mistake of, as common parlance would have it, *putting the boot in* to a supine officer of the law.

It is never a good idea to kick a policeman when he's down. One day he will rise again. Memory intact.

The constable, meanwhile, lifted his hand in salute.

'It's nice to see the general public joining in with the police in the pursuance of their duties, sir.'

Archibald Carstairs nodded gravely, but a dark humour was not far from either man's eyes.

As the runaways were dragged off, the felled accuser draped over Mulholland's shoulder like a bedraggled plaidie, Tom murmured that perhaps they might take one of the side-streets to avoid further confrontation.

His father nodded agreement, but the man's gaze was fixed on the debris of distant warfare.

His fist clenched as if to deliver another blow, but who would be the target now?

A distant figure waved at him. McLevy in his element.

All that had gone for the major now.

An anguished parting.

Yet a compensation holds for those who miss the heat of battle — death is never far away.

It aye lurks close at hand.

36

Suns that set, may rise again;
But if once we lose this light,
'Tis with us, perpetual night.

Ben Johnson, *Volpone*

As she climbed the stairs to her boudoir, Jean Brash was wondering if that last wee gurgle of champagne might have been an error of judgement.

It had left her giddy after a riotous evening.

The Worshipful Society of Engineers, having assembled for the funeral of an august member, had made their first visit en masse to the Just Land and belied a sober sounding name with maniacal energy, erotic curiosity and a never-ending thirst for expensive sparkling wine.

They were to a man lean-shanked, above average height and had a profound interest in how things worked.

Especially a bawdy-hoose.

How did the inner mechanisms function?

The nuts and bolts, as it were?

The magpies were only too keen to supply practical exposure, but as the evening wore on and sated couples returned to the main salon, having explored the nooks and crannies of sensual construction, an ancient one-eyed fiddler struck up the starting notes of a frolicsome jig.

'A Mile to Ride' was the tune and in a matter

of moments, and not for the first time, sofas and chairs were dragged aside and the carpet rolled up, as the salon was transformed for a ceilidh.

Annie MacManus was a soft-hearted and bounteously framed female, whose form had become not unlike the cream buns she was so fond of devouring, but who also possessed a delicate yet firm touch appreciated by the older clients. Now, she plumped herself down at the piano and, instead of soothing background melodies, let the stirring notes of the fiddler's tune echo in the ivory keys she struck with both abandon and precision.

Hannah Semple had a soft spot for auld Mally Duncan, a rapscallion when young, rogue through the middle years and in his helter-skelter journey down the brae of dissipation, an unreconstructed snaffler.

But he could play, one eye darting amongst the increasingly bared limbs of the magpies like a randy sparrow, while his fingers leapt to ribald conclusions upon the roused and rousing strings.

There was a time he had played that music for Hannah alone, but the man wasnae tae be trusted — he would follow the notes out the window and never be seen again.

Yet still — she poured a generous dram and slid it near enough that he could smell the quality.

Mally grinned and did not even look down — he knew his women and he knew his fiddle.

He brought the tune to a close and then launched into an Irish jig this time. 'Wild Oats'. Wander the earth, sow them well and reap your fill.

Hannah's face split into an unaccustomed smile. That had been their melody.

On with the dance.

Later, after a hectic and lung-bursting strip jig that near bounced Jean's expensive painting of a lecherous octopus dragging a scantily clad female under the foaming sea from its pride of place on the wall — when the music became less frenetic — Jean was tempted onto the floor for a slow waltz by a stoop-shouldered lighthouse designer, tall and solemn, not unlike an owl, who had nonetheless assiduously plied her with the best champagne on the principle of oiling the moving parts.

As she danced in his arms and the lights dimmed a little, Jean closed her eyes and who knows what dreams fluttered behind those lidded curtains?

There was a vague, fragrant, pipe-tobacco smell from his evening jacket that she found not unattractive.

However when the music stopped, so did she.

A bawdy-hoose keeper can play no favourites amangst the clients; lovers she can pick and choose, but not from those who enter by the front door.

Jean had made that mistake once, disastrously, lost a most precious piece of jewellery to the blaggard's treachery, and if it wasn't for that miserable swine McLevy, her bonny Tahitian pearls would have been gone forever.

But the inspector brought them back. That was the trouble with James McLevy. He brought things back.

She looked at the man before her — decent, respectable, married no doubt but they all are — and sighed to admit that he was the civilised opposite to what she desired.

What a bugger.

Still, a waltz is a waltz.

While events unfolded above, in the cellars Lily and Maisie were having the time of their life, showing two of the younger brethren exactly how the Berkeley Horse worked its particular magic.

The ingenuity of the pulley system for those who enjoyed being hauled up and scourged on a circular basis also ignited their interest, but the engineers returned in fascination to the structure of the Horse itself; after some persuasion one allowed himself to be inserted into the various apertures, fitted for head, nether regions, and feet. Adjustable of course.

Maisie then 'whipped' him gently on the backside with a sturdy but dull cane, while Lily crouched on the other side explaining her part in the proceeding by hand signs.

She mimed milking a cow with great earnestness, while both the young men were near overcome with the giggles.

Maisie smiled grimly. She could have told them a few tales of deep-desired and blood curdling flagellant activity that would have wiped the smiles from their faces.

Mostly inflicted upon those who inflicted their will upon others, rather like pirate captains walking their own plank.

And she took them right to the edge.

It was the best job Maisie had ever had in her life.

Having led the young men on a guided tour of whips, spikes, and cruel implements of torture that lined the walls both girls felt more like museum curators.

There was a moment of some discomfort at the end as in — *well what shall we do now?*

Lily instinctively leant back her head till it rested on Maisie's swelling bosom — lifted for the purposes of the profession by a corseted costume that combined domination with jagged gratification.

The jutting mother of night and pain.

One of the young men bowed his own head in response to Lily's movement and let it come to rest upon his friend's shoulder.

Both couples stood there.

Entwined.

Innocence personified.

It may be found in the strangest currency.

However there are two sides to the coin.

Back to the higher reaches.

At the end of the evening Jean Brash, having bid a chaste enough farewell to her solemn owl plus a more formal goodbye to the Worshipful Body, left the exhausted magpies and detritus of the night for Hannah Semple to knock into shape, then slipped into her boudoir and closed the door.

She took a deep breath to control the giddy whirling in her head and smiled a little foolishly.

Then the Mistress of the Just Land frowned.

A draught of damp breeze. She could have

sworn she'd closed that window.

Ah well. A wee bit of fresh air wouldn't kill her.

She threw clothes aside carelessly, till she reached a very fashionable soft satin corselet, then crossed the room to don her peignoir.

Fancy name for a skimpy auld scrap o' silk, according to Hannah Semple, but Jean loved the feeling of the material as it caressed her bare skin.

However, ruffles were no protection when the cane whipped into the side of her neck.

From behind the curtains where he had waited for some hours in the dimly lit room, marking the time with sweet imaginings, the slight figure had emerged and struck from behind like a snake.

The pain paralysed her as if the whole body had frozen in shock, and then a precise kick, delivered with the toe-end of a polished boot, smacked into the back of her knee and sent her tumbling onto the thick carpet.

Jean's mouth opened and closed but no sound emerged.

She lay on her front like a stricken animal in the slaughterhouse, hit with a bolt between the eyes.

In the semi-dark, oil lamp burning low, the killer's white-painted face hung in the gloom like a ghost. The pale-grey figure turned her over with one casual foot to expose her body for punishment.

It was silk clad.

The body.

As a whore's should be.

Now where to commence?

Ah, yes. He took a scrap of paper from his pocket, smoothed it out and then dropped it onto the creamy quilt of the bed.

Later.

In her mouth, it would find a home.

Jean's eyes could hardly focus. She saw above a shimmering, silver figure, the face a blur of white. A shoe trod on her face, turning it to the side. Her neck was bared for the next blow.

She lay on the carpet just beside her bed, and underneath the frame she could see something glinting in the dark, just behind where the edges of the quilt touched the floor.

A small, empty cut-glass scent bottle with a silver top that must have been knocked under by a careless hand and now was her only hope of salvation.

A hand grabbed the collar of her peignoir and ripped it from her body.

The naked whore.

Jean gathered all her strength and reached out her fingers to grasp the heavy little bottle. Through half open lids she could see the silver cane rise into the air.

She threw the bottle with every ounce of power in that arm. Not at the figure. But at the window to the side.

The pane shattered as the bottle smashed through it, falling into the garden.

After a long moment the silence was broken by a voice calling in alarm from below.

The killer moved swiftly to the window and,

using the curtain as cover, glanced beneath.

Two women, one large, one small. For a moment they gazed up, then together dashed towards the garden door back into the house.

Not much time but at least it left his way of escape free.

Voices approaching up the stairs. A gaggle of females, he could kill them all — but perhaps not.

Just time for one strike.

It might be enough.

He crossed back to the recumbent body that was by now huddled on its side, pulled it so that the front was open to a lethal blow, took careful sighting —

The noise was nearer.

Kill the whore.

Hammer down!

37

Now I saw in my dream, that [...] they drew nigh to a very miry Slough that was in the midst of the plain; and they, being heedless, did both fall suddenly into the bog; the name of the Slough was Despond.

John Bunyan, *The Pilgrim's Progress*

The cat lapped carefully at a saucer of weak coffee, one ear aye cocked for danger.

McLevy had named the beast Bathsheba, since she often bathed and groomed herself on the wet roofs in the manner of that biblical temptress.

Now and again, he would see her from the window padding on the damp slates, sliding between chimney breasts and then launching into a sudden swoop, which signalled the demise of something smaller of frame and slower on the uptake.

For the moment she was content to lap, while the coffee provider scratched on a page inside a large, red ledger.

The exploits at the rammy had provided the inspector with some much needed release, and cramming the dishevelled, dispirited, bruised remnants of the Scarlets and Whites into the holding cells also had its compensations but now — at the end of the day — he was left with himself.

That is if you didn't count the cat.

They both had whiskers. That much might be shared.

Diary of James McLevy.
12th May, 1887.

Shakespeare wrote, 'The whirligig of time brings in his revenges,' and by God he wasnae far wrong.

I seem no further on in both cases.

Every moment I turn around something else smacks me in the face.

I feel like one of these matchstick boats wee boys sail in the gutter. Borne on by a torrent of dirty water till the vessel meets its nemesis by some open drain.

A dismal prospect.

And I have a foreboding there's more to come.

Furthermore, I am haunted —

And there he stopped.

How could he write he was haunted by a pair of eyes?

That was daft.

And yet true.

It was all right when he was in motion, but as soon as he stopped, this feeling of dreadful unease — as if a hunger had been aggravated that would never be satisfied — took possession of his solar plexus and dallied with the nerve ends. All to do with seeing the damned woman's face where there should have been a man's!

When her hair had fallen down over those red lips and dark eyes it had stuck a knife right into his guts.

A guilty twist.

And the more he saw her, the worse it got.

Whit was it Jean said?

Love is the very devil.

She wasnae far wrong either.

When would this sorcery leave him?

He let out a long growl of anguish that startled the cat into flattening its ears and yowling low in response.

For a moment they stared at each other, then Bathsheba jumped up and exited huffily by the window.

Good. One less female.

Back to the scratching.

Try to find a wee bit of dignity. Somewhere.

I return to Edgar Allan Poe. 'The Tell-Tale Heart'.

Never mind the victim in the story.

Never mind my own fallible organ of flesh.

And emotion.

Whit else is there beneath the floorboards?

Two murders.

What connects them?

Stevenson, it has tae be.

The bugger's lying under there.

By hook or by crook.

McLevy called a halt there to close the ledger.

Not only that, the man knows it.

McLevy could see it in his eyes.

Not knowing in a factual concrete sense but in a way with which the inspector himself found resonance, in the murky depths of intuition, where the monsters lie.

They cough up their secrets like a black toad.

And yet was he being unfair to lay it upon the writer? Do they not inherit the blame when folk look at them and bitterly resent their connection to the darkness?

Not unlike McLevy himself had suffered.

When a child, an odd child with a secret world in his slate-grey eyes, bigger boys had mercilessly chased him down and left him in a misshapen and bloody heap.

So be it.

The past aye comes back tae torment.

Out of the mist.

But he'd be waiting.

By hook or by crook.

38

I played with fire, did counsel spurn,
But never thought that fire would burn.
Or that a soul could ake.
> H. Vaughan, *Silex Scintillans*

Hannah Semple looked into the scorched, furious eyes of James McLevy and sighed, a tendril of hair hanging lank on her forehead.

She had not slept a wink all night, endured a morning fraught with anxiety and guilt — now she had the majesty of the law with which to contend.

They were standing in the kitchen of the Just Land; she had hauled him in there as soon as he came bursting in the back garden door, before he started knocking lumps out of the solemn-faced doctors milling in the hall.

For some reason the kitchen stove had been lit and the place was boiling — Hannah felt the sweat running down her oxters, but the inspector was like an ice-man.

Save for the eyes. And the burning fury.

And the Keeper of the Keys was struggling with hellish remorse, because she had lingered the night previous, joshing with Mally Duncan the auld fiddler at the front door before sending him packing out into the street, well paid and well provided with good whisky.

If she had gone about her lawful business, she

might have heard something above, been quicker on the scene, saved the mistress a fearsome beating — all this because she stood on the step with a toothless auld bugger to relive the past.

Now it was a bitter present.

'How is your mistress?'

'The doctors say, no' too good.'

'Very medical.'

'She needs rest.'

'I have to question.'

Hannah made no answer — whit fur did the man no' admit he was worried tae hell about the one person still alive who might care for his miserable soul?

Mulholland slipped in to report his findings, having judged it apposite to leave his inspector a moment private with Hannah and incidentally examine the lie of the land.

'Easy to reach the window,' he said. 'A rain pipe up the side and there's a big thick vine as well.'

'Did ye climb it?'

'I did. The curtains are drawn but — you can see where he forced the window. Light frame. Easy meat.'

McLevy nodded and turned unfriendly eyes back to Hannah as if he blamed her for all that had befallen.

Or was it a dark figure in her own mind pointing the long finger?

'Tell me the story,' McLevy said.

Hannah took a breath — as the images flashed through her head, she looked like the old crone in the fairy tale who has bad news for the hero.

'Thank God Lily and Maisie were out in the

garden last thing tae feed the peacocks. Jean's window crashed through, a bottle landit at their feet. A wee perfume glass.'

McLevy did not respond. Mulholland removed his helmet in the heat and filled the gap.

'Not a usual occurrence?'

'By God, no. They came in howlin' blue murder, we ran up the stairs, I had my razor, in the door and she was — she was — the mistress was a terrible sight.'

The old woman caught her breath as the picture of Jean's crumpled body imprinted itself once more.

McLevy's face was like stone.

'The killer? What about the killer?'

'Jumped out the window jist afore we came in. A high distance up. I hoped the swine would break his neck but no — across the wet grass, shinned up the wall lik' a monkey.'

'Check for footprints. Soft earth below that wall.'

Mulholland nodded assent to the terse instructions.

'The killer. Did ye catch a look? Would you know him again?'

Hannah shook her head. The constable had never seen her look so anguished and forlorn.

'A pale coat. A stick. He turned top o' the wall and waved it goodbye. I'll swear the bastard was smiling!'

'The face?'

'White. Painted white. I couldnae make out a thing.'

She added this to the list of failure — guilt

attracts such dark thoughts.

As the heat rose, the inspector finally removed his low-brimmed bowler.

'I'll need tae see her.'

'She's no' supposed tae talk much.'

'I'll look in anyway.'

'No' much tae see. A' bandaged up.'

'Nevertheless. A witness.'

'Is that all you've got to say?'

'A *material* witness.'

Hannah stuck her face pugnaciously into the inspector's, all remorse forgotten, glad of the chance to let rip, and who is to say that McLevy in his perverse way was not offering her the chance?

This thought occurred to Mulholland as Hannah accepted what was in no way an olive branch.

'Ye're a miserable swine, McLevy, and for two pins I'd roast ye in this kitchen like a hog on hellfire, but — '

A memory of Jean's last whispered command echoed in her mind.

You will admit one person and one person only.

'For some reason, she wants to see you. God knows why. A mystery tae me. I'd rather have the pox onyday.'

Silence, then McLevy walked out of the door, closing it quietly behind.

Silence.

'Oh here,' Hannah delved into her pockets and passed a note to Mulholland. 'I was supposed tae gie this tae Angus to hand in at the station this very morning.'

'Before all hell broke loose, eh?'

'Uhuh. It's tae McLevy but you might as well open it. Ye're one and the same.'

The constable was not quite sure how to take this, but slipped open the note and read it in any case.

The contents had some interest regarding Carnegie, but nothing immediate to the matter in hand.

The matter in hand cut through everything.

'If you can show me,' remarked Mulholland, 'where the killer scaled the wall?'

'Near enough,' replied Hannah. 'I'll get my heavy boots.'

She departed also, and Mulholland was left alone in the kitchen, with the heat rising.

39

Ah, none but I discerned her looks,
When in the throng she passed me by,
For love is like a ghost, and brooks,
Only the chosen seer's eye.

Coventry Patmore,
The Angel in the House

The door creaked open and Jean opened one bleary eye. She had a large, prescribed amount of laudanum swirling around in her system; a powerful dosage that distanced pain, though one side effect was confused imaginings.

Was this a hairy animal taking refuge in her bedroom?

Lie still. Hope for the best.

McLevy could see her red hair spread out on the pillow. The face seemed relatively untouched, but when he moved a little closer the inspector could see in the dimness, the curtains drawn and just one oil lamp emanating, white bandages swathed down the left-hand side of her neck

From the two corpses witnessed, he could imagine the livid welt on that milk and honey skin.

What other wounds had she suffered?

An irrational shaft of trespass stabbed him. He might have been on hand but no — there he was with another woman in his heart.

Like a leech, guilt will attach to any movement of the blood.

Jean opened the other eye and attained some purchase on the wavering image beside her bed.

'Is that you, James?' she whispered in a broken, harsh croak. 'I thought it was a hairy beast.'

'Not far wrong,' he muttered.

She signalled at a jug of water to the side and he hastened to pour from it into a tumbler and hold it to her lips.

Jean sipped and groaned as the water trickled down her throat, then lay back on the pillow.

McLevy replaced the tumbler and stood indecisively, before remembering he was an investigating officer.

'How many times did he strike you?'

'Twice. Lucky, eh?'

'Ye don't look lucky.'

She laughed hoarsely, then coughed up a spasm of pain that had him shifting helplessly from foot to foot.

'No jokes, James,' she murmured. 'Pain and pleasure. They don't mix this day.'

'Wisnae a joke. Jist . . . observation.'

She said nothing and he glanced longingly at the jug of water.

'Ye mind if I have a wee sook? That kitchen was like an inferno.'

She closed her eyes in what McLevy took for assent and he saw that there was only the one tumbler. Of course he could slug it straight from the jug, but was that not lacking in sickroom etiquette?

So he refilled the glass and slurped it back noisily in some confusion, while she kept her eyes shut and tried not to register the awful noise.

Finally, when he was done, he replaced the tumbler, wiped the rim clean with a hankie, and then reached out a tentative finger towards the bandages at her throat.

'Are they not too tight?'

'They're fine.'

McLevy moved restlessly to the window and checked where it had been forced. Mulholland was right. Easy meat.

'Ye should have better safeguard.'

'Not many visitors. That entry.'

'So he hid behind the curtains. Out he stepped. Made his move, eh? Out of the blue.'

Jean nodded, eyes still closed.

'Did ye not think to keek in case? Aye a good idea tae keek behind curtains.'

A foolish statement that deserved no response.

He twitched back the hanging to see Mulholland and Hannah by the garden wall. The constable clambered up and dropped over the other side, while Hannah looked back and scowled when she saw McLevy's face at the window.

One of the peacocks approached her and she scuffed her boot to send the bird scuttling back to its fellows, making a detour round the boy Cupid, who seemed short of things to do at this moment.

McLevy returned to the bedside. With her eyes closed, he could look his fill at the wraithlike figure, and he experienced a weird lump in his throat, as some unexpected emotion welled up like a blister.

Was it all his fault?

Somehow.

Feelings creep up on men and then jump out of the shadows like an assassin.

'The second blow — where?'

Her eyes snapped open to find his close scrutiny.

'Are you gawking at me?'

'Whit the hell else am I supposed to do — *where* did he strike?'

She licked dry lips and he quickly pulled a handkerchief from his inside pocket, dipped it in the jug, then dabbed it across her mouth.

'It's clean this morning,' he announced. 'The hankie.'

Jean smiled wanly for a moment, then her face changed as she relived the last blow.

'He turned me over. To hit me down the front. I saw the cane jump. Silver. Turned away. Got it in the back.'

Salve and laudanum had numbed the agony, but she still felt it burning down her spine.

'The doctors said — if he'd hit me. Front. It would have been a whole lot worse. Bad enough.'

'Did he . . . touch you at all?'

A shaft of dark humour entered her eyes, pupils inflamed with the ordeal.

'Ye mean — privately?'

'Uhuh.'

'He ripped my gown. Left me naked. But that was just — for the blow.'

She began coughing again, shuddering as her body registered the memory of that cruel invasion; he poured more water and offered up the tumbler but she shook her head.

James McLevy, nursemaid. Didnae fit somehow.

The hairy beast spoke through a thick moustache.

'Then you must have seen him, eh?'

'What?'

'His face. You saw his face.'

'Did I?'

'If ye saw the cane, ye saw the face!'

Whatever thrawn compassion had been in his eyes was replaced by a look of fierce intent.

Of course it might be to avenge her, but more likely it was just a policeman on the trail.

And now he had a live victim.

For some reason her eyes brimmed up, so she closed them again. Tears get you nowhere.

'I saw little. Face — white. A phantom. Never still. Only the eyes. Like the devil.'

'Devil — how?'

'Hate. Nothing but hate.'

The inspector was beginning to wonder if the man had some sort of refracting shield that blighted others' vision.

'If ye saw him again — would ye know that face?'

'Not a hope.'

'Even a wee bit?'

'Not a hope.'

A flat statement.

Jean lay there with a curious sense of grim satisfaction. Bugger him. Hardly an ounce of sympathy did the man show, and anyway, it was the truth.

329

The killer's face swam before her, melting like jelly.

Whereas McLevy's was only too ugly and sticking out a mile. Thank God it was moving back, out of sight.

He looked round the boudoir; it was all very feminine.

Perfumed.

What must it be like to live in perfume?

The stink of death followed him like a black dog.

'Why?'

A quiet lethal question, unlike the rest.

'Why whit?'

'Why did he attack you, Jeannie — out of the blue? What had you done to provoke his wrath?'

That was what she hated about the man, these changes! And whit did he look like? An ill-farrant Toby Jug or was that the laudanum talking?

For the inspector was right.

It was also the thought that had plagued her. Every time her body ached, every time she saw the silver cane above, the swimming, swirling vision of that melting face, eyes slanty with evil intent — why?

Why?

Even killers have their reasons.

She pointed to a small drawer in the bedside cabinet, where the jug was standing on a copper tray.

McLevy opened it to find a scrap of paper.

'He left it behind. Keepsake maybe.'

A page from the bible, again underlined with a score of the nail.

Whoso loveth wisdom rejoiceth his father: but he that keepeth company with harlots spendeth his substance.

The inspector's mind did not exactly leap to a conclusion, more gathered it in like part of a harvest.

'When you rendezvoused with Stevenson, was it a public place?'

'In the garden. The gazebo. Like yourself. Gentlemen callers.'

'Open to all eyes, then?'

'If you keek through the gates.'

'Or hide across the street?'

Was Robert Louis the key? Whit kind of maniac would kill you for having coffee wi' somebody?

Pain jagged into her thoughts as the laudanum began to lose effect — she'd need another dose, but damned if she'd do it in front of McLevy.

'When you leave. Send Hannah up.'

He seemed lost in deep thought and provided no kind of answer.

It annoyed her for some reason, like the memory of their last meeting — the braw gallant, but not for her.

'And for God's sake get rid of that moustache. It's an affright tae one and all.'

She almost giggled, then winced as the pain flamed her neck and back.

Again he made no answer, but reached out to her dressing-table mirror, where she had jammed a small crumpled photograph into one of the ornate fixings.

'Where did you find this?'

'Night we shot the students. It cheers me up.'

He looked at the image of a military man with his fragile son and law-abiding wife.

'Mind if I take such?'

'Is it a clue?'

'Not material, I doubt.'

She waved her hand wearily.

'Please go now.'

He moved to the door then, instead of opening the damned thing, spoke to the wooden panels.

Whit the hell was the point of talking tae a door?

In such solemn tones?

'I swear to you, Jean Brash, that I will find this man and bring him to justice. I have no family, I have no kin; I have nothing except the law and I will bring it to bear.'

Then he was out the room.

In the silence, his words echoed in her mind.

I have no family, I have no kin.

Liquid welled up once more.

Though as she knew to the bone — tears get you nowhere.

And love is the very devil.

40

Do wrong once, and you'll never hear the
end of it.
Seventeenth-century proverb

Robert Louis lay under the covers and shivered.
This very morning, the funeral morning, as the
house stirred and every floorboard creaked with
intent to inter, the ague had struck like a
hammer blow.

One moment he had been half-listening to the
scurry of various bodies as they sped through the
house with a perfect entombment in mind — fingers twitching idly at a black but rather limp bow
tie — and the next he had been jack-knifed
towards the nearest privy, where he vomited copi-
ously and then had to switch like lightning as the
other orifice began to expel with the same velocity.

Stevenson had called faintly for a bucket, lest
both might join forces to leave him in perilous
mid-stream. There ensued an acerbic, more than
ridiculous conversation with Fanny, conducted
through the privy door.

His wife, not to put too fine a point on it, had
deep suspicion that her beloved yet slippery
husband was evading his filial responsibilities,
but the sounds of what might have been a swamp
emptying, with attendant odours, finally persuaded her that even his chameleon ability had
limits.

Stevenson had then spent an eternity of evacuation before tottering to his bed, a now anxious Fanny behind, an arm on Lloyd's strong young shoulder, and had not budged an inch since.

Was it the oysters from last night? He and Lloyd had consumed a dozen each, but the young man, admittedly the possessor of a cast-iron stomach, showed no sign of galvanic upheaval.

Or was some virulent airborne messenger sent by one of his Brownies who sensed his deep ambivalence, deeper as the event loomed, with regard to witnessing his father's coffin being lowered into the earth, himself holding one of the ropes, with the eyes of the world upon him and a maelstrom of grief and anger in his breast?

He had sought to provide an elaborate display of mourning — a hundred invited guests, carriages galore — but it was only an outward show.

For two days his father had gazed at him and seen nothing, and for two days Stevenson had done the same.

What do we see when we regard death in waiting?

And what do we remember, as the child looks up and the father looks down?

All those writhing thoughts and agonised doubts had been blown away to the four winds.

He was now beset with bucket and basin, arranged round his bed like sentinels. Mercifully, the writer had expurgated his meagre breakfast, plus whatever remnants of food may have resided in his seething innards from the previous day, so all that was now left was what in common parlance was termed *the dry boak*. This consisted of retching to no great purpose, the stomach heaving with nothing to show for it.

Some unkind Calvinist critics might describe authorship as such activity; those who root themselves in fundamental righteousness have their noses perpetually out of joint.

The precipitous defecation had also ceased, though Robert Louis had discovered to his cost that the slightest sip of water rushed through his system like a mighty flood.

A doctor had been summoned and prescribed a calming potion, but no sooner swallowed then it was spewed out like the Whale did Jonah, a tin bucket taking the place of biblical dry land, and had Stevenson the strength he would have emptied it over the damned quack.

Meanwhile life went on for the dead.

Servants were already ferrying out vast amounts of funeral meats and whisky for the eventual return of the sorrowful mourners. The house not being large enough, the wake was to be held in a nearby civic hall where sherry, port wine and ale linked up with John Barleycorn, and the tables were loaded to the brim with cold meats, pickles, cheese, hefty loaves of bread, cakes of all denomination, and funeral biscuits baked by the widow's own hand. All of this based on the premise that there's nothing like the filling of a grave to give folk a healthy appetite.

This cornucopia for the sad at heart was

guarded by beady-eyed butlers, some hired, some borrowed from neighbours, but all watchful that the help — also in the main hired — did not untimely reap the harvest of sorrow.

Luckily, given his internal tribulation, Stevenson saw nothing of this, but he could hear horses neighing, reins jingling, and the sound drove him deeper under the covers.

> *Full fathom five thy father lies;*
> *Of his bones are coral made:*
> *Those are pearls that were his eyes*

The Watcher across the street observed the principal funeral carriage, four black horses tossing their heads, the coffin behind glass, a solid burnished casket, brass gleaming in the pale sunlight, for the weather had relented somewhat upon this momentous day.

Other carriages ranged behind all the way down Heriot Row stretching back to Abercrombie Place, horses stamping their hooves, whinnying and whickering, steam rising from their flanks, for it was a good day to raise a gallop.

Sadly they were all headed for the New Calton Burying Ground, where galloping was not the norm.

None of this interested the Watcher.

He had eyes only for the carriage directly behind the funeral coach.

A murmur from some spectators — the assemblage had attracted a curious crowd — signalled figures emerging from number 17.

Bob Stevenson, a tall elegant gentleman, cousin of Robert, took the lead with the widow Margaret, wife of the departed Thomas, veiled from vulgar scrutiny, holding firmly to his manly arm.

Another couple followed.

Fanny Osbourne, striking features obscured by the swaddling clothes of mourning, had her arm equally firmly hooked into the elbow crook of a tall, thin fellow with a lean and hungry face.

But it was not *him*!

Lloyd Osbourne, the woman's son. A usurper. Imposter.

And not *him*!

The carriage was entered, both men ensuring the delicate sex to be safely ensconced before Lloyd followed suit; then Bob Stevenson walked to the funeral carriage and gravely — as befitted the privileged status of Chief Mourner — spoke quietly to the coachman.

The vehicle jolted into motion, then cousin Bob swung lithely into the family coach with undeniable elegance, and off went the procession.

Minus the one who must be found.

The Watcher also moved, for he had business to pursue and duties to observe, but would return with time to spare.

He had no plan as such but he could feel the powers gathering within.

Fate.

Destiny.

Finally in hand.

Like a silver cane.

41

Out of the mouths of very babes and sucklings hast thou ordained strength, because of thine enemies.

The Bible, *Psalms*

Mulholland entered the station to find bedlam, as various self-important citizens gathered round the ominously still figure of Lieutenant Roach. The more sensible fathers, who had decided their sons deserved what they got and hell mend them, were no doubt occupied with affairs of commerce, but there were enough paternal petitioners, with various lawyers at hand, to keep the pot boiling.

The new arrival towered over the swarming crowd, caught Roach's gaze from the back, and was gratified to see that there was a certain flinty obduracy to his superior that did not bode well for the hectoring horde, had they but the wit to realise it.

Mulholland skirted the edges and slid in behind his beleaguered commander, signalling up one of the constables, Ewan Sinclair, a hefty specimen who sported the mid-burgeoning of a prize keeker from the student rammy.

Folk high, low, lawful or otherwise often took Mulholland for a soft mark, due to smooth skin and blue eyes, but these latter were like chips of ice as he trained them on the nearest

338

combatants. With the bruised but hulking figure of Sinclair looming up on the other side, the two caused more than a little unease, as if arrest were merely waiting in the wings.

When policemen gather, no-one stands safe.

A silence fell, or rather there was a cessation of clamour and Roach took full advantage. Mind you, to be truthful, though it was useful to have men at each arm, he would not in fact have been disquieted to face the yammering host on his own, for he had awoken that morning and announced to his wife — *enough is enough!*

Mistress Roach lay unsure whether this referred to their marriage, the opera, or life in general. She had little chance to question her husband further, because he levered himself out of bed, donned slippers, struggled into a far from flamboyant dressing gown, then stalked off to the dining room where two cold, hard boiled eggs and a small mound of salt awaited the pleasure of his company.

The memory of those eggs, smoothly composed behind the shell, now sustained him.

He took a deep breath.

Robert Roach was about to make a speech of sorts.

'Your offspring,' he began crisply, 'have broken the peace and assaulted my officers. If by chance you harbour any doubts, please look around you.'

Indeed throughout the station many a plastered eyebrow, bandaged jaw, and discoloured cheekbone was manifest, in addition to the afore-mentioned bruised keeker.

'The injuries caused have not so far threatened life, though who knows what complications may ensue, but at least two of my men have had to be dispatched to the infirmary.'

Like so much in life, factually accurate yet not *quite* true.

Ballantyne had indeed been sent to the nearest hospital, but that was because his mother worked there as head nurse, and since the station cupboard had run short of supplies the constable had been instructed to scrounge what he could in the way of salves, plasters and bandages.

Sinclair, despite being a Highlander with little sense of urban direction, had been posted along to make sure the other did not get lost in the dark.

They had returned laden with contraband, and while Ballantyne basked in the unaccustomed acclaim, the young constable was somewhat reserved, as if something was on his mind.

Of course none of these supplies was passed through to the equally bruised and battered students in the cells.

The force looks after its own.

Only natural.

'In view of the severity of physical damage incurred by my officers in pursuance of their duty,' Roach continued, 'I have no option but to press charges, and I will do so without fear or favour!'

In fact there was no pretext to this attitude; the lieutenant had seethed through the whole night and opened his eyes to a fury cold as the boiled eggs.

This was a violent affray, lives could have been lost, especially those of his own foot-soldiers, and it would be a mistake to think that the rigid cast of his normal demeanour encased a heart of pure stone.

These were *his* men.

Not the cream of the crop perhaps, but they had laid their bodies on the line for justice.

Spoiled brats notwithstanding.

One of the loudest supplicants for these whippersnappers, a man who shared the same Lodge as the lieutenant and mistakenly presumed this to give him some edge, being of a higher Masonic rank than Roach, stuck his florid countenance to the fore, with what he took to be a valid and unanswerable complaint.

His business was tobacco — the more yellow smoke the populace drew into their lungs, the richer he waxed.

'I spoke with my son — he has been bitten by fleas all night!'

'Let us hope the fleas survive,' said Roach dryly.

'How dare you allow this to happen?'

'I might ask you the same question,' was the unyielding response.

'If you break the law, sir,' remarked Mulholland, 'you take the consequence. All or nothing.'

The demanding throng suddenly became aware of an ominous stillness, not only from the three facing. When they glanced around the other constables were ranged throughout the station, obviously in attention, and, to a man, facing directly towards the contending parties.

It is always wise to look behind — it may be only a shadow, but something will always be on your trail.

Roach pitched his voice a little louder, aware of a wider audience.

'I will not have my men assaulted by a rabble who fondly imagine themselves to be privileged above justice and I will press charges — as previously stated and at the risk of repeating myself — without fear or favour!'

Then a smile crossed his face for the first time.

Wintry, but a smile.

'Furthermore it is my pleasure to inform you that this will be heard in court within the next few days, and that the presiding official will be Sheriff Hunter.'

An indrawn breath from the lawyers present.

Hunter was a nuggety little man, fierce in the sentence, who would snap a legal head from its shoulders, who was no lover of Masonic ritual; not a man who might view student revels as a gay whirl.

A bushy-eyebrowed, granite nemesis.

'If you wish your clients or progeny released on surety of bail, Sergeant Murdoch will be attending at the desk with relevant forms. I will then decide each case on its intrinsic merit.'

Now the smile was more that of a crocodile.

'It will be a long day, gentlemen. Goodbye.'

As the disconsolate pack headed towards the desk where Murdoch, whose blood coursed at a speed that would put a sloth to shame, waited, Roach dismissed Sinclair with a nod of thanks and addressed himself to Mulholland.

'And where is McLevy, if I may be so bold?'

'The inspector dispatched me post-haste to bring you the latest developments, sir.'

'You mean he's up to something he doesn't want me to know about or you to witness?'

'That would be about the fist of it.'

The constable then, as directed, brought Roach up to date with what had been gleaned from the Just Land. Sadly not a great deal, in that he had been unable to find any footmarks, and a thorough examination on both sides of the garden wall had produced nothing either.

The killer had come and gone, leaving not a trace behind.

Save on the body of Jean Brash.

'You begin to wonder if the man is somehow anointed with the devil's luck,' muttered Roach.

'Had crossed my mind.'

'But no. He is of this earth and we will find him.'

'I hope so,' Mulholland replied, the memory of his inspector's grim figure disappearing into the pale light of a treacherous May sun with hardly a word of farewell clear in his mind.

'I take it the Mistress of the Just Land will survive?'

'Not by too much. It was a vile attack.'

The lieutenant shook his head in frustration.

'Could she identify the man?'

'No. Neither from the past, in the present, nor might she recognise him in the future.'

'She could supply no reason for the assault?'

'According to the inspector, not a one.'

Roach almost stamped his feet in temper, such

was the irritation, for he had something rustling in his inside pocket like a canker on the skin.

And his small victory was over.

'Surely there must be some motive that links these three crimes?'

'That's what I keep telling myself.'

Mulholland's face gave nothing away, but he had a notion that McLevy was brooding to some effect.

Or was the constable just grasping at straws?

Like his inspector.

The lieutenant cast a bleak glance over the station.

'When word of this latest depredation gets out on the streets, there will be no place to hide.'

He then fished something out of his jacket pocket.

'Here — just to cheer you up.'

It was a folded copy of the *Leith Herald*, morning edition, with yet another flaming accusation.

WHERE IS THE KILLER? HE LAUGHS AT THE POLICE!

Their visit to Carnegie had not obviously discouraged the man from flaunting his banner headlines.

As Mulholland read on, Roach tapped a long bony finger to indicate a worrying sub-heading.

Rumours of another killing. What is being concealed?

'I hope to God McLevy can pull a rabbit out the hat,' muttered Roach. 'We are running out of time.'

The lieutenant cast an eye over the crowd at

the desk, which had not diminished one jot, as Murdoch licked his thumb and laboriously separated one sheet from another.

'A minor triumph,' he said soberly. 'Compared to what is coming. You can keep the paper.'

Roach then disappeared into his room, leaving Mulholland a little bereft.

The constable had been, in truth, taken aback at McLevy's sudden departure, though it was certainly not the first time his inspector had pursued his own ends.

But now, for the life of him, Mulholland could not think quite where to direct his own steps.

All the other constables had returned to their various tasks save Ballantyne, who was gazing his way with a strange expression on his face.

Mulholland glanced once more at the paper; it did not make pretty reading, so he hurled it into the nearest wastepaper-basket and, for want of something better to do, stalked over to the constable's desk.

For a change there were no insects, dead or otherwise, on the surface as the young man averted his eyes, birth-mark pulsing — a sure sign of emotional upheaval.

'Is something bothering you, Ballantyne?'

The constable nodded.

'McWhirter,' he replied.

'You'll have to help me here,' muttered Mulholland, telling himself for the umpteenth time he was dealing with a strange labyrinth of a mind, and that howling abuse or wrenching the boy up by the scruff of the neck would not help matters.

'My mammy told me. Last night. In confidence.'

'Go on.'

'An auld woman. Wi' bellythraw. McWhirter.'

'Well enough named,' said Mulholland. 'I know you'll get there eventually, Ballantyne, but if you wouldn't mind while the Queen still reigns.'

'Wind mostly,' was the response. 'An auld woman. Frae the church. St Stephens'.'

A bell of sorts rang in Mulholland's mind. There were two old biddies who had entered the church along with the minister's wife, and was not one of them named McWhirter?

They had been questioned right enough, but though both McLevy and he had the impression the dead woman was not universally popular, lips were locked tight and holy praise won the day.

'She knew Agnes Carnegie,' Ballantyne said, as if confirming the other's line of thought. 'And Agnes tellt the auld woman something about her son. No' very nice.'

'Sadly,' rejoined Mulholland, wondering if he should go and lie down somewhere, 'Sim Carnegie has an alibi for the murder night.'

'It's been on her conscience. She should have told ye. But dirty linen. When she saw me last night, wi' my uniform and my mammy told her . . .'

Here Ballantyne looked abashed.

'Told her what?'

'That I was . . . a son tae . . . stick by his mother. The auld woman tellt her. And my

346

mammy tellt me. In confidence.'

'And you're worried about breaking that confidence. The patient to the nurse, the nurse to her son?'

'A wee bit.'

Finally they had reached the goal, and Mulholland had a reasoned response to the constable's misgivings.

'Nothing is private where the law is concerned, Ballantyne. Now spit it out!'

And the constable did.

Some ten minutes later, when Roach opened his office door to see the continuing stasis at Murdoch's desk, he noted the absence of these two men.

Without so much as a by-your-leave.

And McLevy gone as well.

He tried to rid himself of the feeling of being a sinking ship, with rats streaming off in all directions.

He closed the door again and looked at Victoria on the wall.

Only the Queen holds true.

Everything else is fabrication.

42

Stop and consider! life is but a day;
A fragile dew-drop on its perilous way.
>   Keats, 'Sleep and Poetry'

Another vile dream and Stevenson wrenched out of it basted with perspiration.

His father and he had been astride a log, floating on dark, deep water, paddles to hand.

It seemed to be an underground cavern, with pale clay walls, and the sinuous current bore them onward with little effort on their behalf.

Thomas was at the back, old and frail, but accoutred in his Sunday best, a fierce expression of determination on his face. Louis had only a shirt for covering, dangling legs bare, and he sported a nightcap with some foolish bobble on the end, which obscured his vision as it danced in front.

There was a feeling of menace in the dark waters, and various large, snakelike shapes swam near the surface, now and again breaking surface and disclosing flat, reptilian heads with sickly yellow eyes that seemed not to focus on the paddling pair, as if they were of no interest.

The heads then dipped below again, but the malevolent ripples that spread on the viscous tide showed the length of the creatures.

Stevenson's naked legs were freezing in the flow, but his father seemed unaffected, stout

Sabbath serge repelling all evil machinations.

'You are the lawful son!'

This strong shout from Thomas echoed and bounced off the cavern walls, before disappearing behind as the motion of the water drove them onwards.

The lawful son, the lawful son, the lawful son.

Robert Louis tried to nod his head in acknowledgement, but the nightcap slipped over his eyes and disaster struck.

He had been guiding from the front, but this temporary blindness caused him to steer the log into a treacherous rock, black and slimy, sticking part out of the water like a knife. The log struck with a bone-shaking blow and the jolt skewed the primitive craft sideways so that, agonisingly slowly, Thomas began to slip from the rough bark.

'A lighthouse! See the need!'

As his father howled and pointed, the log now travelling sideways while both scrabbled desperately to hold firm, the writer jerked his head round to see a pure white structure looming out of the darkness ahead.

A beautiful, phallic pharos, so cunningly jointed that the surface seemed unbroken, rising from the waves like an alabaster beacon, like a warning —

These poetic musings were broken by a strangled cry.

Stevenson turned back in time to see his father slide off the rear end of the log and be swallowed up by the icy waters.

Thomas maintained a brave front, no trace of

fear as he called out once more.

'*YOU ARE THE LAWFUL SON!*'

Robert Louis could not move. His legs were clamped round the log, skin frozen to the rind of the dead tree.

His mouth opened and closed, but no sound emerged. He watched horror-struck, while his dauntless father sank below, going down bolt upright, so that the son's last view was that of a valiant right arm which plummeted like Excalibur.

Then the deadly ripples gathered as the serpents feasted and the water boiled.

A few scraps floated to the surface: the fragments of a Sunday suit, a shred of white cotton, gobbets of a striped tie that once denoted the Worshipful Society of Engineers. All wisps of law-abiding material that whirled in the water until they too sank back into mindless oblivion.

And then the log hurtled into the foot of the lighthouse, tipping Stevenson from his rooted base to sprawl, arms outstretched like one crucified, onto the black, smooth steps that led to the entrance of the edifice.

The breath was knocked from his body — he did not dare turn round to see the sullen, slobbering element that was now his father's tomb.

With an angry gesture he snatched the ridiculous nightcap from his head and threw it to the side.

His bare shanks shivered. What a pale, useless worm had been cast to shore.

Then the door of the building opened and a

ray of blinding light shot out in the darkness.

A figure was silhouetted by that light, but Stevenson was mostly dazzled and deprived of vision.

The oscillating shape stretched out a questing hand and the writer screamed.

To come awake.

Sweating like a pig.

The house was eerily silent, all servants departed for the repast-to-be, and Stevenson was grateful enough for such diversion as he struggled into his clothing, having decided it would be better to stagger round the place than lie in bed and risk another trip into the unconscious obliquities of filial remorse.

Guilt.

It never leaves the generations.

Find a way to sever your own shadow and you may kiss the beast goodbye,

What was it the old man had called out?

'*You are the lawful son!*'

What might that mean?

At the frontal lobe of the conscious ego, as it nestles in the pineal gland, the meaning was clear.

But in the depths, where the flat-headed ones slither with their own truth to tell, where the Brownies raise hell and hurl lightning bolts of mischief, another meaning might well present itself.

Damned if he knew.

Damned if he did not.

Time would tell.

Who was the figure?

Life — or death?

And what was it searching out?

Stevenson shrugged on a burgundy velvet jacket, though his feet were encased in rather large, shapeless slippers that had once belonged to the man of the house, borrowed by nature of the sudden infirmity, that flapped side to side to render him a duck waddling to market.

That was, however, better. He had caught sight of himself in a long mirror. Skin and bones but upright.

To celebrate he pulled out a thin cigarette he had rolled just before catastrophe struck, and as he wandered to the window, he lit up, luxuriating in the silence of the house.

And the pure emptiness.

A drag of scented tobacco, though not too deep, just enough to tickle the innards.

And yes — he was still standing. Wavering, but ready for a very small adventure.

Such as staying upright.

Robert Louis smiled at that idea, drew in a deeper drag, coughed just to restore further normality, and gazed from the window at the infidel sunshine that dared to lay a faithless sheen upon Heriot Row.

Where was the rain?

Where was the dark cloud?

The tombstones of New Calton surely would resent being so presented — naked to the light.

But the family vault would shroud his father's coffin, lest the sun stripe a natural pattern through the blossoming trees. A gloomy but righteous cradle.

Just then a covered carriage came into view, with a single horse clip-clopping quietly in the vacant street.

The driver looked up to the window and seemed not at all surprised to see the ghostly apparition staring back.

He waved something in the air. It was a book, quite large, and olive green with fine ribbed cloth.

Robert Louis recognised not only the tome, but a promise made. The coachman was also familiar and equally welcome to the eye, as he smiled an invitation.

Stevenson nodded eagerly and walked away from the window, most carefully down the stairs, along the narrow hall, opened the front door and stepped into the unknown.

In his father's slippers.

43

Something will come of this. I hope it mayen't
be human gore.

Charles Dickens, *Barnaby Rudge*

The story Mrs McWhirter had told Ballantyne's
mother, who had told Ballantyne, who told
Mulholland, was as follows.

The auld woman had some days before come
across Agnes Carnegie sitting in one of the side
vestries of the church, with a satisfied smile upon
her face.

It shamed McWhirter to confess to the nurse
that she did not like the woman, aye sneaking
her fingers into every wee nook and cranny.

Agnes had obviously discovered something
that had given her great pleasure, but she would
not share the secret, content to say that a book
once found, cannot be put aside should sin have
been revealed.

But then, as if the pleasure had spilled into
other hidden crevices, she confided at length to
McWhirter that she no longer believed in the
Christian redemption of her errant son, and
knew that Sim only waited for her to die so that
he could lay his greedy hands on her
hard-earned money.

Sons were not to be trusted.

Agnes had taken precautions that this would
not happen, and her deceitful offspring would

354

get what he deserved.

That very night, however, Agnes herself received, if not what she deserved, then perhaps an enactment of the Scots saying.

Ye can never see whit's comin' roon the corner.

This pithy adage was meant to indicate the unexpected and inexorable working of Fate, though in the Carnegie case what came round the corner was a vicious and violent murder.

Ballantyne's earnest but laborious rendition was attended with mounting impatience by Mulholland, but the young man had the last word, or rather his mother had, or rather auld Mrs McWhirter had, when she repeated the final statement of Agnes.

The young constable delivered the words, sitting at his desk in the station, birth-mark radiating as if to defy contradiction.

The voice of God has warnt me no' tae hesitate or scruple. And I aye listen tae the voice of God. Whit I have done, I have hidden well.

And now Mulholland was back in the grim little lodging of Agnes Carnegie, this time searching with more attention and a fierce resolve.

'Whit are we looking for, exactly?' questioned Ballantyne, who had been brought along for luck.

'Paper. A sheet probably. Folded, I have no doubt. Concealed until she could get it to the lawyer.'

'Lawyer?'

Mulholland did not yet reply directly,

muttering to himself as he took each drawer from the rickety chest, brusquely emptied it of clothing, then turned it over to make certain nothing was taped beneath.

'When the inspector and I first saw this room, we thought it might well have been searched, but for what? And then, though Carnegie has been boasting about his inheritance, I felt in my bones he was making noise to pump up his own balloon. Now I know the reason.'

He moved to a little wooden box where the lock had been slightly skewed and began to leaf through the church papers one by one, shaking each as if some revelation might fall to the floor.

'The reason? A will. If Agnes made a new will and cut the legs from under him — Jean Brash left a note that Sim is in a fathom deep to the moneylenders — Mister Carnegie would have a different headline to write.'

There was one threadbare rug in the middle of the floor, which Mulholland pulled aside and turned over, but nothing was attached to the backing side.

Ballantyne watched. He had never been on an official search before and did not wish to miss a thing.

There was much to observe, as Mulholland painstakingly examined the floorboards uncovered by the rug. None seemed loose, even when levered at by his trusty penknife.

He looked at Ballantyne's solemn face.

'If you were an old woman,' he asked suddenly. 'Where would you hide something?'

The young constable gave this great thought

and, just before Mulholland despaired of hearing an answer this side of Christmas, responded as follows.

'My granny went funny in the head.'

It was no wonder, was the unkind thought.

But Ballantyne had more to relate.

'She hid things. It was aye in a place that meant something to her. That she took tae heart.'

The voice of God has warnt me no' tae hesitate or scruple. And I aye listen tae the voice of God. Whit I have done, I have hidden well.

Mulholland brought these words of Agnes to mind as he looked at the two holy pictures; one of the sorrowful, kind Redeemer, the other of God Almighty casting those unredeemed into hell.

Father and son.

He indicated both to Ballantyne.

'Take your pick.'

The constable creased his eyes in deep thought.

'From whit ye hear, Mistress Carnegie wasnae much in the way of forgiveness.'

God it was then.

Mulholland, with due reverence, removed the Creator of All Things from the wall and turned the picture over, as the younger man came over to join him.

It did not look promising.

The back was dusty, with a brown paper wrapping gnarled and warped by time.

'My granny was dead cunning,' said Ballantyne. 'She'd never leave a new sign. Aye stick things back by spit and detritus. Wait!'

His sharp eyes had detected the merest flicker of movement under the brown paper.

They both waited until the curled edge of one corner lifted infinitesimally and a very small cockroach crawled out into the light.

'It might be an omen,' said Ballantyne. 'Cockroaches are curious creatures. The Egypts swore by them.'

Mulholland once more unsheathed his penknife and carefully scraped the insect to safety, while the young constable nodded approval, hoping he'd found another convert to the cause.

Then the knife was inserted down the edge of the wrapping and gentle pressure applied, causing the whole side to lift back.

Behind it, and also, incidentally, behind the wrathful face of God who guarded the other vantage, was a sheet of carefully folded good quality vellum pepper.

As Mulholland shook it, a few more cockroaches tumbled out to scurry for safer refuge.

Ballantyne whistled.

'Lucky it wasnae beetles. They eat paper. Not out of badness, mind you — jist the mandibles.'

This piece of arthropodal folklore slipped past Mulholland as he carefully opened the paper to read therein.

Little could be gauged from his countenance and the young man, worried it had all been in vain, cast a glance at the merciful face of Jesus.

'We've still got the Son,' he said. 'If all else fails.'

44

A guiltie conscience is a worme that bites and neuer ceaseth. A guiltie conscience is neuer without fear.

Politeuphuia 10

It had been an exhilarating ride, short and circular, that brought them back not far from where they'd started.

Stevenson loved carriages. He loved being safely enclosed, yet with an open window on the world, puffing tobacco smoke that trailed behind like that of a steam train and occasionally waving a lordly hand at pedestrians.

Indeed, as they had sped past the Queen Street Gardens, he had been amused at the sight of a man in some kind of hurry, tripping over the lead of a fashionable lady's dog and sprawling headlong on the pavement.

Accidents will happen.

He had been conducted from a small, hidden entrance at the back door to the catacombs of a place he knew only too well, and deposited, after the door was unlocked, with the utmost courtesy in a cell-like, windowless room that might have served a monk for existence.

He had, thereafter, been seated at a small table where, ceremoniously, the olive green edition was presented.

Stevenson signed his name with a flourish.

During all this, his driver, guide to the underworld, had uttered not a word and Robert Louis had been delighted to join in the silence.

This elaborate healing ritual of mime was to be welcomed after the lethal images of his dream.

The signed book was removed and his guide then moved to some concealed corner shelving to bring back a gold embossed volume, which he laid in front of the writer.

It was large, heavy, the front cover engraved and scrolled with elegant designs, but what immediately caught Stevenson's attention were his initials, elaborately worked into the centre of the piece.

R. L. S.

The silent conductor pulled back a curtain, laid some vestments over his arm, fetched something from the corner, withdrew and exited, closing the door behind him to lock it with a quiet metallic sound.

More silence.

R. L. S.

The writer ran his fingers over the cover to trace the raised letters that depicted his identity; the whole episode had taken on a mysterious, dreamlike quality, but when he glanced at the misshapen slippers at the end of his skinny ankles, reality reasserted itself.

Therefore he opened the book.

And perused with growing amazement.

A collection of press cuttings, writings, excerpts from the earliest days when the young Robert Louis was making his way in the world, hand-written copies of his qualification to the bar, even election to the Speculative Society, each meticulously noted with time and place. And then, as his craft took root, a list of every publication up to the present day. Fascinating in a forensic fashion. Stevenson laid out, stripped of flesh, bones arranged in an orderly structure.

As if the skeleton had meaning.

An obscure resentment began to fester within him — the writer does not necessarily wish himself to be the subject of dissection.

He is the one who looks over the shoulder, like Long John's parrot.

And yet who could resist the care and scholarship that had gone into the labour?

So, turn the page.

Photographs from the papers, drawings, articles as fame slid round him like a serpent, especially when *Doctor Jekyll and Mister Hyde* danced the Paddington Two-step.

All of it seemed so consequential and to some plan compared to the chaos and maelstrom of his life.

How absurd it is to try to impose order upon chaos.

Chaos is natural.

As these and other thoughts flooded his mind, Stevenson was aware of a growing unease.

Was he being manipulated? An unwilling player as he himself, the impatient youthful creator, had once pulled and pushed the paper puppets from Skelt's Juvenile Drama?

Out flashed the cutlass, down went Ben
Dead and rotten there and then.

Dead and rotten. That's the ticket.

He continued to leaf through the Great Book in the monk's cell, only halting progress to light an accompanying cigarette.

The very last page had but one photograph.

A strange and sulky boy gawped out past the camera, his hand resting awkwardly on another's shoulder, but this person had been cut out, so that only the lad remained.

Himself at nine years.

The excised human other, his father Thomas.

'I stole it, I'm afraid.'

First words spoken. An affected drawl.

The guide had returned, the click of the opening lock lost upon Stevenson, rapt in study.

The figure had not yet entered fully, staying in the shadow of the doorway, his voice his presence so far.

'I was in your house. Official business. No-one was watching and I could not resist.'

Yes, now Robert Louis remembered. That image in a small stand-up frame had always rested upon the piano.

Not any more.

His mother would have missed it no doubt, but would have blamed a careless maid.

'Why did you — sunder the photograph?'

'Because the man concerned was not you,'

Silence.

The guide's tone changed.

'If you please — look inside the front cover.

Behind the facing page.'

Stevenson leafed back through the book.

There was a hidden inscription he had missed in his haste to open the beginning pages.

To my rightful father,
Robert Louis Stevenson.
From his lawful son.

The writer looked at the figure who now stepped through the doorway, who had changed out of all recognition.

His dream had tried to warn him.

A Lawful Son.

And the square-built, sandy-haired John Gibbons, admirer of *Treasure Island* and toasted cheese had vanished.

In his place was a slimmer effigy, in a light suit that seemed to shimmer in the candlelight, face painted white, a silver cane twirling in his hand.

The Killer.

45

God is on the side not of the heavy battal-
ions, but of the best shots.

Voltaire, *The Piccini Notebooks*

*The dark night had fallen, but to the dead girl it
made no odds. Her neck was snapped; Rose
Dundas, one pale, bare arm outflung, the mouth
twisted.*

*A young constable knelt beside the body, and
shifted it so that the ashen, pretty face was
caught by a random beam of light.*

*He knew her. He knew the reason for her
death. He knew the man who had killed her and
the man who had caused it to happen.*

*But evidencing this, my friend, would be a
different matter.*

*Gash Mitchell looked at the young policeman
and laughed in his face.*

*'She was a wee whoor, hingin' about in the
wynds, anyone could have kill't her. I have been
wi' my freens, all this day and all this night.'*

*The giant looked round his companions in the
tavern who nodded acquiescence, and leant
forward so that his rancid breath blew like
poison smoke over the figure opposite.*

'We have played cards. I won well.'

His tongue played over thick, rubbery lips.

'And you — have nothing.'

The man laughed like a drain gurgling with

scum from the slaughterhouse.

'Not a scrap o'proof.'

Gash picked up a sturdy piece of wood from some kindling near the tavern fire and snapped it between his blunt, powerful fingers like a twig.

A sharp, savage crack.

That sound echoed in Mulholland's mind as he gazed down at the two surprised faces in the lawyer's office.

Herbert Lawson and Sim Carnegie.

The lawyer of Agnes Carnegie, deceased had been in the throes of reading out the terms of the will deposited with him some years ago to the only surviving relative, who stood to inherit a considerable sum, when the door burst open and two policemen tumbled into the small, arid office.

The tall one, without a word, extended his hand with a sheet of good quality paper, whilst his companion looked around the dry woodwork with some interest.

A fine hidey-hole for eariewigs and the like.

Lawson took the paper and read.

Mulholland gazed bleakly at Sim Carnegie, whose sallow complexion had turned a yellowish, insanitary hue.

Lawson finished his perusal, minutely scrutinised the written name at the bottom of the sheet, and then looked up at Mulholland.

'May I ask where this document was — discovered?'

'In the continuing course of our murder investigation,' came the solemn and smooth reply, 'we took it upon ourselves to once more examine the quarters of Mistress Carnegie. The aforesaid article, as it were, came to light.'

'Behind the Almighty,' Ballantyne piped up.

Lawson decided to let that remark pass and nodded gravely.

'This is without doubt the signature of Mistress Carnegie, witnessed by two churchgoers through indication of address. In fact I know one of them, Donal Darwin, stripping clerk and lay preacher. *Highly* respectable man.'

'Whit's that tae me?'

To Sim's brusque interjection, Lawson traced the date on the sheet with one lizard-like finger, before response.

'I am afraid — your mother has — em — perhaps I might just read an excerpt . . . '

Was there a slight perverse enjoyment that Mister Herbert Lawson might be experiencing?

Such as when poking at a loose tooth with the tongue, enjoying the sensation, unable to leave it alone, realising a weak foundation might suffer incremental damage?

Let well alone. A sore-neglected adage.

The lawyer read aloud, his dry tones in contrast to the sniping condemnation of the written words.

'*The Voice of God has warned me that my son, Simeon Carnegie, wants my money for himself and detests my religiosity, being a man who lacks the smallest scruples of devout worship.*

'*He tries to hide it but his sinful profanity cannot be denied. Like the stink of whisky.*

'*I now change my will to leave all my estate to*

366

the Church of Scotland, in the sure and certain knowledge that the money will be used for holy purpose.

'As for Simeon, I shall look down from heaven and see him in the flames. Burning eternally.

'This in God's name — Agnes Carnegie.'

For a moment there was silence except for a faint clicking that Ballantyne thought might be a deithwatch beetle lurking in some dusty crevice.

'The woman was unhinged!'

'Unhinged or not,' Lawson observed dryly, 'the will is properly constituted and witnessed. I fear, Mister Carnegie, that your visit has been rendered null and void.'

Sim snarled as he found himself under Mulholland's steady gaze.

Bad blood between.

A young magpie had been savagely beaten. Her friend, a girl called Rose Dundas, promised to the police that she would identify the man, the girl's pimp, Gash Mitchell.

The assaulted girl was too terrified, but Rose had courage enough.

Somehow Carnegie had got wind of the story and the next afternoon's edition of the Leith Herald *had a first article by their new reporter.*

It was heavy hinted that a witness was coming forward, and by that night Rose was dead.

And the alibi of Gash Mitchell could not be broken.

Unlike the neck of a splayed corpse.

McLevy had been ill, taken to his bed with fever, so this was Mulholland's case.

Lieutenant Roach had aided as best he could

with the investigation, but eventually they had to admit defeat.

No-one dared speak against Mitchell now.

Mulholland had failed.

Rose Dundas was dead.

And the bitter taste never left.

Carnegie on no account took responsibility for what he had caused, claiming, like Mitchell, that it could have been anyone who killed her. She was, after all, a causey paiker.

A streetwalker.

Hell mend you now, Carnegie.

'This is a dirty spite!'

'This is the truth. Take or leave it.'

A near howl and a calm response, but it was nothing much of a triumph. Undoubtedly the moneylenders owed were the lowest type, and Sim would suffer violence until he somehow scraped up the money.

If he managed it at all.

A brick through the newspaper window would no doubt be one of their first reminders.

With luck he might lose his job and spend a great deal of his life looking over his shoulder.

But Rose Dundas still lay unavenged.

'I have a headline for you,' said Mulholland. 'Just deserts for a dirty dog.'

Carnegie let out an outraged yelp and launched himself at the constable.

For his pains he received one punch straight to the mouth, which rendered him groaning and bloody on the floor.

'I'll get it cleared in no time,' remarked an unperturbed Lawson. 'You'd be surprised what

368

ends up on a lawyer's planking.'

On the way back down the stairs, Ballantyne suddenly stopped as if revelation had struck.

'D'ye think that wee cockroach was an instrument of God?'

'In what way?'

'It led us tae the path of righteousness.'

Mulholland gazed at the guileless face before him.

'I'm not certain sure, Ballantyne,' he said. 'But I'll tell you one thing for nothing. There may be more to you than meets the eye. I hope so — for all our sakes.'

46

What is this world? what asketh man to have?
Now with his love, now in his colde grave.
Chaucer, The Knight's Tale

Now it was the storyteller's turn to listen. He was acutely conscious of being severely depleted in energy, so no chance of running for his life, especially in these slippers — no — Robert Louis was a captive audience.

And also a fascinated one.

The murderer of two human beings stood before him.

Not from distance, like musket fire on a remote island, but a close-quarters killer.

Edward Hyde, take a bow.

Yet this was not a literary fancy. This was real. Best to remember that as the tale wore on.

'Do you admire my Golden Book?' the effigy asked.

'It is . . . remarkably constituted. A work of art.'

'A work of love.'

The effigy stepped a touch nearer and laid the cane lightly upon the open pages of the sacred volume.

'She found it. The skulking old witch. I always kept the door locked, but the dull one must have — forgotten.'

Who was the dull one?

The effigy's speech pattern had now a liturgical tinge, but Stevenson kept that observation to himself.

'Here — in the deep cellars that I had made my own. Where no-one ever sets foot. She did. She did not lay filthy hands upon the book — I came upon her before that. But she had seen — my secret.'

The cane slid from the exposed page, and took its part in a jaunty pose, in contrast to the formality of the delivery.

'I *knew* what she would do. Not tell the witless worshippers, or more especially the man of God — no — but threaten. Hang it over my head, make me dance to her tune.'

Then the effigy laughed with glee and skipped daintily around the seated Robert Louis.

'She thought she was dealing with the dull one, the stupid one. She did not realise there was another to hand!'

'And so you killed her?'

'Of course. I followed her that night. She knew the secret. She had to die.'

The cane cut through the air in a series of chilling blows, and Stevenson could almost see the old woman huddled like a dumb animal in the rain.

Yet he had to hammer this through.

The writer was a part of it, after all.

The cigarette had died in his fingers, so he lit another and blew a puff of smoke that hung in the small cell like a cloud of incense.

Two performers in a play, but now that Stevenson remembered, he had never had much luck with theatrical productions.

But keep up the act.

'What of the bible — the pages from — ' he had almost said *your father's bible*, not a good idea — 'that were left on the bodies?'

'A mere diversion. A present from the witch. Fell from her to the ground. It amused me to leave a holy keepsake on the dear departed souls, but — not for long.'

He indicated a small pile of ashes in the corner.

'Burnt at the stake, I'm afraid.'

'And Mary Dougan — what of her?'

This time the laughter was manic, harsh, a bitter black thread running under.

'She *was* the secret, my dear friend. Why I left her on your doorstep. She *was* the secret!'

The Foul Anchor was heaving, air like chunks of grime, as John Gibbons moved quietly amongst the feral bodies of a lost tribe.

He had been instructed to spread the word, by process of pious pamphlets that were to he handed to men and women alike, in the hope that salvation might stir in their damned souls. The young man was greeted with sly courtesy and downright insults, hit pursued a dogged course, until he ended at a table where an old woman was slumped upon the surface.

As he slid the pamphlet into her outstretched palm, the woman stirred and opened her watery eyes.

Then her face creased up in shock and anguish.

She reached up a clawed hand and pulled him

down so that their faces were almost touching, her breath fetid and reeking of raw cheap whisky.

'You are my child!' she hissed. 'My boy. My bonny boy. I've watched ye grow. You are my bonny boy!'

Her mouth opened and closed as if she wanted to swallow him whole, like some creature from the deep.

He wrenched away from this nightmare vision and the old woman stumbled to her feet, clinging to his coat.

The fracas attracted some interest, with the barmen trying to peer over through the crowded room.

One of her cronies tried to haul the grappling parasite away and he heard her mutter.

'Leave him be, Mary — he's too holy fur fornication.'

Then he pulled back, almost using violence to extricate himself, and burrowed his way through the mostly unheeding throng, the pamphlets already trampled upon the floor.

Outside the tavern he paused and took great gulps of air — a drunken old besom; why should he be so disconcerted?

And what nonsense she had spoken.

'John?'

His name. He turned. She was standing there, but now subdued, shrunken, timid almost. He put out a hand as if to keep her at bay, and the woman nodded acceptance, kept her distance. Then she spoke quietly.

'That was the name bestowed on you. I

wanted another, but I gave away your birthright. Not tae sell. Jist tae find a better life for my bonny boy.'

He said nothing.

She was encouraged enough to speak on.

'A good woman. The wife of a holy man. No children. God had not seen fit, she said, tae grant her that boon. The night you were born, she came and took you away. I hardly even saw your face.'

Then she smiled. It transformed her and for the first time he wondered if there might be some macabre truth in what she was relating. But surely not?

'I watched ye grow. I would hide and watch. In the street at your home. Outside the church. With the holy man. A fine boy. A decent boy. My son.'

Tears began to run down her face and he felt a disgust and fury boil up inside — had his whole life been some kind of despicable trick?

How could he spring from a tavern whore?

'There is no truth in what you say!'

'Ask the good woman. She cannot lie. By dint of God.'

That part told, the effigy laughed.

'I was born that night. In the moment when the dull one wished to strike her down but did not. Buried it deep. Where he had buried me. All these years under all that goodness, strangled and buried me — there was I born!'

He raised both arms into the air, as if receiving some blessing, and slapped around to some merry, mental tune.

'She was left there like a scarecrow in the field. But her last words whispered the name of the real father. A man she had loved. Her plight known only a certain time after he had gone. To pursue a different life. A life of fame and fortune.'

Stevenson was silent, his mind racing. He was dealing with a candidate for Bedlam, but there was a weird, touching vulnerability, as if a protective skin had been wrenched away that invited pity, yet had an attendant danger that one wrong move might unleash a psychotic killing fury.

Father or no father, my friend.

So keep your mouth shut and wits sharp. In addition, whatever happens, don't forget to smoke.

The effigy was pleased enough with the writer's silence — it signalled belief, for who could not believe such a history? Now it may pour out like a cleansing stream.

'The dull one, the stupid one, he went to the good woman and asked. More tears, but she confessed. Yes, it was true. Her womb was sterile. By grace of God.'

The effigy poked with his cane at the small heap of ashes that lay in the corner.

'The good woman was persuaded not to tell the man of God what she confessed to the son they never created. Keep it between — their little secret. Bury it deep, eh?'

Robert Louis blew out a puff of encouraging smoke. It was the least he could do.

'Of course, the dull one adored him. Even

when he knew the truth. But not I. The man of God. *Fruit of my loins.* His words often. *Fruit of my loins. Liar!'*

A sudden, vicious slash of the cane scattered the ashes, some of which floated up into the air.

'And so the lie was lived and I grew stronger. I searched the markets, found myself gay clothes to wear, a silver cane. I changed my face, pomaded my hair to darken down the colour, what perfection! I ruled the roost. I came and went — as I pleased.'

For almost the first time he gazed directly at Stevenson, and it took all of the writer's steel to meet those eyes and hold his nerve.

'So you kept the Golden Book? And then when you heard I was coming back . . . ?'

'I gave thanks unto the Lord.'

Savage irony in the tone, but Stevenson had a more pertinent question in mind — a perilous enquiry, but one he might not avoid and live with his conscience.

'Mary Dougan. She would not harm a living soul. Why did you end her life?' The effigy seemed surprised.

'It was for your sake. For *our* sake. As soon as you returned, I knew. She had to die.'

'But she loved you.'

'She had to die.'

'For what reason?'

'She was not worthy of us.'

The chilling simplicity of response almost took the breath away, but what followed was more than a match.

'And for that I need your blessing.'

The effigy knelt before the seated figure, who had frozen, cigarette to lips.

'I am your son. Give me your blessing.'

This was the moment Stevenson had feared; the moment that could not be avoided.

Mary Dougan's face, twisted in pain, racked with a suffering that was never deserved, swam into his mind.

A blessing?

'I'm afraid that may come at too high a cost,' he murmured.

'I'll give you it for nothing,' said James McLevy.

He stepped into the room from where he had crushed himself by the side of the door, witnessing without daring to move.

A listener split in two.

The inspector, no doubt, taking the part of the dull one.

47

The garlands wither on your brow;
Then boast no more your mighty deeds!
James Shirley, *Ajax and Ulysses*

McLevy had lurked opposite the house to watch the funeral procession leave, cursing himself for a fool.

Then he had cursed some more as the empty street mocked the great Thieftaker and late spring blossoms drooped down from the trees of Queen's Street Gardens where he had chosen to conceal himself.

Yet Stevenson was in the house — he had not left to throw the dirt on his father's grave — and McLevy had this deep, or was it more desperate, conviction that the writer was the centre of it all.

But conviction demands belief.

A feeling in the bones — does that constitute belief?

The park was full of well-upholstered wifies walking their glaikit wee dogs, both parties giving him an affronted glance as they traipsed past.

Then like a ghost Stevenson appeared at the window, and as if summonsed a carriage drew up.

It fitted the description provided by Tom Carstairs but the driver was no howling spectre — just the minister's son.

Yet the funeral could not yet be over, not

378

unless they slid in the coffin and banged down the sods? The Church of Scotland was not noted for such lack of decorum.

While the inspector puzzled this, Robert Louis shuffled out of the house and slipped into the coach.

The carriage took off suddenly heading past McLevy's vantage spot towards Albany Street and as he jumped out to follow best he could, a Cairn terrier dashed in front of him trailing back a long lead to its dumpy but fashionably garbed female owner.

His foot caught the line and the inspector fell flat on his face.

Had he time he would have first kicked the dog and then the woman but, ignoring her apologies though she seemed more concerned with the yelping canine, McLevy scrambled to his feet and ran off in hot pursuit.

It was an unequal contest and the inspector was scarce fleet of foot — he puffed along in time to see the carriage far in the distance turn left at the end of Albany Street and disappear.

The pursuer let out a howl of frustration and the woman with the dog retreated rapidly back into the park until this mustachioed madman had quit the scene.

For a moment McLevy thought to run the length of the long thoroughfare in the hope that he might catch a glimpse of the vehicle to the left but common sense told him this was not an option.

He stopped; his hands fell loosely by his side and he closed his eyes.

Think, damn you.

Never mind whether it was a conspiracy or accidental meeting, where the hell might they be going?

His mind flipped back over the events of this case with a speed that belied the stolid set of his features.

The church. St Stephen's. It had tae be. That's where it began, that's where it would end.

It had tae be.

He turned and walked slowly in the opposite direction to that which the carriage had taken.

It would swing back.

It had tae be.

Besides, it was his only hope, and when you have just the one hope — dress it up as best you can.

McLevy had retraced his footsteps and made his way deliberately towards St Stephen's. Eventually he stood before the uncompromisingly dour face and decided to try his luck at the rear of the building.

And there it was.

It had tae be.

The empty carriage reins tied to a stone post, horse munching contentedly at a nosebag of oats. There was a small stables nearby, so the carriage would be for the minister's usage — to visit the poor, no doubt.

But to what other uses might it lend a hand?

A small door was directly opposite the coach, but when he tried the handle, it was tight locked.

Nothing, however, can withstand the might of the law.

Or a criminal craftsman's lockpicks.

How McLevy had come by them was another tale, but he could use them like a born thief.

Though he had never broken into a church before.

Moments later, he was inside.

The interior was gloomy, the sun having given up the ghost, though some grey light filtered through the tall, narrow windows.

But sight was not at a premium.

He could hear the faint murmur of voices from the bowels of the empty church and followed them down a series of deep, winding staircases, until he came to a partially opened door. Through the aperture he could see Robert Louis sitting, puffing calmly at a cigarette.

Did the man ever stop smoking?

Then he saw the other figure.

Then he listened for a long, long time.

Then he walked into the room.

'I'll give you the blessing of the law,' James McLevy stated, with a heavy old revolver now hanging loosely in his right hand.

It looked like a museum piece, yet had put an end to more than one life, especially at close quarters.

The effigy moved back into the gloom, but Stevenson seemed unsurprised — indeed since his chair faced directly to the door, he had remarked what might have been a shadow of sorts, and was desperately hoping that it might help him get out of this predicament alive.

For he was in no doubt that to provoke that psychotic fury was to kiss the girls goodbye.

It was the best of all possible worlds that, instead of being some old biddy from the church, the shadow had turned out to be none other than the Thieftaker.

Or had he somehow always known?

'I am pleased to see you, inspector,' he said. 'Visitors are always welcome.'

McLevy was in no mood for politesse.

He must not be distracted for a moment from the pale outline that had moved to the side of the cell.

'Whatever your changing form, I will address you by the name known tae me — John Gibbons, I charge you with two vicious, cowardly murders and one attempted.'

'Jean Brash?'

'Ye damned near killed her.'

'What a pity. Just another whore.'

Stevenson observed McLevy's body stiffen with fury, but the policeman's concentration was unwavering as he raised the revolver while his other hand reached into an overcoat pocket for the restrainers.

'You will drop the cane and turn your back to me.'

The effigy ignored this and spoke only to Stevenson.

'Give me your blessing. You are my father.'

Robert Louis provided no answer.

'Turn before I bring you to your knees!'

At McLevy's command the effigy drooped as if winded, began to turn as bidden, but then whirled and lashed out with the cane — a ferocious blow which cut the inspector just above the eye, drawing blood at once.

Another blow sent the revolver scudding out of McLevy's hand. A howl of rage issued from the policeman as his fist smashed into the guts of his adversary, doubling over the effigy and sending him reeling backwards, a look of pain and astonishment on the mask of a face.

This was not part of his world.

By chance his trajectory ended beside the open door and before the inspector could continue his furious response, the figure darted out of the doorway into the darkness beyond.

McLevy scrabbled for the revolver and cursed to see that the firing-pin had been knocked askew so that the weapon would not fire.

He hefted it anyway to give appearance of a lethal authority and prepared to follow the effigy; the blood was running freely down his face from the lacerated eye and he cast one scornful, savage glance at the writer, who sat as if frozen to the chair.

'You are a bloody menace, Stevenson!'

And with that he was out of the door.

Robert Louis sat for a long moment, the cigarette dead in his fingers, and then let out a long gasp of air.

He bowed his head in pain and anguish.

This also was not his world.

48

Shield-breakings, and the clash of brands,
   the crash
Of battleaxes on shattered helms, and shrieks,
After the Christ, of those who falling down,
Looked up for heaven, and only saw the mist.
                Tennyson, *The Passing of Arthur*

McLevy burst into the body of the kirk
— blood-spattered, wild eyed, revolver in hand.

The place was empty, pews gaping, organ
pipes huddled together for company, the bare
stone floor showing no sign of recent passage,
and the pulpit looming overhead like the prow of
a ghost ship.

The inspector mopped at his eye with a hankie
and gasped for breath. He had hurtled up the
narrow staircase from the cell with best speed,
but emerged to find nothing.

His quarry could be anywhere; there was a
plethora of side doors, some of which might even
lead to the outside street, but McLevy had an
instinct the man was still here.

He calmed his breathing, held the hankie tight
against welted, weeping skin, and waited.

A hollow church.

Silence.

Then a faint scrape took McLevy's gaze high
up to the bell tower, part of which looked down
upon the interior and a balustrade of sorts

fenced off an area where a well-like staircase led even higher into the campanile.

As the inspector strained his eyes, he thought he glimpsed a grey smear amid the dark surroundings of stained oak above, yet he could not be sure.

There was a small access door on the south side, which no doubt led to the vestibule under the tower.

So be it.

He crossed swiftly, and began to ascend the constricted stairwell, which gradually became pitch black.

McLevy walked like a blind man, hands outstretched, fingers hooking into the rough surface of the brick wall.

At last the journey ended at a door, which gave way reluctantly with a faint screech.

Was that not the sound he had earlier heard?

The portal opened out to a cramped space enclosed at one end by the balustrade.

There was also a man-sized rectangular opening that led to what appeared to be another flight of steps. But the inspector had no need to explore further.

The effigy leant against the wall opposite in the dim light cast from the narrow windows.

He still had his cane and McLevy still had his useless revolver.

'I think,' said the figure in some pain, 'you have cracked one of my ribs.'

'Only one? I'm getting old.'

For a moment they looked into each other's eyes, though inspector's right was near closed with drying blood and swollen skin.

And the effigy?

There was a curious glitter that shone like winter sun on cold water — in fact his whole presence seemed to flicker with a strange inner light that rendered the watcher unsure whether this was a corporeal being or some strange projection from a magic lantern show.

And yet McLevy could see sadness.

Quickly as it materialised in the creature's face, so swiftly did it disappear.

A desire to belong.

The fugitive could have easily found his way outside and disappeared into the streets while a fruitless search was made within the building.

But he did not. Had not. Would not.

Too late now.

'Murder,' said McLevy, lifting the defunct weapon, 'is a vile business. I must ask you to accompany an officer of the law.'

'You may have to kill me first,' the effigy replied, skipping oddly this way and that.

'That would be a last resort.'

'My assumption also. You have had your chance and not done so. Do you lack the nerve to kill?'

'I would not wish to do it.'

Nor did he have the wherewithal, unless it was a bare-handit proposition.

While he pondered the odds on that, the effigy made his move.

He whipped the cane high up and down, aiming at his favourite target, the side of the neck.

The inspector hunched up to deflect the blow, but as he did so, the missile changed direction and slashed into the knee of his standing leg.

Despite the trouser covering, this savage cut numbed his leg and as he lunged forward the effigy swivelled around so that McLevy now had his back to the low balustrade.

This was a parlous predicament.

One push and he would fall to the pious flagstones below and they would have no mercy; it was a steep plunge that would break neck, back, and any other bone that was in the vicinity.

Life or death.

The effigy could not know McLevy's fangs had been drawn and so he was also playing with his own life.

Only one chance.

Bluff and be buggered.

He lifted the revolver and cocked back the hammer.

'You leave me no option.'

The figure seemed unafraid.

'I will back my reflexes against the move of your finger. One cut, one thrust, and goodbye.'

Whit a caper, eh?

The blood was running freely once more, so that the inspector had to turn his head grotesquely to the side in order to get a decent view of his protagonist.

Throw the gun and make a rush, though with just the one working leg that might be difficult.

Surely he wasnae going tae hop towards death?

The effigy made a dart forward and as

McLevy automatically crabbed back in retreat, he felt the polished wood of the balustrade against his legs.

The cane whistled through the air again, to land with jarring force on his collarbone, and though he grabbed at it, his hand was too slippery with his own blood.

His head was swimming, as previous exertion began to take its toll and the inhabited world seemed to be fading, swirling, like a nightmare.

The effigy bared its teeth.

Killing time.

McLevy gathered his strength.

Survival.

Then a voice floated up from beneath.

The thin personage of Robert Louis Stevenson had emerged to see them high above and had taken a hand.

In the empty church his voice echoed with a strange foreboding, as he stood isolated on the flagstones.

'John — my boy — I must tell the truth, no matter the cost!'

Words that froze the combatants for different reasons, the effigy jolted at being thus addressed, and McLevy wiped at his eye with his sleeve and wondered what the hell the man was up to now?

It had better be good.

Stevenson cut an anguished figure as he struggled for words to address the pale, distant outline.

'I have been to see many doctors and they have told me the same thing. My wife — '

He broke off. An abject confessional figure in

the church where he was raised.

'My wife and I — have tried for children these many years. She has two progeny from previous liaisons, a fertile womb, but — the fault — is mine.'

The effigy was stock still as if paralysed.

'I am sterile,' the regretful but inexorable voice rose in the air. 'The seed cannot find a path. It has no strength and I — I must tell you. You — could never be my son. Fate has decreed it otherwise.'

A terrible silence.

'Mary Dougan knew many men, rest her soul. Never, never could you be my son.'

A sudden scream issued from the effigy and he hurtled forward.

McLevy realised his intention and tried to intercept the man before he hurled himself over.

As they struggled, the effigy twisted round so that he was underneath, with McLevy grappling to retain some hold on the man, who was as slippery as a snake.

Now the death that the killer sought might well be his own, and the perversity of this attempted rescue would have amused Old Nick himself.

As McLevy looked down, the blood pouring from his wound, his opponent smiled and then spat deliberately into the inspector's one good eye.

The shock blinded McLevy for a moment and that was enough.

The effigy twisted gracefully out of his grasp and then slipped away to let gravity take its course, spiralling headfirst through the air to land with a sickening crunch, arms outstretched like a cruel parody of the crucified Christ.

Stevenson, with a very shaky hand, lit up another of his thin cigarettes and gazed at the newly-dead arrival.

There was another howl as a man ran forward from the front of the church. Jonas Gibbons in full ministerial garb, his mane of hair near electric at what he had just witnessed.

He cradled his son's body up against his chest and turned a grief-stricken face upwards.

'Murderer!' he screamed at McLevy, who with hands and face awash with blood seemed to justify denunciation.

'Murderer!'

49

Some circumstantial evidence is very strong,
as when you find a trout in the milk.

Thoreau, *Journal*

Queen Victoria looked down with clear features
on the three men who had gathered at an hour
far beyond her bedtime.

'What a mess,' was Roach's somewhat
ungrateful comment on the story thus told.

McLevy said nothing. His eye was killing him,
despite the pastoral care of Ballantyne, who had
during the salving of deep lesions excitedly
brought the inspector up to date with the
Carnegie outcome. A triumph of detection that
had been accomplished by Constable Mulholland with the aid of a wee toatie insect and
Ballantyne's gimlet scrutiny.

The inspector's leg was hurting also, but if he
stuck the thing out straight, it behaved better.

Mulholland himself sat quietly enough in the
office. He felt no great sense of achievement and
besides there was no need to rub the battered
bride's neb in the bowl of barley.

One of his Aunt Katy's sayings. Strange he
had not thought of her in a long time. Perhaps
he was developing a mind of his own?

'And what is *your* verdict, McLevy?' asked
Roach querulously. In fact the only more
annoying occurrence than the inspector laying

down his version of the law was when he took the opposite course and said nothing at all.

For a moment the anguished face of Jonas Gibbons brought itself into McLevy's mind.

'Don't keep secrets,' grunted the inspector. 'They come back tae bite ye.'

'I'll keep vigil on such as regards my future conduct,' Roach muttered.

'What a nest of vipers,' announced Mulholland. 'God knows how you got through it, sir.'

McLevy tried to flex his leg and winced at the pain.

'It wasnae easy.'

'But you solved the case!'

'I'm sure congratulations are in order,' said Roach dourly. 'I take it Stevenson will make a statement tomorrow?'

'Unless he has some other sleight of hand tae perform.'

McLevy puffed out his cheeks.

'The only thing ye can rely on with that will o' the wisp is that he'll hae tobacco on the go.'

The inspector then surprised his colleagues by banging the flat of his hand upon the lieutenant's desk. Not in temper — more as if he were trying to banish a troublesome imp of hell.

'I've met some souple creatures in my time, but that mannie takes them all!'

His recollection switched back to one of the last moments he had spent with Stevenson.

While Jonas Gibbons wept over his dead boy, McLevy limped up beside Robert Louis, who had extinguished his puff so as not to appear sacrilegious.

'Wis that true?' the policeman asked aside.

'What exactly do you mean?'

'About the seed. And the path?'

'My dear inspector — *who can believe what a writer tells?*'

That lie, if it was a lie, and the bugger is you would never know, had most probably saved his life.

'The damnedest thing, though,' he said.

'What was that?

In response to Mulholland's query, McLevy shook his head in genuine perplexity.

'When we looked at the boy's face, it had changed back. It wasnae — the other thing. Just — what we all had known. A minister's son.'

He grimaced as a shaft of pain from his eye ran down the side of his face.

'He had told his father he was feeling unwell at the funeral and taken the family carriage. Jonas had done his duty, buried the patriarch and then followed back to check the welfare of his boy.'

The inspector sighed heavily.

'A wee bit late. The welfare.'

'It may be, of course,' Roach uttered carefully, 'that the authorities decide not to prosecute the case. The poor father has suffered enough, the killer is no more — I can just envisage Sandy Robb looking at me as if to say, *let sleeping dogs lie.*'

'The two auld women might not think so,' replied McLevy with some weariness. 'Especially Mary Dougan who died with an innocent heart. But it's all gone now. A'body's deid and the case is solved.'

'And what of Jean Brash?' Roach asked slyly.

'From what I hear, she is . . . on the mend.'

'Good,' was the lieutenant's brisk retort. 'Well at this juncture, let me direct your attention to a small matter that has completely escaped your notice, McLevy.'

He leant across the desk while both McLevy and Mulholland tried to puzzle out this cryptic remark.

'Completely escaped your notice!'

50

Always present your front to the world.
                    Molière, *L'Avare*

And so James McLevy, late afternoon next day, with a newly pounding heart, found himself in the Drummond drawing room, clutching at a badly wrapped parcel.

The frantic activity of murder and mayhem had kept these jellyfish feelings at bay, but now they were back with a vengeance.

A swirling sea for a matchstick boat.

He wondered whether to remove his bowler, but that might indicate an intention to take root.

Then if he didnae remove it, would that not portray a man of low breeding?

A lumpen Lothario?

Ach tae hell with such; he'd keep it on.

The door handle turned to end this welter of indecision and Jessica Drummond entered.

'My God!' she exclaimed. 'You look like a Quasimodo.'

Not the most promising of starts.

'What on earth has happened?'

The swollen eye and the bulge beside it had indeed rendered the inspector's face somewhat misshapen, but surely there was no need to compare him to a creature wha hobnobbed wi' gargoyles?

'A hazard o' the trade,' he muttered. 'Where is your brother?'

'Daniel is . . . resting.'

'Resting?'

'For the last two days. He cannot stand the light.'

McLevy could have pursued this and put Jessica on the back foot, because they both knew the weakness and potential danger hidden behind that statement, but he decided to play the bluff inspector.

'Well ye can tell him tae stick his head out the window. The case is over.'

'You found the killer?'

Quasimodo nodded a painful assent.

'And he found me.'

'I shall inform Daniel. He will be much relieved.'

'Good. Now we can get down to business.'

He unwrapped the parcel and with solemn if battered mien, laid its contents on the table before them.

It was a top hat. With a severe dent not unlike some on the inspector's own physiognomy.

'This belongs tae Lieutenant Roach. It was damaged the night of the rammy by the harbour. Your brother caused such and he can pay for it.'

Her lips twitched in amusement and he wished she wouldn't do that. For some reason it brought back the moment when he had watched the curls come tumbling down in such sweet disarray.

And looked into those dark eyes.

Drowned at sea.

'I will arrange for the hat to be . . . reconstituted, cleaned spotless, buffed up and then

— delivered to the station.'

'Make sure ye pay the bill first.'

'That will be done.'

She shook her head sadly.

'You still have that awful moustache.'

'Ye noticed?'

'Who could not? Like a hedge.'

The memory of their close-quarter encounter had come into her mind also and Miss Jessica Drummond found McLevy's presence oddly disturbing.

As he found hers.

An uneasy silence fell between them.

How long they would have remained in this mutually dislocated state is a matter of conjecture, but the impasse was broken by the door opening and Alan Grant poking his head inside.

He seemed surprised to find the inspector, but nodded pleasantly enough before addressing himself wholly to the young woman.

'I was wondering — Jessica — when we might talk with your mother? She is — waiting, I believe.'

'Not long,' was the firm response. 'I will not be long.'

With a rather jerky inclination of acknowledgement, the young man withdrew.

'He's awfy polite, Mister Grant.'

This deadpan remark of the inspector's met its match.

'It runs in the family.'

James McLevy often said of himself that he was a nosy man, and so it proved.

'Whit was it — ye were tae talk with your mother concerning?'

Jessica did not blink.

'Alan has asked me to marry him and I have accepted.'

His face betrayed nothing, but it was as if a mule had kicked him in the guts.

'That's nice,' he said finally.

'He will make a good husband. And father.'

'Ye're thinking ahead then?'

'Of course,' she said with an ironic edge. 'I am a woman.'

'I remember you told me such. You had just wiped a dod o' mud from off your neb.'

This remark broke the tension between them, at least on her side, and she laughed.

Jessica moved over to a side cupboard and fished inside a small drawer, while McLevy remained frozen to the spot — the less movement the less agony.

'I took the liberty of assembling a small token of my gratitude for your . . . understanding in this matter.'

She turned with something concealed in her small fist.

'If you would be so kind as to extend your hand and close your eyes.'

'Is it a dead toad?'

'Do as you are bidden,' she retorted.

He did so and felt something press into his palm. His skin also registered the warmth of her hand.

'You are a strange man, James McLevy,' she murmured softly. 'I will not forget you.'

For a moment she leant in close and he could smell that strange mixture of woodsmoke and scented soap.

And then she vanished.

When he at last opened his eyes, he stood alone in the middle of the room and in his hand was a small locket.

Silver in colour with her minute likeness inside.

A photograph.

It was in fact not very flattering, posed in some studio, but you could recognise the face right enough.

Especially the eyes.

Roach's top hat was still sitting on the table, so life goes on, eh?

But Jessica was gone.

Love is cruel — the older you get, the deeper it bites.

51

Do men gather grapes of thorns, or figs of thistles?

St Matthew, ch7, v13.i, *The Bible*

The sleek revolver gleamed in the pale lamplight as McLevy sighted down its length and nodded approvingly.

A good piece of business — ye exchange a portrait for a weapon of destruction.

Not Jessica's photo, however; that was nestling in its locket wrapped in a clean hankie within his inside pocket.

He had left the Drummond house and wandered the streets with a heavy heart, while the rain paid yet another visit in a fine, drenching smirr and his leg began to pain him badly.

In no time his overcoat was as heavy as the aforesaid organ, and it must have been in the spirit of self-preservation that his boots directed him to Albany Street just before utter darkness closed in.

In his coat outside pocket was a crumpled photograph left behind in the Scarlet Runners' mad scramble at the Just Land.

Jean Brash had given it him and he knew the provenance.

So he knocked upon the Carstairs family door, was admitted by the maid, met the son, kept the likeness in his pocket, and was conducted to the lion's den.

Tom Carstairs seemed troubled, his open candid face unable to hide the disquiet.

'My father is not himself,' he said softly. 'I hope that you can help.'

McLevy's name was announced, Tom opened the door, and in went the inspector.

The room was full of shadows, curtains drawn, only one oil lamp burning to illuminate the burly figure of Major Archibald Carstairs sitting bolt upright in an armchair.

A bottle of whisky and a glass was beside him on the small table, but the bottle seemed hardly touched.

A good sign, thought McLevy, already wary, for there was a certain edge to the atmosphere.

He also noted the glass case that had contained the army revolver was now empty.

'Have you come to arrest me, inspector?'

Bleak irony undermined any humour in the tone.

'No. Not at all.'

McLevy decided to play this hale and hearty, though it was not at all how he felt.

'The case is closed!'

'I am glad to hear it. A swift enough conclusion. Not all things can be solved so . . . expeditiously.'

'No,' agreed the inspector soberly. 'Some things linger on — like a fell curse.'

Then he blinked somewhat askew.

'I cannae see ower well wi' this bad eye.'

Taking suitable action, he pulled back the curtains to admit the fading light of an Edinburgh dusk.

401

'That's the ticket.'

There was now enough light for Carstairs to see the policeman's battered countenance, and for McLevy to note the revolver, held in his lap by that broad, military hand.

While the useless arm still hung by the side.

'Wounded warriors!' the inspector declared.

'Yours will heal.'

McLevy scrabbled somewhat comically in his pocket.

'I have a wee present for you, sir.'

He limped across to hand over the photograph.

'Abandoned under duress. When your boy was shot in the backside scaling the wall of a bawdy-hoose.'

As Carstairs studied the picture, McLevy circled around so that he was peering nosily over the other's shoulder.

'A fine wee family, eh?'

Indeed it was a proud portrait, one of the major's arms resting protectively round the back of his wife's chair, the other with hand fixed to the hip, elbow jutting.

Both limbs vibrant.

Ready for battle.

The boy's eyes were fixed upon his father, one of the hands timidly upon his mother's shoulder.

'That laddie. Apple of your eye, eh?'

The major was momentarily annoyed by the familiarity of McLevy's tone and position, but he was well aware what the real focus of the policeman might be, and just to illustrate this, brought the revolver in his hand up into the light.

'Afraid I was going to use this, inspector?'

'Shoot who ye like — long as it's not me.'

McLevy walked slowly over to the glass case and laid his hand upon it, as if about to perform a conjuring trick.

Silence fell.

The inspector was fine with that. For a sometime garrulous man, he could pipe down with the best.

The silence lengthened,

At last Archibald Carstairs spoke.

'I look out on this world. And I see no place for myself. Nothing.'

McLevy nodded, face serious and reflective.

'There is a darkness in all of us, jist waiting for the chance. I have it also.'

'But you are a policeman. You have a function.'

'Not always. Sometimes I'm a man sitting alone in an attic room. No family. No footstep on the stair. Nothing.'

Their eyes met and held — no quarter.

Then McLevy grinned like a wolf and let out a whoop of wild laughter.

'But I have a dangerous appointment this night and I lack a certain wherewithal.'

'Such as?'

'My old redoubtable is at the gunsmith's. It got battered along wi' me.'

His eyes were fixed upon the revolver grasped in Carstairs' hand.

For a moment the military man hesitated, and then flipped the weapon round so that he had it by the barrel, the butt extended towards the policeman.

'The safety catch is on.'

'I noted that.'

'And it shoots straight,' said the major.

'Given the owner — I am not surprised.'

McLevy took a clean handkerchief from his inside pocket and carefully wrapped the gun before sliding it back into place.

The nozzle rested somewhat uneasily on Jessica's locket, but first things first.

'The chamber is fully loaded,' warned Carstairs.

McLevy gestured his thanks, walked to the door and then turned.

'There's a boy downstairs needs your help to grow. I envy him the chance and you the privilege.'

Then he threw back his hand in the parody of a salute.

'I'll bring your wee pistol back, sir. Safe and sound!'

'Keep it. Until requested. That is an order.'

For the first time a quirk of humour twisted the lips of the seated man.

McLevy nodded like a new recruit and was out of the door.

Carstairs looked down at the photograph — a moment frozen in time.

Tom was waiting at the bottom of the stairs as the inspector came hirpling down.

'Your father has something tae show you,' said he. 'Now on ye go up!'

As Tom moved past rapidly in response McLevy called after.

'Oh and by the way, ye might warn him that I

404

intend to pop in frae time tae time — coffee is
my predilection.'

'His also.'

'Decent quality?'

'Only the best.'

'Away ye go then!'

The boy bolted up the stairs and shot through
the door.

McLevy squinted cheerfully.

Now and again his miserable existence was
justified.

A sound brought him out of these thoughts.
Footsteps echoing in the damp night.

He hefted the new revolver and turned to his
companion.

'I hope you're in fettle,' he said quietly. 'For I
do believe we have company.'

52

Their injustice will return upon them. Curses,
like chickens, come home to roost.

S. Smiles, *Duty IV*

Gash Mitchell had progressed a tolerable
evening. A deal of drink taken in the Foul
Anchor, none of it paid for by him, some bought
by those wishing to curry favour with a man of
his reputation, some chalked up behind the bar
for a reckoning he had no intention of honouring
in the foreseeable future.

His three cohorts were, like himself, firm
enough on their feet, for to be staggering fou in
this grim back area of the harbour where he had
his lodgings might invite a gang of nichtwalkers,
and though Gash relished a vicious onset, he
liked it to be on his own terms.

He had wondered whether to haul along some
tavern whores for amusement, but even the
hard-bitten cowclinks of the Foul Anchor
seemed reluctant to walk out into the night with
him.

Fear in their eyes.

Gash laughed aloud.

That was the best. Fear in another's eyes.
Himself the cause.

Take it to the limit.

He was in the lead and so was first to see the
figure up ahead; tall in stature, a white shirt, the

sleeves rolled up, standing under one of the few working streetlights.

Mulholland.

'I'm waiting for you, Mitchell!'

The policeman's voice rang out in the night.

'Just the two of us. Man to man, I'm prepared to soil my hands with you.'

Gash Mitchell could not believe his luck. Man to man, eh? A lamb tae the slaughter.

'No holds barred?' he jeered back.

'If that's how you want it,' came the resolute response, and Gash near pissed himself with delight.

He spoke aside to his confederates.

'*Wait for yer chance then kick in till the bones come through. We can leave him by the slaughterhoose.*'

He grinned at that prospect, but then something happened to change the game.

James McLevy had emerged to join his constable, making sure that the revolver hanging loose in his hand caught the light enough to be unmistakable.

'No holds barred — are ye certain sure?' he muttered to Mulholland. 'He's a dirty fighter.'

'I'm not afraid,' was the proud response.

'It's not a matter of fear,' replied McLevy grumpily. 'It's a matter of survival.'

When Mulholland had spoken that very morning about his intention to bring retribution to Mitchell the inspector was by no means knocked down with a feather.

This had been festering like a canker.

Of course he had insisted on being on hand,

and the fortunate advent of the revolver was a bonus, but the venture was still fraught with peril.

The constable was accustomed to his hornbeam stick wreaking havoc amongst the Fraternity, but McLevy was a close-quarter man when necessary and knew the dark arts of that species of encounter.

Somewhere Mulholland still believed in fair play.

A hellish misconception.

'A wee word, Gash!' McLevy bellowed. 'If your snivelling scunnerbags interfere in any way, I'll shoot them where they stand. You hae my word upon it.'

'Don't you worry, McLevy,' came a cry in response. 'I willnae need them. Tend tae yer own midden!'

With that contemptuous gibe, Mitchell turned to huddle with his crew.

'Watch his eyes,' said McLevy to the set-faced Mulholland. 'His first move will signal there.'

For the constable it was as if his whole life had led him to this point.

One time, in the hills above the village, a young boy, he had come upon a March Hare. The beast showed no fear, bounded up and looked him in the eyes.

He knew by country lore he should kill it. Knife or gun or in his case a catapult, but he gawped and did nothing.

The hare looked him in the eyes and bounded off.

He felt then the throbbing life in the beast.

A precious gift.

So even when he stood side by side with McLevy and meted out the hammer blows of his hornbeam stick, it was without Satan's violence driving.

Though, to be sure, those who felt the whacks possibly did not notice the difference.

But he did.

And now he was face to face with dark brutality. The memory of a young girl's pitiful dead body his own driving force.

Bare handed.

He and Gash Mitchell stood not far apart, a watchful McLevy to the side and Mitchell's men a respectful distance behind their man.

What was it the inspector said?

At that moment the apelike figure of Gash Mitchell made his move.

Under cover of the huddle, he had bent down and scraped up a mixture of gravel and dirt, saturated with dirty water.

For a moment his eyes narrowed and then from a massive paw he threw the mixture directly into Mulholland's face, to sting and blind.

Gash now aimed a kick straight at the groin, that just missed to land on the fleshy inside of the upper thigh, and then went to work.

He butted his head in under Mulholland's chin and hammered blows into the guts and belly, revelling the while that his opponent could hardly see.

Mitchell had also managed to crunch his heel on top of Mulholland's boot, which not only anchored and agonised as Gash cruelly twisted but gave him purchase for the brutal thrash of his fists.

At the moment Mulholland's arms were absorbing some of the force, but soon he would become weakened and all his attention would be caught in that area — and then Gash would draw back his head and smash the granite top of it into the unprotected face, breaking the nose, blooding the already damaged eyes. After that, it would just be the boot.

The constable gasped in pain and Mitchell judged it time to make the cranial strike.

Draw back — in like a battering ram!

Then a terrifying crack close by split the heavens and pinned all of them to the spot.

McLevy stood with the revolver pointing at the sky where he had aimed the shot.

The noise, near to hand, was deafening and both combatants staggered back for a brief moment — but the inspector seemed unperturbed.

'The round is over,' he announced.

Mitchell was outraged, while Mulholland simply gasped for agonised breath.

'It's no' a bastard boxing match!' howled Gash.

McLevy negligently waved the revolver to indicate a further parting, the barrel pointing at Mitchell and his men, who shuffled back while the inspector pulled his constable to the side.

As Mulholland bent over trying to coax some air into his bruised and crippled body, he became aware that McLevy was talking quietly into his ear.

'You are fighting a monster, a brute, a barbarian. Unless you find the same within, there will be nothing left tae pick up. No holds barred, ye gave him that. I cannot stop it again mid-stream. This time it's to the end.'

'I'm not the same as him!'

'We all are. It is merely a matter of how deep you wish to delve. In order to survive.'

McLevy's one good eye had its cold lupine stare; there was no pity to be found.

Anywhere.

And no hiding place.

Martin Mulholland said goodbye to the civilised man and finally nodded assent.

'Good. Now — a wee word before ye go.'

The inspector whispered for a moment, then left him to it, turning away abruptly.

'I can do no more for you!' he announced loudly. 'On your own. No mercy, remember!'

Gash Mitchell grinned, taking this as condemnation rather than salutary advice.

He shifted with a swagger as Mulholland shuffled painfully towards him — easy meat.

The strike was fast and ruthless.

The constable's body was in sore distress but his legs, honed on the saunter and wild hurling matches of his youth in Ireland, were not.

McLevy's guidance had also given him an edge.

Act worse than ye are. Then hammer in. No mercy.

One foot was pained, but that was the left, thank God, and it was the other that swept forward.

411

The instep of his boot hit Gash Mitchell flush in the groin; the squat massive frame shuddered in shock and then the man doubled over as the agony shot through his body like a lightning bolt. But there was more to come.

God is bountiful.

Mulholland held him by the back of the neck while unleashing a series of uppercuts with his right fist.

Into the face and he never missed once.

Then he hauled the groaning monster up by his straw coloured hair and smashed his knuckles into the exposed throat before standing back to watch the man collapse to his knees.

Another kick sent Mitchell sprawling onto his back, then the constable leapt onto the recumbent body to batter in with a further series of blows.

No holds barred.

Rose Dundas. Her corpse lies still. The face white, the eyes closed, the neck snapped.

Her corpse lies still.

How long Mulholland lambasted like a madman he lost track, but another thunderclap shot rang out to bring him out of his frenzy.

'End of the bout,' announced McLevy.

One of the constable's hands was still clamped around Mitchell's inflamed throat and the inspector carefully prised it loose.

Mulholland's eyes were dazed, almost bewildered, as if he had been in a far country.

'I've jist been chased stupid wi' two murders so far,' said McLevy stolidly. 'I don't need witnessed manslaughter tae boot.'

He pulled the assailant up and away, led him aside to recover his wits, then returned to stand over the unmoving body of Gash Mitchell and address his confederates.

McLevy, with his half closed eye and fell expression, resembled something dragged from the depths of hell.

'He is naething now. My constable cut him tae bits.'

He prodded the body with the toe of his boot.

'Ye can pick him up and take him home or ye can leave him lay. Tae lie there in the muck. Where he belongs.'

The three men turned without a word and quit the scene.

McLevy leant down and whispered a malediction into Mitchell's ear, and only by the merest flicker of the eyelids might it be discerned that the man was conscious at all.

But the inspector knew better.

His words would penetrate like a gutty knife.

'*As previously stated, Gash Mitchell, you are nothing now. The word will fly round. A'body will know. The young keelies will laugh in your face. No-one will fear you — you have lost it all. Teeth will fasten round your throat and the herd will tear you to pieces. You are nothing. A dead man walking. Welcome tae the prospect.*'

McLevy straightened up and walked over to where Mulholland wavered uncertainly on his feet.

'I lost myself,' he muttered.

'Easy found again,' was the breezy response. 'Time tae get ye home.'

413

The constable did not move, his eyes deflecting back to the prone figure of Mitchell.

McLevy frowned. 'I warned ye not tae wear that white shirt; it shows the blood something terrible.'

'I have a last word to say — '

'It's already been said. Come on!'

And none too gently he shoved Mulholland into his policeman's cloak from where it had been neatly laid aside and stuck on the helmet.

'A sight for sore eyes,' was McLevy's verdict.

For a moment Mulholland's gaze met with his inspector's.

'I am not that beast,' he said quietly.

'So long as ye know where to find him,' replied James McLevy. 'That's the main thing.'

'I have done my best by Rose Dundas.'

'That ye have. Now let us take our leave.'

As the two made their way out of the wynd into the harbour streets, seagulls screeching overhead, the inspector burst into song.

In truth he could scarce carry a tune, but had never let this hinder him in any way.

However, instead of one of his usual Jacobite refrains, McLevy let rip with a favourite of the tarry-breeks, the sailors flooding off the ships into the Leith taverns, who could be wild as a brattling gale or innocent as children.

What shall we do with the drunken sailor?
What shall we do with the drunken sailor?
What shall we do with the drunken sailor?
Earl-aye in the morning?

414

Scrape his guts with a hoop-iron razor,
Scrape his guts with a hoop-iron razor,
Scrape his guts with a hoop-iron razor,
Earl-aye in the morning!

As his voice faded into the night, one arm hooked firmly into his constable's to guarantee safe passage, a rat came creeping out of a nearby drain and cautiously approached the unmoving body.

A hank of Mitchell's dirty blond hair lay in one of the puddles, and the rodent had a wary nibble before scuttling off a little, as a groan emitted from the lumpen carcass.

The rat would return later.

Everything comes to he who waits.

53

I'll sing thee songs of Araby,
And tales of fair Cashmere,
Wild tales to cheat thee of a sigh,
Or charm thee to a tear.
                    William Wills, 'I'll Sing Thee
                              Songs of Araby'

Diary of James McLevy.
15th May, 1887.

Having headed the page, James McLevy paused
for thought. The cat Bathsheba had already
come and gone, turning up her nose at the
mixture of cold coffee and milk he had so
diligently prepared.

Fair's fair. He couldnae blame the beast. When
he looked in the tin mug, there were unidentifi-
able flakes that seemed — or was it his imagination?
— to be growing larger by each making in his
iron pot.

He slurped, caught a flake in his teeth, sniffed
at it, then flicked it away towards the fireplace.

The inspector was sitting at his rickety table,
facing the large window that looked over the city.

He could make out the outline of a few scabby
Edinburgh pigeons sliding on the oily slates. One
in particular had a crabbed foot that tilted it
comically from side to side and put McLevy in
mind of Mulholland's enduring torment of the

sharp cobblestones upon his injured foot.

The constable was not used to being amongst the halt and the lame, and another thing that seemed to perturb him was his inspector's high spirits.

After a rousing if tuneless version of 'The Drunken Sailor' McLevy had then sought the safety of dry land with 'The Piper o' Dundee' and much to Mulholland's relief, this ditty lasted sufficient to bring them to his lodgings.

The constable's ribs were on fire and his guts and belly a maelstrom of conflicting distress — it did little to quell the suffering to hear his superior say that he could have the day off tomorrow and Lieutenant Roach be told that one of Mulholland's bees had stung him in parts private.

While McLevy roared with laughter at such a fancy the constable's face was sombrous as a church door.

And yet?

And yet.

A different outcome without this hooligan.

Having managed to open the portal, Mulholland turned back to the grinning eyesore.

'I'll lie one day in bed but — day after tomorrow. On the saunter?'

'On the saunter.'

For a moment they held each other's gaze.

It would seem they had spent a lifetime together blowing smoke in the devil's face.

McLevy grinned and tapped the crown of his bowler.

'Here's tae murder and mayhem!'

'And more to come.'

Mulholland's sober response was a signal for the two to part company without another word, the door closing while James McLevy walked off into the night.

And now?

What of this present moment in his wee attic room?

Jessica Drummond's locket had been placed in the cupboard to lodge beside strangler's gloves, a cricket ball with darker red smears than natural, a sliver from a piece of driftwood that had saved McLevy's life in an empty ocean, a small but murderously sharp axe, a pulley rope that had ended a decent but weak man's existence, and various other artefacts pervaded with past criminality.

McLevy hoped the keepsake wouldn't be too upset by its surroundings, but as the bard put it,

Misery acquaints a man with strange bedfellows.

Though the remarkable happenstance was that he himself, James McLevy, felt anything but miserable.

With that in mind, he picked up his pen and began to write in the red ledger.

Is violence more important to me than love? It is as if these feelings of desperation and need have been scoured from my system by the searing necessity of life or death.

Had Mulholland fallen the second time, he would not have risen.

I would have had to kill or at least maim Gash

Mitchell and if not watch my comrade splintered to pieces.

Thus breaking the very rules I had set into motion.

And when it was over I felt release, as if I had triumphed over the most heinous adversity.

An exultation that blew the sticky cobwebs from my heart and left me dancing with abandon.

That may be a wee bit far fetched.

For a start, Mulholland did all the work.

But it is as if a curtain was lifted.

Maybe I was suffering an illusion?

They say dry men in the desert see fountains of water.

Now when I think of Jessica Drummond, I feel nothing — I see in my mind a bonny face and strong bones, but that fades away like a glimmering snip of light.

I am free.

Like the hero in a fairy tale under a magic spell, though that usually involves some ugly auld besom.

What was it Jean Brash said?

'Love is the very devil.'

Perhaps that's what she meant. Jean is deep, no doubt.

Time will pass.

Time will pass, her wounds will heal, and the savage attack she suffered has met with due retribution.

Mulholland has avenged Rose Dundas.

Agnes Carnegie, a miserable old besom, nevertheless had her will delivered and murder solved.

Mary Dougan, poor soul, has also been avenged, though I fear she will find it sma' comfort. Killed by her own son, father unproven.

And the twisted, tortured spirit of John Gibbons may have found some peace, but I doubt it.

And how did Stevenson feel about his part in all this, or did he somehow see it as a story from imagination spilled into real life?

We'll never know, for he's a devious bugger.

And me?

As Mulholland said — I've done my best.

To the limit of my compromised ability.

As regards the jellyfish, I think the best thing is to let well alone.

McLevy laid aside the pen and walked to the window. His city sparkled in the darkness.

Above in a clear sky, the stars did likewise.

Take the light and love the dark.

What more could a man desire?

54

Is not old wine wholesomest, old pippins toothsomest, old wood burn brightest, old linen wash whitest? Old soldiers, sweethearts, are surest, and old lovers are soundest.

John Webster, *Westward Ho*

Some two weeks later at the Just Land, Hannah Semple, in a rare flurry, burst in on Jean Brash as she laboured over accounts in the small office next door to her boudoir.

'There's a muckle great body in the garden!'

'Talk sense, woman,' snapped Jean, who was never in the best of moods when confronted by arithmetical challenge.

'See for yourself.'

Jean waited for further elucidation, but when none came heaved up from the desk and made for the window.

She had a slight stiffness still in neck and back, but was dressed to kill, accounts or no accounts.

And there he was. In the garden. Staring with great concentration at a robin redbreast that had found itself a perch on the curly head of Cupid.

The bird's tail flew up as it deposited an avian verdict on the boy god, and then it departed in search of a worm worthy of disengaging from the soil.

As the inspector turned to follow the flight his eyes scanned the upstairs window. Jean Brash withdrew abruptly, leaving Hannah gawping out like an idiot.

'Whit does he want?' Jean hissed.

'How would I know?'

While Hannah scrutinised further Jean's mind replayed the fact that McLevy had visited a fortnight back to bring her tidings of the solved murders.

This, of course, included the conclusion of what lay behind the brutal assault on her own person.

Having delivered the relevant summation, the inspector had abruptly left.

Not even scrounged a coffee.

And not been seen since.

Now he was.

Seen.

'He's no wearing his hat,' observed Hannah. 'And his heid's a' flat.'

'You mean the hair?'

'Aye. Pomade it must be.'

'Pomade?'

'Or he fell in a cow pat.'

One of the peacocks approached and, instead of his usual practice of booting the bird out of sight, McLevy allowed it to peck ineffectually at his foot before moving on.

The policeman did rehearse a kick but did not follow through.

'Oh, I see his hat,' Hannah announced. 'In his hand.'

'Whit else?'

'My Goad. His fusker's gone!'

'Thank the Lord. How does he look?'

422

'Younger. Ugly as hell though.'

Hannah was further puzzled by something, while Jean had a thought gnawing at her like a harvest mouse.

'He's awfy tidy dressed. Wedding or funeral maybe?'

'Clean shirt?'

'Looks like so.'

'Tie?'

'Purple.'

'Hannah?' Jean spoke with a queasy belly. 'You don't think he's come . . . *calling*?'

'How the hell would I know?'

'Is he holding flowers?'

'No. Not even a pee-the-bed.'

'Go and ask him.'

'Whit?'

'What he wants!'

Some time later, James McLevy, like an ill-farrant Narcissus, regarded his reflection in the pond that housed Jean's loitering tropical fish.

Although it was a fine day and the sun was shining, these piscine shirkers lurked obstinately at the bottom, keeping their bright colours to themselves.

There was no wind, so he had no escape from his watery image. The only ripples were the near-healed bumps and lumps on his face.

Hannah had arrived and departed with his request to Jean, muttering to herself like a harbinger of doom.

The inspector's mind rolled back to Doctor Seward Ramsay. In his consulting room the fierce little man, tufted eyebrows, mouth like a snapping turtle, did not spare the inspector from his withering verdict.

'You're a damned fool to yourself. Who was that fellow you saw in Glasgow?'

'Alexander Pettigrew.'

'The man's mistaken. There is nothing wrong with your heart. This is the problem!'

Ramsay emptied the iron coffee mug by hammering it out on a spread newspaper.

After the exhilaration of the case being solved, McLevy had begun experiencing the shafts of pains again, as if the frenetic activity had merely kept them at bay.

He had sworn Ballantyne to silence and sent the boy to ask his mother for a medical man recommended.

Ramsay was her choice.

Close-mouthed, diligent, sharp as a tack.

The wee man had given the inspector a worse going over than the effigy's cane, found nothing, then honed in on what went down the McLevy gullet.

The tavern fodder was indeed a heavy load and the irregularity of his meals another, but when McLevy described his late night slurping, Ramsay demanded that he bring in the implements concerned.

And there on the newspaper were great wodges of flaked iron, some smaller versions of which had reappeared in the tin mug, itself a crusted bearer of ill fortune.

'That is poison!'

Ramsay tapped the pile of ferrous cartilage.

'Going into your guts on a regular basis. God knows how your digestive system had coped, but that's the source of your pain!'

The little man screwed up the paper and threw it into a wastebasket, along with pot and mug.

'Now — Pettigrew was right in one thing — improve the way you live or you'll die like a dog!'

Jean's image appeared beside his own in the water — all dolled up with a concoction on her head that might have been a hat or some French meringue.

He looked circumspectly at her footwear, the latest fashion no doubt but —

'Are we not taking my carriage?' she demanded.

'I thought we'd go on the saunter.'

'Whit's the destination?'

'Princes Street.'

'We can take the coach and walk the length.'

He nodded at a sensible compromise, shoved his bowler onto a newly flattened head and crooked an elbow in habitual fashion that more suggested arrest than affection.

She slid her arm through his, opened up her parasol and they walked to the iron gates as the carriage drew up with the giant Angus sitting dourly atop.

Jean was still testing the boundaries.

'Ye don't mind the carriage being open?'

'Not at all.'

'Ye don't mind being seen wi' me — a woman of easy virtue?'

'Virtue — where does that bide?'

'So you don't mind?'

'I wouldnae hae asked ye for high tea else.'

He helped her up and in, followed suit and the carriage disappeared down the street.

The big fish were unconcerned — only the shadow of a heron would provoke them to movement.

The peacocks' impossibly small heads all whipped round as the back door disclosed Lily Baxter and Maisie Powers with their mid-afternoon provender.

Hannah watched for a moment from the window, then stumped out to the top of the stairs inside and bawled out a message to one and all.

'I hope you girls are fit for purpose this coming night, because we have a bawdy-hoose tae run!'

55

In nature there are neither rewards nor
punishments — there are consequences.
Robert Ingersoll, *Some Reasons Why*

As the carriage rattled along at a leisurely pace
towards Leith Walk to turn up for Princes Street,
Jean made a covert study of the man sitting
opposite. He could have sat by her side, of
course, but that might be too much to expect.

Hannah was right, the absence of moustache
gave a less careworn look and uncovered the full
lips that sat somewhat strangely with a battered
exterior.

His eye had near healed up, but both optics
were trained on the passing vista and did not
meet hers.

Ye wouldnae call the man ugly though, just
. . . not all at once immediately prepossessing.

'I have some news for you, James,' she murmured. 'Sim Carnegie?'

'Uhuh?'

Now she had his attention.

'He welshed on his debts and is no longer in
the city.'

'With luck on a fish cart tae Stranraer, given
the boys he owed the money.'

'That's always possible.'

'Wi' a nine-eyed-eel stuck up his backside.'

'I hope the fish doesn't mind,' said Jean demurely.

They exchanged a smile, but any further intimacy was shattered by the advent of a hansom cab that went hurtling past them, piled to the gunnels with luggage, and containing three people also laden with the detritus of travel.

Angus let out a curse and the man in the open cab abruptly rose to his feet, balancing precariously, and waved a large, velvet hat.

Stevenson having the last word as usual, with Fanny grasping firmly to the sides, and her son holding onto the sliding chaos of cases.

'We are late for the train,' called Robert Louis. 'I doubt they will delay. Goodbye, goodbye!'

He fell back with a peal of laughter as the cab picked up speed and just as suddenly was gone, scattering all in its wake, heading for Waverley Station.

Both Jean and McLevy lifted theft hands in farewell.

'The man's a menace,' said the inspector.

'He leaves his mark,' was the cryptic response.

It was the last time Stevenson saw his beloved, intractable city — the writer never returned and died seven years later in Samoa of cerebral haemorrhage.

The last sentence he wrote in the unfinished Weir of Hermiston *might well have described his death.*

'It seemed unprovoked, a wilful convulsion of brute nature . . . '

The last word.

As usual.

They disembarked the carriage in Princes Street and Jean, more naturally this time, slipped her hand through his crooked arm as they walked in the mid-afternoon sunshine.

It might have been her imagination, but folk seemed to turn and at times downright gawk as they made their passage.

Were they all that well known — the Thieftaker and bawdy-hoose keeper?

McLevy seemed oblivious and whistled absent-mindedly under his breath — 'Charlie is my Darling, the Young Chevalier'.

Half way down Princes Street was an establishment called Miss Lavinia's Tea Room, and it was there McLevy guided them.

Jean had been inside once before with Hannah, but both women found it too knabby.

'Hoachin' wi' genteelity,' was the Semple verdict.

Again this did not seem to perturb the inspector, as a dainty little waitress shimmied towards them.

'Would Sir and Madam desire a table?' she asked in affected tones.

'Sir and Madam would,' replied McLevy; then as the waitress turned to survey the room that was three quarters full of women with various lap dogs, he added, 'Do I not know you?'

'I beg your pardon?'

'Nettie Burns! Your mother, you're the spitting image. How is she these days?'

'She — she — very well. She lives with my brother now.'

'Oh, that's nice. Give her my regards. James McLevy, Inspector of Police.'

He had raised his voice slightly and the

discreet hum of the tearoom dropped a notch as the inhabitants gauged the social standing of these two strange arrivals.

Jean, for the few who did not know her profession or reputation, cut an acceptable if exotic figure in her finery, but McLevy, pomade and purple tie notwithstanding, was like a hairy animal in his heavy overcoat.

They were led to a corner table, but he would have none of it.

'That's too pokey, hen,' he boomed, as if to an old family friend. 'There's the mission!'

He pointed at a table right in the centre of the room, underneath one of the hanging lamps.

Prime position.

And soon after, there they sat in all their glory, cakes and coffee even though it was high tea.

But tea was not a taste they shared.

Jean did the honours, pouring what looked like a gey spleuterie offering from the coffee pot.

McLevy surprised her by adding only three lumps of sugar to the weak mixture.

She picked out a French cake and he a decent slice of gingerbread.

'Nettie Burns?' asked Jean.

'A cleaner at the station. Nice wee woman.'

They drank and munched as one of the lap dogs, a Cairn terrier, sneaked out from below its table and approached, hopeful of fallen crumbs.

'Hamish?' called the owner. 'Come back to Mummy!'

McLevy recognised the woman from the park; Hamish recognised the inspector and scuttled back to safety.

His mind shot back to that moment in the church when he tried to hold the killer from hurtling to his death.

The inspector wiped at his face with a napkin as if the effigy had just spat straight in.

'Awfy nice in here, eh?'

Jean made no reply — she was acutely conscious of sly glances and whispered behind-the-hand remarks aimed in her direction; and though she would usually brush these off with contempt, for some reason her hackles were rising.

'What do you want, James?'

'Me?'

'You.'

'Me?'

'You — you aye want *something*.'

McLevy considered. He'd risen that morning after a straight six hours' sleep without a besom rider to haunt his dreams, noted it was his day off, decided to shave away the moustache and then spiffed himself up.

Next thing he knew, he was in the garden of the Just Land.

With high tea on the agenda.

'*What do you want, James?*'

McLevy considered once more.

What did he want?

'Your company,' he answered finally.

Jean sighed. He'd get round tae the truth eventually.

Or *was* such the truth?

'D'ye remember,' McLevy said suddenly, 'when you lost that pearl necklace?'

431

Jean winced. She had fallen most inappropriately in love and the man concerned not only had a woman on the side but they were both swindlers.

They swindled her. Like a fool.

And the necklace was beyond price.

'I near droont myself getting it back for you.'

'Ye were after him for something else. The pearls were incidental!'

'I still endit up near droont.'

'And who brought coffee and sugar biscuits to your sick bed?'

Jean swirled her cup disparagingly.

'Better brew than this peely-wally rubbish.'

McLevy, now launched, would not turn back.

'What about when you were in the frame for murder — who got you out of that?'

'The guilty party had knifed three people and thrown acid over one of my girls.'

'So?'

'So you were after him for something else!'

McLevy chewed resolutely on his gingerbread, but she was not finished either.

Women rarely are.

Finished.

'And what about when you were shot in the belly? Who gave you the wee bit of paper where to find the man?'

'You did. Inside a rotten apple, though.'

'It wasnae rotten. Jist soft!'

In her vigorous response, the shawl-neck of her dress had separated and he saw to his surprise that she was wearing the very same pearl necklace. He also noted the lingering scar left by

432

the silver cane, just above her collarbone.

His healing eye ached all at once.

'Whit's the matter wi' your face?'

'I was just thinking. One way or another, we've been battered tae buggery right enough.'

'True,' said Jean thoughtfully. 'No mercy.'

They looked at each other in silence before he pronounced judgement.

'Whit a pair of shipwrecks, eh?'

McLevy's aggrieved expression suddenly struck her as very comical and Jean began to laugh.

He looked even more aggrieved and this provoked a further explosion.

It must be said that her laughter was not at all ladylike. In fact it could have been mistaken for that of a tarry-breeks on the randan.

Whatever, it set McLevy off and he began to whoop in that odd fashion that always had an edge of menace.

The little waitress started to panic at the racket and darted into the kitchen, returning at speed, accompanied by the eponymous Miss Lavinia — a tall bony woman with lantern jaw and sour disposition.

It put McLevy in mind of someone he knew only too well.

'God Almighty,' he muttered. 'It's the lieutenant in a bustle and corset.'

Off they went again into howling laughter and the tight-arsed, purse-lipped Edinburgh tearoom was shaken to the core, as if two lions had escaped from the zoo.

Then just as suddenly, they both stopped.

Jean because something had struck her deeply,

433

and McLevy's reason being that he had spotted Mulholland's face gazing in through the window like a man staring into a goldfish bowl.

The inspector muttered some excuse and made his way to the outside street.

'How did ye know I was here?' he asked, with no discernible trace of cordiality.

'I approached your landlady and she said you had enquired of her after a decent tearoom. This was her recommendation.'

McLevy nodded. That made sense. But why was the constable chasing to his lodgings and furthermore looming over him in Princes Street?

'Daniel Drummond,' said Mulholland.

'Whit of him?'

'Bad blood between himself and Gregor Gillespie — leader of the Scarlets.'

'A' that stuff is over now.'

'Not for them. A duel. Foils. Early this morning.'

'But Drummond's a champion!'

'So it proved. Straight through the lungs. Gillespie's at the hospital in a bad way.'

McLevy stroked where his moustache used to be.

'You deal with it,' he said.

'I just thought since you'd been involved — '

'Is Drummond in the cells?'

'He knows them well by now.'

'You and the lieutenant sort the thing. It's my day off.'

Mulholland looked past him into the tearoom where Jean sat in isolation.

'Right enough. I'll be on my way.'

434

And without more ado, his lanky frame strode like a giraffe down the street and out of sight.

McLevy thought for a moment about the look in Jessica's eyes as she talked about her brother, and the darkness he had sensed in the young man's soul.

Darkness will out.

Back he went and sat down.

'Crime,' he remarked. 'Never at peace.'

'What was it?'

'Jist the usual. Could ye pour me another of that shilpit coffee?'

She did so.

He added three more sugar lumps and slurped noisily through his teeth.

Jean winced, but at least she was spared that drookit moustache.

'So,' she announced. 'You desired my company?'

'Uhuh.'

'Well, you have it on hand.'

'That I do.'

There was a long silence between the two while the tearoom babbled with exchanged inanities.

Her thoughts went back to when she'd been looking at Cupid in the garden and McLevy had asked her a question that had stopped her dead.

God knows what he'd been going through at the time, but she was buggered if she'd ask him about it now.

However Jean did have another subject in mind.

'What about us, James?' she asked quietly.

'What about what?'

'You know what I mean!'

He took a deep breath and named the unnamable.

'Ye mean love, Jeanie?'

The wee dog Hamish lifted a sly leg under the table and urinated on the hem of his mistress's garment.

'Love is the very devil,' said James McLevy.

We do hope that you have enjoyed reading this large print book.

Did you know that all of our titles are available for purchase?

We publish a wide range of high quality large print books including:
Romances, Mysteries, Classics
General Fiction
Non Fiction and Westerns

Special interest titles available in large print are:
The Little Oxford Dictionary
Music Book
Song Book
Hymn Book
Service Book

Also available from us courtesy of Oxford University Press:
Young Readers' Dictionary
(large print edition)
Young Readers' Thesaurus
(large print edition)

For further information or a free brochure, please contact us at:
Ulverscroft Large Print Books Ltd.,
The Green, Bradgate Road, Anstey,
Leicester, LE7 7FU, England.
Tel: (00 44) 0116 236 4325
Fax: (00 44) 0116 234 0205

FALL FROM GRACE

David Ashton

A burglary and murder at the home of Sir Thomas Bouch, the enigmatic architect of the ill-fated Tay Bridge, sets Inspector James McLevy off on a trail of brutal killings, lethal liaisons, and a double suicide that leads to a violent encounter with an old enemy, Hercules Dunbar. Caught up in a terrifying storm as he tracks his foe to Dundee, McLevy watches the rail bridge collapse and plunge into the icy depths of the Tay. The aftermath brings the destruction of reputation and love, as the inspector uncovers the secret passions that have led to murder . . .

A TRICK OF THE LIGHT

David Ashton

Halloween, 1881. Edinburgh. And the dead are restless. Inspector James McLevy is called to action when Muriel Grierson, an outwardly genteel widow, is robbed at home. Her knight in shining armour — one Arthur Conan Doyle, recently graduated from medical school — is keen to learn from such a master of detection as the renowned inspector, but McLevy is less sure that he requires a new acolyte. When a vicious murder occurs with evidence of supernatural strength, all roads lead to Sophia Adler, a beautiful young American spiritualist, and the inspector becomes involved with one of the most dangerous women he has ever encountered . . .

SHADOW OF THE SERPENT

David Ashton

1880, Edinburgh: Election fever grips the city. But while the rich and educated argue about politics, in the dank wynds of the docks it's a struggle just to stay alive. When a prostitute is brutally murdered, disturbing memories from thirty years ago are stirred in Inspector McLevy, who is soon lured into a murky world of politics, perversion and deception — and the shadow of the serpent.